The Dancer

The Dancer

First published in Indonesian by
PT Gramedia Pustaka Utama (Jakarta, Indonesia) under the titles:
Ronggeng Dukuh Paruk © 1982 Ahmad Tohari;
Lintang Kemukus Dini Hari © 1985 Ahmad Tohari;
and *Jantera Bianglala* © 1986 Ahmad Tohari.

Publication of the Modern Library of Indonesia Series, of which this book is one title,
is made possible by the generous assistance of the Djarum Foundation.

Jl. Danau Laut Tawar No. 53
Jakarta 10210 Indonesia
www.lontar.org

Template design by DesignLab; layout and cover by Cyprianus Jaya Napiun.
Cover illustration detail of *Berkemben* (*Putting on a Sash*) by Suprobo;
image courtesy of Hadiprana Gallery.

Printed in Indonesia by PT Suburmitra Grafistama

ISBN No. 978-602-9144-21-5

MODERN LIBRARY OF INDONESIA

AHMAD TOHARI

The Dancer

a trilogy of novels

translated by René T. A. Lysloff

Jakarta, Indonesia

Contents

Introduction

I first discovered the fiction of Ahmad Tohari in 1986 when I was conducting PhD research in the region of Banyumas, Central Java. I was living in Purwokerto, the capital of the Banyumas regency at the time and, after a few weeks of fieldwork, I decided to visit Yogyakarta, which is a much larger city, about seven hours away. There, while browsing in a bookstore, I came across a slim pocket-sized novel entitled *Ronggeng Dukuh Paruk* (*The Dancer of Paruk Village*). Because I was gathering materials on rural performance traditions, I was intrigued by the word *ronggeng* in the title, a term that refers to itinerant or village female dancers. The book, I learned, was the first in a trilogy and when I began reading it I was pleased to discover that the story was set in the very same region that I was conducting my fieldwork. Reading more, I was impressed by the incredibly rich detail with which the author portrayed both place and people within the story. (I did not know at the time that the author originated from Tinggarjaya, a village only twenty minutes from where I was living.) While on the one hand, the novel related the romantic account of the lives of a young village dancer and the man she loved, on the other it also provided a meticulous description of both the social and natural order (or sometimes disorder) of their world.

After my return to the US several months later I became obsessed with the first book, translating it into English in an attempt to fathom every word of the narrative. I tried to learn everything I could about the author and the place he described. I pondered the ethnographic truth of the novel: wondering where fiction could be separated from fact in its depiction of an isolated Javanese village and the people who lived there. Indeed, knowing what I already did about the region, I felt certain that he had described a real world within the fiction of his novel. Henceforth, I embarked on a mission to understand how and why he did it. By the time I returned to Java in 1994, I had read the other two books in the trilogy as well as other novels and short stories by the author. I was determined to get to know this extraordinary writer.

Ahmad Tohari is one of Indonesia's preeminent writers and to date has published eight novels, three anthologies of essays, and two collections of short stories. His trilogy of novels, combined under one cover here, has already been published in Dutch, German, Japanese, and Chinese. He is the recipient of several national and international literary awards, including the Southeast Asian Writers Award, and a fellowship through the International Writers Program in Iowa City. He is also an experienced and respected journalist. From 1979 to 1981 he served as staff editor for the Jakarta daily *Merdeka* and, from 1986 to 1993, held the position of general editor at *Amanah*, a national magazine focusing on religious and political affairs. Presently, he contributes political essays to *Suara Merdeka*, another daily published in Jakarta. He is also a religious intellectual and leader. He and his family run an Islamic school (*pesantren*) and community center. Finally, he is a well-known expert of Javanese folk arts and often serves as a consultant for the regional office of the Indonesian Ministry of Culture and Education (now the Ministry of National Education).

He was born June 13, 1948, the fourth of twelve children. Though both his parents came from farm families, his father received an education and worked for the government as director of the regional office for the Ministry of Religious Affairs. It was his parents who established the *pesantrèn* in Tinggarjaya. Thus, when growing up, the author received a religious education at home while also attending local public schools. Because his father was a progressive intellectual who firmly believed in keeping up with national affairs, he developed a sophisticated understanding of Indonesian politics even while being thoroughly inculcated to local values and norms.

When I returned to Java in 1994, I learned to my delight that the author had recently moved back to his village. Following Javanese etiquette, I sent word through an intermediary that I hoped to visit him at his home. Once I received his permission, I drove to his house armed with my translation of his first novel as proof of my interest in his work. I found his house easily enough; it was the only two-story house in the area and near the main road that cuts through the village. The large front yard was dominated by a lush but carefully maintained garden of tropical flowers and fruit trees. The garden attenuated the traffic noise from the nearby street and provided cool shade for us as we sat on the front veranda.

After chatting for a while, he invited me into the house and showed me where he did most of his writing: a spacious and comfortable den, his desk placed near a front window so that he could gaze out on his garden as he worked. The den was filled with the kind of technology taken for granted by Westerners but still considered luxury items in Java: a personal computer and printer, and a stereo system with an extensive collection of recordings of both Javanese *gamelan* music and Western classical symphonies.

My research in Java mainly consisted of spending time with rural musicians, most with little more than a grade school education. Thus, my visits with him proved to be exhilarating times for me. During our discussions, he always asked probing questions about my work. He also offered valuable suggestions and, with his wealth of knowledge about local traditions and customs, soon came to be a very important informant for me. In the years that followed we also became close friends and, through that friendship, I learned why he was so deeply respected by other intellectuals as well as his fellow villagers. It was, I believe, because he lived by his principles. Not only was he an astute political theorist, he was also a community activist. Because of his efforts, primarily, the area had telephone service and he often lobbied on behalf of his village for state-supported development projects, including the construction of schools, roads, and so on.

The author sees himself as a progressive religious intellectual whose aim is to nurture what he calls a post-modern Islam, one that honors indigenous culture and tradition yet follows the teachings of the Koran. He advocates not the modernist orthodoxy of many Indonesian Muslims today but a more tolerant form that places emphasis on moral and ethical behavior over the formal aspects of Islamic practices. As a result of this perspective, he has developed a strong sense of social and environmental responsibility which, as is evident in his writings, colors his fictional work and his views of the Indonesian state. Because of his political, religious, and social convictions, he has come under fire from both orthodox Muslims for advocating Indonesian nationalism (as opposed to Islamic piety) and the government for pointing out social injustice and political corruption.

One day, in an interview, he explained his politics to me:

> "I'm not a communist and I'm certainly not an atheist. Perhaps I am what you'd call a socialist, but one who honors humanistic liberalism, which is bound up in my sense of social responsibility.
>
> "My beliefs go back to childhood experience. I was born in a very poor agricultural community. There was

> no irrigation, no agricultural technology, no chemical additives for fertilizers; there was nothing. Farming depended entirely on rainfall and during times of drought many of my friends and neighbors suffered from malnutrition and its effects.
>
> "Fortunately, because my father worked for the government, my family had enough to eat, but many of my friends went hungry. And when I looked into their eyes, I saw a great wrong. I had to ask myself how this could be.
>
> "The answer, I saw, could be traced to ignorance, which was frequently fostered by religious leaders who wrongly said that the poor had no work ethic. In fact, the problem was in the system of production. The agricultural system wasn't fair and the government administration was feudalistic. These factors combined to keep people poor."

Perhaps because he was raised in the *pesantren* that his parents established, the author harbors deep religious convictions. Even so, his views regarding the place of religion in society are considered, by some of his critics to be out of line with the status quo. In that regard, he says:

> "I have serious reservations about religion being used as a model for social progress. From what I can see around me, it is obvious that religion has become little more than a system of laws. Meanwhile, the general understanding of religion is so shallow that its very essence is completely absent.
>
> "I advocate a return to the kind of Islam that was first brought to Indonesia, one that is inclusive, not just of a set of rules. Islam when it came here was not a commitment

> to formal procedures; instead, it emphasized ethical and moral teachings. The ancients who brought Islam to these shores put the ethical and moral at the forefront and made dogma and ritual duty secondary. This gets at the basis of my own ideas. I believe that I must establish an understanding of Islam that is holistic: one that embraces existing forms of culture. Not only should Islam tolerate these existing cultures but it should also nurture them."

This profound emphasis on essence over form underlies his religious convictions. It also informs his political convictions. He avoids being too overtly political in his fiction, emphasizing fundamental moral and ethical issues even in his sharpest attacks on the Indonesian state. He argues that overly politicized writing is, generally speaking, poor literature. Nevertheless, he himself must be described as a political novelist. He advocates tolerance and religious pluralism in his writing because he, like other progressive post-modernist Muslims, is deeply aware of the past excesses of Islamic followers against the communists in 1965 and the role of Islamic political parties in undermining Indonesian democracy during the 1950s.

During my last trip to Java, I found to my chagrin that the growth of Islamic fundamentalism in Central Java had caused Ahmad Tohari, with his "post-modern" religious views, to become a very controversial figure in the region. While it became clear during my stay that he was still loved in his own village, a growing number of people in the region disapproved of his views. Specifically in regard to this novel, many now contended that he had misrepresented the ronggeng dance tradition. There was no truth to his description of the tradition, several informants told me.

Thus, I felt deeply disturbed that the author whom I had grown to admire and respect so much seemed completely at odds with the surrounding community. Selfishly, I also worried that the criticism aimed at his novel could also apply, perhaps even more aptly, to my own research on the traditional performing arts of Banyumas. My interviews of elderly musicians and dancers supported his depiction of the ronggeng tradition but younger artists rejected his story as pure fiction. I began to wonder then if either of us was qualified to present our readers with an ethnographic and historical account of what it means to be a dancer or musician in the region of Banyumas.

I spoke with the author about this during one of my last meetings with him that summer. He simply replied by asking me the following questions: "What constitutes ethnographic or historic truth in a text? Can an author convey this truth if readers don't want to see it? Perhaps the issue isn't that the novel misrepresents the ronggeng tradition but that it describes a truth about Indonesia's past: a truth regarding the injustice of rural poverty and ignorance which is too painful for some readers to bear."

In closing I would like to thank Ahmad Tohari for both his friendship and the tremendous educational opportunity that he presented me when giving me permission to translate this trilogy of novels. I must also mention the assistance of Penelope Lane, whose editorial advice was always true, and John McGlynn, whose constant and unflagging support enabled me to complete my work.

I

Notes for Momma

1

A pair of herons sailed high in the sky, supported by the slightest breeze. Without once beating their wings, they floated in the air for hours. Their calls were strident, long mournful laments. Water. The herons had flown hundreds of kilometers in search of water, even a puddle. For an eternity they had yearned for a muddy bank where they might find sustenance: frogs, fish, shrimp, possibly a few water insects.

But the drought was far from over. Thousands of hectares of wet rice fields surrounding the village of Paruk had been bone dry for seven months. The herons would not find any water, not even a pool a foot wide. Entire paddy fields had been transformed into dry, gray-colored plains. Grassy plants had all withered and died. The only spots of green here and there were the cactus-like *kerokot* that appeared in the fields only during a drought, nature's sacrifice to the sundry forms of locusts and crickets.

In another part of the sky, a sparrow was struggling to stay alive. It flew like a stone released from a slingshot, screeching incessantly. Behind it, with greater speed, flew a hawk. The air, pierced by these two birds, crackled and hissed. A scream sounded from the little sparrow as the hawk bit into its head. Small, fine feathers floated down to the ground, a murder in the desolate sky above Paruk.

From the southeast a breeze blew. Arid. The top branches of the trees around the tiny hamlet swayed. Yellow leaves and dry twigs fell to the ground. Groves of bamboo rustled. Bamboo windmills, built by the children who herded goats on the outskirts of the village, squeaked in the wind. Kites made of turnip leaves rose upwards into the air. And the warbling of birds dispelled the desolation of the sky above the village.

The lingering hot weather had dried all the seeds months before. The boll of the kapok plant grew black as its shell broke open into three sections. With the gusting breeze, minute tufts of cotton were scattered, drifting in the wind. Each tiny cotton wisp held a ripe seed, eager to germinate wherever it landed on the earth. Such was the wisdom of nature, ensuring that no new kapok shrub grew too close to its parent plant.

The *dadap* tree had a similar method for dispersing its young. After ripening, the seeds used the skin of their pods like wings and, whenever the wind blew, it looked as though thousands of butterflies were taking off from the tree. These seeds, borne aloft and carried away by the air currents, took root far from their mother tree. Thus was the law of nature.

From the high vantage point of the two herons, the village of Paruk would have looked like a small thicket in the middle of a broad field. A tiny area of settlement, situated almost two kilometers from the nearest road, Paruk could only be reached by traversing the network of dikes bordering the wet rice fields. It was, perhaps, because of this relative isolation that the inhabitants of Paruk, over the years, had developed a unique way of life.

Twenty-three homes made up this tiny community, inhabited by people with a common genealogy. It was believed that all the villagers were descended from a man by the name of Ki Secamenggala, a shaman and mystic of ages past who, it was said, had sought out this very isolated area as a place to retire from his villainous career. To this place, the village of Paruk, Ki Secamenggala had entrusted his descendants, his flesh and blood.

The people of Paruk were aware of their ancestor's dubious reputation, yet they still paid homage to him. His grave, located on the crest of a small hill in the center of the village, was the focus of their spiritual lives, with constantly burning coals of incense on his gravestone bearing mute evidence of their devotion.

As the herons searched in vain for water from their lofty heights, three young boys could be seen on the outskirts of the village struggling to pull a cassava plant from the hardened and gravelly earth. Its roots were buried deep and, despite their efforts, the cassava stubbornly remained fixed in place. They had almost given up hope. Then Rasus, one of the boys, said to his two companions, "Go and find a shovel. Otherwise, we'll never get this damn cassava out."

Warta, one of the other boys, scoffed at that idea. "Forget it. You'd need a crowbar to break through ground as hard as this. Maybe water would work. If we had some water, we could wet the plant around its base. It'd be easy to pull out then."

Darsun, the third boy, sneered, "Water? Where are you going to get water?"

"I've got an idea," Rasus announced. "We can piss on it and, if that doesn't work, to hell with it."

Immediately, three small, uncircumcised penises were pulled from their owners' shorts and pointed at the base of the plant. Whizzzz... Afterwards, Rasus, Warta, and Darsun stepped back to consider the effects of their action, each wiping the palms of his hands on his shorts. With a final burst of desperation, they once again tried to pull out the cassava.

Small arm and shoulder muscles heaved while straining legs pushed mightily against the earth. Fine roots began to part and the earth slowly cracked. When the last roots broke, the three boys fell back on their behinds. But their cheers quickly subsided. The cassava tubers they had pulled out were no bigger than their own small fingers.

Village custom dictated that cooperation among the three boys would now have to end and, immediately, the three began to wrestle, fighting over the tubers they had found. In the end, Rasus and Warta got two, but Darsun only one. The fight had been fair and there were no protests. The three busily peeled their winning portions with their teeth and began to chew on them, tasting the saltiness of the earth and the bitterness of their own urine.

Wiping his mouth with the back of his forearm, Rasus invited his two friends to go with him to check on the goats they were tending. After checking that their charges were not destroying anyone's garden, the three walked towards a jackfruit tree, a spot where they often played. There, beneath the tree, they found another playmate, a young girl by the name of Srintil, absorbed in a game by herself. She was making a garland by tying jackfruit leaves together with a piece of palm leaf fiber.

Sitting on the ground with her legs tucked under and engrossed in her work, Srintil sang happily. The people of Paruk knew only two kinds of music: the classical kidung poetry that old people chanted, and the songs of ronggeng dancers that were popular among the children. Srintil, in her young girl's voice, was singing a favorite song of ronggeng dancers: "*Sénggot timbané ranté, tiwas ngégot ora suwé.*"

"Sénggot" was an erotic song but Srintil, a girl of only eleven years, sang it heartily. It wasn't likely that she was able to fully fathom the meaning of the lyrics, but that didn't matter, and the people of Paruk wouldn't have been bothered about a young child singing such an indecent song.

Srintil was so absorbed in her singing that she didn't notice the three boys standing behind her. She only became aware of them as she placed the crown of jackfruit leaves on her head.

"Too big," remarked Rasus, startling her. The girl raised her head.

"I'd be glad to make a *badongan* for you," continued Rasus, offering his services.

"No need. But if you want, you could get me some mango leaves. Then, this badongan will be better," answered Srintil.

Rasus smiled. He liked doing things for Srintil. He turned and looked around, searching for a mango tree. When he found one, he climbed it, scampering up like a monkey, and picked several large leaves. Rasus thought to himself that with these leaves in her headdress, Srintil would look even prettier.

With the help of the three boys, Srintil was able to finish her garland of leaves. It fitted perfectly.

"That's great," said Rasus after examining the crown of leaves adorning her head.

"Honestly?" asked Srintil coyly.

"No kidding. Don't you think, Warta? Darsun?"

"Yeah, it's true. You really look beautiful now."

"Like a ronggeng dancer?" asked Srintil again, flirtatiously.

"Exactly."

"No you don't," Darsun hissed, "not unless you can dance like a ronggeng."

Srintil was silent. She gazed at the three boys standing in front of her, feeling slightly annoyed.

"Okay. I'll dance," she finally said. "But you have to make the music to accompany me. How about it?"

"Well, in that case," answered Rasus quickly, "I'll be the drum. Warta can be the *calung* xylophone and Darsun the blown gong. Let's go!"

On the stony ground beneath the jackfruit tree, as the southeast wind blew the perfume of the coffee flowers that were always in bloom in the dry season, and as the sunshine grew hazy in the western sky, Srintil danced and sang, accompanied by the vocalized sounds of drum, blown gong, and xylophone. Rasus sat on the ground, his legs crossed, slapping his knees to imitate the movements of a drummer. Warta swung his hands from left to right as if there were a xylophone in front of him. Darsun filled his cheeks with air, his voice sounding low to imitate the resonance of a gong.

No one seeing Srintil dance that afternoon would have believed that she had never been taught dancing and singing, nor would they have imagined that she had never even seen a performance of ronggeng. The last ronggeng dancer in Paruk Village had died when Srintil was a baby. Yet, Srintil was able to dance with skill and conviction.

Vague feelings of lust and desire, always engendered by true ronggeng dancers, were aroused in her young audience by Srintil while she danced. The sweep of her neck, the glance of her eyes, even the way she swayed her shoulders would have mesmerized any adult male that saw her.

The fact that Srintil, a naive little girl, was able to imitate a ronggeng dancer's style with considerable skill would not have come as a surprise to anyone from Paruk. In the hamlet there was a powerful belief that a true ronggeng dancer was not the result of teaching.

No matter how she was trained, a young woman could not become a ronggeng dancer without being possessed by the *indang* spirit. In the world of ronggeng, the indang was revered as a kind of supernatural godmother.

And so, Srintil danced that afternoon, with half-closed eyes. The fingers of her hands were bent back coquettishly. The three young boys accompanying her bore witness to the fact that she was able to sing many of the ronggeng songs.

The mouths of Rasus and his two friends grew weary, yet still Srintil swayed and undulated, her singing flowing continuously like a water spout in the rainy season.

Nevertheless, she did eventually have to stop because her three accompanists grew silent. If Srintil was tired, she showed no evidence of it. She even continued to demand more of her friends.

"Come on, again!" she urged.

"Let's rest first. My mouth is tired," answered Rasus.

"Yeah, let's stop for a while. We'll start playing again only if you promise to pay us," said Warta.

"All right, all right. What kind of payment would you like?"

Warta was silent. Rasus smiled, and looked at Darsun.

"What kind of payment would you like?" repeated Srintil.

As she spoke, Srintil stepped toward Rasus. Very close. Unable to avoid it, Rasus received a kiss on the cheek. Then, Warta and Darsun were given a kiss as well. "There. You got your payment. Now I'll dance and you have to accompany me."

The three gave in. The pact beneath the jackfruit tree continued until the sun touched the horizon. Actually, Srintil didn't want to stop dancing even then, but Rasus said that he had to drive his three goats home to their pen. At the end of the game, Rasus, Warta and Darsun demanded payment again. This time they vied to kiss Srintil's cheek. The little girl accommodated them just as a ronggeng dancer might have done. Before running home, Srintil made Rasus and his two friends agree to come the next day to play together again.

Because Paruk was located in the middle of a large expanse of rice fields, the setting sun was clearly visible. A soft wind breathed, just enough to shed the branches of some of their leaves. Clumps of dry grass rolled along the ground, stopping only when they were blocked by the dikes surrounding the rice fields.

The disappearing light of the sun was anticipated by small bats and flying foxes. One by one, they flew out of nests and knotholes, ascending out of the midst of coconut fronds, or emerging from the still rolled-up sprouts of banana palms. These fluttering creatures did not like the dry season. They were unable to find fruit to eat, and even insects became scarce. In such times, the bats were forced to eat the leaves of the hibiscus trees to survive.

In the village, small lanterns were lit. From afar, the flickering lights were the only indication that the remote hamlet was inhabited. An oval-shaped moon almost reached the top of the sky. Unhampered by clouds, its light created murky shadows on the chalky ground. The sky was clear and the dry air grew colder as the night wore on.

Like a kind of natural stage, the dusty dry village square was a magnet to the children, and had become their arena for play. The light of the moon created an intimacy between the humans and the surrounding natural world. Being little creatures still pure of heart, the children were appropriate visitors to the village square in its moonlit splendor. Typically, they would run after one another, play games and sing songs. Perhaps they knew instinctively that childhood is an idyllic, sustained moment, experienced only once in a lifetime.

But this perfect evening was not filled with the shrill sounds of village children playing. The dry season had gone on too long this year. For the past two months, there had been no rice for the villagers. They had been reduced to a diet of tapioca made from dried cassava. The children ate a tapioca gruel for dinner, but the carbohydrates had been mostly cooked out, and as a result they had little energy to play in the evenings, preferring to roll themselves up in a sarong and sleep. They would wake again in the morning when the sunlight pierced the gaps in the wall and kissed their skin.

Usually, by mid-morning, the adults were already hard at work. During the dry season, most of their time was spent irrigating thirsty plants like vegetables, tobacco and other food crops with water drawn from deep artesian wells. When evening fell, the adults, tired from the day's work, sat resting and rolling cigarettes from dried banana leaves or corn husks. Close to midnight they would go to bed. In long dry seasons like this one, it was unlikely that any of the village women would become pregnant.

Around midnight, Sakarya was probably the only person still nodding under the dim light of an oil lamp. A respected elder of the village, Sakarya was musing over the behavior of his granddaughter earlier that afternoon. Unseen, he had been watching Srintil as she danced beneath the jackfruit tree, and he was convinced that she was possessed by the ronggeng spirit.

Sakarya smiled to himself. For a long time, this elder among Ki Secamenggala's descendants had felt that life in the village had become dull because of the lack of a ronggeng dancer. "Paruk Village without a ronggeng dancer isn't Paruk Village. Srintil, my own granddaughter, will bring back the true greatness of this village," said Sakarya to himself. He believed that the soul of Ki Secamenggala would chuckle, knowing there was now a ronggeng in Paruk.

For a Paruk villager, such thoughts were natural. Indeed, with the shrine of Ki Secamenggala, some dirty jokes, a few curses, and a ronggeng dancer accompanied by her calung ensemble of bamboo xylophones, life in Paruk could indeed be considered complete by its inhabitants. Outsiders viewed the people of the village with disdain, which was evident in their often-uttered words: "Don't glorify misery like the people of Paruk," or "Hey, you kids, take a shower. If you don't, your ears will leak pus and your legs will be covered in scabies like the children of Paruk!"

The following day, Sakarya went to visit Kartareja, a man his own age who, through his lineage, had become the village *dukun* for ronggeng. He, too, had been waiting for years for a candidate to train as a ronggeng. A set of calung instruments had been waiting in the attic above his kitchen for over a decade. On hearing Sakarya's news, the ronggeng trainer began to entertain the hope that the dazzling sounds of calung would once again be heard in Paruk.

"If what you say is true, we'll be able to enjoy living in this little hamlet again," said Kartareja.

"You'll see for yourself," answered Sakarya. "Srintil's dancing will be even more titillating accompanied by your calung."

Kartareja shook his head vigorously. His red lips, blackened by chewing betelnut, tobacco, and lime, jiggled from left to right. As he spoke, bits of tobacco and other debris sprayed from his mouth.

"I won't be needed, if that's the case, "Kartareja remarked. Do you think Srintil has been a ronggeng since birth?" he then asked with a trace of annoyance, feeling that his expertise as a trainer of ronggeng dancers was being devalued.

"Hey, don't you get what I'm saying? What I meant was that Srintil truly has got the indang. Surely, you can understand that."

"Oh, so that's it."

"Yeah, and of course you'll need to refine Srintil's dancing. She seems to be having trouble flipping her scarf properly. And, there's another thing: the problem of *rangkep*, of course. That's right up your alley, isn't it?"

Kartareja chuckled. Sakarya was referring to the black magic, love charms, body piercing with talismans and other procedures that make a ronggeng dancer popular. Kartareja and his wife were experts in that field.

"The bottom line is that Paruk Village will once again have a ronggeng dancer."

Kartareja sighed. "I hope it is as you say. Those of us in this hamlet who are elderly don't want to die before seeing Paruk return to what it once was. I've been worried that Ki Secamenggala might even refuse me a spot in the cemetery if I don't preserve the ronggeng tradition of this hamlet."

"Not only that. Ronggeng dancers help us to enjoy life, don't they?"

The two old men chuckled knowingly. Between guffaws, Sakarya ruefully asked why he couldn't turn back the years and become twenty again instead of his actual age of seventy.

For the next several days, Sakarya and Kartareja secretly watched Srintil dancing beneath the jackfruit tree. The two old men let the young girl dance to her heart's content to the accompaniment of the vocalized calung ensemble made up of Rasus and his two friends. After seeing her dance, Kartareja believed what Sakarya had told him: Srintil was indeed possessed by the ronggeng spirit.

Thereafter, they decided that, on an auspicious day, Srintil would be presented by her grandfather to Kartareja. The custom in the village for handling a potential ronggeng dancer was for the family of the candidate to give her over to the dukun to become his adopted child.

It was eleven years since the last ronggeng dancer of Paruk had died. Since then, the people of the village had not heard the sound of the calung ensemble. The bamboo xylophones lay covered in dust and soot in the attic above Kartareja's kitchen. The fiber strings which stretched over each instrument, holding the bamboo keys in a taut row, had been cut by nibbling mice and moths.

Fortunately, worms and termites had not weakened the bamboo keys of the xylophones. Fortunately, too, Venerable Matchmaker—*Kyai Comblang*—the heirloom drum owned by Kartareja's family, had been specially treated before being stored, and the instrument was ready to be used even after its very long rest.

The main problem facing Kartareja was not repairing the various musical instruments, but finding the musicians to play them. His favorite drummer had died two years earlier during a famine. Another musician, who used to play one of the calung xylophones, had left the village. Nevertheless, Kartareja was fortunate in one respect. He managed to locate Sakum, a man who had useless eyes, but who possessed the special skills to play the main xylophone of the calung ensemble.

Sakum, despite his blindness, could follow a ronggeng performance with precision. As if he could see, Sakum would let out a bawdy shout exactly when the ronggeng dancer swiveled her hips back and forth. At the precise moment the ronggeng aroused her male audience, Sakum's sharp voice would make a sound that had become renowned: Chisss! People said that, without Sakum accompanying, a ronggeng performance would be dull and flat.

The drought continued endlessly. But finally, Kartareja found a suitable day to begin Srintil's training. The villagers waited impatiently for nightfall. Kartareja ordered the village square to be cleaned and four rolls of pandamus leaf matting to be spread on the dry sandy ground near the center. When the day grew dark, a large oil lamp was lit. Reflectors surrounding the blazing wick enhanced the illumination, making the area bright and inviting to the children who gathered around to watch the people preparing the stage. Everyone knew that Srintil would dance that night.

In the Kartareja house, Srintil was being adorned in the style of a ronggeng dancer by Nyai Kartareja. Her small thin body was covered to her chest with a wrap-around batik *kain* held closed with a yellow waistband. A bright orange sash hung loosely from each side of her hips. Her skin glowed from the application of a mixture of powder and turmeric water. The wife of the dukun had ordered Srintil to chew betel, and her young lips had turned bright red.

Women and children filled the Kartareja house to watch Srintil being dressed. For the first time in her life, Srintil was under the close scrutiny of a crowd of people, and she felt embarrassed. She giggled a little when she heard people whispering together, praising her beauty, her sweet mouth. The fine hairs behind her cheeks near her ears became more apparent after Srintil was powdered. Her thin eyebrows were thickened with a mixture of root and papaya resin, making her look like a doll.

But Nyai Kartareja kept some of her procedures hidden from sight. Over the top of Srintil's head, she had blown a love mantra, an incantation considered in Paruk to make any woman appear more beautiful than she actually was:

Uluk-uluk perkutut manggung
Teka saka ngendi,
Teka saka tanah sabrang
Pakanmu apa,
Pakanmu madu tawon
Manis madu tawon,
Ora manis kaya putuku, Srintil.

Warbling turtle dove,
Where did you come from?
I came from a far-away land.
What do you eat?
I eat the honey of bees.
Yet even the sweet honey of bees
Is not as sweet as my grandchild, Srintil.

But that wasn't all.. To make her even more desirable, Nyai Kartareja had also inserted several gold talismans under Srintil's skin.

The people who had gathered to see Srintil dance began to grow restless. They were impatient to hear the calung ensemble. For over a decade they hadn't seen a ronggeng, performance and their hearts filled with joy when they finally heard Kartareja announce that the concert would begin.

They quickly formed a circle around the four musicians who sat crossed-legged facing their instruments: a drum, two xylophones, and a large tube of bamboo which, when blown, sounded like a gong. A large mat was unrolled for Srintil to dance on. Sitting at the main xylophone, Sakum drew stares from the audience because of his strange eyes. He didn't seem bothered, and just sat there, smiling disdainfully. His hands held the calung beaters ready as he sat waiting for a signal from the drummer.

When Srintil emerged, led by Nyai Kartareja, all eyes turned toward her. Rasus stood spellbound at the very front of the large mass of spectators. He couldn't believe that he had kissed Srintil only a few days earlier. Nyai Kartareja seated Srintil in the center of the rattan mat. The girl remained motionless, not even moving her eyes. Kartareja appeared with a pot of burning incense, carrying it around the circumference of the performance area. He placed the small charcoal burner, billowing with aromatic smoke, alongside the drum.

Silence.

Soft whispering could be heard, a woman nudging her nearby friend and commenting on Srintil's beauty. Rasus, Warta, and Darsun stared at the doll in the center of the woven mat. Srintil, who had often danced for them beneath the jackfruit tree, was now the star of a public performance.

Kartareja signaled the drummer. The seconds that followed echoed with the percussive music of the calung ensemble, matched by the clapping of almost every inhabitant of the village. Sakum began clowning around, swinging and swaying comically as he played his xylophone, his bawdy shouts drawing noisy applause.

As Srintil rose to her feet, the spectators fell silent, staring. Guided only by her instincts, Srintil began to dance, her eyes half closed. Sakarya, standing next to Kartareja, anxiously watched his granddaughter's movements. He wanted her performance to prove what he had claimed, that Srintil did indeed possess the indang spirit, forcing Kartareja to acknowledge the evidence.

When he heard Srintil sing a particularly difficult song, one that she could never have studied, Kartareja was convinced that she had received the spirit and that she had been born with the blessing of Ki Secamenggala to become a ronggeng dancer. Kartareja kept nodding his head. "Sakarya wasn't exaggerating when he told me about her," he thought.

During her performance, Srintil remained cool and calm, the audience completely in the grip of her enchantment. They were amazed at the way she flicked her scarf and curved her fingers back, the most difficult hand position for a ronggeng dancer. Sakum continually spiced her performance with lewd shouts and calls, the sound of "chisss" always perfectly timed with the thrusting of Srintil's hips.

When the first set was finished, the calung ensemble stopped playing and Srintil sat down. The admiration of the audience was obvious. One woman was so moved, she began to sob.

"I never knew Srintil could dance so well," she said. "I just want to cradle her in my arms and rock her until she falls fast asleep on my lap."

"I want to wash her clothes and help her with her morning bath," another woman said.

"Srintil doesn't belong to any one person. You aren't the only ones that want to pamper her. After the performance, I'm gonna talk to Nyai Kartareja."

"What are you going to do?"

"I want to give Srintil a massage. The child will certainly be tired. I'm gonna give her a good rub down before she goes to bed."

"What a charming and poised little girl! I wish she was my child!" declared yet another woman, dabbing her eyes and wiping the tears which were dripping off her nose.

Rasus, who had been standing motionless from the start of the performance, heard all these remarks. The thirteen-year-old boy felt that propriety had been transgressed and, in the process, Srintil had become the common property of the village people. He realized that never again would he be able to play contentedly with Srintil under the jackfruit tree. Yet he didn't say a word. He stayed there, unable to move, until the performance finally ended around midnight.

The villagers went back to their homes, profoundly impressed that night. However, a specter haunted them, bringing back memories of a calamity that had struck the hamlet eleven years before, a disaster which had left many of the village children orphans.

On that night, the village of Paruk was soaked by heavy rains. And in the dark night the isolated village was lonesome, truly lonesome.

The only indications that the village was inhabited were a baby's cries and the hiss of a small lamp. The only other sounds were the croaking frogs which debauched all night long in frenzied copulation. The following morning, the aftermath of their revelry would be seen in the long strands of eggs left by the females, the green frog depositing her eggs in clusters that floated on the surface of the water, the leaf frog storing hers in foamy clumps that stuck to the shrubbery.

An educated person could have worked out what happened that night, at about midnight in the year 1946. All the inhabitants of the village were fast asleep, except for Santayib, Srintil's father. He was just finishing his work. For some years Santayib had provided the people of Paruk with a particular kind of tempeh, called *bongkrek,* made from *bungkil,* the dregs of finely-ground coconut. Each evening he rinsed, drained and then steamed bungkil until it was cooked. He then spread it evenly in a large, flat, winnowing basket made of bamboo, where it cooled. Finally he sprinkled it with yeast. Overnight the bungkil fermented; the following morning it would be ready to be sold in its final form, bongkrek.

Finished with his night's work, Santayib went to bed. Before he slept, Santayib checked Srintil's diaper and, after changing her swaddling, returned her, still sound asleep, to her mother's arms. Stillness. Paruk and all its inhabitants seemed to have dissolved into the cold and damp night.

Rainwater, collected on the foliage, fell to the earth in dripping beads that made steady tick-tock sounds when they struck banana or taro leaves. An owl perched quietly on a low branch, its watchful eyes surveying the watery surface of a mud hole. When it saw a frog, the owl dived soundlessly towards it, returning to its perch with its victim in its beak. The owl repeated its hunt throughout the night until its gullet was adequately filled with fresh meat, expressing its contentment by crying out in a heavy voice: *guk-guk-guk, hrrrrr.* The sound of a ghost. A sound that causes every child that hears it to quickly seek the safety of his mother's arms.

The moonlight, too weak to pierce the blanket of clouds, tinged the eastern sky with a pale yellow glow. Lightning occasionally produced momentary daylight, leaving searing after-images of jagged and glittering striations, followed by prolonged reverberations of thunder. When the echoes died away, Paruk was once again ruled by the voices of the frogs. The continuing rainfall made the village seem even smaller and stiller.

No one in the village was aware of what then happened: A reddish ball of light raced through the sky toward the village. Above the hamlet, it exploded, scattering fragments in all directions. If the villagers had seen it, they would have screamed at the top of their voices, "The rain of death! The rain of death! Watch out, it's the rain of death! Cover the water cisterns! Cover all the food!"

Villagers believed that such an unearthly light was a carrier of misfortune but that night not a single person was awake to ward it off with magic or prayers. Only the goats bleated in their pens. A small commotion arose in the chicken coop, with the owl suddenly hooting in response. From the leafy banyan tree towering over Ki Secamenggala's grave, other owls cried out with powerful echoes.

The stillness held until dawn began to break. The cry of a baby pierced the silence, and goats started bleating as they grew hungry. The rain became a misty drizzle and created a rainbow in the east. The croaking of the frogs continued into the morning. Roosters crowed and rats squeaked as they rooted for insects hidden beneath rocks.

Although Santayib had been the last person in the village to go to sleep the previous night, he was also the first to awaken, followed by his wife and baby. Srintil was left on her own as her parents began their busy routine, preparing the bongkrek for sale. Before the sun rose much higher in the sky, the neighbors would be coming to purchase the bongkrek. Except for market days, Santayib always sold his product to his neighbors.

The day grew brighter. In the yard in front of Santayib's house, a frog hopped around seeking a dark place under the verandah. Others of his kind were still swimming and mating in the nearby pond. Bats and flying foxes squabbled as they returned to their nests. It could be that they were still hungry as the rain would have disrupted their hunting. Yet, such flying creatures were regulated by nature. If they dallied, and returned to their homes too late, they would become prey for the crows.

Several children had already emerged from their respective porches, some running to the bamboo front gate and peeing there. Others ran to an outhouse behind the house. Flies scattered. A jay screeched as it swooped down on its dinner, a greenbottle fly. Occasionally, the adroit little bird would swoop down and catch a mosquito circling around the head of one of the children.

Burrows of dung beetles surrounded the outhouses. This revolting insect, whose unique life cycle revolved around the collection of feces, would crawl backwards until its rear legs struck against a small turd about the size of a seed. It would then push the turd backwards until it reached the mouth of a burrow. There, the turd would be pushed into the earth. And in the turd, the dung beetle would lay it eggs and perpetuate its kind.

A couple of people had already come to purchase bongkrek from Santayib's wife. The women chatted with ease and intimacy, one of the delights of simple village life.

"Srintil up yet?"

"No," answered Santayib's wife "She knows that I sell bongkrek every morning, and she knows how to behave."

"You're lucky to have such a quiet baby."

"If she weren't, we'd have a problem."

"Your bongkrek isn't mixed with bran, is it?"

"Oh my, no. Yesterday, Mr Santayib got a good batch of coconut meat. Dry and aromatic. Try some, the bongkrek is really sweet today."

"Thank God. This morning, everyone at home is eating river paddy rice. We're pounding the last of what we've been saving for planting. What else can we do? We've been eating tapioca gruel for a month. Today we're cooking rice."

"Hmmm... Bongkrek and vegetables mixed with beansprouts on cooked river rice. Served hot. Can I eat at your house?" joked Santayib's wife.

"Of course you can. Come on over."

"Thanks, but I was just kidding."

The village slowly came alive with the booming sound of cassava being pounded into powder in immense mortars carved out of logs; the sizzling of hot vegetable oil in big pans as battered bongkrek was fried; the ringing of a small bell on the neck of a lamb as it suckled its mother's chapping nipple. A hen squawked loudly as a hawk made off with one of her young. Women in their kitchens scolded their children who whined while waiting impatiently for still-cooking gruel.

When the children dashed outside to tear off a wide banana leaf to use as a plate, it meant that breakfast was ready. They ate on the verandah, the door step, or wherever they could find a spot to sit. To the village children, all food was delicious as their stomachs were rarely full.

The sun rose in the sky, its heat beginning to burn. The strong sunlight had bleached the hair of the villagers to a deep, dark red, and burnt their skin to a scaly blackness. The previous night the village had been saturated with rain, but now it boiled, hot and humid. Yet, the village people always followed the natural order of things. The adults resolutely worked in the fields or the rice paddies and the children tended the livestock. The beginning of this day was no different from any other in the small, isolated hamlet.

However, everything changed around noon.

A child came running from the paddy field holding his gut. In the yard in front of his home, he vomited and staggered about until he fainted. His mother, her head aching, screamed and called out to her neighbors. By the time they arrived, the child was almost dead.

The mother fell, unconscious, her face turning blue. Mother and child lay sprawled on the ground. The screams from their house started a panic in the village.

Hearing the cries, people working in the fields rushed home. In some cases they, themselves, felt their heads reeling. One man had to be carried by his friend because he couldn't walk. In the village, cries for help could be heard from every home. Eventually, almost every family was involved in its own pandemonium, its own horror, so that finding assistance from others became impossible. Mothers helplessly watched their children and husbands dying, as they themselves hovered between life and death.

The people of Paruk were not very clever, but some people thought they could figure out the cause of the disaster. Not every family was affected. Families not affected were those who hadn't eaten Santayib's bongkrek.

In the commotion and panic, people began cry out "*Wuru bongkrek!* The bongkrek is bad! "

Santayib heard the cries, first with disbelief, then dread. In his heart, he strongly denied such accusations, but his mind told him the accusation might be true.

Struggling and raging inside, Santayib trembled under the emotional stress which was quickly engulfing him. His lips were pale; he was breathing rapidly. His wife wept in terror. They themselves hadn't eaten any of the bongkrek as they were tired of its taste. Santayib's wife drew closer to her husband as he sat trembling on a bamboo couch on the verandah.

"Everybody's in a panic. Many of the neighbors are sick or unconscious. What's it all about?" she asked.

Santayib was mute, his stress increasing by the minute. Watching him sit, silent and still, his wife cried out again, "Haven't you heard people say that they've been poisoned by our bongkrek? What's it all about?"

Still, Santayib kept silent. Only his chest heaved faster. The inner struggle between his heart and his mind grew more violent. His basic nature wanted to deny what was happening. Yet Santayib understood that the facts he faced were almost impossible to deny.

He also knew that he would be held responsible for the bongkrek that had caused this disaster.

Santayib's father, Sakarya, appeared at the door. With him, were three other men, their faces dark with fury.

"Oh my god! Oh my god, Santayib! The people are dying from eating contaminated bongkrek. Your bongkrek!"

As he spoke, Sakarya entered his son's house to see the contaminated bongkrek for himself. Suddenly Santayib stood up. The struggle between his feelings of accepting and rejecting responsibility for what was happening emerged as a flash of anger. Santayib stood, trembling, shouting to the four men facing him.

"No! My bongkrek can't be poisonous! It was made from dried coconut meat. It wasn't mixed with anything. Father, how can you allow people to accuse me of such a thing?"

"The evidence speaks for itself," one of the men said. "My children, my wife, my mother, they're all overcome. They ate your bongkrek this morning."

"It can't be! Maybe it's a coincidence or a curse from Ki Secamenggala because he hasn't received an offering for a long time."

"Or maybe you rinsed your coconut in an old copper bowl," yelled another of the men, running to the well. Sure enough, there he found a brass bowl. And on it was a layer of blue, the color of corroding copper. He held up the bowl to show the large crowd of people gathering in front of the house, then screamed like a lunatic, "You son of a bitch! You bastard! Look, this bowl is blue with poison. You bastard! You've murdered all those people."

The man tried to throw the bowl at Santayib, but he didn't have the strength to do it. His head was spinning and his bowels were twisting. His face and chest felt hot. Shuddering, he toppled over. The panic of the crowd increased to a frenzy when a woman appeared, running, with her skirt hiked up high and her accusing finger pointed directly at Santayib.

"Santayib! Two of my grandchildren are sick from eating your bongkrek. They're going to die. What do you say to that, Santayib? I demand you admit responsibility. You owe me their lives. Help my grandchildren! Now!"

Bitterness, disbelief, and distress gripped Santayib's heart. He was bewildered, completely bewildered. The confusion in his heart was reflected by the undecided look on his face. His wife ran back and forth with Srintil in her arms, weeping. As if she understood what was going on, Srintil joined in and bawled loudly.

Santayib, probably only half aware of what he was doing, ran into the house, coming back out with clumps of bongkrek in his hands. His voice, shrill and harsh, made everyone's hair stand on end.

"Assholes! You're a bunch of rotten assholes! My bongkrek has nothing to do with this disaster. Look! I'm going to eat this bongkrek. If it really is poisoned, then I'll die too."

Santayib shoveled bongkrek into his mouth, swallowing it without chewing. At first, his wife was stunned, but then feelings of loyalty commanded her to act. Still holding Srintil, the woman followed her husband's lead, snatching pieces of bongkrek from his hands and quickly swallowing them.

For a moment, Sakarya was thunderstruck. In front of his own eyes, his son and daughter-in-law were defying the poison. Panic-stricken, the old man cried, "Don't! My god, Santayib, don't! Don't play with death."

Sakarya lurched forward, intending to knock the bongkrek out of Santayib's hands and scoop the poisonous food out of the mouths of his son and daughter-in-law. But in his rush, he tripped on the doorframe, his head striking a wooden pillar. He fell down next to the man who had tried to throw the copper bowl at Santayib.

The bodies of the two men lay sprawled on the ground, one overcome by the poisonous tempeh and the other knocked out by a blow to the head. The other two men quickly left the house, carrying vivid images in their minds of the two bodies and the young couple who had deliberately swallowed the poisonous food.

Santayib swallowed the last of the bongkrek. He looked around for his wife who had been next to him. But she had disappeared, taking Srintil into the house.

Stillness gripped Santayib's home. He felt dazed. He knew he had done nothing to harm the two men lying sprawled on the ground and he left them, lying there unconscious.

What happened then could only have been madness. Santayib roared with laughter and ran out of his house. As he jumped and capered along, he was heckled and sworn at by the crowd which quickly surrounded him. Santayib ignored the general panic that had infected his neighbors. His eyes were wild as he raged.

"You, people. Open your eyes. I've swallowed handfuls of the bongkrek you say is poisoned. You're all sons of bitches! I'm still healthy even though my stomach's full of bongkrek. You wanna die, go ahead and die. Just don't say my tempeh is poisonous. You're all cursed by Ki Secamenggala. You're all sons of bitches and deserve to die!"

Finally, weary from shouting, Santayib returned home. At the front of his house several people were trying to help the man who had attempted to throw the copper bowl at him. His father was still sprawled on the ground near the door.

Santayib stopped briefly and shook his father's unconscious body. As he stood up his head started to swim and a thousand butterflies fluttered before his eyes. He felt the first stabs of pain in his stomach.

Santayib went into the bedroom, the door creaking as he opened it. He could see his wife lying on the bed staring up at the ceiling, her body bathed in sweat and her face pale. Occasionally she grimaced as the muscles in her stomach cramped.

Srintil lay chattering and gurgling happily next to her.

Although the room seemed to be spinning around her, his wife was aware that her husband had come back. With great difficulty, she struggled to sit up on the edge of the bed.

Husband and wife looked at one another. They both firmly believed that they had received an omen from the founder of Paruk. They looked questioningly at each other, but said nothing. Santayib's image registered in the eyes of his wife, but it shattered chaotically in her fevered optic nerves. And what she saw wasn't Santayib, but a terrifying shadow advancing toward her.

Her face grew deathly pale. Her eyes bulged so much that her irises looked like black dots in the middle of white spheres. Her mouth gaped as if she wanted to scream out.

It was the same with Santayib. While the sound coming to his ears was actually the chuckles and gurgles of his baby girl, all Santayib registered was the cacophony of a thousand screaming monkeys from the village cemetery. He saw hundreds of corpses rising from their graves, playing bamboo xylophones with such violence that their bones fell like branches from a windblown tree. Santayib's eyes bulged and his mouth gaped. When he saw a vision of Ki Secamenggala with his hands reaching out to throttle him, he wanted to scream, but the muscles of his neck were rigid and he couldn't produce a sound.

In the suffocating silence, Santayib stood teetering, his wife sat shivering. The two could not bear to look at one another. Only with one final superhuman effort could they speak, their voices rising out of swollen throats.

"My dear," she said with bulging eyes staring directly ahead.

"Hhhheh?"

"Srintil ... Who will care for her?"

"Hhhheh?"

"I can't bear to leave her."

Santayib had only enough strength to swallow. At that moment, Srintil squirmed and cried out, demanding their attention. He wanted to gaze upon her one last time, but he was hallucinating. Her movements, usually amusing to him, now seemed like those of a terrifying demon. In the final moments of his life Santayib saw his wife topple backwards onto the bed. He too soon collapsed, but only after mumbling the curse, "Fuckin' bongkrek." His wife died while struggling to turn her body to hug her baby.

Crows smelled the stench of death, evil black birds flying in circles amongst the trees around the village. That day their hoarse cries sounded to the villagers like a macabre celebration as they cawed from afternoon until night.

Death works deliberately and determinedly. Death is experienced in its vocation, having conducted such business since the very first mortality. Undeterred by screams and mourning, death called upon the people of Paruk. That day, nine adults died, two of these being Santayib and his wife. Eleven children were also beyond help, more than half of the village youngsters. The other ten or so became orphans.

Although Santayib and his wife died that afternoon, their bodies were not buried immediately. The other families were busy burying their own dead, or helping those people still clinging to life. The villagers had simple methods for treating stomach poisoning: administration of coconut milk mixed with salt, or water mixed with kitchen ashes, both being relatively effective purgatives. Unfortunately, unrestrained use of such concoctions brought about death as often as it offered hope of survival. Unbeknown to the villagers, many of their friends didn't die from bongkrek poisoning that day, but from dehydration: the result of too much vomiting.

That night, Sakarya, together with his wife, stood watching over the bodies of their son and his wife. Srintil cried a great deal, but she was too young to grieve. She cried because she was hungry for her mother's milk. To quieten her, Nyai Sakarya fed her rice porridge. Although he was supposed to keep watch over the bodies of his son and daughter-in-law, Sakarya went out in the middle of the night to Ki Secamenggala's grave. There, the old man wept in solitude. In his grief, Sakarya prayed to the ancestors of Paruk, mourning the catastrophe that had struck his people. This was his duty as the village elder.

After leaving the cemetery, Sakarya walked around the village, visiting every home. At every door he found tragedy. Not infrequently, he was received ungraciously, as if he were responsible for the sins of his son. Despite such rudeness, not one home was left without a visit by the village elder.

After he had visited every house, Sakarya resumed his walk, this time tracing the perimeter of the village. At the foot of the small hill that marked the grave of Ki Secamenggala, he stood with his arms folded. In meditative concentration, the old man tried to commune with the spirit of Ki Secamenggala, or with any of the other spirits that lived in the realm of the village. His ancestors had taught him to communicate with the spirits by reciting a kidung poem, which he sang from the depths of his heart:

Ana kidhung rumeksa ing wengi
Teguh hayu luputing lara
Liputa bilahi kabèh
Jin sétan datan purun
Paneluhan datan ana wani
Miwah penggawé tirta
Maling adoh tan ana ngarah mring mami
Guna dukuk pan sirna...

This is a song to guard the night,
Keep me safe from harm, free from all suffering,
Let me forget all misfortune,
May devils and demons not torment me,
May black magic not strike me, as well as deeds of evil,

Or the workings of misguided humans,
Quench them like fire in water,
Let the designs of thieves be directed elsewhere,
May spells and disease be destroyed...

The world was silent, listening to Sakarya's lament. The only sounds from the village were the occasional moans of the sick, or the weeping of the living for the dying and the dead. The fragrance of night flowers was overpowered by the acrid smoke of incense, billowing from every house in the village, a community deep in grief.

Srintil was five months old.

2

The tragedy was still fresh in the memories of the people of Paruk. An old woman told the story to her grandson, Rasus, dozens of times. That old woman was my grandmother. In Paruk there was only one person named Rasus, and that was me.

I wasn't able to write down Grandma's stories until after I grew up. And those things which I experienced in my childhood I now recall as a multitude of childlike memories. Yet, even as a small child, I began to piece together the whole story from bits and pieces I heard here and there. Only after reaching the age of twenty years or so, could I compile these into a set of notes. These notes are really nothing more than the story of a youngster living in the village. But, I couldn't possibly have written them without first completing the long twists and turns of my life and finally discovering who I really was. It was like crossing a long and dangerously narrow bridge which I could only describe and write about after I had reached the other side.

I believe that much of Grandma's story is true. Parts of the story, I think, were drawn from the legends unique to Paruk, and other parts I believe to be a rather unsatisfactory fabrication.

One of these village legends was the story Grandma told me about certain phenomena in the cemetery on the night of the catastrophe. Grandma said that lights had been seen above the banyan tree growing over Ki Secamenggala's grave, and that the sounds of weeping, echoing sobs, had been heard coming from the cemetery. Grandma said that the ghost of Ki Secamenggala had emerged, visiting each corpse before it was buried.

She told me that Sakarya said Ki Secamenggala had communed to him that the death of the eighteen inhabitants of the village was his wish. Ki Secamenggala claimed that, during his evil life, he had murdered the same number of people. The lives of his descendants were being offered as compensation.

Several days before the disaster, Grandma told me, unusual things had happened, that were later interpreted as omens. Water in the village well had developed a foul odor. The *puring* trees in the cemetery had withered, while neighboring *kemboja* trees had flowered. Wild dogs had unexpectedly invaded the village, the males fighting over the females amidst a terrifying din. The cuckoo bird had sounded from nightfall to dawn.

The people of Paruk believed these stories and nobody could convince them otherwise. Neither, I considered, should the villagers be blamed for believing that oxidized copper was the primary cause of the disaster. I learned later that while oxidized copper could have been the cause of the fatal food poisonings, there was in fact no hard evidence that this was the case. The real culprit might have been a bacteria named *pseudomonas coccovenenans* that can grow in bongkrek as it ferments. This bacteria creates a powerful poison, which would have killed those that ate the tempeh.

However, it would have been useless to present this information to the villagers, since they were absolutely convinced that copper oxidation was the cause of the poisoning. Although they now avoid using copper implements, the people of Paruk continue to make tempeh bongkrek. The disaster that struck the village when Srintil was a baby—I was three years old at the time—was not the first such incident, nor will it be the last.

I was saved, according to Grandma, by sheer luck. When my mother and father first began to feel woozy, I had already fallen unconscious. Without anyone to assist her, Grandma dug a hole in the ground next to the house and buried me in an upright position with only my head above the ground. This was a method that people in the village sometimes used to treat stomach poisoning.

After I grew up, I thought about what she had done that day. It may be that, by being buried, the earth drew out and quickly absorbed the poison-filled sweat from the pores of my skin, thus depleting its potency. Naturally, such a theory does not have much basis and would probably be scoffed at by scientists. Perhaps, then, it would be better for me to accept Grandma's notion that I survived because Ki Secamenggala did not yet wish me dead.

The story Grandma told that most intrigued me was one concerning my mother. Both my parents, along with many of the villagers, had eaten the bongkrek that day. While my father died on the first day, my mother and five others became very sick, but lingered on. Three days later, a district health official arrived in the village. Wearing a pith helmet and sporting a mustache, he tried to assist the still-living victims, but scolded them, asking why they had eaten tempeh bongkrek, a food not even fit for dogs?

Mr Health Official took my mother and the five other survivors to a clinic in a town to the east. Several days later, one person came back alive and three others as corpses. Mother was not among them.

Grandma always stopped telling the story at this point. I was sure that she knew what happened to my mother. Yet, like everyone else in the village, Grandma hid from me the truth regarding my mother's fate.

When I reached fourteen years of age, the time when Srintil began her career as a ronggeng dancer, someone told me that my mother had died at the town clinic in the east, and that her body had been taken to the regency capital where it was dissected by doctors trying to find out more about the poison in the tempeh bongkrek. Mother's body was never returned to Paruk. Where she was buried, nobody knew.

However, there were other people who thought that my mother had survived the poisoning, but was too ill to leave the clinic for several days. After Mother recovered, these people said, she left the clinic, but not for Paruk. Instead, she went to an unknown destination with the health official who had taken care of her.

So, there were two versions of the story of my mother. I had always felt unsure about which one to believe but wanted the first version to be true. I wanted to believe that my mother really did die at the clinic and that her body was chopped up in the interests of research. I intentionally allowed myself to dwell on such morbid thoughts, and I hope people will understand why I wanted this version of the story to be true: for me, its implications were easier to face than that of the other version. Unfortunately, both versions left me with many uncertainties, creating more suffering than a parentless child should have to bear.

Throughout the years, I could only speculate about my mother's fate. Let's assume that my mother really did become an object for research on tempeh poisoning: an autopsy would have been performed on her body. Her digestive organs would have been removed, as well as her heart and, most likely, her brain as well. The doctors would have wanted to know the effect of the bongkrek poison on the network of muscles in the heart and on the brain cells, and how the poison destroys the red corpuscles of the blood.

My mother's blood would have been examined to ascertain the amount of poison it took to kill her. I imagine that almost all the organs of her body would have been sliced up and then placed under the lens of a microscope or examined with intricate laboratory instruments. Finally, Mother's messy and formaldehyde-smelling body would have been buried, but where? Who knows where? Those doctors, whoever they were, considered that they had the right to bury my mother in obscurity, and that I, who had been nine months in her womb, did not have the right to know anything about it.

I didn't feel revulsion over the concept of my mother being sliced up. In fact, as I said, I found this version more acceptable than the other fantasy that intruded on my thoughts. Suppose that Mother hadn't died, but had run off with Mr Health Official.

It could be that my mother is living happily somewhere. Outside of Paruk, life is always better. At least, that's what I had always believed. This bureaucrat with the pith helmet, white suit, and long mustache, might have married Mother and together they had many children. Of course, their children would have clear skin and plump legs, and would always wear shoes. Every day, they would eat white rice with a delicious side dish. These children, who lived only in my imagination, would have thought life in Paruk very strange. My mother might have felt embarrassed to tell her new children about her native village.

Because I was sure that Mother was a good woman, I once imagined her wanting to come home to Paruk. Yet, I was certain that the health official would have forbidden it. Or, another possibility was that Mother wasn't able to return because she and the bureaucrat had moved to Delhi, a far-off place once described to me by Grandma.

Who knows the truth? At any rate, I eventually relegated Mother to my memories. Sometimes she would emerge as bitter thoughts. Other times, she would visit to comfort me. In any case, I did know that she had once lived, carried me in her womb, given birth to me, and nursed me with her milk. That would have to be sufficient.

Perhaps it would be better if I turn to a more concrete subject, something I know for fact: Srintil became the ronggeng dancer of Paruk at the age of eleven. I was fourteen years old. From then on, she became like a doll for the women of Paruk. Everyone wanted to coddle her, to dote on her. The women of Paruk took turns to wash Srintil's clothes. They bathed her and shampooed her hair with an ashy substance they made from burnt rice stalks.

If a man happened to cut down a banana tree, he would set aside the best bunch of bananas for Srintil. If a chicken was slaughtered because it was ill (nobody in the village would kill a healthy chicken), Srintil would always get some of the meat. The kids my age, Warta and Darsun, were willing to brave an assault by red army ants high up in a tree just to pick some mangoes or guava for Srintil. But all of that didn't really matter. What disturbed me was that Sakarya and his wife had forbidden Srintil to go outside and play on the outskirts of the village or beneath the jackfruit tree. If I wanted to see her, I had to go to Sakarya's house or peek at her while she was bathing at the fountain. I could understand why Sakarya wanted to keep Srintil secluded. In the space of a month, Srintil had visibly changed. Her hair, no longer bleached by the hot rays of the sun, had become thick and jet black. Her skin glowed ruddy and healthy, the fine scales and abrasions having disappeared. Her cheeks were so clear I could see a delicate network of blue capillaries through the skin. The pervasive dust that settled on our legs had vanished from Srintil's calves. But what amazed me most was that Nyai Sakarya had managed to eliminate the foul smell that used to emanate from Srintil's ears.

Basically, at fourteen years of age, I was bold enough to declare that Srintil was beautiful. It could be that the standards I used to evaluate her beauty were limited to Paruk village norms, but at least my admiration was honest. Indeed, this admiration continued to develop, and I felt no guilt about it. I began to feel anger toward those who treated Srintil as an object, especially Sakarya and his wife, and those young men who put money down Srintil's front when she danced *tholé-tholé*.

The village women were paying so much attention to Srintil that it seemed that she didn't need friends to play with any more. Srintil no longer showed any interest in me or anyone else. And I recognized that it was Srintil's interest that my heart was longing for.

One time, I thought I had found a sly method for regaining her attention. I stole a papaya from someone's field and at an appropriate moment, when Srintil was alone at the fountain, I gave her the stolen fruit. I was taken aback by the cruel thanks I received.

"Actually, I'd like a tangerine," Srintil said coldly. "But I suppose a papaya will do."

I was silent with disappointment, and a little embarrassed, but I found inspiration to help me through the situation. An idea suddenly occurred to me when I saw that her teeth had been filed.

"I know that you like tangerine, but it's not good for your teeth after they've been filed. It'd really make them sting."

"You're right, Rasus. I shouldn't have forgotten that. Lucky you reminded me," answered Srintil. And then she actually looked at me. When Srintil smiled, a soft ray of light reflected from one of her front teeth that had been capped with gold. With such a sparkling gold smile, she would make the heart of anyone with Paruk tastes for beauty beat faster.

I couldn't speak. As we gazed at each other, I was the first to give in and look away. What impudence. That's a ronggeng for you, you just can't stand up to the gaze of her eyes. The strange thing is that the way Srintil gazed at me made me happy. Yet, as I said, Srintil no longer needed friends her age. In fact, without any embarrassment whatsoever, she told me that she wanted to go bathe.

"And you had better go home too," she then added. "If you want, you can watch me later tonight. I'm going to dance again."

"Oh, so you're planning to dance tonight?" I asked, hiding my irritation.

"Yeah, now go home!"

Her order reverberated in my head. As I had been so directly dismissed, I went off, swearing at her underneath my breath. Moments later, however, I realized that I wasn't cursing Srintil. Rather, I was cursing myself for having been born the kind of person that could be summarily dismissed.

I didn't like being treated this way by Srintil, but I let it pass. I didn't go home, as directed, but walked a short distance away and sat on a tree stump, from where I could see the fountain through the sparse leaves of some low shrubs.

I saw Srintil remove her clothes. Then, three women arrived at the fountain, one of them bringing rice-stalk shampoo for Srintil's hair. Even in the act of bathing, Srintil really didn't need to bother herself. The three women vied with one another to assist her. Srintil just giggled, or yelped sweetly whenever a hand pinched her breast.

These Paruk women! Later, after I had learned about other women, I could say with more authority that the behavior of the women of Paruk was indeed astonishing. In this respect, I was relieved that my mother was long gone from the hamlet. If she had lived, she would have been just like all the other village women, who competed with one another in this very odd way.

Once, when I was watching Srintil dancing, I overheard the conversation of some women who were standing around the stage. Their words would certainly not have caused their husbands to think that they were shackled in any way by marriage and family.

"When Srintil is allowed to dance socially, my husband will be the first man to touch her," one of the women announced.

"Don't be silly," said another. "The ronggeng's choice will be the man that gives her the most money. And in this regard, my husband is unbeatable."

"But your husband's old. After just one dance, his butt will cramp."

"I know better than anyone else my husband's strength, if you know what I mean."

"Well, don't get too cocky. I could sell a goat so that my husband has enough money. I still believe that my husband will be the man who first kisses Srintil."

"We'll just have to wait and see when the time comes, which husband will win."

So it went on. A professional ronggeng dancer would never become a source of jealousy for the women of the village, rather the reverse. The more a husband dances with a ronggeng dancer, the prouder his wife feels. Her husband would be viewed as powerful by the public in terms of both his financial status and his sexual prowess.

After the papaya incident, I felt that Srintil was growing more and more distant. I often cursed myself for allowing myself to feel tortured by her neglect. I had to keep reminding myself that Srintil's beauty did not belong to me, but was hers alone. The soft, fine hairs in front of her ears, more pleasurable to behold than ever, were also hers alone. If Srintil smiled while she danced, I would tremble. Yet, her smiles were not for me. They were for everyone. Nevertheless, such reasoning did little to comfort me. I still felt deeply disappointed that I could no longer play with her.

Perhaps it was out of this anguish that I was able to devise another, more successful, method of gaining her attention. I had often heard people criticize Srintil's closing number, the Baladéwan dance, in which she assumed the role of a divine male character. They said that her body was still too small and slight for the dagger that was strapped in a sheath behind her back. This gave me an idea; at home there was a very small *keris* dagger which had belonged to my father.

I thought long and hard about that keris, and was a little apprehensive about giving it to Srintil knowing that Grandma would be against the idea. Fortunately, some wicked spirits showed me how to fool my old grandmother. One day. I told her my father had appeared to me in a dream. "He made me swear to carry out his wish," I reported.

"What was your father's wish?" Grandma answered, drawn into my fabrication.

"It was about the keris, Grandma. Father said I should give the keris to the one who is to become the village ronggeng."

Grandma's brow furrowed, making her look ugly beyond belief. This woman had given birth to my mother, but I hoped her grotesque looks weren't hereditary. However, such wretched thoughts didn't last long in my mind. I reminded myself that it was Grandma who, with boundless patience, had taken over the difficult task of raising me. Whenever she managed to find unhulled rice to pound, she allocated none for herself so that I would always get enough to eat.

"Is it because we haven't been taking good enough care of the keris that we have to give it to someone else?"

"It could be," I answered with conviction, pleased that my deception had been successful. People in Paruk believed that a command from the dead should never be circumvented.

The length of my father's keris was no more than twice the span of my hand, and its sheath was layered with brass and gold. The handle was made from a very hard wood called *walikukun*, carved into a strange shape which, if you looked at it closely, resembled a penis. Although I was a native of Paruk, I knew virtually nothing about the keris and its purpose. Consequently, I had no qualms about giving it to Srintil. I only needed to find an opportune time to do it.

Every day, when the sun was high in the sky, Sakarya and his wife went out to work their field, leaving Srintil at the house, either alone, or with some of the village women, who would come to pick lice from her hair. Sometimes, if she had danced the night before, she would be sleeping. I chose just such a time to enter the house through the back door and to steal into her room. Sakarya's house was utterly quiet, and Srintil lay sprawled on her bed, fast asleep. Near her pillow, several coins were scattered about. I felt angry when I remembered that this money had been inserted into Srintil's blouse by lecherous young men, who would have undoubtedly taken the opportunity to paw her breasts.

I stood watching Srintil as she slept. I've already said that my age was thirteen, almost fourteen, at that time. My knowledge of women, either as individuals or as a collective concept, didn't amount to much. However, I did have the ability, albeit still naive, to appreciate the impression a woman makes when she is sleeping, as opposed to when she is awake.

Srintil, asleep, was more at peace, more calm. Her closed eyes and expression, devoid of all emotion, made her even more delightful to behold. Her innocent lips, drawing breath slowly and regularly, made me feel as though I was beholding the image of the quintessential woman. Later, I learned that many artists have attempted, using paint, sculpture or words, to capture the image of true womanhood. I believe that these artists would have done better, if they wished to represent the very essence of woman, by capturing her sound asleep.

I didn't want to waken Srintil, but I couldn't stop myself from caressing the fine hairs in front of her ears and gently touching the tip of her nose. A fleeting thought passed through my mind of the way that my goats behaved before copulating, and the way forest pigeons bite one another's beaks just before they mate. I felt a sudden desire to do as these animals did, but resisted the urge, for fear Srintil would awaken. In reality, I was disgusted at the idea of being reduced to behaving like an animal.

The keris I had carried from home was tucked under my arm, carefully rolled up in a shirt. I felt that it would be better for me to give the keris to her while she was asleep. I assumed that such an offering would make a deep impression on her. I didn't feel that I was simply giving a keris to a young ronggeng dancer. Not at all. I was surrendering the keris to a true woman, one who lived only in the realm of my fantasy, but was embodied in the sleeping Srintil.

I laid the keris, still wrapped in my shirt, near her pillow, and gently moved Srintil's arm so that it covered the little dagger. Before leaving, I gazed at Srintil one more time. I wanted to keep the image of this beautiful, sleeping dancer in my mind forever.

Afterwards, I couldn't go straight back to tending my herd of goats. I let them run wild, not caring if they got into people's fields. All I wanted to do was to sit quietly beneath the jackfruit tree, which was still a peaceful place for me: even though I hadn't played there with Srintil for a long time. There I sat alone, musing.

A short distance to the west I could see the village cemetery. The sight of the gravestones there made me sad, reminding me that my mother's grave wasn't among them. I was surprised that the villagers hadn't made an agreement amongst themselves when I was a child to deceive me about my mother's fate. If they had told me that she was buried in the village cemetery, I would have believed them. It would have been better than having to conjecture what was true and what was not about my mother's story. Was Mother still alive? Did she run off with the health official who had taken care of her? Or, was she dead and her body dissected by doctors?

Indeed, it would have been far better for me to have been certain that Mother was dead. If she were alive, she'd be as beautiful as Srintil. Asleep, she would be the true woman I fantasized about, one who was attractive, calm, and the source of all virtue: like the sleeping Srintil who at that moment would be snuggling with the little keris I had placed next to her.

Or, perhaps Srintil was already awake. If she was, she would be surprised to find a keris next to her. But she would recognize the shirt in which it was wrapped, and would know who had left the keris on her bed.

Proof that my scheme was not just an empty fantasy was soon borne out when a pair of hands reached around from behind me and covered my eyes. For a moment I couldn't guess who it was, but when I smelled the fragrance of the *kenanga* flower and felt the smooth skin of a girl's hands, I knew that it was Srintil.

"Were you daydreaming, Rasus?" asked Srintil, sitting down next to me.

"No..."

"Admit it, you were!"

"I was just..."

"Never mind. Don't make up excuses. I know you were daydreaming about the shirt you lost. And here it is. Put it on!"

Srintil didn't simply hand me the shirt that had covered the keris.

She helped me put it on, carefully fastening the buttons for me. The backs of her hands were white, and her fingertips red from chewing betelnut, a new practice for her. I could feel my heart beating faster.

"Rasus, please tell me about the keris. And why you put it next to me while I was sleeping," said Srintil very close to my ear.

I couldn't answer right away. Neither could I bring myself to raise my head and gaze at Srintil's face.

"Tell me, Rasus."

"The keris is for you," I said softly, without looking at her.

"I know, Rasus. But why did you give it to me. Do you like me?"

Again, I couldn't answer. But, after she urged me several times, I finally said, "This keris is small, so it's right for you. The dagger you've been using is too big. With the keris I gave you, you'll look more beautiful when you dance the Baladéwan."

"So, you would like me to look more beautiful?"

I nodded.

"But do you know anything about the keris you're giving me?"

"No."

"Grandpa and Kartareja know something about it."

"What? Did you tell them I gave it to you?"

"No, I didn't. I kept that part a secret."

"And?"

"They said that the keris is called Kyai Jaran Guyang—Venerable Potion of Love—and that it is a village heirloom which disappeared long ago. It is a love charm, used as a talisman by ronggeng dancers in the past. They also said that it is because of my success that the keris came into my hands. With this keris, I'll become a famous ronggeng. At least, that's what Grandpa and Kartareja said."

"You'll become a famous ronggeng dancer?" I asked, repeating her words.

"That's what they said."

"So, do you like my present to you?"

"Oh, yes, Rasus I do."

Then Srintil embraced me. I knew she was expressing her thanks, and I didn't try to stop her. At the same time, I remained silent when she began to kiss my cheeks. Srintil didn't appear to feel at all uneasy behaving like this. It seemed she was already quite accustomed to it. When had she learned to kiss and embrace I asked myself. Or was a ronggeng like this by nature? Even when she was only eleven years old?

Srintil had been a ronggeng dancer for two months, but village custom dictated that there were two more stages for her to pass through before she could call herself a real ronggeng. One of them was a ritual bath, traditionally carried out in front of Ki Secamenggala's grave.

One morning, Paruk was adorned with the blossoms of the *bungur* tree, a brilliant shade of purple gracing almost every corner of the tiny village.

The sun had begun to return to its path along the line of the equator. The southeast wind no longer blew, and the sky, always clear and blue during the dry season, began to be spotted with clumps of clouds. The end of the dry season was approaching.

The morning was quiet; thin rays of sunlight pierced the leafy gloom of the cemetery. Drops of dew on the tips of leaves captured the light like prisms and splintered it into soft, glittering rainbows. A squirrel crept down from the top of a tree, spiraling down the trunk until it reached the ground. With watchful eyes, it leapt about, then climbed up the tree again, holding a millipede in its mouth.

In the dense foliage of parasitic vines, a pair of hummingbirds were chasing one another, the dark red male pursuing its mate. After he had caught her, the two birds struggled briefly and then let themselves plunge to the earth, mating in freefall. Only split seconds before their bodies struck the ground, the birds separated, having accomplished their primal function. The male flew off, now completely fulfilled, and returned to his perch in the thick foliage. His life ended abruptly there, where he was caught and eaten by a green snake.

The great banyan tree crowning the cemetery was like a sanctuary for birds. On one of the leafy branches a long-eared owl perched, almost invisible, sleepy after a long night of hunting mice and lizards. Only the little magpie robin dared to annoy this king of owls. Other birds, the pitch black *seling* and the green *katik* perched in groups. They quietly waited, warming themselves in the morning heat, before flying off in search of food.

That day, nobody worked in Paruk. The ritual bathing of a ronggeng dancer was a rare and important event. No one would miss it. By early morning the whole village had gathered in Kartareja's front yard. They would accompany Srintil from the house as she walked to Ki Secamenggala's grave, where she would be bathed.

Srintil was dressed as an adult ronggeng. I could see the little keris I had given her, tucked away behind her back. It suited her body perfectly, and this wasn't just my own assessment. I heard several people commenting, "Srintil has a new, smaller keris. It's just right, and so cute."

I was sure Srintil heard those words of praise, and I waited for her reaction. She didn't look at the people who praised her, but glanced at me and smiled. Unfortunately, I couldn't bring myself to return her smile because my heart was beating too fast. People might have wondered but I knew that, except for Srintil and my aged grandmother, no one else knew anything about the origin of the keris she wore that morning. Even if anyone did know that it was I who had given Srintil the keris, I didn't care. As a result of giving her this heirloom, Srintil had taken an interest in me again. This meant that there was a woman in my life, something I had missed for many years.

I couldn't be sure whether I longed for a woman to fall in love with, or a woman to represent a mother: my mother. Although she wasn't aware of it, Srintil had played a part in forming my fantasies about the woman who had given birth to me, even as to what she looked like. That much was clear to me. I felt that my mother would have had a nice smile like Srintil; that her voice would have been soft, fresh, like a true woman. Yet I couldn't be sure whether Mother would have had soft, fine sideburns like Srintil's, or if Mother, too, had a dimple on her left cheek. When Srintil laughed, that dimple made her look lovelier than ever. However, in my mind, my mother only generally resembled Srintil. I couldn't really remember what she looked like and, over the years, bit by bit, I had created in my mind these fabrications of her appearance, and they had eventually become realities for me.

In the front yard of Kartareja's house, Srintil began her first set. This time the performance was different, lacking both the singing and the erotic elements. Sakum remained silent, uttering no bawdy shouts. Everyone knew that this was not a normal ronggeng performance, but part of a sacred ritual blessed by the ancestors of the village.

After the first set finished, the remainder of the ritual was to take place in the village cemetery. Kartareja headed the procession to the cemetery, carrying a burner of incense. Srintil walked behind him, followed by the troupe, with Sakum being led by one of the other musicians. Behind them, the entire population followed, from children to the elderly. Babies were carried and small children led by adults, all heading towards Ki Secamenggala's grave.

When he reached the cemetery, Kartareja set down the incense burner at the gate of the ancestral mausoleum. Two men brought a jar filled with perfumed water, with which Srintil was to be bathed. Nyai Kartareja brought Srintil forward and, while two other older women provided a screen, she removed Srintil's clothes, leaving only a sheet of batik material to cover the girl's body.

Nyai Kartareja recited several incantations and blew puffs of air at Srintil's forehead. Then she sprinkled her body with the perfumed water, dipperful by dipperful. The villagers watched. The musicians prepared themselves, arranging their respective instruments and sitting cross-legged on the ground, waiting.

After the ritual bathing had finished, Nyai Kartareja dried Srintil's hair with a batik cloth. Three woman helped her dress Srintil again. They combed and powdered her, and helped her with her wrap-around batik skirt, tying a sash around her waist. Finally, they tied Srintil's hair on top of her head in a knot. Then, Srintil was led to the gate of the mausoleum, where she prostrated herself in prayer. Afterwards she stood up and walked over to the waiting musicians.

It was now Kartareja's turn to act. After briefly mumbling a silent prayer, he signaled the drummer. The silence in the cemetery exploded into music. The sounds of drumming and calung xylophones reverberated together in musical rhythms.

The dozens of birds that had been perching in the trees flew off in unison. Unlike the people of Paruk, the birds disliked calung music. And unlike me, watching spellbound as my mother appeared in the form of Srintil, the birds disliked ronggeng dancers.

The villagers believed that the spirits in the cemetery awoke at times like this to watch the performance. They also believed that Ki Secamenggala's ghost stood at the threshold of the mausoleum to watch Srintil dance. No one stood in front of the gate as this would have obstructed the spirit's view of the proceedings.

I stood near the front of the crowd, thinking. If there had been people in the village who could discuss things like artistic appreciation or, even better, a means to evaluate it, whose appreciation of Srintil's performance would have been the most profound? I arrogantly believed that my admiration was the deepest. I didn't just see Srintil swinging and swaying as she danced and sang. I didn't just hear the harmonious sounds of the drum, xylophones, and blown gong creating beautiful rhythms. I wasn't just impressed by the graceful curve of her neck, her swaying hips, or her bent back fingers. It was more than that. I saw Srintil as more than a small girl in the process of becoming a ronggeng dancer. While I watched her performance, I felt as if my longing for Mother had been quenched. Thoughts of whether Mother had run off with the health official, or had died and been sliced up into pieces, vanished from my mind. What filled my soul was the fact that Srintil was dancing and smiling at me. This was enough to vanquish, even if only for a moment, my suffering in not having known my mother.

People said that, during his life, Ki Secamenggala had greatly enjoyed a particular song, "Gunung Sari." It was this song that Srintil sang immediately after her ritual bathing, repeating it several times. Like the start of the ritual earlier at Kartareja's house, the performance in the cemetery did not include any bawdy songs. Sakum was silent. However, during the third set, something unexpected happened, something I will never forget.

Kartareja, who was standing, watching, suddenly convulsed with tension. The dukun's eyes stared wide open at the sky, his face became pale and soaked with perspiration, and his body went rigid. With his eyes partially closed, he took a few staggering steps towards the stage.

The crowd gasped. The calung music died away. Srintil stopped dancing as the drum and xylophones fell silent. Kartareja kept moving forward until he reached the center of the stage, where he began to dance and sing a love song.

Only Sakarya seemed to grasp what was happening. He believed that Ki Secamenggala's spirit had taken possession of Kartareja's body and wanted to dance with the ronggeng. Sakarya saw this as an acceptance of the ronggeng by Ki Secamenggala. He shouted out, "Start playing the drum and xylophones again. Ki Secamenggala wants to dance. Srintil, come on, start dancing again. Dance with Ki Secamenggala."

The calung music started up and Srintil began dancing again, but the atmosphere remained tense. The villagers, believing that Kartareja was indeed possessed by the ghost of their ancestor, drew back in fright.

Then the calung ensemble, picking up the mood of Kartareja's entranced state, started playing songs of a raunchier nature, and the somber atmosphere of the sacred ritual vanished. Sakum resumed his usual role, pursing his lips when Srintil thrust her hips and blowing out a bawdy hiss. "Chissss...chisss."

Kartareja's dancing became more and more sensual. Gyrating, he stepped closer to Srintil. First his left, then his right hand encircled her waist and, with surprising strength, he suddenly lifted her up high. Setting her down again, he lustily kissed her.

The audience cheered and clapped with delight, but I stood still, my heart pounding. I watched this spectacle, with hate and anger filling my heart, unaware that my hands were tightly clenched. I didn't do a thing. I didn't dare do a thing. Kartareja continued to kiss Srintil, unperturbed by the dozens of pairs of eyes watching him.

Suddenly the cheering and clapping stopped. Horrified, the village watched as Kartareja embraced Srintil so powerfully that the young girl gasped for breath. Srintil groaned in pain, as if she felt her ribs breaking from the pressure of Kartareja's powerful arms.

The situation was terrifying, but the only person to act was Sakarya, who suddenly leapt to the stage, shouting, "Stop the music! Stop the music!"

Sakarya slowly approached Kartareja who was still holding Srintil in a tight embrace. He could see his granddaughter's bulging eyes as she struggled to breathe. He began to chant, softly and slowly, "Release this child, Grandfather Secamenggala. I beg you to release Srintil. Have pity on her, Grandfather. She's your own flesh and blood," chanted Sakarya over and over.

Sakarya turned around and picked up the incense burner, waving its smoke toward the possessed Kartareja. Nyai Kartareja took a dipper of the perfumed water and sprinkled some of it onto her husband's head. "Remember, my dear," she started to say, but Sakarya interrupted.

"Don't call him 'my dear'! Call him 'Grandfather'!" he shouted. Don't you realize that your husband is possessed?"

No one knows whether it was due to the sprinkling of perfumed water or the billowing incense smoke, but Kartareja slowly eased his embrace, and his arms dropped to his sides. For a moment he tottered unsteadily, then crumpled to the ground. His arms and legs convulsed, and his eyes rolled into his head, only the whites visible.

I moved up to the stage, anxious to help Srintil out of her terror. I put my arm around her shoulders.

"Are you okay?" I asked.

Srintil shook her head. Her body felt cold and her hands trembled.

I led her away. The attention of the villagers was centered on Kartareja who was still sprawled on the ground, but slowly beginning to relax. He gasped. His eyes opened. He gazed around and then sat up, looking confused.

"It's okay, it's okay," Sakarya said. "Are you back with us, now?"

"What's happening? How come I'm all sweaty? Why has the calung music stopped?" asked Kartareja anxiously. The people surrounding him watched as he stood up.

"What's going on?" he asked again.

"Grandfather Secamenggala was just here. He danced with Srintil," explained Sakarya.

"Grandfather Secamenggala?"

"That's right. His spirit entered your body. You wouldn't have been aware of it though. This means that our prayers this morning have been accepted by him. Srintil has been given his blessing to become a ronggeng."

I didn't hear the rest of the conversation between Sakarya and Kartareja. Neither did I hear the bawdy jokes and remarks made by the villagers about the incident. All I wanted to do was remove Srintil from the scene. I took her hand and we went down the hill, away from the cemetery. I didn't take Srintil to her home, but to mine, with a boldness I never would have imagined of myself. Strangely enough, Srintil meekly followed, and my heart swelled.

"Rasus, if you only knew how terrified I was," she said, as I sat her down on a bench.

"Kartareja is a bastard and a son of a bitch," I swore.

"Hush, Rasus. Don't talk like that. You heard my grandfather, didn't you? Kartareja was possessed by the spirit of Ki Secamenggala."

"I don't care. The old bastard went too far. He was squeezing you too tightly. If someone hadn't helped, you would have suffocated."

"Would you be sad if I were to die?" asked Srintil.

I was silenced by her question. It wasn't her fault if she didn't understand what I was feeling. She wouldn't understand that, for me, she was a mirror through which I was desperately trying to see the image of my mother. I knew I couldn't expect her to understand. In answer to her question, I finally said, "You and I have been orphans since we were small children. We share the same destiny and I don't want to see you hurt. If you were to die, I'd lose my best friend. Do you understand?"

3

I thought the bathing ritual in the cemetery was the last requirement for a girl to become a ronggeng dancer, but I was wrong. The people of Paruk believed that Srintil still had to fulfill one more condition before she could be a paid performer.

The last ritual was called *bukak klambu:* "opening of the mosquito net." My hackles rose when I learned what this requirement was about. *Bukak klambu* is a type of competition, open to all men. What they compete for is the virginity of the candidate wishing to become a ronggeng dancer. The man who can pay the amount of money determined by the dancer's trainer has the right to take his pleasure with this virgin.

Srintil's maidenhood was to be the prize in a contest. "Sons-of-bitches! Bastards!" I thought.

I wasn't just jealous. Neither was I simply upset that, because of my young age and impoverishment, I couldn't possibly win such a contest. It was more than that. I believed that Srintil was born to be a ronggeng dancer, a woman who was possessed by all men. Yet, hearing that her maidenhood would be the prize of a contest filled me with rage. The bukak klambu ritual that she must undergo was an established custom in Paruk, and no one could change it, much less someone like me. I could only wait bitterly while events took their course.

Well beforehand, Kartareja had decided on the particular night on which Srintil was to lose her virginity. Kartareja himself was required to spend money for the event. He sold three goats at the market, and with the money bought a new bed for her, complete with mattress, pillow and mosquito net. In this bed, Srintil would be deflowered by the man who won the contest.

For many days the sound of the calung ensemble had not been heard in the village. Kartareja was busy preparing for the night of the bukak-klambu. He travelled far and wide, spreading the news that his determined fee was one gold piece.

"I have decided that the time will be next Saturday," said Kartareja, addressing a large group of men at the market.

"And you want a gold piece?"

"That's right. I believe it's a fair price," answered Kartareja.

The man who asked the question gasped.

"What's the matter? Too much for you? Think carefully. Was there ever a ronggeng as pretty as Srintil?"

"Maybe not but who in Paruk has a gold piece?"

"Well, I never dreamed of someone from Paruk winning the contest. No man here has a silver rupiah to his name, let alone a gold piece. I'm not expecting anyone from Paruk to enter the contest."

News of the night of passion quickly spread to other villages far from Paruk, arousing the excitement of many married and unmarried men alike. However, the enthusiasm of most was quickly dampened when they learned of the stipulation for sleeping with Srintil: a gold piece, worth approximately the price of a large water buffalo. Very few young men felt they could rise to such a challenge.

Three days before the ritual evening an oil lamp burned brightly in Kartareja's home. The door to one of the rooms remained open so that the new mosquito-netted bed could be seen by people from outside the house. The bed had been freshly made up with clean white sheets. For the villagers, who usually slept on simple bamboo pallets, such a sight was most unusual. That evening, many of the village women and children came to Kartareja's home just to see the magnificent bed.

I was there too. I didn't go into the house because, from where I stood at the corner of the yard, I could see the bed with the mosquito netting. While others viewed it with admiration, I stared at the bed with dread and revulsion, mixed with anger.

For me, the bed where Srintil would undergo the bukak-klambu ritual was nothing more than a sacrificial altar, or something even more repulsive. There, in another two days, the butchery would take place. I'm not talking about matters of passion. There, inside the cage of mosquito netting, which was visible from where I stood, the destruction of something precious, something that I'd always valued, would take place. Srintil would no longer be pure. As such, the matter of the loss of her virginity did not bother me greatly. Yet, as the mirror in which I sought an image of my mother, Srintil would be tarnished, even shattered completely.

To imagine Srintil sleeping with some man was as repugnant for me as it was to imagine my mother running off with the government official. I felt nauseated, unable to bear the thought of such an ugly and hateful thing happening. Yet, time and again, I reminded myself that a child of Paruk like me was powerless to stop it. So, I could only spit on the ground and curse them all silently, those sons of bitches!

Still standing at the same spot in the corner of the yard, I saw Srintil come out, her lips red from chewing betel. Her lustrous hair cascaded downward, partly covering her ripening shoulders. Women and children quickly surrounded her on the porch, words of praise echoing among the females. I watched Srintil as she laughed gaily. What could be wrong with a girl her age finding pleasure in hearing so much praise?

Seeing the way in which the village women praised her, convinced me that every one of them wanted their daughters to be exactly like Srintil, a ronggeng dancer. Would they be disappointed if their own daughters' legs were bowed, or their cheeks fat, or their lips as ugly as those of the water buffalo, so that they couldn't be ronggeng dancers. I just couldn't understand it!

I would probably have continued my angry daydreaming if it hadn't begun to rain. I would have never thought that the rain could be so fortuitous. The women and children who were crowding round Srintil quickly left to go home. As I moved forward a few steps and took shelter under the eaves of Kartareja's porch, Srintil caught sight of me.

"Is that you, Rasus?" she asked, her voice sounding glad.

"Yeah."

"Have you been here long?"

"Since before it began to rain."

"Come on in and keep me company. Grandpa and Grandma Kartareja have gone to see my own grandfather. I'm all alone now."

Srintil pulled my hand.

I followed and we sat together on the bench. Srintil chatted gaily, gesticulating like a small child. In fact, she was still a child, only eleven or twelve years old. Suddenly she became aware of the apathy that had overtaken me.

"You sure don't seem to want to chat," she remarked. "Don't you like being here with me?"

"No, it's not that at all."

"But you only talk when I ask you something. Why?"

"First close the door to the bedroom"

"Why?"

"I don't want to look at it!" I said crankily.

Srintil was momentarily taken aback, but it didn't take long for her to realize why I spoke the way I did. A woman's instinct. I waited a long time for her response but her sweet red mouth remained closed. She stood up to close the door as I had requested. The bamboo door squeaked and the bed, the site where Srintil was to lose her virginity, disappeared from sight.

"I understand, Rasus. I already know why you hate the bed."

I stared at her quizzically.

"But you know that I want to become a ronggeng dancer, don't you?"

I nodded.

"So?"

"Well, I want to ask you, how can you face Saturday night?"

I didn't get an immediate answer. I saw a young girl thinking about something totally new to her. But not only new, it was also something that was to become one of the pillars of her biological history. Maybe Srintil was only intoxicated with Kartareja's promise that she would possess the gold piece offered by the winner of the contest. Her thoughts could only go that far.

"So?" I asked again.

"I don't know, Rasus. I don't understand," Srintil answered with her head bowed.

"Of course, I'm glad that you'll get a gold piece. I have thought of that."

"I don't understand, Rasus. All I know is that I'm a ronggeng dancer and to become one I have to go through the night of bukak-klambu. You know that, don't you?"

I nodded again.

"Look at it like this, Rasus. You've been circumcised, haven't you?"

"For three years now. Why?"

Srintil tossed her head to shake her hair back. She bowed her head and then, without looking at me, the ronggeng dancer spoke: "It's an example, Rasus, just example. Do you own a gold coin?" she then asked.

"I've never had a gold piece in my life," I said quickly. "The only thing I have owned is a small keris that I inherited from my father. And that one possession, which was of any value, I gave to you. You know I have nothing else. You must know that."

Srintil looked directly at me, her eyes those of a child. Strange. I realized that I expected too much from those eyes, but I didn't feel guilty about it. Not at all, because, when Srintil looked at me closely, I remembered my mother. My dead mother whose body was dissected. Or, my mother who ran off with the government official and now lives in Delhi.

I glanced at Srintil. She was still staring at me dumbfounded, realizing that I had hoped for her to announce that she would not go through bukak-klambu because she had decided not to become a ronggeng dancer. It was an impossible and crazy fantasy and it was funny that I understood this as well as I did.

I couldn't bear the silence and could see that Srintil was also uncomfortable. I didn't know what else to do or say to her, so I stood up without saying another word and walked to the door.

"Where're you going, Rasus?" asked Srintil.

"Home."

"Really?"

"Yes."

"But it's still raining."

I kept walking. Once outside, I raised my sarong and tied it over my head. When I turned around, I saw Srintil standing under the eaves of the porch. Although I didn't really want to leave her, I continued walking. When I arrived at home I threw myself down on my bed.

The rain grew heavier. A slow leak from a hole in the roof dripped onto my sarong-wrapped body, nature's way of distracting me from myself. I eventually fell asleep curled up in a ball and, after a while, the tension in my body slowly relaxed. To fall asleep while the rain fell outside was an enduring memory for a child of Paruk. I slept soundly, dissolving into the natural course of the small village.

Friday night. The dry season was coming to an end. Earlier in the day, the rain had fallen in a deluge. Dirt clods, previously rock hard, were now saturated, and the rice fields surrounding the village had become stagnant pools. Paruk had become a lake. Only the network of dikes separating the different fields were visible, forming innumerable squares in the water, but the dikes were now soft mud, and the earth collapsed if anyone tried to walk on them.

Water birds, the *bluwak*, *kuntul* and *trintil*, reappeared. During the dry season they fled to the swampy lands at the mouth of the Citanduy River. Soon the bamboo forest would be alive with them, reproducing there as their forebears have done since time immemorial.

Paruk would go through months of humidity. Mildew would grow on the bamboo fences and damp wooden posts. Mushrooms would sprout on dead tree trunks and moldy branches. Worms would climb up on the porch roofs. Mole crickets would tunnel underground until they reemerged beneath porches. Ringworms and scabies would return with a vengeance to the arms and legs of the village children. And the people would accept all this as the natural order of things.

In the late afternoon, when Paruk was covered with stagnant pools of water from yet another downpour, a young man by the name of Dower could be seen hurrying towards the village. He wasn't bothered by the muddy dikes, and continued walking, his feet making slurping sounds as he lifted them from the muck. He wasn't wearing his sarong, but had it folded up over his shoulder so it wouldn't become stained with mud.

Dower only had one thing on his mind: to reach Paruk and knock on Kartareja's door. The closer he got to the village, the more he fantasized about a mosquito-netted bed with a clean white mattress and pillow and, paramount in his mind, a young virgin girl lying in the bed.

Winning the bukak-klambu contest did not only involve passion, nor was it simply about the celebratory rite of passage of a young girl. It was a matter of pride for the winner. Dower's main objective was for people to talk about him: "Dower isn't just anybody, you know, he's the young man who won the bukak-klambu contest over the ronggeng dancer, Srintil."

As he entered the village, Dower became increasingly nervous. It had become very dark and the lanterns had been lit. Since the ground was wet, locusts and grasshoppers weren't singing, but the tunneling mole cricket took over for them, vibrating its wings to create a deep, grating sound. Tree frogs shouted continuously. Unlike bullfrogs and green frogs, tree frogs croak with few pauses.

There was a nightwatchman's shelter at the main intersection of the village. Dower could hear the mutterings of several young men inside the shelter. Dower didn't know it, but these men had, like him, come from outside the village, lured by the bukak-klambu contest. However, they were only there to see how things developed if someone failed to come up with a gold piece as stipulated by Kartareja. They didn't have that kind of wealth, but still had a remote chance to compete if nobody else was able to fulfill the stipulation. They hoped that, if this were the case, then perhaps Kartareja would lower the amount.

Unlike on previous nights, Kartareja's house had been quiet all afternoon. The dukun had chased away any children that had come by, but he hadn't had to chase away the adults; the people of Paruk knew that Kartareja was about to face an important celebratory ritual and they didn't want to bother him.

The light of the oil lamp fell on Dower as he reached the yard in front of Kartareja's house. The young man paused. He could see Kartareja sitting alone in a cloud of cigarette smoke. In addition to chewing betel, the old man was a heavy smoker.

Although his feelings were hidden by his outward calm, Kartareja was restless. It was already Friday and no young man had come to offer a gold piece for Srintil's maidenhood. What an embarrassment it would be if the bukak-klambu contest he had arranged didn't work out. The three goats he had sold to pay for the ritual would have been for nothing. Kartareja's thoughts were suddenly interrupted by the creaking of the front door.

"*Kula nuwun*," Dower declared, politely announcing his request to come in.

"*Mangga*," welcomed Kartareja, in customary response. He bobbed his head, squinting in the glare of the oil lamp. "Please come in."

Dower walked past Kartareja, and sat down next to him, the bamboo boards creaking as he settled himself the bench. Kartareja knew from Dower's winded breathing that he had come a long way.

"You look tired. Where have you come from?" asked Kartareja.

"From Pecikalan. My name is Dower."

"Pecikalan? That's a long way."

"It is. I came because I heard the news."

"About the bukak-klambu?"

"That's right."

"It's happening tomorrow. You know my stipulation, don't you?" asked Kartareja, not looking at his guest.

"I know," answered Dower flatly.

"Well, did you bring it with you?"

Dower was embarrassed, unable to lift his head. Kartareja let out a long breath and groaned to himself. The gold piece he wanted still hadn't appeared.

Dower finally said, "Right now, all I have are two silver rupiah. I want to offer these to you as an advance. There's still another day left and probably by then I can get the gold piece."

Kartareja didn't answer straight away. He drew deeply from his cigarette to hide his disappointment. When he exhaled, the smoke came out with a long hiss. He considered the facts at hand: two silver rupiah was more than any candidates had come up with so far.

"So that's your intention, boy?"

"Yes, sir."

"All right. I'll accept your cash advance, but tomorrow you have to bring a gold piece. If not, you lose the contest and your cash advance."

"You mean, if I fail to bring a gold piece I lose my cash advance?"

"Yes!" replied Kartareja curtly, his face tinged with cunning. Dower was silent, apparently considering the matter carefully.

"It's your decision. Think about it and, if you're not interested, go back to Pacikalan quickly while the night is young. I'm expecting some other young men; several will be arriving soon."

Evidently, Kartareja's bluffing hit home. Dower answered anxiously, "Okay, I'll accept your terms. Here's my cash advance."

Dower stood up and groped in the pocket of his trousers, the coins jingling. The two silver coins he placed on the table sparkled in the light of the oil lamp. Kartareja scooped them up and slipped them into a pocket in his belt. At that moment Srintil appeared carrying a tray with a teapot, two cups and a plate of fried cassava. She bit her lip lightly as she set the tray down. Without even looking in his direction, Srintil had made the young man from Pecikalan even more resolved to win the contest.

Kartareja smiled, seeing Dower fidget in his seat.

I knew every secret corner of the village and, as Kartareja chatted with Dower, I listened, hidden behind a clump of banana trees next to the house. I gathered from the conversation that in all probability it would be Dower who would win the bukak-klambu contest. Without even knowing him, I immediately hated him intensely.

I imagined Dower treating Srintil badly in that mosquito-netted bed. I was sure, absolutely sure, that he wouldn't respect her as I always had. Over the years, Srintil had come to represent all that I held noble in my life. But, with Dower, it wouldn't be like that. He would feel that he had bought Srintil. For one night she would become an object he had purchased, and he could treat her as he liked. The son of a bitch! I spat on the ground hatefully.

No stars were visible the evening sky. A faint light colored the sky in the west, where the moon was hidden by clouds. The weak glow was just enough to reveal the shadow of a flying fox as it flew lazily to the south, its wings flapping slowly. As it flew beyond the pale light of the moon, it disappeared from sight.

My attention returned to Dower when the front door of Kartareja's house creaked and the young man came out. I assumed that he would do his best to fulfill the promise he had made to Kartareja. Either that, or he would lose the two silver rupiah he had put up as collateral.

I don't know why I suddenly decided to leave my hiding place and follow Dower. While creeping quietly behind him, I imagined a fight with him, how I would punch him in the neck, or kick him in the crotch. Dominating my thoughts was the idea of destroying this interloper from Pecikalan who intended to molest Srintil.

I never actually intended to carry out my desire to hurt Dower, but when he drew near the guard house he stopped and cursed. The three young men who had been hanging around the shelter earlier had thrown a dirt clod at him.

"Son of a bitch! Who threw that dirt at me?" Dower yelled.

There was no answer, but several more dirt clods followed, hitting him on the back. His shirt and sarong were smeared with mud. Dower became even more angry. He spun round in my direction, only a few feet in front of me.

"Hey, you bastard! If you want a fight, come on out! Come out and face me!"

Still no answer. I moved to the side, out of his line of sight. The feeling of wanting to hurt Dower arose in me again, and I bent down to look for something to throw at him. My hand felt a soft pile: cow dung. I scooped some up and threw it at him. I heard him cursing repeatedly. He tried to continue on his way, but couldn't because more and more dirt clods were being thrown at him. Finally, he could do little else but try to protect his head from the hail of clods.

Unable to face this attack in the dark, Dower finally turned to flee, but hearing the young men guffaw, he reeled around to chase his attackers. As he didn't know the various alleys of Paruk, he soon lost the trail of his assailants. With rage and desire for revenge driving him, Dower ran blindly into the darkness. But then he tripped and fell into a deep mud hole. He bellowed like a man possessed.

Saturday arrived, a day I'll never forget because of the outrage I felt. I don't think I could ever adequately describe it, either because I wasn't able to find the words to express my feelings, or because nobody could fathom the sufferings of a child who knew his mother only through his dreams. Srintil, who in so many ways had become the embodiment of my mother, was about to be defiled. I put it this way even though in reality I knew it was somewhat different. For me, if Srintil was sold for a gold piece, she was no longer Srintil. She was the ronggeng of Paruk. Nothing more than that. I couldn't have a ronggeng dancer represent my mother.

I felt as though I was losing my mother for a second time. If there had been people with whom I could talk about my problems or who could have understood the bitterness I felt, my sorrow might have been lessened. But I was alone in this. To make matters worse, I believed that Srintil didn't fully comprehend the level of distress I was feeling at her being sold for a gold piece. As she had told me, she was born to become a ronggeng dancer and for that to happen she had to go through the bukak-klambu ritual.

I should be able to say that I went out that morning and released the goats to graze as usual, but actually I had long been ignoring the animals. That morning was no different. I wasn't concerned about the goats getting into other people's fields. I sat alone near the outskirts of the village and gazed at the rice fields now flooded with water.

Above me, at the top of a *sengon* tree, *keket* birds were perched: a male and a female with their young which were continuously flapping their wings begging for food. The female bird dove down looking for dragonflies or locusts, and then returned to her perch. She would tear up her prey, not for herself but for her young. An ideal family, I thought.

I liked to think that my mother would have been like that *keket* bird. She would have protected me and found food for me while I was still a child. Together with my father, she would have invited me to join in their chatter, the way those keket birds chattered. But I knew it was only a dream. Like a dozen or so other children in the village, I was an orphan.

I would have continued my daydream, carried along by the sight of the keket birds and the sound of water flowing over the lip of the mud walls separating the small plots of wet rice fields, if Warta hadn't come and intruded.

"You've been sitting here brooding for a quite a while," he said. "Didn't your grandma make your rice gruel this morning? If she didn't, why don't we go look for some taro root and roast it right here?"

"I'm not hungry," I answered, distracted.

"So?"

"Go away. Don't bother me."

"This is the first time I've heard you tell me to go away, Rasus. I want to know what's really on your mind."

"That's my business. Even if I were to tell you, you couldn't help me, so I'm not going to tell you anything. It would be better if you just go and look after your goats."

"If you're feeling that way, I can guess what's up. You've been affected by the love charm that Nyai Kartareja gave to Srintil, haven't you? Come on, admit it! Your secret is safe with me."

I laughed hollowly. Warta's words were cruel, but true. He had guessed accurately. Seeing my reaction, he knew he was right and laughed loudly.

"Oh, my poor friend. You've got a crush on Srintil, but tonight she's going to be mounted..."

"Damn you, Warta."

"Well? Isn't what I say the truth?"

"Yeah, but don't make it any worse for me."

"Rasus, you can feel unhappy. You can feel jealousy. But as long as you don't have a gold piece, it's all pointless."

"Sure, buddy, but you could distract me a little. Sing something, like you always do."

If you were prepared to say a few words of praise, it wasn't hard to get Warta to sing. Of all the village children, Warta had the best voice. His favorite *tembang*, or traditional sung poetry, was also the favorite of the other children, and had become known as the song of the village orphans. Nobody knows who wrote the song, but it captured the sorrow of all the children who had lost their parents as a result of the tempeh poisoning eleven years before.

Bedhug tiga datab arsa guling
Padhang bulan kekencar ing latar
Thenguk-thenguk lungguh dhéwé
Anginé ngidid mangidul
Saya nggreses rasaning ati
Rumasa yèn wus lola
Tanpa bapa biyung
Tanpa Sanak tanpa kadang
Duh nyawa gondhèlana

It's three in the morning and I'm not asleep.
The moon spreads its light on the yard.
While I sit here alone with my thoughts,
A breeze gently blows to the south,
Making me suffer all the more.
This is the way for those of us all alone,
Without a mother and father, without kin,
Without family: a life of destitution filled with sorrow.
Lord, help this hopeless spirit.

Warta had sung this song hundreds of times and no longer took much notice of the meaning of the words. For him, only the melody was important. After singing the song, Warta glanced at me. He saw me bite my lips, and may have noticed that my eyes were glistening.

"What's this all about?" he asked mystified.

"It's nothing, Warta. Believe me. I'm moved, that's all. Everyone who hears you sing is moved.

"Is that all? What about Srintil losing her virginity tonight?"

Although I tried not to react to Warta's words, I felt pain, profound pain, unable to speak. I stood and started to walk away.

I could feel Warta watching me as I left him. I didn't pay much attention to where I was going, but just walked wherever my legs carried me. My aimless wandering brought me to the path which led to the cemetery. I saw someone moving furtively amongst the shrubs. Srintil!

Without realizing that I was following her, Srintil continued through the shrubs, her route circuitous to avoid the headstones and the dense growth of kemboja trees. She turned left and made straight for Ki Secamenggala's tomb. I saw her squat down and place an offering in front of the gate to the mausoleum. When she stood up and turned around, she was startled. I was standing only a couple of steps behind her.

"Oh, it's you, Rasus."

"I was following you."

"Nyai Kartareja told me to put out an offering here. Because tonight..."

"Stop! I don't want to hear any more about that, "I said tersely. I turned to go but Srintil grasped my shirt.

"Rasus, where are you going?"

"Home."

"Don't go yet. Don't be like this. Let's sit here for a while."

She then took my hand and we sat down on the root of a large banyan tree, but both of us remained silent. Srintil must have sensed that I was experiencing a great deal of hurt. Surely she must have known that I was fond of her. And she must have known that I deeply resented the idea of bukak-klambu. I thought to myself, perhaps I should speak frankly and tell Srintil I respected her more than I would have if she were just my lover? No. I didn't have the courage to tell her all of that. Let Srintil know only a part of me.

Finally, it took a small insect to break the ice and offer an opening for conversation. A mosquito settled on Srintil's cheek, its belly swollen with blood.

"Srin, slap that mosquito on your right cheek."

"I can't see it."

"Of course not, but if you slap your right cheek, high up, you'll get it."

"I don't want to. You have to kill it."

"My hands are dirty."

"That's all right. Go on, kill it."

I complied with her request. My movements were tentative, but the mosquito was filled with blood and its movements were sluggish, and I killed it with ease. I pressed the palm of my hand against Srintil's cheek and when I removed it a drop of blood remained, a stain of red on a white cheek.

It was lonely and quiet. A twig fell from a nearby tree and made a ticking sound as it struck a leaf. A small lizard appeared in front of me and quickly ran off in pursuit of a dragonfly resting on the ground. The stillness resumed. Srintil and I were silent. A breeze blew slowly while a grasshopper scraped a response from the slope south of the cemetery.

I don't know what Srintil was thinking, but in the silence of Paruk cemetery I felt that I had become part of the natural surroundings. I was no different from the moss-covered rocks in front of me, or the scores of jagged gravestones held in place by death and scattered throughout the cemetery. Perhaps my common sense had stopped functioning and had been replaced by instinctive desire.

I remained absolutely motionless as Srintil put her arms around me. I could hear my rapid breaths and felt the palms of my hands grow sweaty. When I glanced sideways, I saw that Srintil's face was tense. Although I had no experience in such matters, I guessed that Srintil was in the grip of passionate desire. It was I who didn't want her in these circumstances. Without removing her arm from my shoulder, Srintil looked around and checked to see if there were any other people in the area. She needn't have worried; the trees in the cemetery formed a dense wall around us.

Srintil released me from her embrace and I realized that she had done this to undress herself with greater ease.

I had often seen women bathing in the nude at the fountain. I knew the difference between male and female bodies. However, what I was seeing here was a female still untouched, a female who was not yet a woman: Srintil's chest and waist were yet undeveloped.

I knew that Srintil wanted me to undress as well. If I were Darsun or Warta, I certainly would have done so. I would have seized the initiative. Well, I wasn't Darsun, nor was I Warta. I was Rasus, a most unfortunate child whose mother had disappeared without a clue. I was a child full of doubts: doubts about my mother which had nearly driven me insane.

I believed that I was a normally functioning male. Seeing Srintil completely naked in front of me, I recalled how my male goat became excited when it was about to mate. My own heart pumped blood to my extremities, reaching that particular organ so that it was filled, tight and swollen. Powerful natural urges demanded that I act on them.

Srintil pulled my hand.

I looked at her blushing red face and her glistening eyes. I looked at her small nose, drops of perspiration forming on the tip. Gradually, everything in front of my eyes began to tremble and then merge together. The image of Srintil disappeared and was replaced by a blur.

I believe that ever since I was a child I had fantasized about my mother to such an extent because I was desperate to see her. This lifelong fantasizing now caused me to believe that it was not Srintil, the ronggeng of Paruk, standing naked in front of me, but the dream woman who had given birth to me. On her breast I saw that nipple from which I had nursed for almost two years. I had resided for nine months in her womb and when I saw the passage from which I emerged into the world my eyes grew dim and my body broke out into a cold sweat. I could do nothing else except cover my face with my hands.

"Rasus, don't you want to do it?" asked Srintil, her voice barely audible. "Nobody can see us here."

I had a sudden inspiration: "These are cemetery grounds," I told her. "Ki Secamenggala could curse us for this."

I could see that Srintil was confused; her breathing was rapid and her face flushed. She seemed disappointed and stood immobile, like the gravestones behind her.

"We can't do something reckless in a place like this," I continued, while picking up her clothes.

"Sure, but you're the one acting crazy."

"Forgive me. Don't be angry with me," I pleaded, like a servant asking pity from his master.

I waited as Srintil regained her composure. Her taut features slowly became more relaxed.

"Okay, Rasus, I'm not mad anymore."

"It has to be like this, especially if you think of the legend..."

"I know. You're right. I'm glad you reminded me. If you hadn't, who knows what could have happened."

The legend I was referring to was part of Paruk lore. According to the story, a couple once died in this cemetery in scandalous circumstances. They were struck by a curse after committing adultery on top of Ki Secamenggala's grave. Most everyone in the village believed this legend but I myself wasn't sure. Even at my age I had my doubts about its truth, suspecting that it was just another attempt to perpetuate local attitudes regarding the supernatural power of the ancestral grave.

I wasn't conscious of the length of time Srintil and I were alone in the cemetery. From where I was sitting, I was unable to see the sun, which was obscured by the leafy branches of a banyan tree. Thus, I was startled to hear someone calling from the distance I recognized the voice of Nyai Kartareja.

"I have to go home," Srintil told me. "Nyai Kartareja is calling. I've been away too long."

I could only nod my head to indicate that I understood. Srintil stood up and wound her way through the stumps of gravestones. Puring bushes swayed and swarms of butterflies took flight from the flowering kemboja trees as Srintil rushed from the grounds. I stood and watched her as she bobbed in and out of view among the trees and bushes. When she reached open terrain, she ran off into the distance, her hair streaming behind her. I felt as though I had lost something, but I didn't know what it was.

That afternoon was the worst of my life. When I went back to the village, I didn't go home. I ignored my grandmother who called and called for me because the food she had prepared for me had lain untouched since lunchtime. I sat near the goat pen watching the storks returning to the bamboo groves. The arc of a rainbow in the western sky made a peaceful and beautiful scene, but I couldn't enjoy it. The part of me that normally appreciated beauty was overwhelmed by the anxiety of knowing that, in a few more hours, Srintil would no longer be Srintil.

That afternoon, everything proceeded as usual, making me acutely aware of my insignificance in relation to the world, even in relation to a small village like Paruk. I watched the sun as it set, and scores of bats and flying foxes emerged to rule the darkening skies over the village, supplanting all the flying and soaring birds of the daytime. Small lamps were lit, illuminating the bamboo-walled verandahs of the village houses. Mosquitoes and gnats took to the air and began to swarm around my head. When it finally grew dark, I moved to go home.

It seemed as if the entire population of the village had decided to go to sleep that night. Not a single child was to be seen, or even heard. At one point I heard a minor scuffle in the goat pen and guessed the animals had been made restless by the biting of mosquitoes or because they had seen a pair blue eyes glowing in the dark: the eyes of a prowling cat.

The twenty-three houses of Paruk village seemed lifeless. The only exception was the Kartareja home. For several nights, the house had been illuminated by a large lantern, and tonight was no different. Nyai Kartareja was just finishing preparing Srintil, dressing her in a wrap-around batik kain and a new blouse, and arranging her hair in a chignon. Kartareja, was performing a ritual to ward off potential rain. He had lit an incense burner and placed it in a corner of the yard. In the same spot, he planted a water dipper with its handle in the ground. He threw old panties, brassieres, and other items of underwear onto the tiled roof of his house. Finally, he stood in the center of his yard with his face upturned to the sky.

I was sitting on my porch in the dark because I felt too sluggish to get up and light the lantern. I became aware of the bellowing of a water buffalo as it was guided along the narrow path which led to Kartareja's house. This was not a typical occurrence in Paruk. In fact, nobody in the village could even afford to keep such a beast. When the buffalo and its guide were struck by light from the porch of one of the houses, I recognized the person as Dower.

The young man from Pecikalan made his way toward Kartareja's house. I knew at once that this was related to the bukak-klambu event. I seized a sarong from the clothes hook and stealthily crept to the dukun's house, approaching it from the back. I could see the large beast tethered next to the house. Wanting to hear the conversation between Kartareja and Dower, I tiptoed to the porch from the side of the house and, through a hole in the bamboo wall, peered in. Dower, wearing a new shirt, had just sat down in front of his host. Srintil was not visible but I could hear whispering between her and Nyai Kartareja from inside the house.

Wiping the sweat from his face, Dover began the discussion. "As you can see, sir, I've come back, but what I bring isn't a gold piece. Nevertheless I hope that you'll accept it."

"What! No gold piece?" asked Kartareja.

"No. I bring you a large female water buffalo, the value of which far surpasses that of a gold piece," Dower explained.

Kartareja received this news with a sour smile. Dower fidgeted in his chair.

"But I can fit a gold coin in my pants pocket. I don't need to give it a stable or feed it hay and it doesn't smell," Kartareja replied scornfully.

"You're right, sir but if you add in the two silver rupiah I put down in advance then I think the offer is enough, more than enough."

Kartareja didn't change his expression, although he knew he had succeeded. He had won a female water buffalo *and* two pieces of silver. The dukun felt like crowing with delight, but controlled his elation.

"Even so, I don't consider that you have fulfilled the conditions I set down. A water buffalo and two silver rupiah are not the same as a gold piece."

"Are you turning down my offer?" Dower asked nervously.

"Yes, unless..."

"Unless what?"

"Unless you accept that you will be an alternative candidate. If nobody brings a gold piece by midnight tonight, then you'll be the winner. If you don't agree to this, you can have your two silver rupiah back. And take your water buffalo, too."

Dower hadn't imagined that Kartareja would respond to his offer with such harsh terms. The young man from Pecikalan was stunned, and the disappointment he felt in his heart went beyond words. He felt that he had done everything to deserve winning the bukak-klambu and to sleep the whole night on a soft bed with the young ronggeng. He thought of how he had broken into his parents' cabinet to steal the silver coins, and how he had succeeded in fooling his father by bringing his largest water buffalo to Paruk, instead of leading it home from the fields. Now he realized that, despite all his cunning strategies, his success wasn't by any means assured. The specter of possible failure emerged in front of his eyes. To himself, Dower bitterly cursed Kartareja.

From my dark place behind the wall, I could feel the tension between Dower and Kartareja. There was no further talk between them. Dower was reluctant to accept the new terms Kartareja had set down. On the other hand, the dukun did not wish to back down.

The tension was broken by the arrival of someone on a motorcycle. It was Sulam, the son of the wealthy headman of a neighboring village. Dower grew nervous, realizing that a serious competitor had arrived. On the other hand, Kartareja smiled. He also knew who Sulam was. Although still quite young, Sulam was known to be a gambler and a scoundrel. But Kartareja didn't feel compelled to look for someone virtuous to win the contest: his only requirement was a gold piece as payment for Srintil's virginity.

Sulam entered the doorway boldly, without a customary greeting. He carried his pride in being the son of a village headman everywhere he went. He stopped momentarily when he saw another young man sitting with Kartareja.

The two young men glared at each other.

"What's he doing here?" asked Sulam, arrogantly.

Before their host could respond, Dower answered. "And why not? I've offered an ox and two silver coins. Together, they're worth more than a gold piece," said Dower proudly.

The statement infuriated Sulam.

"Is he lying?" Sulam asked.

Kartareja did not answer immediately. Without looking at either Sulam or Dower, he finally spoke: "No, Dower is not lying, but sit down first, Sulam. You haven't said what your purpose is in coming here."

"You organized the bukak-klambu for this evening, didn't you?" Sulam asked, still arrogant.

"That's right."

"So, why are you asking why I'm here? Do you think I'd come all the way to Paruk if I didn't plan to have some fun with the ronggeng?"

"If that's the case you must have the gold piece with you," Kartareja replied.

"That's an insult, You don't seem to know who I am. Of course I brought the gold piece: not silver coins or an ox," retorted Sulam, glancing scornfully at Dower.

Stung by Sulam's words, Dower glowered back at him.

"Sulam! You can boast all you want, but not to me. My offer to Kartareja is worth a lot more than a gold piece." Dower turned to Kartareja. "And, you, you'd be stupid to reject my offer and take Sulam's."

"You're the one that's stupid!" Sulam retorted "The only thing Kartareja asked for as a condition to win the contest was this, nothing else in any shape or form." He threw a gleaming gold piece onto the table.

"Give him more, if you're so rich!" challenged Dower.

"If Kartareja had asked for more, I would. So you can quit your chattering and go back home. Go herd your ox in the field."

"You bastard!"

The two young men jumped to their feet and glared at one another angrily, clenching their fists, ready to fight.

Kartareja remained calm, slowly taking his cigarette from his lips. "Relax, boys. Sit down and we'll talk this through like adults."

"I'll sit down only after this kid gets the hell out of here!" Sulam shouted loudly.

Dower stared at Kartareja. "Don't tell me to sit down unless you admit my offer is worth more than his."

Aware of the growing tension, Kartareja stood and placed himself between his two guests. Nyai Kartareja came out of the house, and Srintil appeared at the door, quickly withdrawing again. Strangely, after catching sight of Srintil, the anger of both young men subsided a little.

"Boys," said Nyai Kartareja. "Don't argue here. I'm worried the neighbors will complain if they hear fighting. Please sit down. If you continue quarreling, Srintil will be frightened. What if she were to refuse to go through with the bukak-klambu?"

With the style of an experienced brothel madam, Nyai Kartareja was able to calm Sulam and Dower. The two resumed their seats, each with a sour look on his face. Silence. Kartareja sat thoughtfully. His furrowed brow indicated that he was thinking hard about something. When the old man stood up, his words came slowly and were full of authority.

"You two have brought a problem to this house. If you don't want me to postpone my plans, give us a chance to solve this problem. I want you to sit quietly for a while. I'm going inside to think about this."

"Yes, do what he says," his wife added. "Remember, Srintil is still very young. She's not used to hearing to people quarrel."

The old man and his wife went inside and left their guests on the porch. The two stole glances at one another, but did nothing more. They were cowed by Kartareja's reprimand and the threat that he would postpone the bukak-klambu.

Inside, the husband and wife did not see Srintil, but they knew she was near. Most likely, they thought, she was lying down in her room, her heart pounding. Nyai Kartareja could imagine how the girl was feeling. She was, after all, still a virgin.

"Get me two glasses," said Kartareja to his wife.

"What are you gonna do?"

"You'll see."

Kartareja went to the cupboard and brought out two bottles. One was full of *ciu*, a brandy made from fermented cassava. The second bottle was only a quarter full. He topped up second bottle with water from a jar, and told his wife, who had brought out glasses, to offer the liquor to Sulam and Dower.

"But, don't mix them up! The unmixed one is for Sulam and the other is for Dower."

His wife smiled. Although not as cunning as Kartareja, the woman realized what her husband's intentions were.

Sulam and Dower could smell the alcohol. Nervousness and liquor: two things that went well together anywhere. Both Sulam and Dower wanted to down the contents of the bottles Nyai Kartareja offered as quickly as they could, especially after her challenge.

"The most manly one of you is the one who can finish this liquor first."

"Hey, lady. Why just give me one bottle? Make it two or three. Don't think that I'll leave any for you," cried Sulam.

His desire to prove himself no less inflamed, Dower took his glass and bottle. He didn't want to be seen as second best. He wanted to prove that he was not just a hick who would gag at the taste of liquor.

Sulam had already gulped down the first glass. Ignoring the pain of the shriveling muscles in his throat, he gulped down a second glass, then a third, and a fourth. In only a few moments, the whole content of the bottle was settling in his stomach. Suddenly, Sulam's face flushed. Hot. His ears were ringing. His body felt light. His eyes began to blur. The world around him turned tipsy, yet Sulam felt his strength doubling.

Stone sober, along with Kartareja and his wife, Dower watched Sulam become delirious. In his fantasy world, Sulam saw thousands of stars falling from the sky, his ears hearing the sounds of a love song. In front of him, Srintil appeared, inviting him to dance. The odor of *ciu* steaming out of his own mouth smelt to him like a perfume worn by the ronggeng of Paruk. His lust awakening, Sulam staggered to his feet. In the middle of the verandah, he began to dance. Nyai Kartareja, standing next to him, was an old woman no longer. To Sulam, she was Srintil beckoning him to dance with her.

Kartareja ordered his wife to entertain the raving Sulam. She needed no instruction. She had great experience in the art of dancing. Simple. Remembering her own youth, Nyai Kartareja took great pleasure in attending to Sulam. She let herself be swept off her feet in dance, even to be kissed by Sulam.

The passion that arose in Sulam didn't last long. The ciu had already taken over his body. His movements grew increasingly slow and faltering. In the arms of Nyai Kartareja, he was just able to mutter several foul words as his legs began to buckle. With Dower's help, the dukun lifted Sulam and laid him on the bench: just another horny goat conquered by the power of *ciu* and deceit.

"He's done for," said Nyai Kartareja, out of breath.

"Sure is," her husband agreed.

"You're not drunk, are you?" Nyai Kartareja asked Dower.

"No, Ma'am. No."

"Good. So what are you waiting for?"

"Uh, what do you mean?" asked Dower, confused.

"You dummy. Don't you understand why we worked so hard to get Sulam drunk? You're the winner!"

"I am?"

"Yes, you can sleep with Srintil now. But you only have until Sulam comes to his senses. Understand?"

"I guess so," Dower muttered.

A long creak could be heard as Dower closed the door to the room that held the bed with the mosquito netting. Silence. Kartareja and his wife went into their own bedroom. There, the couple giggled with glee. A gold piece, two silver coins, and an ox were almost in their hands.

Who could blame Kartareja for feeling that he had done so well? And who could blame Dower for later claiming that he was the one who had deflowered Srintil? But something had happened behind Kartareja's house before Dower opened the mosquito netting that encircled Srintil. Only Srintil and I knew what it was.

While I was peering into the porch from the side of the house, listening to the quarrel between Dower and Sulam, I saw someone come out of the back door and squat beneath the banana tree. From the shape of the small body, I could see that it was Srintil. I approached her, quietly and carefully.

"Srintil?" I called out in a whisper. "Don't be afraid. It's only me, Rasus."

"Oh!" cried Srintil, breathlessly. She stood up quickly and hugged me with all her might. "Rasus. Listen, they're fighting over there. I'm afraid so afraid I had to pee!"

"Did you pee?"

"Yes, but I'm still afraid. Rasus. You're so good to be here while I'm being bought and sold."

Still holding me tightly, Srintil sobbed. I let her because I didn't know what else to do. I could feel her body hot and trembling.

"I hate this. I'd rather give myself to you, Rasus. You can't turn me away like you did this afternoon. This isn't a graveyard and we're not going to be cursed. You do want to, don't you?"

I couldn't say a word. I felt a lump in my throat. Since it was dark, I couldn't see clearly, but I felt Srintil release her hold on me and was aware of her taking off her clothes.

It was not unlike my experience that afternoon in the cemetery. Only now something happened in the dark. I couldn't see Srintil's body, but I knew the moment she was naked.

I believe that one's sense of virtue changes in the dark. A person thinks more primitively when there is no daylight. And something primitive happened between Srintil and me there in the darkness. No vision of Momma appeared to me that time. Something profound happened during which Srintil and I were instructed by nature alone. It may have been that Srintil felt pleasure, but who knows? All I knew was that I had experienced something strange.

The experience didn't last very long.

I helped Srintil dress, then I accompanied her to the door. Peering through the hole in the bamboo wall, I could see Srintil open the mosquito netting and lay down to sleep. I went home with my heart in turmoil.

Later, Srintil told me that she was awakened by Dower, huffing like a horny bull. She didn't say anything about the rape that followed, only commenting that the requirements for becoming the ronggeng of Paruk Village were truly harsh.

After Dower left her room, Srintil heard Nyai Kartareja speaking to him.

"You've now received your reward in the bukak-klambu competition. The two silver coins and the ox belong to my husband and me. You're satisfied, aren't you?"

Dower smiled. He had attained his goal, and would now be known as the young man who had deflowered the ronggeng of Paruk. Whether the ronggeng he slept with was really a virgin or not, remained beyond his comprehension.

"Ma'am, I'd like to go home now," he said.

"Go home? Hold on!" answered Nyai Kartareja. "If Sulam wakes up and sees that you're not here, he'll become suspicious."

"Okay, I got it, and I can see that the two of you are a wise old pair: sly and rotten to the core. But sure, I'll sleep here. I'm tired anyway."

In Kartareja's home silence prevailed, although the dukun and his wife did not sleep. Srintil lay nervously in her bed. The slats of the bench squeaked as Dower settled down to sleep, exhausted.

In the middle of the night, Nyai Kartareja went into Srintil's bedroom and opened the mosquito netting. By the light of the lamp she carried in her hand, the woman saw that Srintil's eyes were still open. In a gentle, soothing manner, Nyai Kartareja stroked Srintil's hair.

"Two silver coins and a buffalo now belong to you. You're a wealthy child. Aren't you happy?"

Srintil nodded her head, although her abdomen ached.

"You still have yet to receive a gold piece. You want that, don't you? When Sulam awakens later, he'll come in here."

Srintil's eyes opened wide and her voice was hoarse as she spoke to Nyai Kartareja.

"You mean I have to entertain Sulam, too?"

"It's not anything to worry about, is it? You'll be the only child in Paruk to have a gold piece."

"But my belly hurts, Grandma. It really hurts."

"I once experienced something like this. My beautiful child, believe me. It's nothing to worry about. Just think, a gold piece! Rest now, as long as Sulam is still snoring."

Srintil sobbed to herself. For her, time seemed to be interminable and she desperately hoped for morning to come. She wanted to find herself finished with the whole ritual. She didn't care any longer for the gold piece or the other things. The only thing she cared about was her belly which felt as if it had been ripped to shreds. The ronggeng couldn't stop crying, knowing that soon another heavy-breathing male would arrive and unveil the mosquito netting.

Outside, a light drizzle fell. Srintil would have dozed off if she hadn't heard the squeak of the bench out on the verandah. Sulam stretched and groaned. He started to close his eyes again, but suddenly they flew open and he got up. For a few moments he sat in a daze, bewildered.

Nyai Kartareja came out of her bedroom and approached him.

“Oh, my handsome boy. So, you’ve awakened?” asked Nyai Kartareja in a sweet voice.

“What time is it, Grandma?” said Sulam, rubbing his eyes with the backs of his hands.

“Uh, it’s still early,” the woman lied.

When Sulam recalled the reason for his coming to Paruk, he stood up. “So, what about it? What about the matter we discussed?”

“Relax. The Pecikalan kid is still sleeping soundly. Srintil is waiting for you.”

“Where is she?” asked Sulam enthusiastically.

“She’s in bed under the mosquito netting. Come on, quickly, before Dower wakes.”

“Oh, yeah. But wait a minute. I have to pee.”

4

No one knows when the small, isolated settlement of Paruk got its name. Impoverished and backward, the thin, sickly, foulmouthed inhabitants had, at some time in history, become officially incorporated, and the shrine of Ki Secamenggala on the top of the small hill in the middle of the village became the eternal guardian of all their deficiencies. Paruk was surrounded by a carpet of rice fields bordered by the horizon, but not a single resident owned even a small granary. Paruk, because of the ignorance of its people, had never once rejected the fate bestowed upon it.

The Almighty created me out of the dusty essence of Paruk. When I began to be aware of myself, my life comprised a grandma, three goats, and a basket of dried cassava in the corner of a tiny house. Small children at an early age would refer to the closest woman in their lives as "Momma." But the old woman who was closest to me refused to allow me to call her that, insisting that I call her "Grandma." This left a big question mark in my heart. Fortunately for me, there were about a dozen children like me in Paruk. Warta, Darsun, and even Srintil, I later learned, didn't have a momma. Nor did I have a father. Yet, none of this bothered me greatly. Don't blame me, because I have no idea why I felt like this.

My memories of the story of the tempeh bongkrek tragedy go back to the time I was about five or six years old. Grandma and other people had told me various parts until eventually I put the whole story together. In the story were bits and pieces about

Momma, my mother, that I won't repeat again. The memory of Momma left a mark, like a prolonged punishment, on my soul.

In my heart, there was a place that remained empty, where Momma should have been. I had created this space, but I knew that it would never be filled. This emptiness, developing along with me since my childhood, instilled a bleakness and restlessness in me. The desire to have and to hold Momma left a black stain on my life.

The people in Paruk didn't understand my problem. However, the village provided me with the chance to fill this empty space with a little girl named Srintil. But before long, because of the night of *bukak-klambu*, Srintil had been ripped out of my heart. Paruk had acted cruelly in doing this to me, and I swore that I would never forgive it and its people.

So, when the village celebrated Srintil's official status as a ronggeng with the sounds of the calung xylophones and Srintil's dancing, I began to hate the hamlet. The ties that bound me to Paruk had been yanked away. I no longer had a mirror in which I could see the image of Momma. My bitterness was now more acute than before the time I had come to know Srintil.

One morning, I told Grandma that I was going to look for an uncle who lived in a distant village, and that I might not return. Grandma cried, begging me to stay. "Who will take care of me if I get sick and die?" she asked.

Grandma had become a victim of the revenge I aimed at the village. But what could I do? She belonged to Paruk and would remain thus until she joined Ki Secamenggala in the graveyard. I took one of my goats, leaving her with the remainder of the herd.

I sold the goat in the market of a nearby town, and with the money I lived for a few days at the vendors' stalls. Whenever I heard someone talking about the night of *bukak-klambu* held recently in Paruk, I moved on to a different stall.

After a few days I became acquainted with a cassava vendor who gave me a chance to make some money. In Paruk, every child grows up familiar with cassava and its various uses, and the vendor was impressed with the speed at which I could peel the tuber. In addition to making money for food, I was allocated a quiet corner in the market place where I could spread out some gunny sacks to use as a bed.

Dawuan, the place I moved to from Paruk, is located near the district seat. I later realized that the Dawuan market was in fact a perfect place for me to live. There, I could watch people from the villages of the county come and go, including people from Paruk. The market was the hub for news that traveled by word of mouth through the district. Things that happened even in the most remote hamlets were talked about in that market.

It was almost as if I were still living in Paruk.

I learned about everything that happened in the village, without having to go there. Paruk had returned to its former glory with the emergence of a ronggeng troupe directed by the famous dukun, Kartareja. The wishes of Sakarya and Kartareja that Srintil become a well-known ronggeng, had become a reality. What the two old men had said may have been true, that the keris dagger I gave to Srintil had a role in her present fame. Who knows?

One time I saw Srintil in the Dawuan market. She had come with Nyai Kartareja to shop. Before I even caught sight of her, I knew of her presence from the chatter of the people at the market.

"There she is, the ronggeng of Paruk. She sure is pretty."

"Is it true that the girls of Paruk have clear skin and shapely legs without scabs?"

"Srintil is proof of that. And, look at how fast she has grown!"

"Don't be stupid. It's the scent of men that's made her grow up fast."

"Look. It's only been a few months since she's become a ronggeng and already she's wearing a gold necklace. Her pendant is also made of gold," noted a woman who sold betel nut.

"You may know where that ronggeng got the pendant, but I bet you don't know who gave Srintil her necklace," replied another woman.

"That adulterous headman from Pecikalan?"

"No, he replaced the grass roof of Sakarya's house with zinc sheeting. He didn't give the ronggeng a necklace."

"So, who did?"

"Le Hian! The Chinese man who owns the ciu distillery. Just you watch, soon Srintil will be wearing gold bangles or maybe even diamond earrings."

"How come you know so much about her?"

"I also know that there's a regional administrator who's sleeping with her. What's more, I heard that his wife wants to divorce him."

"Those must be some incredibly powerful love charms that Kartareja and his wife used. You gotta believe in them now," remarked the betel nut vendor.

"Even without the love charms, men would like sleeping with Srintil. I can sure understand why Sulam would be willing to lose a gold piece to win the virginity of that ronggeng," said a young rattan mat seller from his stand.

I was taken aback on hearing these words. Other people had claimed that it was Sulam who had deflowered Srintil. I knew that Dower, by rights, was the first to sleep with the ronggeng of Paruk. Apparently though, this news had not been publicized. In fact, only Srintil and I knew the whole story. Yet, what happened behind Kartareja's house that night had not left me with any romantic memories. It had simply been a spontaneous act.

Srintil entered the market place.

I hid behind some heaps of cassava and gunny sacks. The vendors treated her like a celebrity. A clothes seller offered her a bright red blouse for an unusually high price. If she hadn't been restrained by Nyai Kartareja, Srintil would have bought it without bargaining. Another vendor held out her wares, offering a mirror to Srintil.

This time, Nyai Kartareja did not stop the ronggeng from buying it, along with several packages of face powder and some scented oil.

An old woman ran up to Srintil from behind, holding out a chemise.

"Oh, my pretty girl, you must wear this chemise. You will look beautiful wearing it. Your breasts are filling out."

"How much is it?" Srintil asked.

"I don't want to sell it to you. Go ahead and take it. Every time you dance, I stand at the edge of the stage and watch. You probably haven't ever noticed me, have you?"

Srintil responded with a sweet smile. She picked out a bright yellow chemise and then gave it to Nyai Kartareja to carry. But it was not only the chemise vendor who gave merchandise to Srintil. Others followed suit. A woman selling fruit presented her with some ripe mangos "to refresh you when you stay awake all those nights". A traditional herbal medicine specialist quickly concocted a special brew. "So that your muscles remain firm. Those young men are so rude and they hate flabbiness!"

While the market women appeared to be honest and straightforward with Srintil, the men obviously had other intentions. Simbar, a soap seller, spoke to her, with his eyes gleaming: "Hey, lovely lady, I know that in Paruk the people use a stone to scrub themselves when they wash. But that's not suitable for you. Wash yourself with my soap. I won't charge you anything if you leave your bedroom door open for me."

As he spoke, Simbar's hand reached out toward Srintil's buttocks. Bastard! I saw this with my own eyes, and Srintil didn't slap his hands away.

Babah Pincang, sitting in his stall, almost engulfed by piles of merchandise, joined in the conversation. His face, too, was wild and his eyes gleaming.

"I have leather sandals for sale. Velly cheap. Good quality. So, you girl not walk with naked feet. You have velly good legs. Take my sandals. Later I want pay when I sleep in Paluk."

Just like Simbar, Babah Pincang had itchy fingers. He didn't simply grope her buttocks, but also her cheeks. Another bastard! This time, as well, I noticed that Srintil made no attempt to fend him off.

The heaps of cassava and gunny sacks hid me from Srintil's view as she went around the market. Behind her, Nyai Kartareja carried a woven basket filled with purchases. As she left the central market area, all male eyes were trained on Srintil's buttocks or legs, or the pale nape of her neck below her black hair which was tied up in a knot. Coarse remarks could be heard coming from every corner of the market. Occasionally Srintil glanced back, with an inviting look, while the women muttered to themselves as they pretended to be occupied with their wares.

The bells of a small, two-wheeled carriage and trotting hoof beats could be heard as Srintil and Nyai Kartareja left the market. The carriage would take them to an intersection of the dikes which separated the wet rice fields. Srintil and her escort would then walk along the dikes in the stifling hot sun until they reached Paruk. The walk took about half an hour and there wasn't a single tree for shade.

In my hiding place behind the piles of cassava, I was lost in fantasies about Srintil. The fantasies were filled with dark images. Srintil had come into her own in a manner which was difficult for me to criticize. Fully aware and proud of herself, she had become a ronggeng and a prostitute. The two were in fact synonymous. I knew that Srintil had the right to seek whatever calling she wished. What's more, Paruk Village would be doomed without a ronggeng and calung ensemble.

Indeed, seeing Srintil as she was now, I found that I had trouble evoking even a hazy image of Momma. Momma was a woman of Paruk. I had never once imagined Momma not to be a part of that little hamlet. So, Momma, like the women of Paruk, was not against prostitution. Although she lived only in my imagination, she was not really one of those pure women I read about in storybooks. Yet, because her womb once enveloped me, I could not bring myself to imagine Momma as the kind of woman who would be friendly with men, who would not slap away the hands of a man who groped at her. No. No matter what, I still couldn't imagine that.

Little by little, as time went on, my living at Dawuan market put a distance between me and Srintil, not only physically, but also, more significantly, emotionally and spiritually. Dawuan market provided me with wider horizons on many fronts. Previously, my only world had been Paruk with all its cursing and swearing, its poverty, and its sanctioned indecencies. Until I took up residence in Dawuan market, I had assumed that the values I brought from Paruk were those which were common to all places.

I found out that the values of the wider world were not the same as those I had learned in Paruk. My experience with Siti would prove this. And Siti also taught me, indirectly, that women were not best represented by someone like Srintil.

Siti was a young girl about Srintil's age. Every morning she came to the market to buy cassava. I knew that her mother made and sold various kinds of dishes made from cassava, not just at the market, but elsewhere as well. One can easily get all sorts of information about people, and I already knew a great deal about Siti and her mother.

Every morning I waited on Siti, and had grown to like her. Her shyness and restraint aroused in me a desire to tease her. One time I couldn't stop my bold hand pulling away the veil that covered her head. Her white cheeks and the beauty of her neck were no longer concealed. Without hesitating, I pinched her white cheek.

I felt absolutely no shame at doing this. When I had lived in Paruk, pinching a girl's cheek wasn't by any means considered a social taboo, let alone a sin. Even the word "sin" I learned only after I had left Paruk. But, because of this bold act, I had a new and bitter experience. Siti looked at me in shock, her cheeks reddening. The girl stood momentarily fixed in disbelief, her eyes boring straight into my heart. At first, I was pleased because, with her reddening cheeks, Siti looked prettier than ever. However, I was shocked when she ran off, throwing away the cassava she had bought.

The incident drew laughter from the people around me. I stood motionless, amazed. I had only pinched her cheek. What was so bad about doing that? In Paruk, hadn't I often kissed Srintil's cheek? She hadn't become angry at all, and had even giggled.

"Hey, don't think that Siti is the same as the girls of Paruk. She got mad because what you did was improper," somebody said. I don't know who it was because I didn't dare raise my head to look.

"Look around if you want to tease a girl, Rasus!" somebody else said. "This is a market. The women who come here to shop aren't all from Paruk. Even a prostitute, if she's not from Paruk, is going to get mad if you touch her cheek in front of a lot of people, even though she may only be pretending. Yet, that's the way it is."

I heard the bystanders telling a lot of other dirty jokes but I couldn't pay attention to any of them. I was overwhelmed by the lesson I had just learned, that pinching the cheek of a girl outside of Paruk can bring about trouble. It was so different from Paruk. There, for example, a husband wouldn't even get upset if he found his wife sleeping with his neighbor. The husband would know that the practical way of taking action was to go to the neighbor's wife and sleep with her. All the problems would then be resolved!

Paruk, that tiny place of my birth, had given me a social understanding: but one without any morality. For instance, the fact that people did not know for sure which child belonged to whom never caused problems. I also knew of a treatment for childless women which was common in the village. The treatment was called *lingga*: a combination of the abbreviation of two Javanese words meaning "neighbor's penis." And this treatment was, in the spirit of Ki Secamenggala, not considered taboo or even strange. So, why did people laugh at me when I pinched Siti's cheek?

Obviously, I had to accept the reality that, beyond my place of birth, there are different values. Many of them. The word "bastard," for example, is uttered in Paruk as a matter of course, while in other areas is considered to be highly insulting and abusive.

My experience with the women of Dawuan market also broadened my horizons. Most of the girls who worked in the various food stalls near the market liked to kid around with men. Their behavior was really not much different from that of the women of Paruk. Several of them were willing to accept money from me and didn't object to my carrying them off for the night.

The longer I lived away from my tiny homeland, the more I was able to critically evaluate life in Paruk. I realized that the poverty there was maintained in perpetuity by the ignorance and laziness of the inhabitants. They were satisfied with just being farm workers or with small-scale cultivation of cassava. Whenever there was a small harvest, liquor could be found in every home. The sounds of the calung ensemble and the singing of the ronggeng dancer were the lullabies of the people. Indeed, Sakarya had been correct when he said that, without calung and ronggeng, life was dreary for the people of Paruk. Calung and ronggeng performances also provided people with an opportunity to dance socially and drink ciu to their heart's content.

My acquaintance with women other than Srintil also brought about changes in my thinking. The idea of women as idols or as mirrors where I sought a reflection of Momma eventually diminished, and finally disappeared altogether.

With a heavy heart, I realized that I had to cast off the image of Momma that I had created in my imagination over the years. Before, I had been fairly sure that Momma had fine hairs near her ears, or a dimple on her left cheek, a soft and cool, voice and a smile that could relieve the sorrow of a child that had always yearned for her. Her skin was white, and her breasts were full.

Although painful, I had to destroy the figure of Momma and replace it with another image. To do this, I ignited a large heap of firewood in my mind. I imagined myself throwing a woman into the flames. In that scenario the woman, representing everything that was noble and fine, burned and disappeared, consumed by the fire.

Her replacement, another woman, appeared, possessing characteristics typical in Paruk. Her hair tousled and the ends reddish. Her face pinched and drawn from the constant lack of adequate food. Breasts with black nipples, and full only at harvest time. Her feet splayed, and covered by a layer of dust. Her words coarse, filled with foul curses. This was my image of the women of Paruk, an image that made more sense to me. I had to accept the reality that all the women of Paruk had these characteristics. A bureaucrat who wanted to run off with a woman like that would certainly have to have something wrong with him.

Well, I now had a more realistic image of my momma. Although ugly, it was formed from the impression I got from almost all of the women of Paruk and the women who shopped at the Dawuan market. However, I found that I still couldn't forget Srintil. The times we had had together since our early childhood could not easily be erased from my mind. Yet, little by little, the predominance of her place in my soul shifted to a more normal perspective. Maybe, sometime in the future, I would miss her, and seek her out to satisfy my lust. Who knows, perhaps someday I would have enough money in my pocket. I have never heard of a ronggeng who turned down the wishes of a man who gave her money, especially a lot of it.

The success or otherwise of my new way of thinking about Srintil was tested several months later, when I saw her again in the Dawuan market. On this occasion, as usual, the attitudes of the market people towards her were as I had come to expect: the ronggeng was a female who belongs to the public, especially to the men. And I thought, if Simbar and Babah Pincang were bold enough to tease Srintil, why not me? I wasn't embarrassed to have Srintil find out that my job was to watch over somebody else's cassava. My hands and clothes were dirty. At the market, I seldom washed as I was usually too lazy to go to the river.

This time, when people hailed the arrival of the ronggeng of Paruk, I didn't hide, but drew close. Without any hesitation, I approached Srintil and guided her to a less crowded spot, ignoring the shouts and stares of the surrounding people.

"You still remember me, Srin?"

"Rasus, it's you!"

"You haven't forgotten what happened that night behind Kartareja's house?"

"Don't talk so loud. Of course, I haven't forgotten. What a foolish half-wit you were."

"Yeah? Well now I'd like to try again."

"Quit talking so loud. If you want to brag, let's go and get something to eat. That little food stall is empty."

"Sure! If I'm with a ronggeng, my stomach is guaranteed to be filled. Right?"

"That's enough. Don't prattle like Nyai Kartareja."

Several people made coarse comments when they saw me, arm in arm with Srintil, leaving the market place and heading towards the food stall. I didn't pay any heed to them. What's more, Srintil herself silenced their annoying words.

"You market people, don't be jealous. Rasus is an old friend from Paruk. Wait here. You'll get a turn later."

Srintil had once given herself to me in a dark place behind Kartareja's house. For me, looking back, that event was almost unimaginable because, for me at that time, Srintil wasn't a ronggeng dancer. I had also believed, at that time, that Srintil had given herself to me in return for my giving her the little keris.

That day, at the food stall, I realized that I was mistaken. From the way she spoke, from the way she sat close to me, and from the look in her eyes, I knew that Srintil regarded what happened behind Kartareja's house as something special. Thus, I was compelled to believe what people say about girls: they never forget the time they gave up their virginity. I also realized the truth of words I had once heard: no matter what, a ronggeng is still a woman. She wants true love. And the man who is her true love never need give her money.

"You disappeared from Paruk right after that night. Why did you do that?" Srintil asked me.

If Srintil had asked me this question a few months earlier, I would have had trouble answering it. Although I could have come up with an answer, it would have sounded pompous, because at that time I still connected Momma with Srintil. Yet now, at the food stall, I was able to explain myself to her.

"Because you'd officially become a ronggeng. I didn't want to see you again until I had some money."

"So, that's the way it is, Rasus?"

"Yeah, why?"

"Did I ask you for money back then?"

Srintil lowered her head when she said these words. Before I could speak, she stood up and left me. I was deeply moved, and could only watch as she lifted her shopping basket into the carriage. When the coachman cracked his whip to urge his horse forward, I felt as if it was my heart that was being whipped.

I didn't set foot in Paruk for a whole year. The news I received that Grandma was still chopping cassava to make tapioca and leading the goats out to the vacant land to graze them was enough for me. I didn't need to go there. During that year, Dawuan market became an occasional rendezvous place for Srintil and me. Sometimes she would invite me to a house not far from the market. Although Srintil hated being called a prostitute, she nevertheless knew every house that could be rented for illicit behavior. She remained true to her words that she didn't expect money from me. Once, she even began to chat about getting married and having a baby.

Strange.

A ronggeng chatting about marriage, about having a baby. As a child of Paruk, I should have been suspicious. I knew for sure that marriage in Paruk was not something momentous, much less sacred. Women there had no reason to glorify it. Arranged marriages could easily be obtained, especially for someone beautiful like Srintil. If Srintil only wanted to have a baby, what did she have to be concerned about? Weren't there dozens of men already sowing their seeds?

People outside Paruk wouldn't understand what the problem was. Even though the women of Paruk lived in a world apart, their instincts to have offspring were the same as women elsewhere. They despised the poor souls who couldn't bear children, especially those who were barren. They believed that they carried the sacred trust of Ki Secamenggala to protect his descendants from extinction as a result of disaster or poverty. This meant having babies.

I had a strong feeling that Srintil had begun to be haunted by the realization that Nyai Kartareja had massaged her in a way that had somehow destroyed her ability to reproduce. The dukun and his wife would have believed that they had to do this because the custom in Paruk dictates that a ronggeng's career would be finished with her first pregnancy. I believed that Srintil had begun to regard her apparent infertility as a frightening ghost that would haunt her for the rest of her life. Or perhaps she had heard stories about those ronggeng who never even reached old age because they had succumbed to syphilis or other forms of venereal disease. Who could say for sure?

In my view, Srintil's chattering about babies and marriage was emotional, intuitive, and without any reasonable basis. Moreover, I felt insignificant beside her now because Srintil had become a truly wealthy ronggeng. Still, if it were true that Srintil's desire to have a baby was brought on by her fear of old age, I couldn't do anything but feel pity, profound pity, for her.

In 1960, the region around Dawuan was becoming a dangerous area. Armed robberies were common, and bandits often burned down the houses of their victims. Because I always slept in a corner of the market, I began to feel afraid. I began to worry, too, about what was happening in Paruk. I hoped that the bandits would not be drawn to the village because of its isolated location in the middle of the rice fields. By my estimate though, if a robbery were to happen there, the police could easily surround the hamlet.

As it turned out, I didn't return to Paruk for another two years. Fate brought about a miraculous change in my life. I left the Dawuan market and began a life on the move with a troop of army soldiers under the command of a Sergeant Slamet.

It all began one evening at the entrance to the market place. There were few people around. Robberies had been occurring with greater frequency day by day. A truck filled with soldiers pulled up and about twenty men stepped down, each with a steel helmet and a rifle. A number of children who had been attracted to the gates of the market by the arrival of the truck, drew aside, watching from a safe distance as the soldiers disembarked. They were especially afraid of the rifles.

I stood at the main gate to the market, observing the troops. I saw a soldier, who I later learned was Sergeant Slamet, looking around for someone to help unload cases and other equipment. I was the only suitable person in sight, and he waved his arm in my direction.

There's not a child of Paruk Village that wouldn't tremble at being summoned by a soldier. I would have slunk off to my corner if Sergeant Slamet hadn't waved again. His smile alleviated some of my fear.

"What's your name?" asked Sergeant Slamet, his manner friendly and fatherly.

"Rasus."

"If you're not busy at the moment, can you help us?"

"No, I'm not busy," I answered, still a little fearful.

"Good. Let's begin. Carry the chests over to that house. Later, you'll be rewarded for your work."

I lifted the metal chests on to my shoulders and carried them to a brick house that had, it turned out, been arranged as headquarters for the troops. My fears slowly changed to feelings of pride. A child of Paruk Village working among army troops! Although I didn't have a uniform like they did, I was nevertheless working with them. I had even spoken to their leader, Sergeant Slamet. I already knew an army soldier.

My sense of pride in working with the army troops made me feel stronger than usual. While the soldiers carried one chest at a time, I lifted two to my shoulders. In the time they took to carry things from the truck to the headquarters, I had already gone there and back twice. I wasn't aware of it but, Sergeant Slamet was taking note of this.

After all the equipment had been carried to the headquarters, I took my leave, intending to return to my usual spot in the market. But Sergeant Slamet stopped me and said there was more work to do. He asked me to sweep out the big house that was to become the headquarters. While I was sweeping, he gave me some used army clothes and said I could put them on straight away. I was now dressed in a green military uniform.

I thought that the patched clothes were the payment that Sergeant Slamet had promised me when I agreed to work for him. However, this was not the case. The sergeant had more work for me to do. He asked me to wait on him and the army troops. Fortunately for him, I was not connected with the gang of bandits making trouble in the Dawuan area.

As evening approached, and I had finished all of my work, Sergeant Slamet asked me to sit down. In front of the soldiers who were present, he said to me.

"Rasus, by wearing those fatigues, it's fitting that you become a *tobang*. We need someone to wait on us as we carry out our duties. Naturally, if you're prepared to do this work, you'll receive a salary. What do you say?"

I couldn't answer immediately, but in my heart I was cheering. If I were to accept this offer, then I'd probably be the first kid from Paruk to wear army fatigues, speak Indonesian, and earn a salary. Incredible! Srintil would see the person she once knew as Rasus, wearing army fatigues, albeit without rank. Sakarya and Kartareja, who had made Srintil into a ronggeng, causing me to lose the vision of my mother, would be speechless if one day I were to go back to the village as an army aide.

"You're not saying anything, Rasus. Are you rejecting the offer or just thinking about it?"

"It's not that, sir. I just don't know whether I have the qualifications to carry out the duties I would be accepting."

"Anyone with sufficient strength and honesty could carry out the job. Regarding strength, I believe that you're strong enough, and I can see that you are honest by the look in your face and eyes.

"If that's your judgment, I can only obey," I answered, looking up at him.

"Answer 'Yes, sir!' We're an army and we do everything with authority," Sergeant Slamet commanded. Yet, I didn't detect any harshness in his tone of voice.

"Yes, sir. I accept your offer."

"Good. You're beginning to talk like a soldier."

"But..."

"Rasus, soldiers never say 'but' when they make a decision."

"Well then, sir, I must, with authority and decisiveness, return the cassava I've been guarding to its owner!"

During my first days as a tobang, I had many new experiences. During the day, I washed the soldiers' clothes and polished their shoes. I also worked in the kitchen. I did this with pleasure because, as well as cooking, I had the opportunity to go shopping in the Dawuan market. There, I could show off my army fatigues. All the people who had known me at the market were impressed. Even the owner of the cassava stall, who for several months had been my boss, no longer had the nerve to call me by my name, but now referred to me as "Mr Tobang." I had hoped Srintil would soon learn of my transformation and come to the market. My only disappointment was that I hadn't met a single person from Paruk there.

A month had passed since the arrival of the army troops, and nothing further had been heard of incidents of theft in the region. Although the army was always on alert, and patrolled the region at night, I sensed that the situation was calm. My relationship with Sergeant Slamet was really more a personal relationship than one between a tobang and a sergeant. He often asked me about myself, my origins, even about my schooling. After learning that I had never gone to school, he taught me how to read and write. He told me many stories, but the tale I liked most was about a novice recruit who, because of his courage, was able to kill three enemy soldiers in one battle. Usually, Sergeant Slamet was gentle toward me, but his military side would sometimes emerge too. For example, several days after I joined his troops, he said, "As a tobang, you must understand that everything you learn here is strictly confidential. You must protect this confidentiality at all costs. You are allowed to speak only as necessary with civilians. If I find out that you've disobeyed, I'll punish you myself: if necessary, with my pistol!"

I learned things I never would have known if I hadn't met Sergeant Slamet. In just two months I learned to read and write. I then began my acquaintance with books, on subjects ranging from *wayang,* the shadow puppet theater, to history and general knowledge. I also learned about the ins and outs of weaponry, becoming familiar with names like Pietro Beretta, Parabellum, Lee

Enfield, Thomson and so forth. Sergeant Slamet taught me how to take apart and reassemble a gun, as well as how to use it.

"You never know when there may be a critical moment and you might need to fire a gun in battle," he said, smiling.

He probably never realized how my heart soared on hearing those words. If only Momma could have heard him!

One morning Sergeant Slamet summoned his subordinates, Even I was called to listen to what he had to say.

"Food and other essentials for us have not yet arrived and our supplies are running short. We need fresh meat. Our stomachs can't take canned rations indefinitely and the budget for buying fresh meat is exhausted. I've decided that we will hunt in the forest for wild boar or deer."

"That's good news, said Corporal Pujo, "I'll come along."

"No. You'll stay here. I'm putting you in command. I need only two men to accompany me, in addition to Rasus who will be our guide."

If Corporal Pujo was pleased with this news, I was delighted that I was being asked along. Hunting with three soldiers in the forest! The villagers from Paruk would see me with the army. They would see me wearing army fatigues. I might even be trusted to wear a gun on my hip. That would double the villagers' admiration for me. On the way back, I'd carry our kill.

I never imagined that this hunt would provide me with an extraordinary experience, but not one that was associated with the hunt itself or even with the gang of bandits that were hiding in the forest.

At eight o'clock the following morning we left Dawuan. On my shoulders I carried a knapsack filled with provisions. On the left side of my waist I hung a thermos and on the right I had a sheathed bowie knife under my belt. I felt uncommonly manly. Indeed, during our journey to the forest, everyone who happened to pass us stopped to admire the kid from Paruk. Small children quickly hid themselves, even though I called out to them in our local language.

As soon as we reached the forest, we began hunting. But I was disappointed, because the three soldiers I was with had absolutely no experience in hunting game. We didn't see a single wild boar and, although we saw a deer, Sergeant Slamet missed his target when he tried to shoot it. At dusk we stopped. We had expended only two bullets, the one which missed the deer and the other to kill a python as thick as a man's thigh, which we saw coiled in a tree.

Right there, in the middle of the forest, I had the job of skinning the large snake, cutting it into small pieces, and packing it all into the three knapsacks we were carrying. I disliked the work like but I did it gladly for Sergeant Slamet, even though I almost threw up several times. The rancid, cloying smell of the snake irritated my stomach and stirred up its contents.

"Go ahead and finish your work," Sergeant Slamet said. "I want to sleep for short while. Wake me up if you see anything suspicious."

"Pig or deer?" I retorted, jokingly. Sergeant Slamet smiled and lay down underneath a tree. The other two soldiers were already sleeping soundly.

I'm a great expert in peeling cassava, but the matter of skinning a snake almost four meters long was entirely new to me. Fortunately, before he went to sleep, Sergeant Slamet had told me how to do it. He had told me to secure the head of the snake with one end of a rope and pull the other end over the branch of a tree. With the snake suspended, I made a slice around its neck. From this slice, I peeled back the snake's skin. It was difficult, and my strength was almost drained by the time I had finished. The result was a long pouch turned inside out. Cutting up the meat didn't require as much strength and, as it turned out, a great deal of it had to be thrown out. I filled two of the knapsacks with the meat and used the third one for the skin.

The work was finished. I stood up to stretch. Silence. Sergeant Slamet and his two men were still asleep. I didn't dare waken them, so I sat quietly in the solitude of the forest that seemed to grow even more silent with the presence of a gentle breeze. I could see the figures of the three sleeping bodies near me. In their sleep, they didn't seem to have the might of soldiers at all.

I gazed at the three rifles propped up against one another, and a brilliant thought suddenly came to me. I'll never know why the inspiration came at that exact moment but, because it did, I was able to put an end, finally, to the long suffering that had marred my life for years.

While the soldiers were sleeping, I decided to use one of their rifles for a particular purpose of my own. I had a long-term enemy. While this enemy had tyrannized only my own imagination, I had long wanted to smash his head to a pulp. When the opportunity arose to smash his head, how could I not immediately take it?

Quickly! Don't wait until the three soldiers awaken. The time for retribution is right now! Such were the voices I heard in my heart.

I submitted to the voices. First, I searched for a piece of sandstone the size of a head. Having found a suitable stone, I set it on top of a tree stump. With my bowie knife I carved eyes, a nose, and lips into the stone, not forgetting to add a long mustache. I placed a teakwood leaf, a hat for the effigy, on top of the stone. In this way, I completed the head of health official who stole Momma.

From a distance of several feet I surveyed the results of my creation. No mistake about it. This was the health official, my enemy since childhood.

I looked around. Silence. The only thing moving was a sparrow hawk in the sky above. Let it be a lone witness to the act I was about to carry out. I was going to take vengeance. Tiptoeing, I reached for one of the rifles, a Lee Enfield. My hands trembled as I picked it up, but not because it was the first time I had touched a weapon. No.

I have already said that I had become familiar with several kinds of guns since I joined up with Sergeant Slamet. My hands shook because of the fire in my heart, trembling because of the hatred that, in a moment, would be released.

Slowly, very slowly, I crept back. I was afraid that one of the three soldiers might awaken. If that were to happen, my plans for revenge would be thwarted. I stood a few feet in front of the health official's head. I drew back the handle to cock the rifle, so silently and slowly that even the mites on my palms couldn't hear the spring as I pulled.

The throbbing of my heart was enough to cause the barrel to pulse as I aimed the gun straight toward the target. I paused, and waited until my heart calmed down a bit.

The moment arrived.

Again I aimed the rifle at the target. I imagined how the member of a firing squad would stand as he carried out his duty to execute a traitor. That's what I pretended to be. I pulled the trigger with an explosion of rage that made the motion of my finger strong and sure. I hardly heard the blast because all my senses were centered on the head as it was thrown backwards. The pith helmet flew off, high into the air.

In the brief seconds that followed, Sergeant Slamet and his two friends awoke. I heard harsh reprimands, and then felt the slap of a hand on my cheek. The rifle I was holding was coarsely jerked away.

I didn't pay attention to any of this. I was experiencing a wonderful spiritual peace. The health official was dead, his head shattered beyond all recognition. Unaware of the three soldiers as they stood gazing at me, confused, I walked forward to see the results of my shot. All that was left of the head were small fragments. A man with a shattered head like this could not run off with Momma. From that moment he became a corpse. Momma was free. I could now invite her to return to Paruk. I had won, and in doing so, had become a real son, successfully freeing Momma from the clutches of Satan.

Awareness gradually returned to me as I stood silently, facing the three soldiers who were looking at me in amazement. My body was drenched in cold sweat. My hands and legs trembled. I struggled to take a step toward Sergeant Slamet, but never reached my goal. Everything turned black.

I don't how long it was before I returned to my senses. The first awareness I had was Sergeant Slamet pouring hot coffee from his thermos into my mouth. Then, from my mouth, not yet completely under my control, came the words, "Mother, you're free now. Please come home!"

"Hey, you're awake. We'll go home soon," Sergeant Slamet remarked. His words made me more alert.

"Oh, Sergeant, I'm sorry. Please forgive me," I said as I sat up.

"I want to know first why you did this. Can you tell me about it now?"

"I'm sorry, Sergeant, I can't explain it right now. Punish me. What I meant to do in firing the gun would be hard for you to understand. Honestly, Sergeant, I'm willing to accept any punishment."

"Good. Let's go home. But, you have to promise that you'll give me the clearest explanation possible."

"Thank you, Sergeant. I promise."

"What about the python?"

"It's cut up and in the knapsacks."

"Do you feel strong enough?"

"I do."

"Get a carrying pole. Your first punishment is to carry those knapsacks all by yourself."

To their friends back at headquarters, the two soldiers on the hunt said that I had been possessed by the devil in the forest. Several people asked me for an explanation, and I more or less complied with the story of the two soldiers. However, in the privacy of his office, I gave Sergeant Slamet the full explanation of why I shot that lump of sandstone. The sergeant understood what I told him.

"I'm truly sorry for all of this, Sergeant."

"I'll let it go this one time, but not again. Fortunately for you I can understand the suffering you've experienced in never having seen your mother. If not, the punishment would be serious. Imagine, taking and using a rifle. Even a soldier would have to be severely disciplined if he did anything like that."

The presence of the army in Dawuan did not always deter the bandits in the region, and as time went on they became bolder. They brazenly began to murder their victims. Overcoming this problem was not an easy task for Sergeant Slamet and his soldiers. The night patrols hadn't been successful in catching even a single bandit. In fact, one soldier had been killed and another wounded when a night patrol was ambushed by a gang of bandits.

Sergeant Slamet changed his strategy. He divided his troops into small units of two or three men, assigning each unit to watch the house of someone thought likely to own gold or precious stones. Such people would always be the targets of robbery. Each small unit would leave the post in Dawuan and take up its position at dusk.

Because the number of soldiers was limited, I too was compelled to become a member of one of the units, although I wasn't yet trusted to carry a weapon. Along with Corporal Pujo, I was assigned to watch Paruk Village. In Paruk I knew there was gold in Srintil's house, so I accepted the assignment gladly, though with a pang of fear as well, knowing that I might come face to face with the bandits.

Each afternoon, before sunset, we set off for Paruk. Corporal Pujo hid his rifle inside a sarong. He didn't wear his army uniform and even went without shoes. I was armed only with a flashlight. We were careful not to draw the attention of the villagers to our arrival. The place we used as our watch post was the corner of the rice field that connected Paruk with the outside world. At dawn, we returned to Dawuan to sleep for the rest of the morning.

In actual fact, I did not want anything to happen in Paruk. No matter what the village had done to me, it had been my home since my birth. However, on the ninth night, a night on which the light from the stars was strong enough to illuminate the village, I could see from my hidden watch post the approaching glare of a flashlight. My eyes opened wide. From the light of the stars I could make out five men, walking in single file along the dikes, each carrying a long object. No mistake about it, rifles.

"Corporal. They've finally come," I whispered.

"How many?"

"Five. They're all armed. Do we confront them?"

"We could, but let's not be rash. We only have one weapon between us. They have five rifles."

"So, what should we do? We'd better decide quickly."

"Wait a minute. I have to piss."

What a disappointment! Corporal Pujo was no braver than me. At that critical moment, he couldn't make up his mind what to do. So, I took the initiative.

"We need help. You stay here and I'll run back as fast as I can to Dawuan. In about twenty minutes, I can be back with Sergeant Slamet and some others."

"Too long. Where's your flashlight? I want to signal headquarters."

"But Sergeant Slamet won't see your signal from here. You'll have run over to the center of the rice field."

"Okay, I'll do that."

"Fine, here's the flashlight. I'll follow the bandits."

"Yeah."

"Be careful. Watch what you shoot."

While Corporal Pujo ran to the middle of the rice field to send the signal, I followed the bandits who had just passed the observation post. My guess was correct. They didn't go to Kartareja's house where Srintil was staying, instead to the home of Sakarya. With the zinc roofing he had received from the headman of Pecikalan, Sakarya's house was the most prominent in the village.

Two of the bandits stayed outside, one at the back and one at the front. The other three went onto the verandah, kicking in the door. The startled Sakarya realized immediately what was happening. He came out and faced the three men threatening him with guns. Nyai Sakarya followed her husband outside and immediately collapsed on the ground.

"This is the home of the ronggeng isn't it?" growled one of the bandits to Sakarya, who was trembling in fear.

"I am indeed Srintil's grandfather, but she doesn't live here," answered Sakarya, his lips quivering. One of the bandits slapped the old man so hard that he staggered back. The others entered the house, searching every corner. Not finding Srintil or her valuables, the bandits again turned their violence toward Sakarya.

"Tell us where she lives! Don't waste our time. Our guns can go off any moment."

"Don't shoot, don't shoot! I'll tell you. Srintil lives in Kartareja's house, three houses that way. But please, don't hurt her. She is our granddaughter. Take whatever you want, just don't hurt her."

Before leaving the house, the bandits knocked the couple out with a blow to their heads. They went straight to Kartareja's house. The dukun had heard the commotion down the street, and had quickly hidden all the gold valuables he owned, and those of Srintil, in the ashes of the fireplace.

Two of the bandits again stayed outside, one at the front, one at the back. I was behind a tree only a few feet from one of them. Harsh voices and the sounds of beating. Several moments afterwards, I heard Srintil scream. I angrily cursed Corporal Pujo for not being there. No longer able to wait, my courage surged.

The bandit standing at the back of the house seemed to be nervous. I looked around on the ground for a weapon, a stone would have been adequate. I found the handle of a hoe. When the bandit had his back turned towards me, I advanced cautiously and struck him hard. He fell down immediately, dead. It was the first time I had killed a man. I've never even seen a human being die, and this first experience made me tremble. I would have run away if I could have. But I heard footsteps approaching. I quickly picked up the weapon of the man I had killed, a Thomson fully automatic with the stock replaced by a homemade one. No matter. I used the automatic for my second killing.

After that, I felt really scared. I ran, turning for a moment to spray Kartareja's house with the bullets remaining in the gun. I kept running. When I reached the fields, I lay prone behind one of the dikes. I had thrown the Thomson into a ditch.

I saw four figures in the gloom, running toward the village. Corporal Pujo had arrived with help.

"Wait. It's me, Rasus."

"Hey, where are they?" asked Sergeant Slamet.

"At Kartareja's house. Quickly. I've killed two of them," I said, shivering.

Sergeant Slamet hastily made a plan of action. He ordered his three subordinates to go into the village and chase the criminals out. Using his Thomson, Sergeant Slamet would intercept them at the edge of the wet rice fields.

We could hear gunfire. The bandits were apprehended by Sergeant Slamet's strategy. When they ran out of Kartareja's house, one of them was shot by Corporal Pujo. One escaped, but Sergeant Slamet succeeded in killing the remaining one.

After all was quiet, Sergeant Slamet invited me to go with him and check Kartareja's house. Corporal Pujo and two of the soldiers were there. Using a flashlight, I searched for the Thomson with the homemade stock that I had thrown into the ditch, and when I found it, hung it over my shoulder in a manly way. Behind Kartareja's house, I showed Sergeant Slamet the two corpses, but I almost threw up when I saw all the blood. Another rifle was lying near one of the bodies.

When Sergeant Slamet and I entered, Kartareja was standing, shivering, in front of Corporal Pujo. His wife was sitting in a daze. Srintil was astounded to see me carrying a gun, and was unsure about approaching me. From Kartareja's explanation we learned that the bandits had succeeded in taking only the jewelry worn by Srintil at the time: a pair of earrings, two rings, and a necklace. Kartareja had told Srintil to wear the jewelry in order to protect the more expensive items from being plundered by the bandits.

The villagers came out of their houses and gathered at Kartareja's house. They were ordered by Sergeant Slamet to collect the four corpses. In front of all the people, Sergeant Slamet praised me as a hero. He didn't know that I was more afraid of seeing blood than anything else. "Rasus is a real soldier. I'm going to see to it that he becomes an official member of my unit," said Sergeant Slamet. The villagers responded with cheers.

The four corpses would be buried the next day after their identities had been established. Sergeant Slamet and his two followers returned to Dawuan that night. Corporal Pujo and I stayed in the village.

Srintil accompanied me as I walked to Grandma's house. I could see that my grandmother was growing older. She was thin and more stooped. A pity. Grandma couldn't ask many questions of me. She hardly recognized me, but I hugged her as I shouted out my name. "It's me, Rasus, Granny."

"Oh, so it's you Rasus?"

"Yeah, Granny."

"Have you eaten?"

"Yes, I have."

"Do you want to sleep here?"

"Yeah, Granny. Tonight, I'll be with you. Now you lie down. Let me help you."

While the villagers were assembling at Kartareja's house, I sat next to Srintil on the verandah of my grandmother's house. I had once read a story about a war hero who came home from battle and was welcomed back by a beautiful girl. I reproached myself continuously, wondering why a story like this came to mind. As I sat with Srintil, I did indeed feel profoundly content. But it wasn't because Srintil wouldn't stop praising me, nor that she had once given herself completely to me. Nor was it because of the lives of two men I had taken that night. My soul was too weak for me to acknowledge this as an accomplishment, although the men I had killed had been violent bandits. I swore to myself, I'd never kill again, even the most violent criminal.

No. My contentment stemmed from the day I had shot the head of the health official in the middle of the forest. Some people would have said that my actions that day were nothing more than the behavior of a snot-nosed kid. Well, I didn't expect anyone to believe that I had executed an enemy who had harassed, even terrorized, me to the depths of my soul over many years. Nobody would even be interested in something so apparently stupid and crazy.

Yet, I knew that a spiritual burden which had been pressing upon my heart had for the most part been lifted. The possibility now that Momma had run off with the health official had been eliminated. In my mind now I was sure that Momma, who had nothing in common with Srintil, had indeed died of food poisoning. Her body was then used in the medical investigation to learn everything possible about the poison. If I had come from a place other than Paruk I would have probably said that Momma's body had been sacrificed for the benefit of humankind. I resigned myself to the fact that Momma was buried in some unknown place. I realized at this time that my world had widened considerably beyond the small, isolated hamlet of Paruk.

In the morning, as the village people busied themselves dealing with the corpses of the four criminals, I stayed at Grandma's house, with no intention of leaving. Srintil who had been with me since the previous night only left me briefly to go home to get some rice. When she learned that there hadn't been rice in Grandma's house for an entire year, not even a handful, she cooked rice and boiled some water for Grandma and me. She also fried omelets, the most expensive and rarely cooked meal in Paruk. That morning, and for the next few days, it was as though Srintil was preparing herself to become my wife. Not only did I make much of her, but so did Grandma. The old woman surely felt that she was experiencing the most pleasurable time of her entire life.

Through Corporal Pujo, who was returning to headquarters in Dawuan the day after the raid, I put in a request to Sergeant Slamet for permission for four or five days' leave. "To look for someone to take care of Grandma who's extremely old," was my request. As it turned out, my efforts to find someone proved to be quite easy. I was amazed when I realized that everyone from my village was now willing to help me with anything they could.

"As for the problem of your grandmother, you don't need to worry at all. We'll take good care of her. We realize that a hero has been born among us, a fine young man who has succeeded in killing two criminals," said Kartareja, indicating me with his thumb. "And I'm willing to provide her with food, as I now own a rice field."

"Asshole!" I said to myself under my breath. "You dried up old bastard, you became rich selling Srintil."

"Will you be returning soon to headquarters, my fine young grandchild?" asked Sakarya.

"Yes, tomorrow morning, Grandpa," I answered.

"So you aren't going to come back to live here in Paruk?" asked a woman, I didn't know.

"That's not possible. Rasus is in the army now. Don't you see his gun hanging on that wooden pole?" another woman replied.

"I have to join up with Sergeant Slamet again. He and his men need me. The region of Dawuan isn't safe yet," I said. Heads nodded in understanding.

During my last night in the village, I barely managed to close my eyes. The whole night I encountered a woman following her natural instincts. A woman who I believe didn't want to be referred to as a ronggeng or a woman of Paruk, but just as a woman. She truly wished to have my child in her womb. She wanted me to stay with her in Paruk, or to go with me to join up with Sergeant Slamet's unit.

"If you want to farm, I could buy a hectare of wet rice field for you to work. If you want to go into business, I could get you the money," pleaded Srintil in the silence of the night.

"I haven't thought that far, "I told Srintil. "In fact I've never even thought about such matters. What's more, I still remember your words when you said that you liked being a ronggeng."

"Oh, Rasus. Why do you bring up things from the past? What I'm asking for is now. Listen, Rasus. I'll stop being a ronggeng because I want to be the wife of a soldier; and you're that soldier."

Srintil continued her outpouring of excuses and promises to me. As a man of just twenty years, I almost gave in. Yet, as a child of Paruk who had come to know a great deal about the world outside, I had a thousand arguments to counterbalance, even to reject, Srintil's entreaties. Srintil could have whatever else she wanted of me, except a baby and marriage. I knew such a stipulation would satisfy any other Paruk woman. But I believed that Srintil's demands stemmed from a moment of need, arising from her natural instincts as a woman.

As morning approached, I heard the *sikatan* bird singing in the bamboo grove behind the house. The ticking of drops of dew sounded as they struck dry leaves. I heard the buzzing of dung beetles as they flew toward the sources of food that were spread throughout the tiny village; the whimpering of a neighbor's baby and a small commotion in the chicken coop; the plop of goat shit as it fell to the floor of the pen; and the flapping of bat wings among the leaves of the guava tree at the side of the house.

I got up slowly. Very quietly. I didn't want to make the bamboo slats of the bed creak and waken Srintil. She was still sleeping soundly exhausted. That night Srintil had sweated too much. Like on another occasion I remembered, Srintil became calmer and even more beautiful while she slept. I carefully straightened the wrinkled sheet. When Srintil stretched and yawned, I gently stroked her cheek, as if I were stroking a small child. After a moment, I stood up and briefly examined the ronggeng of Paruk. I didn't want any foolish sentiments to stop me from leaving.

In the other bedroom, I checked on Grandma, her body askew and somewhat twisted as she slept. In the light of a small oil lamp I could see that she was breathing. Very slowly. For a brief moment I searched for a picture of my mother's face in her. Then I stopped myself. I had learned my lesson. Looking for an image of my mother had only resulted in restlessness. I wouldn't make that mistake ever again. Thus, in peace, I observed the lines of age on Grandma's face. Then, I put all the money I had in my pocket under her pillow.

I turned around. I remembered that I was a soldier, albeit without rank. As such, I had to cast aside all my doubts.

After I put on my uniform, I grabbed the rifle hanging over the couch in my bedroom. Srintil was still sleeping soundly, but I only glanced at her momentarily. The sky was beginning to brighten as I stepped outside. Nobody was out and about in the village. My steps were firm and sure. I, Rasus, had finally found myself. I was leaving Paruk Village, all of its inhabitants and their values. I no longer hated my tiny place of birth, even though I had cursed it at the time it first tore Srintil from my arms. In addition, I had just given my village the chance to return to its original glory. In refusing to accept Srintil's proposal of marriage, I had presented Paruk with what it most valued: a ronggeng!

When I reached the middle of the rice fields, I looked back. I smiled to myself, then briskly continued my journey. Holding the gun to my side, I felt strong and masculine. However, I was

II

A Shooting Star at Dawn

1

The night-time silence of the village was slowly broken by the sounds of animals awakened by signs of the coming day. The goats were growing restless in the stable and one by one the roosters began to crow. The wagtail chirped from its hiding place, ready to take flight as soon as it saw the first insect. Lured by the scent of a female, a squirrel emerged from its nest to make chase. Tree branches swayed in the breeze. Dripping dew created a percussive cacophony of sound. A bat passing over the top of a banana tree stopped suddenly and dropped like a stone into the opening of an unfurling leaf.

The cricket, the grasshopper, and the praying mantis had long been silent. The cricket had hidden itself in a hole in the earth, and closed the entrance from the inside. The praying mantis had camouflaged itself amongst the green leaves, revealing its location only by the distinctive sound it made by rubbing its wings together whenever it sensed a breath of air.

In one corner of the village stood a guava tree. Within its leafy foliage a performance of natural harmonies was taking place: hundreds of honey bees working with astonishing diligence gathering pollen. As their wings buzzed with a chorus of delicate sounds, they filled the loneliness of the still gloomy morning. The ground beneath the tree was carpeted by thousands of white petals. The air was filled with the scent of the earth, the soft sounds of the wings of the honey bee, and the radiance of dew capturing light from the rays of the sun in the east.

The tips of the coconut palms and the bamboo stalks received the first heat of the morning. The sun's rays woke the village by turning back the fog that had blanketed the town. The small hamlet began to stir. The whimpers of hungry children could be heard. A woman went outside to hang up a sheet dampened during the night by her baby. Her husband came out to the yard to pick a dry banana leaf for rolling tobacco. Behind the bushes someone squatted, flapping his hands to chase away the gnats buzzing around his head. Paruk village had awakened.

Only one house remained silent, the smallest in the village. The elderly woman who lived there was awake, but reluctant to get out of bed. She lay dazed and confused. In her hand she was clutching several heavy coins which she had found under her pillow. Rasus's grandmother was bewildered; but in reality, she had been confused for a long time.

The old woman was not alone in her house that morning. In fact, she hadn't been alone now for several days. Srintil, the most prized person in the village, lay on a bed on the other side of the room, dreaming about being with Rasus.

The rays of the sun pierced the bamboo wall and, like a beam, fell on her cheek. A spot of light no larger than a coin revealed the vivacious beauty of Paruk's ronggeng dancer. Her tousled black hair sparkled softly. When the beam of light moved towards her eyes, Srintil stirred. Her breathing changed from the regular, slow rhythm of deep sleep and her eyelashes began to flicker. Finally, with a long sigh, she awoke and stretched slowly.

During this transition from the world of sleep to the world of wakefulness, Srintil's eyes remained closed. Her cheeks flushed as a realization crept up on her: life had passed a threshold. She felt herself dissolve and become one with Rasus.

Because Srintil was lying diagonally across the bed, she assumed that her lover was still next to her. She moved her hand, expecting to feel Rasus's chest. But, her fingertips only felt the coolness of the sleeping mat. She reached further. And found nobody.

Srintil quickly sat up and looked around. Discovering that she was alone on the bed, she immediately thought, or hoped, that Rasus was somewhere around the house. But, that hope was abruptly shattered when she saw that none of Rasus's possessions remained in the room.

Srintil could see the old woman lying on her bed, the only movement being the barely discernible rise and fall of her chest. The gray eyes turned towards Srintil as she approached.

"Where's Rasus, Granny?"

"What?"

"Rasus, your grandson! Where is he?"

"Rasus?"

"Yes, Rasus."

"Rasus? Has Rasus come home?"

"Oh, you've forgotten. You're confused. So, you don't know where Rasus has gone?"

For a long time the old woman remained still. Then she held out her hand to Srintil and opened her fingers, revealing the coins. Srintil looked at them without comprehending, and then gave up. She turned around, wrenched open the door and went out. She searched for a spot from where she could clearly see the fountain. She couldn't see any sign of Rasus. She stared at the empty yard, the place where the village people usually squatted behind the bushes. No sign. All Srintil could see was a pair of wagtails busily swooping down and catching greenbottle flies.

Srintil gazed off into the distance, across the broad rice fields. She could just make out the outline of the town of Dawuan. She could see the thin fog which had blanketed the town wafting away under the heat of the sun. Dawuan, with its market and the army post where Rasus had joined up with Sergeant Slamet. For Srintil, Dawuan now appeared as a smug, self-satisfied shape in the distance.

"So, that's the way it is," she thought, trying to deny the reality that Rasus had left without saying goodbye. In her mind, all men were the same. They were crazy to be with her for one or two days, apparently unconcerned about the cost. Sulam, the chief of Pecikalan Village, and even Mr Assistant District Administrator were just two of a long line of men who had succumbed to the flick of Srintil's dance scarf. The ronggeng felt surprised that there existed one man who felt different to her. Yet, that man had fled to avoid her. She realized then that the only man capable of breaking her heart was Rasus.

For several long moments, Srintil stood there, ignoring the mosquitoes flying around her. Several sucked the blood from her legs. Another one landed behind her ear, its belly filling with blood at each passing moment. The hair on her forehead became damp from the morning fog as it turned to dew. Her eyes glistened with tears.

Two naked children watched Srintil with surprise. They were seeing what nobody in Paruk ever expected to see: a ronggeng dancer crying. In Paruk, the ronggeng was the symbol of passion and joy. Her entire existence was represented by singing and dancing. Her adornments were her smile and the glance of her eyes, pouring forth a natural vivaciousness. She was animated by the same spirit that causes birds to fly and flowers to bloom. The ronggeng was to them the epitome of happiness and laughter.

The two naked children drew back. How could a ronggeng be crying?

Only Srintil knew the reason she felt so disturbed. Somebody had exposed her; it wasn't relevant who he was. But, little by little, she began to see herself from another perspective. No longer as a woman owned by everyone, but as a woman in the simplest sense.

She was beginning to feel a sense of incompleteness without the affirmation of a man in her life: in her heart and in her bed. If it was the case, she thought, that the world is made up of thousands of small worlds and each of these small worlds consists of one man and one woman, Srintil longed only for a small world. A world without Rasus had suddenly become absolutely unimaginable.

It did not take long for the villagers to realize that something was happening to Srintil. It quickly became obvious that she preferred to be alone with her thoughts rather than mix with other people. By the following day, the small hamlet was buzzing with gossip, especially amongst the women. They all realized that Srintil's state of mind was bound up with Rasus, who had left the village to join up with Sergeant Slamet.

"Has it ever happened that a ronggeng fell madly in love with a man?" asked one woman sitting with her friend beneath a jackfruit tree, searching her head for lice.

"As far as I know, there's never been stories like that," her friend answered. "What's more typical is the man being crazy about the ronggeng. After all, she's made to attract men. She can't become attached to anyone. So, how could she fall in love?"

"Well, Srintil sure is a strange one. If that's what really happened, then it must be Nyai Kartareja's fault."

"Nyai Kartareja?"

"Sure. If Nyai Kartareja had been careful to keep an eye on Srintil, this never would have happened. She neglected her responsibility because of greed. Srintil was ordered to service as many men as possible without paying attention to taboo days. Certainly, Nyai Kartareja has become rich, but now look at what has happened."

"Actually, I can understand why Srintil likes Rasus. Nobody's to blame really. The problem is if Srintil keeps moping around and doesn't want to perform, the village will suffer. That's what I'm sad about."

"Yet, I still believe in Nyai Kartareja and her husband. If they are able to create some sort of magic so that a lot of men lust after Srintil, why can't they break the attraction between her and Rasus?"

The last remark was, in fact, quite relevant. The people who had become most worried about Srintil were Nyai Kartareja and her husband. They could not bear to have their adopted child fall for Rasus, or for any other man: and they would be even more worried if Srintil were to think about settling down and having a family. Their status as ronggeng trainers, as traditional healers, and as experts on village female dancers, was at stake, and their source of a prosperous income was seriously threatened.

Nyai Kartareja realized that she had to do something to break the love that bound Srintil to Rasus. She decided to try some magic. She found an unhatched egg which had been left to rot in the chicken coop and secretly buried it under one corner of Srintil's bedroom. Over this spot she recited a spell to break the love:

Niyatingsun matak aji pamurung
Hadi aing tampéan aing cikaruntung Nantung
Ditaburan boèh sana, manci rasa marang
Srintil marang Rasus
Kéné wurung kana wurung, pes minpes déning
Éyang Secamenggala
Pentil alum cucuk layu, angen sira bungker
Si Srintil Si Rasus
Ker bungker, ker bungker kersane Éyang Secamenggala
Ker bungker, ker bungker kersane Sing Murbeng Dumadi

My purpose is to cast a spell of annulment.
An extraordinary gift, an extraordinary boon,
the pinnacle of good fortune.
Disperse, to those places, to those feelings between
Srintil and Rasus.

Here thwarted, there thwarted, a deflating hiss by
Grandfather Secamenggala.
A bud withers, a spout fades, your thoughts thwarted
You Srintil, you Rasus.
Thoughts thwarted, thoughts thwarted, this is the wish of
our ancestor Secamenggala.
Thoughts thwarted, thoughts thwarted, this is the wish of
Almighty God.

The power of the spell was believed to be drawn from the supernatural, and free from dynamic and even physical laws. It was said that this power could only be averted by an equal but opposite force.

However, Nyai Kartareja's efforts were thwarted. One night when Srintil wanted to urinate, she was too lazy to go outdoors and peed in a corner in her bedroom. In that particular corner, part of the floor had recently been dug up. It was quite natural for Srintil to choose this spot since she assumed that the dirt would soak up her urine. But this was the very place Nyai Kartareja had buried the rotten egg after casting her spell over it. And in doing this, Srintil unwittingly neutralized the spell that had been cast against her.

To the disappointment of Nyai Kartareja and her husband, and especially of her sponsors, Srintil had already canceled two dance performances, offering only a lame excuse: she felt lazy!

Yet she was apparently not too lazy to do something that seemed rather strange to the villagers: she began chatting with the goat-herding children, most of whom ran around naked. Without showing any embarrassment, Srintil accompanied them as they chased after goats or sat with them under a tree, and helped them build kites from the leaves of the turnip plant. Srintil found she could share the children's happiness, made more intense by their gaining a special playmate. At first, the children felt awkward, but after a while they all become close friends.

"Once, I was like you, having fun playing in the fields while I tended goats," said Srintil, her hands busily making a whirligig from coconut palm leaves.

"Do you know how to capture a dragonfly with jackfruit tree sap?" asked one child.

"Ah yes, that's easy. In fact, if you use jackfruit tree sap, you can capture a cuckoo bird," answered Srintil knowingly.

"Did you really do that?" asked another child, who was carrying a dried mound of cow manure, part of which was glowing. A grasshopper was being toasted on top of the glowing ember. Srintil smiled.

"Yes, of course. Dear me, toasted grasshoppers really are tasty, aren't they?"

"D'ya want some? Go ahead, have some."

"Really?"

"Go ahead!"

The children stared with rapt interest as Srintil chewed the grasshopper that had been toasted on the cow-pat coals, a symbolic act sealing their friendship. The oldest child came forward and approached Srintil. In his hands he held a joint of bamboo.

"So, it's true, you really did once play like us. But can you guess what's inside this tube?"

"Crickets?"

"No."

"Berries?"

"No,"

"Aphids?"

"No."

"Well, I give up."

The child turned the tube upside down. Srintil shrieked and jumped, like a frightened little girl. A milk snake slithered to freedom after its long imprisonment in the tube. Another shriek, this time from the children as Srintil chased after the rascal who had released the snake. The boy grimaced when she caught him and pinched his thighs, but he didn't seem to mind when she continued to pinch him.

On one occasion, Srintil felt she had to be truly alone. Fed up with being secluded in her room, she walked towards the edge of the village. There, long ago beneath a jackfruit tree, she had filled most of her time playing as a little girl. She picked up a leaf that had fallen from the tree and crushed it in her hand. Strangely, as she did so, she felt that something in her had been released.

Not far off, two young goats were romping, capering about comically. They raced off to their mother, positioning themselves between her legs to nurse. Their actions were crude, yet the mother let them tug and suck at her swollen teats which were filled with the potency of life. Srintil watched the mother in awe. She smiled, and felt a sympathetic tightening in her own breasts, as well as a thrill somewhere in her womb. Suddenly, she was overwhelmed by a powerful desire to hold a baby. Almost at the same time, the thought that Nyai Kartareja had possibly destroyed her ovaries made her gasp in fear. A violent struggle took place in her breast, signified by two wet lines descending down her cheeks. For the first time in her life, she asked herself the question, "Why must I be a ronggeng?" She was beginning to realize that, had she not been a ronggeng, Rasus would never have left in the manner he did.

Srintil's daydreams were shattered by the sound of a motorcycle arriving in the village. There were only two such vehicles in the district. One belonged to a regional administrative official, and the other to Marsusi, the manager of the Wanakeling rubber plantation. It didn't matter which of the two it was, Srintil knew that any man who took the trouble to come to Paruk had only one goal in mind. She sat for a moment, thinking. Then, she stood up and trudged off, away from the center of the village. Her journey took her first to the top of the hill in the village cemetery, where she encountered a brooding silence.

Flying lizards silently sailed from tree to tree. A female starling busily carried fluff from the sugar cane blossom to line her nest. Near a gravestone, a wasp was pulling and tugging at a large worm paralyzed by its sting. Srintil was startled by the sound of a gecko which was hidden in the eaves of Ki Secamenggala's memorial.

The loneliness of the cemetery became the mother to a child trying to understand what was happening in her life. Srintil felt she was at a turning point. Her emotions reached out to the myriad of wild orchids growing on the trunk of a banyan tree, to the ferns that fringed the recesses of a steep incline, and to the sharp rapping of a woodpecker on dead wood. The comfort of their presence made Srintil want to stay in this secret place until sunset or even longer. In the loneliness of the cemetery, nature invited her to stay, enticing her by the smell of the earth and the perfume of the kemboja trees. By the humming of gnats that flew around her head and the softness of the moss covering the damp stones. Srintil dissolved into the comforting lap of her mother, feeling that she was understood and comforted. Her daydreams would have been free to float off and sail away if she hadn't been disturbed.

"Srin, come on home. We have a guest."

For a moment Srintil was startled. Then she was yanked back to reality. She didn't need to look up; she knew whose voice it was.

"Come home, Srin. We've been waiting for you," repeated Nyai Kartareja gently. "It's Marsusi, the manager of the rubber plantation."

Srintil blinked her eyes as a sign that she understood.

"I don't feel like going home yet," answered Srintil in a voice empty of emotion.

Nyai Kartareja sat down next to her. "Don't be like that. You can't just ignore our guests, especially this one."

"Well, I don't want to go home."

"If I were you, Srin, I wouldn't waste this opportunity. You can go to town with Marsusi on his motorcycle. You can go wherever you want, even to a movie. You've never seen a movie, have you? You could ask Marsusi to buy you things too. Wouldn't you like to have a necklace like the one worn by the wife of the Pecikalan Village chief?"

"That's enough, mama. Why don't you go home and I'll follow a bit later. I want to bathe at the fountain first."

"Very good, my little one. But you will come, won't you? We'll be waiting for you."

Srintil nodded slightly.

Nyai Kartareja left her. Not long afterwards, Srintil, too, went down the hill, but she did not follow Nyai Kartareja's footsteps. Instead, she took a route that went neither to the fountain nor to her home. She walked quickly along the road that took her out of the village. She walked with a long, brisk stride, smiling and nodding at the people she happened to pass. Once she reached the long rice-field dikes that lead to Dawuan, she quickened her pace. The sun had already past its zenith, and its rays struck the ronggeng with a torrent of heat that made her head ache. She kept walking, occasionally raising her hand to deflect the hot sunlight from her face.

It soon became evident to Nyai Kartareja, who was waiting at her house, that Srintil had not followed her home. Marsusi, a man of fifty years or so, sat restlessly in his chair. Several times, he put his Stetson hat on his head and then took it off again, without any apparent reason. Finally, he went out and retrieved something from the storage compartment of his motorcycle. He came back inside with a square-shaped bottle. An impatient suitor should always have some gin on hand, he thought. He took a drink directly from the bottle.

"You said that Srintil was home. So, where is she?" he asked, slamming the bottle down on the table.

Nyai Kartareja hid her anxiety behind a friendly smile.

"Well, sir. Srintil told me that she wanted to take a bath. Oh, that girl, where could she be?"

"Try looking for her again," Kartareja suggested. "If she really is bathing, why is it taking her so long?"

"Just a minute," said Marsusi, his patience wearing thin. "You both look after Srintil here, right?"

"That's right, sir."

"So? Do you think that I came here just to sit around and waste time? Just tell me: is Srintil being used by another man or has she gone off somewhere? Don't make me angry!"

Kartareja averted his eyes, glancing nervously left and right. His lips quivered, but he said nothing. The dukun sat there petrified, his eyes giving away his fear when Marsusi stood up and approached him, throwing his hat onto the table.

"You people don't know your own good fortune. Don't forget that you are getting money from me. So why are you treating me this way? Just answer my question: Are you going to bring Srintil here or not? If not, to hell with you. Just don't pretend to be a ronggeng trainer!"

While Kartareja was affronted by Marsusi's rudeness, his wife reacted differently. Nyai Kartareja had considerable experience in the world of men: from small lads to young bachelors, from young pupils just learning about women to those who were quite mature like the angry man in front of her. The work of the wife of a dukun first and foremost required being able to read the emotional state of a man who came to her, hearing his complaints, controlling his longings, and subduing his passions. For the success of her business, Nyai Kartareja never departed from her formula: any man that came to her, even one who was gray-haired, was treated like a baby: a baby whom she knew could be easily pacified by a soft lullaby and effortlessly manipulated by gentle smiles and sweet flattery.

"Oh my dear boy—eh—sir. You've every right to become annoyed, and we understand why you're losing your patience. This is entirely our fault. You came with a passion, a need, that should have been quickly fulfilled in this house. Be assured that we give the wishes of gentlemen like yourself our highest priority. The problem is that the girl you desire, Srintil, is still a child. You must remember, she's still somewhat green, as it were. So, you must be a bit patient with her. Srintil is still fresh, a young sprout," She, lightly touched his chest.

"I'm not looking for a moldy old woman," Marsusi muttered, his voice dropping a tone or two.

"Indeed. We are preparing this sprout just for you. But, you must be patient because Srintil is sulking."

"Sulking?"

Nyai Kartareja smiled, letting Marsusi's question hang in the air momentarily. Had he known what was going on, Marsusi would have realized that Nyai Kartareja's smile was a professional tactic to manipulate him, or at the very least a sign that Nyai Kartareja felt she had succeeded in taking the initial steps to control the situation.

"That's the difficulty of looking after a beautiful child. You see, sir. Srintil is demanding a necklace like the one worn by the wife of the chief of Pacikalan: a gold chain weighing a hundred grams, with a diamond pendulum. I'm sure a gentleman like yourself could fulfill Srintil's wish, but consider us who must endure this situation. Oh, that Srintil. Just because she's young and beautiful, she places heavy demands on us.

"Hmm..."

The negotiations that followed between the two took place in silence. Nyai Kartareja felt herself floating on air. She had succeeded in defusing Marsusi's anger as well as bringing him to a point of wagering his self-esteem. Marsusi was not a naïve man. He knew full well that Nyai Kartareja's words had a specific purpose. The crucial point was that she had indirectly compared him with the village chief. She had also alluded to his status as the manager of a plantation. "A gentleman like yourself..." Her words had struck his heart like whiplashes.

Marsusi went back to his seat and gulped down the rest of his liquor. His features took on a savage look, perhaps because of the alcohol, possibly because of the turmoil in his heart. Silently he cursed Nyai Kartareja for her veiled extortion. But, strangely, he was not powerful enough to break out of this subtle trap, accepting that she had thrown down a challenge. He hurriedly put on his hat and stood up.

"I'm going home, madam."

"Why?" asked Nyai Kartareja, feigning surprise.

"Well, what else can a man do if Srintil keeps moping around," her husband interjected.

"Hold on, sir. Don't you have any message for Srintil? Maybe the day after tomorrow, you will come again?"

Marsusi had already straddled his motorcycle. He glanced up at her, his nostrils quivering and his eyes blazing. His rage was directed through his foot as he savagely kick-started the powerful engine. The Harley Davidson, a vestige of the war, roared into life and he sped off, followed by the admiring stares of the village children.

Nyai Kartareja's shoulder's slumped in relief. She was convinced that she had not only diffused Marsusi's anger over being stood up by Srintil but also trapped the man in a challenge.

"We have a little game going here," she said to her husband.

"What's that?"

"I issued a challenge and tomorrow or the day after, Marsusi will return. And he'll bring a hundred-gram necklace with a diamond pendulum. A suitable challenge for Marsusi, wouldn't you say?"

"What d'you think you're doing? Why don't you worry first about where Srintil is," came the cold but emphatic answer.

The expression on Nyai Kartareja's face changed abruptly, as she realized that there was a more immediate problem to be solved. Momentarily angry, she was rendered speechless. But only briefly, then her face brightened again.

"I bet Srintil is at her grandparents' house right now. I'll go fetch her."

"I'm coming with you," said her husband, scooping up his tobacco.

"Come on then!"

But, when they arrived at Sakarya's house, they were disappointed. Srintil was not there. The two were greeted by Sakarya who was demanding an explanation. A neighbor had reported seeing Srintil walking briskly out of the village.

"Don't you realize that all of this has happened because there's something going on between Srintil and Rasus?" Sakarya said accusingly. "Twice, she's refused to perform. Now she's run off. What are you going to do about it?"

Nyai Kartareja swallowed. She remembered the rotten egg secretly buried in Srintil's room and wondered why her efforts had not been effective.

"Wait a minute," interjected Nyai Sakarya. "If Srintil is attracted to Rasus, what's wrong with us helping them get married?"

Sakarya was silent. He could understand the logic of his wife's question. Having his granddaughter become the wife of a soldier would not likely be rejected by any elder of Paruk. Yet, for Sakarya, the problem was no longer that simple.

"Of course, there's nothing inherently wrong with the idea of Srintil marrying Rasus," Kartareja said to Nyai Sakarya. "Not if she weren't a ronggeng wearing the name Paruk Village on her sash, that is."

"Be careful not to harbor ideas like that," Kartareja warned. "Remember your duties as the caretaker and deputy chief of the descendants of Ki Secamenggala in this village. You're not permitted to place your personal interests above your responsibilities."

Sakarya nodded, coughing. "Right, but you two have to find Srintil and bring her back."

"I'm ready to search for her," replied Nyai Kartareja, full of determination.

"Good. But be careful. You are not to be rough with her, even if she is a bother," ordered Nyai Sakarya.

"Since when have I ever hurt your grandchild? What's more, who was it that gave Srintil the power to own nice things and all that jewelry? You're telling me to be careful, but you had better watch what you say!"

"Okay, okay!" Kartareja's and Sakarya's voices sounded in unison.

The heat from the sun was still intense as Srintil stepped down from a horse-drawn carriage in front of the Dawuan market. Small drops of sweat formed on her nose, but her neck and cheeks were fresh and rosy, giving the impression that hers was the skin of a ten-year-old child. That Srintil wasn't really prepared to visit the market could be seen from the look on her tightly-drawn face, and from her clothes and hair which were somewhat disheveled.

Yet, Srintil's youthfulness seemed quite natural. Only a person with worldly experience would know that she was a fallen woman. The way her eyebrows came together, and the darkening in the hollow of her eyes would have been an indication to those who were worldly wise. These were signs that a woman, whatever her age, had become sexually active.

After paying the carriage driver, Srintil stopped short of entering the market, walking only the few steps to the curb. She had never felt so awkward or out of place at the market as she did then. She stood at the curb for a while, her eyes staring vacantly.

Srintil's arrival at the market of Dawuan usually brought about a spontaneous enthusiastic response from the people there. The men whistled or cracked dirty jokes. The women stole looks at her hands, ears, and neck to see whether she was wearing new jewelry.

And then, afterwards, they would gossip about who her current lovers might be and how rich they were.

But that day the market people restrained themselves as Srintil entered the market with an obvious dark cloud hanging over her. Her mouth was tightly shut and her lips were set in a straight line. Her eyebrows were knitted together, almost meeting in the middle of her forehead. The overall impression was that Srintil was ready to reject any and all forms of jokes and banter.

But there was much whispering, questions quickly filling the air in every corner of the market.

"What could have happened to have made her world so dark?" asked a female sweet potato seller to her colleague next door.

"Well, I can guess," answered her friend. "When a ronggeng is sullen like this, it usually means something has happened between her and her guardian."

"You mean Nyai Kartareja?"

"Yeah. A ronggeng trainer usually wants to take care of every aspect of her charge's life, often even wishing to control her possessions."

"I've heard that. I know that a ronggeng is often considered prime livestock by her guardian. Think of all the times people hold rituals or during the harvest season: a ronggeng has to perform every night. During the day she has to service the men. And the person handling her affairs, especially those involving money, is the dukun. You can't help but feel sorry for Srintil, can you? On the other hand, Kartareja and his wife have become fairly wealthy out of it, haven't they?"

"What are you talking about? asked a third woman, joining in the conversation. "That's nonsense. Listen to me. Srintil's here to escape from a man who can't accept the fact that she is having her monthly period."

"No way. Look at her again. Her skirt isn't stained, the edge isn't even folded. So, she's still clean."

"We're probably reading too much into it. She's probably fed up with men is all. That's probably what's causing her to scowl. She's just sick and tired of men."

The idle gossip in the market soon died away. The women watched as Srintil entered a small food stall. Srintil sat down on a low bamboo bench beside the shopkeeper. Because she seemed aloof, the shopkeeper felt awkward.

"Would you like something to eat, young lady?"

"No, ma'am. I just want something to drink, and to rest here for a while. Would that be okay?" she answered without looking at her.

Srintil drank a large glass of cold clear water, thinking that, if water had the power to return life to dead, dry earth or to enable seeds to grow into sprouts, so too it could calm her restlessness by slowing down her fast-beating heart.

Still feeling dazed, Srintil could feel the refreshing water cooling her body which was overheated by the intense sunlight and fevered by the chaos of her thoughts. Momentarily she re-established the balance between her emotions and her feelings. The silent process of taking control of herself cost her a great deal of effort, as evidenced by the drops of perspiration on her skin. A highly intensive metabolic activity like this demanded that she rest for a while. A vision of Rasus rose up in front of her. At the same time, a slow-moving breeze brought on a sense of great weariness.

"Ma'am, I'm really tired. I'd like to lie down and sleep for a while, is that alright?" she asked, stretching out on the bench, the bamboo slats squeaking.

"Hey, what're you doing? Customers won't like it if I let people sleep in my shop. No way. I'll go out of business."

The proprietor couldn't bring herself to continue when she saw before her the young and lithe Srintil, her face calm in sleep, a vision which reminded her of own baby which she had left with its grandmother at home. Her motherly instincts came to the fore as she watched the peacefully sleeping figure.

In her deep sleep, Srintil's sense of self almost disappeared. It was no longer important to her what her name was or that she was the ronggeng of Paruk. There was no longer any single attribute that defined the person sprawled, like a castaway from a shipwreck, on the bench. She could only be identified as an element of nature called child of man, a child that clearly sought momentary refuge from herself. The impression was one of helplessness, the very helplessness that enables a baby to draw love and sympathy.

Actually, it was not only the shopkeeper who was feeling sympathetic toward Srintil. Many of the market people felt the same. They could see that Srintil was having a rough time and felt protective towards her. It wasn't important to them to know the reason for her misery. This feeling of protectiveness became apparent when Nyai Kartareja appeared at the entrance of the market about an hour later. The taro root sellers saw her set face, the determined look in her wrinkled eyes and the hair piled high on her head, all strengthening the conclusion they had drawn that there was tension between Nyai Kartareja and Srintil. Their basic instincts demanded they do something to protect the young girl.

"Oh, Nyai Kartareja. Are you looking for Srintil? asked one of the sellers.

Nyai Kartareja nodded stiffly.

"Well, she's not here. I saw her heading south earlier."

"By herself?"

"Yes. And she appeared to be quite sad. What's going on?"

This nosy question obviously annoyed Nyai Kartareja. She didn't answer, but turned and strode out of the market.

Most of the activity at the Dawuan market took place in the mornings. After the sun began to set, some of the vendors would go home. Those that stayed were the ones that didn't transport their goods back and forth every day: the sellers of earthenware, grass mats, taro root, or the owners of food stalls that serviced the other vendors in the evenings. Street sellers also used the market as a place to rest.

That afternoon, many of the stalls were filled with people who were stretched out comfortably on mats or sitting in a circle playing cards. The balmy air drained them of their desire to work. They just wanted to rest.

It was the same with the mourning dove in the canary tree behind the market, its body hidden beneath the dense foliage of palm leaves to protect it from the sun's stinging rays. Yet, its lilting song reached its mate far away. When the object of its song approached, the male dove's tune changed, becoming lower and softer. So soft that it seemed to be lost in the sounds of the breeze that swept through the trees. The two doves felt compelled to create a private place to find their unity with nature. The hot air, the soft blowing breeze, and the sound of the mourning dove was a harmony instinctively in tune with nature.

Like the doves, Wirsiter and his wife, Ciplak, a couple who gave kecapi performances for a living, seemed to know instinctively when and where their performances were required. On this particular day, they appeared in the Dawuan market just at the time the people there were at the height of boredom with their work and routine. After working all morning, the market people were ready for some light entertainment.

Wirsiter and his wife didn't like being referred to as street musicians or, even worse, being compared to beggars with musical instruments. They didn't perform their music for just anyone, even for regulars unless they requested it. To maintain their professional image, they always looked clean and neat. This particular day, Wirsiter was wearing a traditional headdress, a jacket of traditional *lurik* fabric, and a neatly folded wrap-around skirt. His wife was also wearing a wrap-around kain, and an embroidered blouse with a sash and a chignon adorned with jasmine flowers on top of her head. Her lips were bright red from chewing betel nut.

There are various musical instruments for interpreting rhythm and harmony, even emotions. The people of Paruk, for example, fully believed that the bamboo xylophone ensemble calung was a perfect tool for depicting the beating of a joyful heart or one excited by passion. If one were to ask where the power of calung music was found, the answer would be immediate: in its simplicity. This does not mean, however, that it was easy to cut and tune the bamboo keys and create a calung instrument. Simplicity in this case means that one must restrain oneself from trying to influence the selection of the bamboo. Natural qualities were considered far more important to calung instruments than the skills to make them.

A perfect calung instrument can only be produced from black bamboo that is properly dried. It should not be dried in the sun, or even worse, baked over a fire. Neither should it be damaged in any way before it is cut down, either by humans, or by animals, for instance, biting or breaking off the young tip. The shoot should be straight and tall. Bamboo that is too thick is not suitable for making a calung. The calung makers wouldn't admit, or even be aware, that the rules they followed were to pay homage to the spirit of the Great Master Craftsman. All they knew was that, by adhering to such rules, they could produce a fine set of calung instruments. Its tones would have the power to interpret the sounds of a host of *blentung* insects, its rhythms would evoke the soft patter of rainfall on a grass roof, and its spirit would emulate the beating of an impassioned heart.

The zither *kecapi* also drew power from its simplicity, shaped like an extended five-sided wooden box, with wire strings stretched along its face, each representing a unique tone. The scale steps are determined by the thickness of the string as well as by thin metal bridges set diagonally underneath, determining the length of the string.

It was no use asking Wirsiter about the preciseness of each tone, general tuning, or the acoustic knowledge needed to play the kecapi. He had never studied music theory. But, with his simple instrument, he and his wife managed to transform the harmony of nature into melodies. Their teachers were the flickering fireflies during an evening drizzle, the flash of foam ebbing and flowing among the boulders on a beach, and raindrops falling on the smooth surface of a lake.

The itinerant duo traveled here and there, peddling music that pampered the senses, sad and melancholic music. Their performances didn't entice people to get up and dance. Rather, it made their listeners muse, looking within themselves or floating away in sentimental fantasy. And so it was, that warm evening, for the people of Dawuan market as they listened contemplatively to Wirsiter plucking his kecapi to accompany Ciplak as she sang *asmara dahana*, a traditional love song:

Li Lali tan bisa lali
Sun lelipur tan sangsaya
Katon baé sapolahé
Kancil désa 'njang talingan
Aku mèlu karo ndika
Lebu séta sari pohung
Becik mati yen kapiran

Forget, Forget, I can't forget
I'm cheered, without a care
Just to see her move
The village mouse deer, long eared
I'll follow her
White dust, essence of cassava
It's good to die with a glad heart.

The people playing poker stopped, slapping down their cards on the table; those who were sprawled on mats floated in an imaginary world between sleep and wakefulness, women chewing betel-nut kept moving their mouths but their thoughts flew back to the most significant moments of their lives.

Wirsiter and Ciplak probably couldn't articulate why they sang so many love songs. In fact, they usually only followed the tastes of their audience. But perhaps it was because kecapi music was indeed the most suitable genre for describing feelings of love.

The market people were so engrossed in the music that they ceased to be aware of anything else, including Srintil lying on the bench at the food stall. The music gently brought Srintil back to consciousness. She slowly opened her eyes but didn't see anything at first because all her senses were focused on listening. Wirsiter and his wife, without intending to, had pierced Srintil's heart with a sad love song. Tears were streaming down her face.

She sat up, wiping her eyes.

The seller turned when she heard the bench creak.

"Oh, you're awake, young lady. You're crying!"

"I'm not, ma'am. I'm not."

"What's the matter? Do you feel ill?"

"It's okay, ma'am. Please, just get me something to drink."

The seller held back. She observed Srintil carefully, as she wiped the tears from her face. She realized that Srintil was not a child and thus kept things to herself: things that were no one else's concern.

"Do you want something to eat?"

"I'm really not hungry, ma'am."

"Come on. I'm an experienced mother, and I can tell when someone is hungry. Your lips have lost their color, your collarbones are sticking out and, while you were sleeping, I noticed that your belly is shrunken. You should eat, so that you don't fall ill. That'd be a shame, wouldn't it?"

Srintil realized that she was, in fact, very hungry. Since the previous day, she had been feeling a growing pain in her stomach. The problem was that she simply felt too tired to feed herself. Yet, as soon as a plate of rice and hot sauce was placed in front of her, Srintil succumbed. She ate the food quickly, her cheeks and lips regaining their red color from the hot sauce and chili peppers. Perspiration and tears began to form, as if her life force was awakening.

"So I was right, wasn't I? My food has brought your strength back. Some more?"

"No, thank you, ma'am. I'm full now."

Srintil left the market while the people were still enjoying Wirsiter's kecapi playing. Some of them glanced at her, but didn't say anything. But they all noted that this was the first time they'd seen Srintil so listless and depressed.

Just clear of the market, Srintil hesitated. Her confused behavior drew the attention of the people around. A man wearing army fatigues approached her from behind, his touch glancing her buttocks. He didn't expect Srintil to turn toward him with such fury in her eyes. "I might have been a ronggeng once and men may have touched me wherever they please, but now I'm no longer a ronggeng. No longer!"

But Srintil's shouts only echoed in her own heart. The army corporal, however, realized that Srintil's anger over his roving hands was genuine.

"About two hours ago Nyai Kartareja came to my post searching for you. Someone looking for a ronggeng at an army post. That's amazing!" Corporal Pujo, grinned foolishly to cover his embarrassment.

"Have you seen Nyai Kartareja?" he then asked.

"No."

"She believes you've gone off with Rasus."

"Oh, really?"

"Yeah. But Rasus hasn't been at the post for three days. He went with Sergeant Slamet to the battalion headquarters."

"Oh? So Rasus isn't around here anymore?"

Corporal Pujo did not pick up the sudden change in Srintil's face.

"He's a lucky kid. When he returns, he'll be a real soldier, with rank and salary. Yeah, just like me."

Srintil lowered her head. How was it that he didn't realize that there was violent confusion in the heart of the young woman before him?

"When do you expect him to return?"

"I have no idea. But, probably not for some time. From what I know, someone like Rasus has to undergo more schooling before he obtains an official rank. Where he'll go to school, I don't know. I'll find out when Sergeant Slamet returns to the post."

"I see," replied Srintil, softly.

At this point Corporal Pujo realized that a change had come over Srintil: her eyes glistened, the light in her face faded, and her breathing became shallow. The corporal frowned.

"Wait a minute, you're from Paruk! I don't understand. Is there something going on between you and ..."

"No. Nothing!"

Srintil turned around and quickly walked away, leaving Corporal Pujo standing there, confused. Then he smiled and nodded to himself. But the only thing he really knew about Rasus and Srintil was that they were both from Paruk. During his entire time at the post, Rasus had never spoken of the ronggeng, nor mentioned anything about a relationship with her.

Srintil returned to the marketplace. She sat down on an empty bench and called Wirsiter and his wife, requesting that they play some music. After they had finished one piece, Srintil asked them to play more. And more, and more, without caring how much money she would be required to pay.

Even when the sun was low in the sky, the sounds of the kecapi music could still be heard in the market. Srintil displayed some unusual emotions during the performance. Sometimes she smiled a strange smile during a song. Other times she sang along with Ciplak, but her voice was hoarse and unnatural. It was obvious that there was conflict in her heart.

But what was it that made Srintil so angry when Ciplak wanted to stop singing?

"We're tired, young lady," said Ciplak. "We've done twenty pieces."

"My wife is right," Wirsiter added. "And it's getting late."

Srintil frowned, her brows deeply furrowed. Her eyes glistened.

"Twenty pieces. What's the matter? Afraid I can't pay? Is that it?" she retorted sharply.

"Don't misunderstand us, young lady," said Wirsiter, in a low voice. "The day is finished!"

What Wirsiter was trying to tell Srintil was that the day was entering its most sensitive period, that of twilight the moment when the ecosystem is teetering between daytime and night-time, undergoing a change in the intensity of cosmic rays that fall on the earth. Wirsiter could never express it in such terms. But he knew that people must rest during the twilight hours, when the demon god, Bathara Kala, came down to earth to feed. Bathara Kala must be worshipped and honored, and this was not negotiable with Wirsiter and his wife. Ignoring this law meant that one was prepared to become fodder for the god of time.

Srintil understood what Wirsiter was saying. She knew that twilight was the time when people withdrew from their daily tasks to fulfill their natural desires. Nevertheless, her face still revealed her anger.

At that moment, an old woman, bent over with age, approached her. Her voice was hoarse and broken, as she gasped for breath after her long walk.

"My beautiful grandchild, is that you?" The voice of Nyai Sakarya immediately doused the fire in Srintil's heart. That voice had been the most familiar to Srintil since she was a very small child. Having been orphaned as a baby, she had never known the voice of her mother.

Nyai Sakarya's eyes, although wrinkled with age, were still able to give strength to Srintil, who stood up slowly. The touch of the ancient hands on her shoulders felt cool and fresh. Embraced by her grandmother, she walked out of the market bowed, biting her lip, her eyes wet with tears.

Both women were silent. Yet in their hearts grew a mutual agreement: they both wished to go home to Paruk. The little hamlet, isolated in the middle of the rice fields was their mother whose lap and embrace were calming and comforting.

They stopped at a bamboo shelter outside the town to wait for the twilight to pass. In the growing darkness, they remained silent. Nyai Sakarya understood why her granddaughter had run away, and Srintil understood, in return, why her grandmother had sought her. The two drifted off into their respective memories of two quite different events. Nyai Sakarya was remembering Srintil's parents, one of whom was her own child, who had died as a result of the mass food poisoning when Srintil was only five months old. The unforgettable sorrow of long ago now transformed into a profound and abiding love for her grandchild.

At the same time, Srintil's thoughts were occupied with Rasus. Rasus had become a kind of puzzle that brought pain every time his image entered her thoughts. Not knowing where he was, Srintil felt that he had callously abandoned her.

When the stars became clear in the sky, the two women continued their journey. Leaving the main road, they walked along the dike separating the rice paddy fields that led straight to the village, now barely visible in the distance. On both sides of the dike the wide open areas were planted with dry season crops. The *bence* bird, which always called when it was disturbed at night, flew just a few yards above the heads of the old woman and her grandchild, its raucous voice insinuating that it owned the entire night and considered them trespassers.

Far ahead a pair of blue lights moved up into the air, crossing over the dike, followed by another pair. Srintil drew close to her grandmother.

"It's just the *belacan* guiding their children," said Nyai Sakarya, understanding Srintil's fear in the darkening night. Not completely soothed, Srintil again drew close to her grandmother as the sounds of rustling in the bushes could be heard nearby. A moment later, in the gloom, a large bird rose into the sky with a field mouse in its claws. The owl had acquired its first meal for the night. The sound of the squealing mouse faded into the distance as the bird flew off.

The night was quite dark by the time Nyai Sakarya and Srintil reached Paruk. The moon, being in its last phase, would rise after midnight, so that the light of the stars ruled the sky unchallenged. The flash of shooting stars gave the impression that there was life in the heavens. As a rule, if the flash continues for several seconds, it engenders feelings of awe and wonderment: how small humans are in the midst of such elemental forces! Beneath this vast curvature of space, Nyai Sakarya and her granddaughter felt like miniscule ants creeping on the surface of the earth, without power or purpose.

2

Tampi walked quickly toward Sakarya's house. Goder, her son of just ten months, was tied to her back in a sling made of cloth. In her right hand Tampi held something wrapped in a rag. It was a bunch of bananas, the large variety known as *pisang raja,* a gift for Srintil who was ill in bed. Srintil's body had begun to grow thin and her face wan. Her vitality, previously her most prominent attribute, had all but disappeared. She didn't want to speak to anyone, didn't want to eat. Even her characteristic smile had almost disappeared.

However, when the baby, Goder, visited with his mother, Srintil always revived. The magic of babies is like the magic of flowers, the magic of areca blossoms that hang loosely from their sepal in the morning, or the magic of flowery blue bungur trees at the beginning of the dry season. Babies are captivating. Even the smell of their small bodies and breath are a miracle of freshness that only nature itself has the power to create. Their eyes, clear and bright, can extinguish a father's rage. Babies are the epitomy of nature and, because of this, a mother never becomes angry when her child dirties itself in her lap. A baby is more than the flesh and blood of its mother; it is the flesh and blood of nature. Anyone who is really honest with his or her instincts would acknowledge that all babies exist in a realm filled with God's mercy. And one who has been overcome by conflicting emotions can find tranquility by slipping away in the world of babies.

Srintil was miserable both physically and spiritually, but she could feel the wondrous joy brought by little Goder. Although she was weak, she struggled to sit up, and asked Tampi to let her hold the baby. It was the same every day when Tampi dropped by to visit Srintil at Sakarya's house.

"*Kula nuwun...*" came the polite Javanese greeting.

"Oh, Tampi, is it? Please come in," Nyai Sakarya replied.

"How is Srintil doing, Nyai?"

"You can see for yourself. She's in the bedroom. Oh dear, I don't know what to do. Srintil still doesn't want to eat. She doesn't want rice cakes. The dish I prepared for her this morning hasn't been touched. She won't even eat rice porridge."

Srintil's real bedroom was actually in Kartareja's house where, as a ronggeng, she received her guests. The room was opulent by Paruk standards. The bed, enclosed within mosquito netting, was of wrought iron, the mattress thick. People like Tampi could never bring themselves to enter a room like that because they would feel totally out of place.

While staying at her grandmother's, however, Srintil slept in a room like those of most of the villagers. Except for the supports, the bed was made of bamboo and was covered with a grass mat with two old worn-out pillows. Tampi felt no hesitation on entering a chamber such as this.

"How are you, Srin?" she asked, entering the bedroom.

The sprawled body gave no response, the eyes empty and sunken.

"I brought you some ripe raja bananas. They smell delicious," Tampi put the package down next to Srintil's body.

"I don't really want to eat anything. The only thing I want is your child. Please, put Goder down so that he can play with me. My hands ache to cradle him."

Tampi could not bring herself to refuse this request, feeling pity when seeing Srintil struggling weakly to sit up. Goder looked at his mother, then stared at Srintil. What those clear eyes sought was a purity of heart. A baby with such a pure heart would quickly recognize false friendliness and any pretense of enthusiasm. He would most surely cry in the hands of anyone who was not sincere.

On Srintil's lap, Goder did not cry, he even bounced up and down happily. He pulled on a string on her camisole, making the ticklish Srintil squeal.

"Hey, you're too small for that. Later, when you grow up!"

"He doesn't mean anything, Srin. He just wants to nurse."

"Yes, I know. But this little boy is a naughty one. Probably like his father."

The two women laughed together. One didn't get the impression, at that time, that one of them was really ill. Nyai Sakarya called Tampi from the other room.

"Come here, Tampi. Let your child play with Srintil."

Tampi obeyed and left Srintil's bedroom happily, feeling the pleasure a mother experiences when her child receives particular attention from someone else: especially someone as special as Srintil.

Outside the bedroom, Tampi and Nyai Sakarya could hear cheerful sounds coming from behind the bamboo walls. They smiled at each other, hearing Srintil chatting to Goder. They could imagine Srintil's movements as she talked to him: "Handsome boy. When you grow up, who will *this* be for? For me, okay?" Or, "Tonight you sleep with me right here. It's okay, really. I'll pinch your cute little cheek like this. Or perhaps, I'll pinch your chubby little butt like this. Hah!"

The whispers in the bedroom continued, alternating with light laughter and sounds of delight. Goder gurgled and babbled happily, only crying when Srintil kissed him too hard. When Srintil herself squealed rather loudly, Tampi and Nyai Sakarya went into the bedroom. They could see Srintil grimacing as she held back feelings of ticklishness and pain. Goder was hanging on to one of the ronggeng's breasts.

"What are you doing?" Nyai Sakarya cried. "You can't possibly breast-feed that baby."

Srintil squirmed, grimacing as she held her breath. She resisted when Tampi tried to take Goder from her arms. Goder cried, either because Srintil's breast had no milk or because he sensed the tension that had come over the three women.

"What did I say?" Nyai Sakarya asked. "You can't possibly feed that child. Your breasts are empty. What's more, a breast-feeding woman should eat a lot, especially vegetables, and you haven't eaten anything in four or five days."

Srintil gave up and held the baby up for Tampi to take. At that moment a spout of urine erupted from the infant and soaked Srintil's stomach. She laughed in delight.

In the days that followed, Srintil increasingly withdrew into the world of Goder, dissolving into the babbling of the captivating little baby. The feel of the baby's skin aroused strange sensations in her. She would hide her nose deep in Goder's cheek, masking her feelings from the world. Sometimes, at those moments, Srintil felt close to Rasus; sometimes she felt as if she were Goder's natural mother, completely content. She felt like a real mother who gladly offered herself to become the earth from which a sprout could grow, a fountain that provided streams of love and comfort, and a protective fence surrounding that sprout. This inexplicable natural mandate resonated within Srintil, and its echoes reached her maternal instincts.

Over the next few days, Srintil grew more attached to Tampi's baby. Often she ordered Tampi to leave Goder with her. The desire to breast-feed Goder transformed into a spiritual, emotional, and physical longing, so that her lactating glands were stimulated to give milk without her ever having given birth. When Srintil realized that her breasts were expressing milk, she cried for joy. Her will to live quickly returned. She began to eat heartily, drinking vegetable juice; even asking for tonics that might help her give more milk.

In just a few days her body became healthy again and her vivacity returned.

If you observe a young woman of seventeen years with breasts filled with milk, you would find both youthful freshness and maternal ripeness: two sources of female enchantment now combining in the body of the ronggeng of Paruk.

Srintil grew even more enchanting. The village people, especially the elders, had to admit that the little hamlet had never had such a beautiful ronggeng. But the people of Paruk were not content with Srintil's beauty alone. They would only be satisfied once Srintil returned to dancing, returned to performing as a ronggeng. Except for Tampi, not one person in the village liked the idea of Srintil going about carrying a baby. They weren't interested in the fact that the baby had become a part of her life, or that it had given her new motivation and a renewed passion in her existence. They weren't concerned because they didn't know that, once Srintil had begun breast-feeding Goder, she had begun to experience a physical contentment which was, in part, fulfilling her sexual needs. In their ignorance, the village people didn't care about that. They just wanted to see Srintil dance. For them, there was no meaning in a ronggeng who did not dance, and what was Paruk Village without the sound of calung music accompanying the swaying hips of the ronggeng? Opinions such as this were especially strong among Sakarya, Kartareja, and Nyai Kartareja. Sakarya was not only Srintil's grandfather, he was also a village elder, and felt he had to carry out the mandate of Ki Secamenggala, to maintain and protect Paruk and its traditions. Ki Secamenggala, the ancestor to all the people of Paruk, had left instructions for his descendants to include the ronggeng and calung as part of the conservation of the village traditions.

On the other hand, Kartareja and his wife, as the shamanistic practitioners of ronggeng, knew all the details related to the world of ronggeng, and used this knowledge and their status as the basis of their livelihood. They took a percentage of Srintil's performance fee that was often more than that which Srintil herself received. Their cut was even larger when they acted as procurers. Young men, filled with desire for Srintil and wishing to sleep with her for a night or two had to go through Nyai Kartareja as intermediary. Thus, for Nyai Kartareja, it didn't matter if Srintil refused to dance, as long as she was willing to service the men who desired her.

When Marsusi appeared again in the village one evening, the time came for Nyai Kartareja to ask Srintil to return to her former activities. Knowing that it was likely that Marsusi had brought a gold necklace with a diamond pendulum, Nyai Kartareja rallied all her powers to influence Srintil. A piece of jewelry like that of the wife of the Pecikalan Village chief had been the focus of her dreams for some time, despite her claims to Marsusi that it was Srintil who yearned for it.

That night Srintil was at her grandfather's house, rocking Goder in his sling. She had heard the roar of a motorcycle entering the village, and knew that Nyai Kartareja would soon come for her. Anxiety was etched on her face, but she wasn't ready to act. All that she knew was that she no longer felt the same. To a considerable degree, her will to live was determined by the fat little baby snuggled in her lap. Her dream life was now so deeply connected to Rasus that she was surprised when she realized that the villagers still expected her to service the men that came to the village. "So, Paruk Village doesn't realize who I am now," she said to herself.

The villagers actually knew very little. They did know that Srintil had fallen in love with Rasus, and that her love was frustrated. They did not know, however, the consequences of Rasus's rejection.

While she had been sick in bed for several days, Srintil had been thinking over her experiences as a ronggeng, during which time she had simply let herself follow Nyai Kartareja's orders, accepting any money or jewelry that was offered. Despite her being a ronggeng, Srintil had felt that she was no different from any other woman.

Now, however, she felt she wanted the opportunity to make choices about what she did with men. It was her fate, however, that the man she had chosen to become the recipient of her love and aspirations happened to be Rasus, the man who had rejected her and abandoned her in a most painful way.

Srintil was still too young to understand the cracks and fissures that were opening up inside her soul. In the beginning, she had felt sorrow and despair. Then she considered all the bitterness she had experienced as a phase of life she had to put behind her. She took this submissively, accepting it as her fate. It was a belief in the village that, in this life, one must accept one's lot in life, whether it be sweet or bitter.

Yet, even Srintil herself did not realize that something had infiltrated her subconscious. That something was a sprouting seed which would later change Srintil's attitude towards all men. First and foremost, an image of men developed in her thoughts, made up of the two types she disliked the most. Firstly, there were men who acted like randy bulls and harassed or abused women, like most of the men who came to her. They snorted and roared like tigers after successfully pouncing upon a deer. Most of these men never even knew Srintil before coming to her. At first, servicing strangers had not presented a moral problem for Srintil. But, the experience that she had shared with Rasus, the young man she had known since she was a child and to whom she was psychologically bonded, provided her with an unsettling comparison. The difference was vast: he had made a profound impression, one that had far more meaning, since her experience with him was not only physical but also spiritual.

The other kind of men she disliked were those who were weak. They grinned sheepishly, were easily dominated, and had no strength when confronted by a beautiful ronggeng like herself. They willingly gave everything they had, but then whined to her afterwards, almost begging. If she had wanted, Srintil could have commanded them to do anything. She treated them like servants.

Men like these were gossipers, revealing the worst about their own wives to Srintil, hoping to get her sympathy, and so create greater intimacy with her. Srintil especially hated men like this.

Another kind of male she disliked, though, were men like Rasus, and he was her only example. He was as agile as a young deer, his self-confidence almost approaching arrogance, and he would never beg or whine. Rasus gave himself to her because she had asked. Rasus was still young, but in Srintil's mind he was a sturdy tree providing shade and shelter.

Unfortunately, despite Srintil's admiration for Rasus, he had created a deep wound in her heart. Like all other men Rasus had also planted seeds of disappointment deep within her subconscious. From this perspective, Srintil saw little difference between these kinds of men. All of them were disappointing; all brought her to draw the same conclusions.

Goder started squirming and Srintil left her musings. She told her grandmother that she wished to return to Kartareja's house. Sakarya and his wife agreed immediately, believing this represented a change for the better. Not only did they believe that it had been far too long since Srintil had dropped by the dukun's home but also because they, too, had heard the sound of the motorcycle as it pulled up to Kartareja's house. They assumed that Srintil intended to meet the guest, and that this meant their granddaughter had decided to return to her true role, indicating that she had forgotten Rasus. They looked at one another and smiled.

"If you want to go meet your guest, you had better return Goder to his mother. Or leave him here with me," said Nyai Sakarya.

"Oh no, Grandma. He can stay with me," answered Srintil as she left.

Srintil walked confidently in the dark. Although the diffuse starlight provided some illumination on the dark earth, the dense foliage absorbed the light leaving almost total blackness beneath.

Srintil walked quickly, hugging Goder closely. Her thoughts were clear and firm as a result of a new-found resolve. She realized it would shock everyone, yet she was determined to stand by it.

In front of her trainer's house, Srintil met Nyai Kartareja, who was just setting out for Sakarya's house to find her.

"Srintil?"

"Yes, Nyai."

"Oh, wonderful! My beauty, a guest has arrived. Do you know who he is?"

"No."

"Marsusi, the rubber plantation manager in Wanakeling. It's best if you take care of him. You're still carrying Tampi's child? Here, give him to me. It's not proper for you to meet an important guest like this while holding a baby."

Srintil said nothing, but her movements clearly indicated that she was not willing to part with the baby. Nyai Kartareja frowned, unsure about how to interpret this new behavior. Finally she relented and went into the house. Srintil followed.

"Marsusi. Here is Srintil. As it turns out, I didn't have to go and look for her as she came herself. I don't think that she'd do that if it were anyone but you. Isn't that right, Srin?"

Srintil paid no attention to the formalities of the introduction. Marsusi's gaze immediately repelled her. Although it was only momentary, Srintil could read the depths of meaning in a look like that, and she felt a shiver of revulsion.

In Marsusi's heart, a fire rose that inflamed the lust he was harboring. His knowledge of Srintil was drawn mainly from what he had gleaned in general conversation. He had also seen her twice on previous occasions. One time was when Srintil had performed in Pecikalan several months before. Then, he had seen her a second time in the Dawuan market. Now Marsusi believed Srintil's arrival in Kartareja's house at that moment meant that she had come just to meet him. "So, that's it!" said Marsusi to himself. Unconsciously he moved his hand up and patted his shirt pocket. In it was a gold chain with a diamond pendulum.

Srintil remained standing, Goder squirming in his sling. Lying there, he could feel the growing unease of the woman who was rocking him. The feelings of the still pure baby could register everything that was happening, not only Srintil's increasingly rapid heartbeat, but also every aspect of her now anxious psychological state.

Why didn't a more obvious sign emerge, demonstrating what the baby was already conscious of: that there was another party competing for a place in Srintil's lap? Why was this natural omen so weak, so that only the baby could pick it up? And why did a baby not have the power to defend its most vital interests: even if only by crying? In fact, this is what did happen. Goder squirmed more vigorously. Then he began to struggle and cry. His cries grew increasingly louder. They were cries laden with meaning, because nature had whispered to Goder, telling him about a pair of bright eyes that wanted to swallow Srintil whole.

It took sharply tuned instincts to understand what was making Goder struggle and cry. Kartareja and his wife appeared again in the guest room. They assumed that Goder wanted to return to Tampi, his natural mother, and they told Srintil to take Goder to her.

"Why are you creating all this bother? You're still a young girl Why carry around someone else's child? And this is your guest! You know who Marsusi is, don't you?"

Srintil didn't want to listen to Nyai Kartareja. She went outside, rocking Goder, her movements comforting his distress. She shushed softly to distract the baby, creating the image of a perfect mother. Marsusi could only swallow and shake his head in disbelief. Along with Nyai Kartareja and her husband, he sat stiffly, listening to Srintil as she hummed a lullaby for the baby.

Yun ayun, ayun turu
Turu lali neng ayunan
Anakku si bocah landhung
Mbésok gedhé dadi rebutan

Yun ayun, ayun turu
Turua si bocah lanang
Ciliké tak ayun-ayun
Gedhèné ngéman biyung

Swaying, swaying, sway to sleep
Sleep in forgetfulness in the cradle
My child, my boy of stamina
Tomorrow, grown up, you'll be the object of feminine competition

Swaying, swaying, sway to sleep
Sleep, my manly child
When you're small, I'll rock you
When you're big, you'll love you mother.

The dark sky remained silent. Its language had no voice, but the flickering stars gave testimony to what was happening beneath the heavens.

Srintil's song was that of a mother. In the background was the sound of the mole cricket, its voice smooth and incessant, music of nature to calm Goder. The baby stirred softly and then fell sound asleep in the refreshing night air.

"Whose child is that?" asked Marsusi, after Srintil had gone back into the house.

"The baby belongs to Tampi," answered Nyai Kartareja. "I don't know why, sir, but Srintil's become very attached to it."

"Yeah, I can see that myself; like a real mother and child."

"Actually, I don't like it. It means that Srintil isn't able to show the respect to her guests that she should."

"Tonight, I want to invite Srintil to come away with me, perhaps for two or three days," replied Marsusi lighting a cigarette.

"What an excellent idea. Srintil's been stuck in Paruk for almost a month, unwilling to dance. At first she was sick but, after she recovered, she simply refused to work. Ah, I think I know why. She's still jealous of the wife of the Pecikalan Village chief, jealous about the necklace."

Well, she doesn't have to be jealous anymore," answered Marsusi, smiling confidently.

Nyai Kartareja did not need to ask the meaning of her guest's smile. In her heart, she felt resonating cheers of victory.

"Yes, take Srintil and make her happy. Srintil has lost her liveliness, her coquettishness. This isn't supposed to happen to a ronggeng. And if that's the case, sir, there is no doubt you'll melt her heart!"

Srintil carefully laid the baby down to sleep on her luxurious bed. When Goder struggled momentarily, she offered him her breast, shushing him softly. Goder went back to sleep with a look of perfect peace on his face, not only from her soft caresses, but also because he felt protected deep within his soul. The baby could accurately interpret Srintil's movements, any tremble in her voice. This deep spiritual bond provided him with the assurance that there was no need to worry about this second mother of his. He would not lose his place in her lap, not even for a second.

Once she was sure that Goder was asleep, Srintil arose. She tied her loosened hair in a tight knot. The baby's face had become a mirror that reflected back a thousand images for her. First, Rasus emerged, followed by what she knew were the faces of her mother and father, even though she had never seen them. Finally her own face emerged.

Srintil bit her lip, confused. The reflection challenged her to ask herself who she was. But the question hung in the air because she was unable to answer it. Other questions followed. Who would take care of her? Nyai Kartareja? The various men that paid her? Or would she have to look after herself? Srintil shut her eyes tightly so that she could commune with her heart without distraction. For a long time, she stood there without moving, the frown on her forehead evidence of the turmoil within.

Yet, when she finally left her bedroom, her face was bright, as if her self-confidence had returned. Her manner was that of a truly mature woman. Moving steadily, she sat down on the bench flanking the guest room. Nyai Kartareja was surprised to see her adopted daughter wearing the same clothes she had worn since morning.

Furthermore, Srintil did not seem very enthusiastic about receiving their guest.

"Don't be angry, sir. Srintil has left you waiting too long. Now please talk to your guest, Srin. Marsusi wants to take you for a trip tonight. Why don't you go get dressed?"

"No," Srintil answered simply.

"What's that?"

Srintil smiled, with the confidence of one who knew she had control of the situation.

"Marsusi, I'm not going anywhere tonight."

"Just a second," Nyai Kartareja cut in. There was a dangerous tone in her voice. "What did you say?"

"I don't wish to go anywhere," came the quiet response.

Nyai Kartareja could not believe her own ears. Momentarily her chest heaved up and down, but her long experience as a procuress gave her the ability to quickly gain control over her emotions.

"My young beauty," said Nyai Kartareja softly. Her hand stroked Srintil's shoulder. "It's not good to refuse someone's helping hand, especially Marsusi's. You haven't asked him where he wants to take you. You don't even know what kind of gift he wants to give you this time."

The sound of a thin metal chain falling on the table could be heard. Srintil and her two trainers stared at the sparkling object. Marsusi's eyes studied the ceiling. In the ensuing silence, Nyai Kartareja's expression changed to one of joy, her eyes overflowing with longing, and her lips quivering soundlessly.

Srintil stared at the gold chain for a long time, as if it was challenging her. She swallowed two or three times. The diamond gave off a bluish light; a temptation difficult to resist for a young women like her.

When she could see that Srintil was at the height of her confusion, Nyai Kartareja urged her with suggestive words. "What do you say now, my young beauty. What a waste if you don't obey Marsusi's wishes. Come on, change your clothes. Change the necklace you're wearing, too, with this one."

"Here. Take it," said Marsusi flatly.

"This one is indeed better. Far better, and of course much more expensive," added Kartareja. "Except for the wife of the Pecikalan village chief, no woman has worn a necklace as nice as this one. Now Srin, it's your turn."

For a moment Srintil remained stock still. Rasus infiltrated her thoughts. Her inner ear heard Ciplak singing a love song.

"No, I don't want to go anywhere," came the slow but steady reply, filled with real certainty.

The three other people in the room were startled. Kartareja raised his head. Marsusi straightened up, his cigarette dropping from his mouth. But the person most upset was Nyai Kartareja.

"You! What's the matter with you? The granddaughter of Sakarya doesn't want to have a necklace as nice as this?"

"There is no need to speak to me like that," replied Srintil, amazingly calm.

"Oh, please excuse this old woman, my young beauty. If you'd rather not take a trip, that's not a problem. Maybe Marsusi wouldn't mind a change of plans. Rather than go off on a trip, he could stay here for two or three days. What do you think, sir?"

Marsusi coughed. He was still getting over his initial shock, and he looked puzzled. This was the first time he had been rejected. His shock was even more profound as he had offered such an expensive gift. In his confusion, Marsusi wanted to scoop up the gold necklace and go home. But a closer look at Srintil made him restrain himself and stay where he was.

The young girl sat next to him on the edge of the seat. Her perfect calm was yet another enchantment. With her hair tied up, she emanated a youthful freshness. Her jaw line was well-shaped. Her cheeks were clear, adorned with fine sideburns. The smooth skin of her nape said it all: that Srintil was only seventeen years old.

Marsusi coughed again. "If you, uh, don't want to go out, that's up to you. I don't mind staying the night here," he said finally.

"Did you hear that, Srin? Marsusi came here for just one purpose: to make you happy. Isn't that so, sir?"

Marsusi smiled his assent. Nyai Kartareja stood up and signaled her husband. The two disappeared into the house, believing that their troubles were over. All they had to do now, they thought, was to provide an opportunity for their guest to enjoy some privacy with Srintil.

The stillness of the night permeated the house. A small bat flew in through the open doorway and circled momentarily before disappearing again via the same route. Two geckos on the wall were competing for the same prey: a bug that had landed close by. When the bug flew off and dizzyingly circled around the lamp, the two predators began chasing each other, a chase that culminated in a brutal mating ritual. Suddenly the roof of the house resounded with a bang. Something hard had fallen from the sky. It could have been a fruit bat dropping its dung or perhaps spitting out a seed as it flew by.

Other than that, all that could be heard was a sound unique to Paruk: the music of the calung. But that evening only the sound of a solitary xylophone could be heard. When there is only the one instrument, the calung xylophone is played like the gamelan instrument called gambang. In the skilled hands of someone like Sakum, the calung actually becomes a gambang, the only difference being that the calung is made from bamboo, while the gambang is made from wood. Whatever the instrument, Sakum usually played energetically, his music full of humor.

Yet that night, Srintil could detect something different in the sound of Sakum's playing. Behind the blending of the music with the night was an implied irony, the irony of a calung player who was without work because the ronggeng no longer wanted to perform. Srintil smiled bitterly as she thought about Sakum's fate. The blind musician was the mascot of the ronggeng troupe. And it was not only he who had lost income as a result of her refusal to perform. Three other musicians were similarly affected.

While the sounds of the calung filled the solitude of the village, the situation at Kartareja's house was becoming more and more uncomfortable. Marsusi was nervous. Beside him, Srintil sat, quite aloof. Several times Marsusi swallowed, while Srintil acted as if she was unaware that there was a lecherous man sitting next to her.

"Young lady," Marsusi finally spoke, his voice hoarse. His smile was artificial, like a small boy begging for candy from his mother. "Here's your necklace. Take it."

Srintil glanced at him and smiled. A smile with no trace of eroticism.

"Why are you giving me the necklace?" she asked.

Marsusi took a deep breath, feeling awkward.

"You must understand, sir," she continued, realizing that Marsusi was unable to speak. "I'll take the necklace if it's to pay me to dance. All you need to do is say when and where. And at the performance, you can ask me to dance with you to your heart's content."

"No, that's not what I want. This necklace isn't payment for you to perform or for you to dance with me."

"If you simply want to give it to me, then go ahead."

"No!"

"I see!" Srintil said abruptly. "You want to give me the necklace not as payment for performing or to dance with you, but for something else. Oh, Marsusi, I can understand why you are doing this, because of what I've done in the past with a number of men. But, sir…"

Marsusi looked straight ahead. Confused, he strained to hear what Srintil would say next.

"You see, I don't want to do that again."

"Huh? Why not?"

"I just don't feel like it, that's all."

"Tell me the truth!" Marsusi's voice grew heavy.

"I just don't want to. If you want me to perform or to dance with you, fine. I am, after all, a ronggeng."

"Wait a minute. Why are you telling me this, and why now? Why not with the men before me?"

"It's simple, sir," said Srintil, still perfectly calm. "You just happened to be the first man to come along after I decided to change my course in life."

"I don't understand! Are you rejecting me?"

"Not entirely, sir. If you want to dance with me, then schedule a performance. It's up to you, when and where."

The muscles of Marsusi's jaw knotted. His eyes blazed at the ronggeng. The lust he had carried from his home began to change into fury. He stood up and strode around the room, his face savage. Srintil prepared herself, expecting her guest to smash something. As it turned out, he didn't. Marsusi just paced back and forth, snorting, gesticulating wildly.

Nyai Kartareja appeared, followed by her husband. They had overheard the stilted conversation. Marsusi pointed at them.

"You two, sit down!" he shouted. "Sit!" he repeated, as the couple hesitated. By then Marsusi was in his element, the foreman of a plantation speaking to his lowly laborers as they tapped the rubber trees.

"There is no way the manager of a plantation would come to this place if it wasn't Paruk, the village famous for its ronggeng," Marsusi began, pacing back and forth. "And there is no way I would come to this house if it wasn't the lair of the ronggeng. If it wasn't the ronggeng named Srintil. Understand?"

Because his finger was pointing directly at her, Srintil looked up. While Kartareja and his wife looked frightened, Srintil showed virtually no emotion at all. As her eyes calmly met his, he lowered his hand.

Marsusi walked over to Nyai Kartareja, speaking vehemently. "You're a cockroach! Who was it that urged me to bring a necklace like the one owned by the wife of the Pacikalan Village chief? There it is, in front of you. What do I get for it?"

"Marsusi," Srintil's voice was flat," Please don't be angry with Nyai Kartareja. This is my doing. Don't turn this simple matter into something more complicated."

"This is not a simple matter! I don't feel it's a simple matter at all!"

"Whatever you might say, sir, it is a simple matter. You want to buy something here but the shop is closed. It's as simple as that, sir."

"So you, and all of you here, have insulted me. And you're Paruk villagers. Don't you realize that I am aware that everything you have here you got from prostitution?"

"Patience, sir. I want to say something..."

"Enough! You old cockroach! You pimp! You Paruk devil! I don't want to hear your voice. Your words are just bullshit!"

Disheveled, Marsusi grabbed his hat and slammed it on his head. With a swift movement of his hand, he swept up the necklace and put it in his shirt pocket. He picked up the half-full bottle of gin and gulped the contents. He threw the bottle against the base of a pillar and the sound of breaking glass shattered the stillness. Moments later, the trio inside heard the sound of Marsusi's motorcycle roaring off.

In the tension following his departure. Nyai Kartareja's face was dark and furious. She gave full reign to her frustration by repeatedly striking her thighs.

"What's the matter with you, Srintil? Why did you reject Marsusi? It's arrogance, that's what it is. You have a few things now but don't forget where you came from. You're the daughter of Santayib. Your parents were nothing better than sellers of tempeh *bongkrek*, and they died of food poisoning!"

Srintil froze, lowering her head and biting her lip. This tirade against her parents tore deeply into her heart. She knew all about her parents, but every time that story was told, it cut her deeply. She began to cry. But Nyai Kartareja paid no heed to her tears.

"So this is the way you repay our kindness? We provided you with the means to be prosperous, but this is what we get in return; completely humiliated by Marsusi. You, offspring of Santayib, you're nothing!

"And yet you have the nerve to reject a hundred-gram gold necklace? Do you think you're rich? If you didn't like the necklace, you should have taken it for me! You should have serviced Marsusi anyway because everyone knows you're a ronggeng and a whore."

"Enough, enough," said Kartareja, trying to restrain his wife's fury.

"Leave me alone! This time she has to be taught a lesson. She has become rude and disrespectful!"

Her chest heaving, Nyai Kartareja released the remainder of her rage by spitting bitterly in Srintil's direction.

Up until this point, Srintil had remained silent. But, as Nyai Kartareja went inside slamming the door loudly, she could no longer restrain herself. Tears poured from her eyes. The determination she had shown in facing Marsusi collapsed, broken down by the references Nyai Kartareja had made to her dead parents.

She was gradually restored to a calmer state of mind by the sound of a solo calung played by Sakum. At first the music was lost in the shrill fury of Nyai Kartareja anger, which continued to buzz in Srintil's ears. This was followed by the rasping of a thousand crickets resounding in her eardrums. Eventually the chaotic sounds subsided, leaving the sound of the calung weaving its way through the night, evoking an image that was complete and perfectly formed. The plinking-plunking tones cascaded, one after another. Sometimes certain tones leapt out, like maggots from an overripe jackfruit, but all were harmoniously tied together.

The sounds of the xylophone keys penetrated the bamboo groves. Bamboo returning to bamboo. Intimate and full of meaning, like a child which hides his face deep in his mother's thighs. When a night breeze made the leaves of the bamboo trees sigh, the sound was the most natural accompaniment for the calung music that poured forth beneath the swaying hands of Sakum. Teet-tweet! Teet-tweet! The sound of the *prit putih* bird, could be heard as usual after sunset, its call completing the song of Paruk. The isolated village was singing an evening song. But this time, the music was not fast and enthusiastic, but sad and melancholy.

Srintil went inside and walked straight to her room. Kartareja, sitting motionless, glanced at her momentarily. He was taken aback when, a few minutes later, she stood before him, holding Goder in her sling. Foster father and daughter looked at one another. Kartareja could only sense why Srintil was standing there. Although he could see her lips moving, he didn't hear a word she was saying. Similarly, Srintil could hear nothing he was saying. Finally, Srintil turned around and went outside to the front yard where all was quiet, apart from the creak of the door and the squeak of a field mouse, startled when Srintil walked close by it.

Leaving the house of her adopted parents, Srintil became aware of a new feeing: a sense of being closer to herself. Her selfhood felt entirely within her grasp: a selfhood made up of herself and the baby she held in her arms. Goder's warm body against her chest was the first warmth of a new spirit that began to take hold of her soul.

Tampi's face lit up when she saw Srintil approaching Sakarya's house. She stood up to greet Srintil at the door.

"Oh Srintil. Bring me my child. I missed him," said Tampi, reaching out with both arms. But Srintil brushed her hands away.

"If you want to see Goder, look at him from here. If you want to touch his chubby little cheeks, go ahead. But don't take him from my sling."

"I mean it. I really missed him. I haven't held him all day. And, who ever said Goder would not cause you trouble? Look at what has just happened."

"What?"

"I know what happened at Kartareja's house. If it wasn't for my child, you'd have gone off on that motorcycle…"

"You're wrong, Tampi. You don't understand. I didn't go with that man because I didn't want to. That's it. It had nothing to do with your child."

"But I heard Nyai Kartareja mentioning Goder's name. You can't imagine what I felt. I wanted to break down the door, take Goder and carry him home as fast as I could. My child is too pure to be involved in adult matters like that."

"You're right. That's why I won't dirty him. Hush. Don't disturb him. And don't call him your child anymore. Call him my child, okay?"

Tampi grumbled a little, objecting, but a smile slowly appeared on her face. She could not honestly deny that she felt proud that her child was the object of affection of the most famous woman in the village.

"Oh, Tampi. You don't have to worry about Goder anymore. I'll be his mother. I can breast-feed him. I can buy him the best clothes at the Dawuan market. The point is, whatever you might be able to give to Goder, I can do better. And don't you worry, when he gets older I'll tell him who gave birth to him. But for now, let him be my child. What you need to do now is take the best possible care of your husband, so that you can quickly have a fifth baby!"

Srintil's witty remark broke the ice. Tampi pinched her friend's arm. Srintil's instincts were right. Her remarks had struck home. For the village women, servicing their husbands wasn't just something they had to do. It was the only other activity outside of the kitchen and child rearing. In reality, the most important aspect of life for Paruk women was on the mattress of their bamboo beds. And, now that Goder was about ten months old, he was starting to restrict her and her husband's activities.

That evening, Srintil found it difficult to sleep. Sometimes she sat on the edge of the bed. Other times she lay restlessly next to the soundly sleeping Goder. At one stage she found, to her fury, a lump as big as a kernel of corn on Goder's leg. She plucked out a flea swollen with blood and crushed it between her thumb and finger. She smeared the blood on the grass mat, the pungent smell filling the air.

Sakum continued to roam the emotions of the night with his solo calung music. Being blind, Sakum could not wander freely in the physical world, but his forays in the realm of feelings were enticing, drawing others to follow him. There was no doubt that many people that evening would have closed their eyes and fantasized with Sakum.

The calung artist performed dozens of songs that evening but Srintil was especially moved by the repeated strains of one particular poem, "Pupuh Sinom":

Bonggan kang tan mrelokena
Mungguh ugering ngaurip
Uripé lan tri prakara
Wirya karta, tri winasis
Kalamun kongsi sepi
Saka wilangan tetelu
Telas tilasing sujalma
Aji godhong jati aking
Temah papa, papariman ngulandara

Its words reminded her that one must never ignore the three essentials of life, those being skillfulness, excellence, and intelligence. If these three are ignored, the superiority of mankind is lost, and man becomes like a dry leaf: miserable, impoverished, and homeless.

It was as though the poem came right from Sakum's heart as he had been without work for a long time. Although he was blind, Sakum had a wife and four children. Srintil increasingly had the feeling that he was making a subtle accusation: how could she refuse to perform when he and his family were forced to go hungry as a result?

The implied accusation added to the burden of Srintil's thoughts, already oppressed by her experience with Marsusi earlier that evening. The faces of Sakum and his wife and children remained in her mind even after the calung player finally fell asleep behind his instrument.

It could have been that Srintil was the only person awake when the first dew drops fell, signaling the moment night turned into early dawn. Staying awake all night was nothing special for a ronggeng. Chatting through the night in passionate encounters involving drinking, money, and sexual desire was a ronggeng's life. This time, however, it was different, very different. While the villagers were sleeping, Srintil sat deep in thought. Her musings began with Rasus, the boy who had played with her beneath the jackfruit tree when they were small children; the lover, to whom she had given her virginity; and the man who had joined the army, and disappeared from her life.

Yet her musing always ended up at a point of speculation, with her asking herself what would happen to her now that Rasus was gone. What would she have to endure—and why—as a result of rejecting Marsusi? Living in Paruk all her life had taught her that existence was like a shadow puppet tale: that humankind consisted of characters controlled by a puppeteer.

In this context, Srintil saw Rasus's departure as nothing other than the wishes of the Puppeteer of Life. Even so, she felt bitterness in her heart. Regarding the matter of Marsusi, Srintil worried that her rejection could constitute a conflict with the Puppeteer. As far as she knew, such conflicts always ended badly. She would probably have continued to worry if she hadn't remembered some of the everyday things she had noticed around the village. For example, not all hens give in to the rooster when he wants to mate. And it was the same with goats, cats, and birds. But one could not claim that, in doing so, these female animals were transgressing some primal law. Surely nature accounted for all forms of behavior among all of its creatures: including Srintil when she had rejected Marsusi's offer.

At the height of her musings, Srintil found some peace with these thoughts, and her eyelids began to grow heavy. She heard the first screeching of the thrush, followed by the crow of a rooster. The leaves of the banana palm rustled as a fruit bat took refuge for its daytime sleep. Her eyes blurring as they began to close, Srintil was still able to see a large frog hopping along, squeezing into a space in the wall near the base of the support pillar. The frog would spend the day hidden in the cool dark space beneath the raised sleeping platform, directly under her head. Crickets and singing insects ceased their sounds. The village greeted the new day with relative silence. The air was quiet enough for the sound of dew dripping on the leaves of a tuber plant growing behind the house to be just audible.

Srintil dreamed about chatting with the goat-herding children; running across a grassy field dotted with wild flowers, the sky filled with birds and butterflies. She could feel herself merging with the animals. Her pleasant dreams, however, were interrupted by a pair of soft hands reaching into her camisole and groping at her breasts. Goder whimpered, wanting to be fed.

3

For several days Sakarya had been lost in thought. His granddaughter, Srintil, was becoming cause for considerable worry. The matter of her rejecting a man who had wanted her wasn't too much of a headache. The problem that was causing him anxiety was the thought of what would happen if Srintil continued to avoid performing as a dancer. Without a ronggeng, Paruk Village would lose its prestige, and that was something Sakarya did not wish to see in his old age.

Sakarya was becoming increasingly concerned by the occurrence of small but significant incidents. The previous day a small, brightly colored bird had flown like the wind through the open door of his house and crashed into the mirror of the wardrobe. The bird had collapsed on the floor and died, blood dripping from its little red beak. Why had this made such an impression on him? A pretty bird, with green feathers and a beak like a small ornamental red pepper, dies in front of him, smeared with blood. The day before, he had witnessed a rare forest fowl landing on a tree near his house. Sakarya always studied the omens of nature, believing that even the smallest event did not happen in isolation but was part of a greater plan. Everything, he was convinced, happens for a reason, with portent. In fact, any of the villagers would interpret the sighting of a rare animal close by—not to mention entering one's house—as an evil omen. And that morning, as he had been sitting quietly in the front room, something soft and cool had landed on his back: a gecko. Both creatures, human and gecko, were equally startled. The gecko had hopped off, dropped to the ground, and then quickly crawled up the wall. Sakarya was just as fast. Grabbing a rag, he lashed out at the gecko—whap!—and then he stomped on it, crying out, "Die, you son of a bitch!"

Another bad omen.

There was only one course of action open to him: to go to Ki Secamenggala's mausoleum with offerings and incense. He began the preparations, ordering his wife to get some flowers from the garden in Kartareja's front yard. He went into his room and fetched a wick. Once lit, the wick would continue to smolder until its entire length was burned.

Sakarya left the house dressed entirely in black. A loose tunic, worn over his trousers, reached to his knees. A length of fabric hung around his neck, and he wore a turban around his head in traditional fashion. In his right hand, held crosswise behind him, he gripped the burning wick. He walked slowly and respectfully with his head bowed. At one time he stopped, drew a deep breath, and shook his head from side to side. A snake had crossed the narrow trail in front of him. The slithering creature stopped for a moment in the middle of the trail. Again and again, obstacles! If there wasn't something amiss, why would that snake be on this trail? And its stomach was distended, meaning that it has recently eaten a mouse. Under normal circumstances, it would be coiled up asleep under some bushes after eating.

Suddenly Sakarya smiled. The thought had just occurred to him that, at more than seventy years of age, he was the oldest man in the village. Perhaps, he reasoned, what he was sensing were omens to remind him of his own mortality, warning him of his predestined day of death. If this was the case, it was fitting that these omens were occurring. Sakarya had contemplated his death more than once or twice recently. Sometimes, he even yearned for it. Several years previously, he had ordered a plot in the village cemetery and had already had a tall gravestone made. When the time of his death came, his body would be buried there.

With his thoughts occupied with death, Sakarya arrived at the cemetery. He paused at the bottom of the steep slope to catch his breath. The cemetery was dark, shaded by the leafy banyan tree that grew on top of the hill, its branches covering most of the grounds. The morning sun was still shrouded by clouds, contributing to the gloomy atmosphere. Sakarya's gray eyes were focused straight ahead as he stood there. The trees were swaying slightly in the gentle breeze, seeming to the old man like a group of people performing a strange dance. Although their faces were terrifying to behold, he could recognize them. They were people who had died from food poisoning seventeen years earlier. There were the faces of Santayib and his wife—his son and daughter-in-law, Srintil's parents—and the faces of the village's dancers who had died decades before.

Sakarya felt a cold breeze blowing on the back of his neck. A confusing racket in his ears was followed by a sudden blinding ray of light which pierced his eyes. The morning sun had emerged from behind the clouds. "It's true. My death is near," he mumbled. Strangely, he felt at peace, accepting this as his fate. As he began climbing up the slope to the graveyard, he felt no different from how he usually felt when walking along the path to his home. His heart was at peace, submissive. His lips moved silently as he stood in front of the door to Ki Secamenggala's mausoleum. Smoke from the incense billowed from the smoldering wick. Sakarya uttered his final requests which were all to do with village matters. He asked that the calung and ronggeng tradition be maintained. He asked that Srintil resume dancing as a ronggeng. The village elder truly could not imagine what would happen if Srintil continued to avoid performing. Paruk without a ronggeng: an ugly reputation for the dwelling place of Ki Secamenggala's descendants.

When he returned to his house, Sakarya found Srintil chatting to a guest in the front room. At first Sakarya thought the visitor had come on personal business with her. But, when he realized who it was, Sakarya sat down with him. It was Ranu, an official from the county office he had met before. Sakarya was sure that someone like Ranu would not visit a ronggeng for purely personal reasons. And thus, after his initial greeting, he asked the visitor if anything was wrong.

"I'm here to discuss something with you and your granddaughter," Ranu told him.

"So, tell us what it is, Ranu. I just hope it's not a legal problem. We here in Paruk have never had problems with the law."

"No, it's not that at all. This is a matter regarding the calung."

"The calung?"

"When an outsider comes to Paruk, what else could it be?"

"Oh, of course. So, have you already spoken to Srintil about this?"

"I have."

Sakarya glanced at his granddaughter. Srintil's face was shrouded in doubt. Sakarya could see that she was confused. Grasping the situation, he took a long breath and leaned back.

"Sakarya," said Ranu. "The Independence Day Celebration Committee wants to hold a performance,

"A celebration with a ronggeng performance? And you've asked Srintil to perform?"

"Yes, that's right. However, I'm rather surprised that Srintil didn't immediately agree to the request."

Again, Sakarya drew a deep breath. Then, with his head bowed, he mumbled as if to himself. "Actually, Srintil should be aware that this isn't just an ordinary invitation to perform. One might say that it's a command, coming from an official committee."

"You're right, Sakarya. And it's better that you said it rather than me."

"Now what do you say, young lady?" asked Ranu, addressing Srintil.

"I haven't danced in a long time, sir."

"Why not?"

Ranu had to repeat the question several times before getting an answer.

"For no particular reason, sir."

"Oh, come on. Where there's a calung ensemble there must be a ronggeng, right?"

"Yes, that's right. But I don't feel like dancing at the moment, sir."

"That's okay, young lady. Sometimes a person can feel lazy or bored with their work. The problem, however, is that this request comes from the Independence Day Celebration Committee, headed by the district supervisor himself. What should we do?"

"When I'm feeling too lazy, my dancing is terrible. What do I do about that?"

Ranu felt annoyed that his question was being thrown back at him, yet he maintained his patience.

"Listen, young lady. On the night of the festival, the plan is that you'll appear with other performers. There'll be a *keroncong* orchestra from the city, a group of comedians, and also a troupe of acrobats. But I'm sure that the ronggeng group from Paruk will be the most popular performance there.

Srintil was not moved by his words. She remained silent when Sakarya pressed her as well. Finally, the envoy from the district office rose to his feet. His next words held a threat.

"Think it over carefully, young lady," he said, as if a threat. "It's no big loss to us if you refuse this request. On the other hand, disappointing district officials may cause trouble for you."

Ranu went outside, his face dark, with Srintil following, looking anxious. Sakarya stayed where he was, not speaking even when Ranu took his leave. Only after the visitor had left could he bring himself to speak, his words of disappointment heavy with blame directed at Srintil. His words held an implicit fear that troubles would come their way, portended by the strange omens that he had witnessed over the past few days.

"You've already disappointed an important person, an act not fitting for villagers like us. Oh God, my grandchild. You don't realize that we're all just servants."

"Grandpa…"

"What?"

"If I refuse, could I be penalized?"

Sakarya interpreted Srintil's question as evidence of a weakening of her stance. He saw that the door had opened a crack, but he hid his feelings.

"Why not? We're servants and are obligated to submit to the command, even the desires, of government officials. Refusing them is like asking to be punished. Is that what we want to do?"

Sakarya intentionally exaggerated his words, hoping that Srintil would quickly change her stance, but her answer shocked him.

"Yes, why not! I'm prepared to be punished, even to be jailed! How can I dance when I don't want to? You know, don't you, that a dance can come to life only if one's heart and soul are dancing as well."

Without waiting for her grandfather to respond, Srintil stood up. She ignored her grandmother who was standing at the door to the front room, took a sash that was hanging on the wall and draped it over her shoulders as she went outside. She walked quickly towards Tampi's house where Goder had been since morning.

On the way, she paused at Sakum's house. The blind calung player was sitting outside, plaiting cane to make a rice steamer. His hands were skilled and confident, as if there were an eye at the end of each finger. Behind him, various items made from cane were stacked neatly in rows, ready to be sold. But everyone knew what little income Sakum made from his cane work. A man with four children.

What Srintil saw was a picture of serious impoverishment. Sakum's house was a slanted structure with just four posts. There were no permanent walls, so that the wind could easily blow right through it and chickens could wander in and out. From the inside, a person could see the clouds in the sky during the day and the stars at night. House? It would be more accurate to call it a shanty, so tattered and broken-down it was.

Sakum's impoverished state was even more evident in his four children. The eldest was a girl of nine years. Her hair was bleached as red as dried corn silk. She had a rash on her cheeks that looked like encrusted lichen. Her eyes were dull and lifeless. Her skin was dry and flaky, and she was covered in grime, especially on her neck and legs. She sat learning against the wall watching over her baby brother who was crawling around on the ground. The other two children were digging in the dirt next to the house. Both were naked and their spines protruded under the skin along their backs. They were digging along a mole cricket's tunnel.

"Son of a bitch!" said the younger boy. "The cricket's tunnel goes straight down. And under a rock, too."

"You're a dumbshit," said his older brother. "Every cricket tunnel ends in a cave. Move aside."

The older boy squatted down and, holding his penis, peed into the hole. Flooded by hot urine, the cricket quickly emerged. Two pairs of hands tried to grab it. The younger child lost and, shoved by his older brother, tumbled backwards. He cried, and tried to fight for his share, but the older boy disappeared into the house to cook the cricket over hot coals. A minute later the burrowing insect was chewed to a paste and swallowed.

Sakum seemed unperturbed by the commotion his children were creating. His fingers kept working, plaiting cane, tying pieces together, cutting those that were too long. "If I can hear my children's voices, that's a good sign. It means they're still alive." This was a joke that Sakum often made.

To keep in touch with things around him, Sakum did not rely just on his sense of hearing. He sometimes had greater confidence in his instincts and feelings. For example, he knew from the tone of her voice when his wife was being, or was about to be, unfaithful. Similarly, he knew when there were unequal servings of food at mealtimes. To discern whether the oil lamp in his house was lit at night. Sakum only need to take a deep breath. His nose could determine this. His instincts, or perhaps his entire body, was sensitive to whatever was happening in close proximity to him. Accordingly, as Srintil approached, Sakum suddenly stopped his work. The eyelids covering his empty sockets moved. He grinned sheepishly. The voice he heard was the voice of the person he accurately predicted would speak.

"Are you busy, Sakum?" asked Srintil, sitting down on a raised platform just a few feet away from him.

"Ah, young lady. How fitting. Since this morning I've been hearing the continuous song of the *prenjak* bird near the house. It told me that I'd have an important guest."

"I'm not important. But the problem I want to talk to you about is."

"In what way? Did Marsusi come again?"

"No. It's not that. We've been asked to perform for the evening celebration of Independence Day."

Srintil waited for Sakum's response, expecting an outburst of joy. A performance meant money for all the members of the ronggeng troupe. Sakum's family, living in such dire circumstances, could only receive this news with gladness. However, the blind man was silent. Only his eyebrows moved up and down. It was true, Sakum had long yearned to perform again. But he could accurately read Srintil's reluctance to dance.

"What do you think?" Srintil asked.

"What do I think? You know what happens if I don't play calung for a long time. I should ask you what you think."

"I'm sure you are hoping that I will accept the committee's request." Srintil said.

"Of course, young lady," Sakum replied.

Srintil felt she was at an impasse. At her grandfather's house, she had refused to fulfill the request to dance. Yet, in reality, Srintil had wanted to take back her words the moment she had spoken them. Now she felt that she had found the only person she could talk to, that she could open up to. Without being aware of it previously, she realized then that Sakum was someone close to her, closer than Kartareja and his wife, even closer than her own grandmother.

"Yes. It would best if I obeyed their request. I want to dance again, but my heart isn't in it."

"I know that the spirit of ronggeng still resides in you," Sakum said quickly. "It could be that your broken heart will mend if you forget about him."

"Him?"

"Rasus."

As he uttered Rasus's name, Sakum's face revealed his true feelings. It was rare for Sakum to do this. His lips drew tightly closed, and the muscles of his cheeks tensed. In this manner, Sakum revealed his own feelings about the relationship between Srintil and Rasus, one that had brought so many problems to the ronggeng troupe, and to the village.

Srintil lowered her head, trying to avoid the look on Sakum's face. Her heart was stung by his words, but she realized his anger was not directed at herself or Rasus. Rather, it was aimed at their relationship, which is what had silenced the sounds of calung in the village.

"Young lady," continued Sakum, in a fatherly manner. "You're not the only ronggeng who has been attracted to a particular man. One time, several decades ago, a ronggeng called Trombol experienced something similar. She married a district chief. But, because the spirit of ronggeng still resided in her, the marriage lasted no longer than it takes to chew betel-nut. So, Trombol returned to being the ronggeng of Paruk, to swinging and swaying her hips as is proper for a ronggeng.

"Another ronggeng, Cepon, fell madly in love with the son of a batik seller. They also married, but her life didn't turn out well. The husband she loved up and left her. Cepon languished, finally dying before she reached the age of twenty.

"And now there's you. Be satisfied with what you had with Rasus. That's what it means to be a ronggeng. You've already felt affection toward him, already slept with him. That's all you can really expect, because you're a ronggeng. And, since the ronggeng spirit resides in you, you won't ever get more than that. It won't happen! That's why I say, forget Rasus, for your own good."

Srintil bowed her head as her eyes filled with tears. Every mention of Rasus' name caused her heart to beat faster. Her memories returned to the approaching hour of her ritual deflowering on that dreadful night. It was Rasus who had taken her virginity, but with an empty and powerless expression on his face. Her ears rang with Rasus's last words that night, "I wouldn't ever marry you because you're a ronggeng. You belong to Paruk."

"So I'm still a ronggeng because within me resides the ronggeng spirit?" asked Srintil slowly.

"Over the decades, I've known a lot of ronggeng. The trembling in your voice is the trembling voice of ronggeng. The smell of your body is the body odor of a ronggeng. Your confident poise is also the poise of a ronggeng. Yes, you're still a ronggeng. Maybe later, at some point, I will know if you cease to be a ronggeng: but that would only be when the spirit of ronggeng leaves you."

Sakum drew a deep breath. His shoulders dropped as if they had just been freed of a heavy burden. For a long time he had wanted to express his feelings to Srintil, to remind her what a ronggeng should be. His intentions were so sincere that he hadn't wanted them associated with his personal concerns.

Feeling that he had said as much as he could, Sakum returned to his work His child continued to cry: a pitiful crying, that of a hungry child who knows that there is no rice to be had. Birds chattered, their voices joyful and melodious, in stark contrast to the crying of the child.

"Where's your wife?"

"She's at Kartareja's house, pounding rice paddy. She'll be coming home soon. I haven't heard any pounding in a while."

"Have you put on the rice?" asked Srintil, looking at the faces of the hungry children. Her question brought them hope.

"Young lady, what are you talking about? The person who pounds the rice hasn't returned home yet."

"Oh, I see. The sun is almost down. Your wife should be home any moment."

"I know the sun is down. I can smell it. The odor of urine gets stronger, because the place where the children pee, on the western side of the house, is being heated by the sun."

Srintil left Sakum and continued on to Tampi's house where she would collect Goder. Not far from the musician's house, she saw a pair of chameleons chasing one another along the small branches of a tree. The female ran along one branch, then leapt to another. The male chased after her and jumped. But he missed the second branch and fell to the ground. He lay quiet as if dead, his bright green skin slowly changing to the color of the earth. The lizard only began to move when Srintil drew close. "If Sakum wasn't blind, no doubt he'd say to me: 'don't go chasing after someone who is running away lest you fall like that chameleon'."

Like Sakum, Tampi also urged Srintil to accept the request by the Independence Day Celebration Committee. She even spiced up her urgings with details that Srintil hadn't been aware of.

"Perhaps you don't know that on festival nights like this one, all the upper crust of Dawuan attend. There'll be district chiefs, police, and soldiers. This government official, that government official. They'll all come. The total number of spectators could reach a thousand people."

"A thousand people?"

"Believe me. That's why you shouldn't waste this opportunity. In fact, you should dance your best number."

"Will you be there?"

"Yeah, for sure. I think everyone will be there. It will be cheek to jowl at the festival grounds. So, why would I stay at home?"

On her way home, Srintil made up her mind. She would fulfill the committee's request. But she found it difficult to determine the reason for her decision. The first person to hear about it was Goder, the baby she held close as she walked home.

"Handsome boy, I'm going to dance again. Is that okay with you? But there's no need to worry. I'll always be your mama. And you'll always be my handsome child!"

As the tide went out in the Anakan Sea, a motor boat with an old diesel engine crawled slowly along the Cilacap-Kalipucang route. On the ebbing tide, the Anakan Sea resembled a river in the middle of a wide estuary, filled with muddy sediment. It was made up of several deltas which were sealed off tightly by mangroves. The passengers in the motor boat could see the vestiges of great aviary kingdoms. On the muddy carpet were several fish-eating fowl. The *trintil,* continuously making rude gestures, ran back and forth with amazing nimbleness. As the motorboat approached they flew off in a broken formation, their calls a cacophony of sound. *Bluwak* chased after them, half-flying, half-running on the sediment. White egrets spread out and then gathered together in slow movements. A solitary crane amongst them stood with its legs almost entirely submerged in the silt. It walked very slowly, with the gait of an old man.

However many forests are destroyed, however many fields smell of insecticides, and however many boys carry air guns to shoot birds, the Anakan Sea and the surrounding marshes will be always be a haven for the birds that inhabit it. The *dadali* bird, now rarely seen inland, still thrives there. Similarly, seed-eating birds like the large and small breeds of turtledove and the banded ground dove, as well as their predators, the various types of hawks, and the many small birds which gather, seemingly intentionally, in concentrations on the small islands dotting the mangrove swamps.

The passengers in the old motorboat did not appear to be impressed by, or even interested in, the enchanting world of birds around them. Perhaps they were too absorbed by their own world, the world of humans. Or, perhaps it was because they couldn't sit comfortably in the boat which was swerving from side to side to follow the channel so that it wouldn't run aground. The boat's skipper, a young teenager, was very adept at his work. The boat turned sharply, and thanks to his skill, closely avoided another boat coming from the opposite direction in the narrow channel.

The boat pulled into the shore and three men alighted. Two of them were traders of *terasi*, a pungent spice made from shrimp, crabs and other seafood. The third person seemed rather out of place. He stood somewhat hesitantly, then walked unsteadily along the bamboo footbridge that connected the pier with solid ground. In the middle of the footbridge he stopped, startled by a monitor lizard crossing beneath him. The lizard ran away splashing, leaving the channel for the putrid black mud that reeked of fish paste.

There was a small shop on the shore that sold cigarettes, drinks and fruit. The man went to the shop, where he bought cigarettes and a banana. He was thirsty, but he was not accustomed to tamarind water, the local drink, which was usually served in a dirty glass, so he tried to ignore his thirst.

What Marsusi really wanted from the shopkeeper was an address that most strangers requested when they arrived at this particular place: that of Pak Tarim. Tarim's neighbors were always surprised that he received so many guests. Tarim was an old man, whose head and fat belly resembled that of Semar, the shadow puppet clown. He spent his days relaxing with a large glass and a plate full of sweet cakes, leaving all the responsibilities of the house to his wife and children. His children and grandchildren were experts at catching the shrimp, crabs and other creatures that make up the mixture for terasi. So unhygienic was the way in which the ingredients for terasi were collected and prepared, that people who disliked the spice argued that it was probably mixed with snails and maggots, even lizard carrion.

However, in this seaside village, the name Tarim was more frequently associated with esoteric knowledge. Only certain elders knew for sure about Tarim's special skills. Outsiders such as Marsusi had only heard about him through rumors. Marsusi had been told by a friend that Tarim was the only person who could carry out the special task he required. And after following long and torturous leads, he had eventually found him.

The heat had begun to abate by the time Marsusi arrived at Tarim's house. Tarim received his guest without any display of emotion, despite Marsusi's being a stranger and his obviously high social status. When Marsusi introduced himself, Tarim did not even look at his face. Nodding his clown-like head, he invited Marsusi to go and rest in an adjacent room behind a closed door.

"Please rest for a while. Later this evening you can speak with me. I don't confer with anyone who is tired."

Marsusi entered the room indicated by Tarim, and found it furnished only with a mat made from pandanus leaf. He was surprised to find another guest there, a man, stretched out on his back, who quickly stood up when Marsusi entered. The two exchanged smiles and nodded at one another. They were aware that they were probably there for the same reason, and a comfortable intimacy quickly developed between them.

"My name is Dilam, and I'm from Warubosok. I came here to ask Grandfather Tarim for help. You too, right?"

Marsusi smiled, lighting a cigarette. He offered one to his new friend. The cigarette smoke made them feel even more intimate, as if they had known one another for a long time.

"So, what's your problem?" asked Marsusi, leaning against the bamboo wall.

Dilam seemed reluctant to say anything. He had brought his personal secret from Warubosok without telling a soul, not even his wife. Should he tell it to someone he had just met? Part of him said no. Yet the feeling of sharing the same fate and tribulations with a person he had just got to know somehow changed everything. Furthermore, to a villager like Dilam, Marsusi had the air of a person who carried considerable authority. And whatever else, Dilam already felt somewhat indebted to him: after all he was smoking one of Marsusi's cigarettes.

"Actually, my problem is quite trivial, sir. It's about water buffaloes!"

"Water buffaloes?"

"That's right. Someone poisoned two of my water buffaloes."

Marsusi nodded, not wanting to interrupt Dilam's story.

"It all began one night when one of my water buffaloes got out of the pen. That night I searched everywhere but couldn't find it. It was morning before I finally found it in someone's corn field, eating and trampling the stalks."

"I led the animal out of the field and went to the owner to make amends. He rejected my apology and refused my offer to pay him for the damage to his crop. Despite my obvious good intentions, a couple nights later, two of my water buffaloes were poisoned and died. It broke my heart, sir."

"You're sure that the water buffaloes died from poisoning?"

"Yes, sir. I've been tending water buffaloes since I was small. I know that they only shit in certain places. I know that when a water buffalo is in heat it rubs its backside against the stable posts. But most importantly, I know when a water buffalo is sick. My water buffaloes died suddenly, their mouths foaming. After they were butchered and their stomachs opened, I could smell poison. We threw the contents of the stomachs into a pond and the fish died. So, what else could it be but poison?"

"You're sure that it was the owner of that field who poisoned them?"

"Who else would it have been?"

Marsusi smiled, and nodded to encourage him to say more. Dilam asked him what problem he was bringing to the old man. Marsusi avoided his question by sliding his body down to a prone position and closing his eyes, feigning fatigue. In the event, weariness and the sea air penetrating into the guest room soon overtook him, and he fell asleep.

When he woke up several hours later, he saw that the room had been lit with an oil lamp. He glanced at his watch "Seven o'clock." As he stood up, his foot almost knocked over a glass. Two glasses of water, two plates of rice and some side dishes had been placed on the floor. However, none of it could whet Marsusi's appetite; his palate was accustomed to better fare. One glass was half-empty, but where was Dilam?

Marsusi could hear two people talking in another part of the house, and he guessed that it was Dilam and their host. Anxious to find out what they were talking about, Marsusi left his room and entered the main part of the house. The front room was in darkness. No sign of Tarim's children or grandchildren, or even of his wife. Silently Marsusi took a seat on a chair close to the source of the voices behind the wall.

In the back room, Dilam sat facing Tarim who was looking serious. Everything his guest said was received by the old man with a deep frown, his eyebrows almost meeting as his forehead wrinkled.

"Once more, think this through first, my child. This is a matter of life and death. And the burden of responsibility will fall entirely on your shoulders," said Tarim, looking piercingly into Dilam's eyes.

"My mind is made up, Grandpa. I'm ready to accept the consequences."

"Consequences in this world as well as in the hereafter?"

"Yes, Grandpa."

"Do you understand that this affair may result in bad consequences for your descendants?"

Dilam did not respond straight away. He lowered his head, and held his breath for a moment. The pain of the rebuff he had felt when his apology had been rejected stung him anew. In his mind's eye he saw the two water buffaloes he loved lying dead on the ground.

"I don't think that far ahead, Grandpa. Let the future take care of itself. In any case, I'm determined to go through with this."

"I'm not accustomed to being rushed, child. Think about it again. Go outside. Maybe the air outside will change your mind."

Reluctantly Dilam stood up. Marsusi quickly tiptoed back to his room.

The air outside was cool. Dilam looked up at the sky, still glowing red in the west as vestiges of the fiery disk grew dark. Harassed by thousands of mosquitoes, he found it difficult to compose his thoughts. But he could at least remember everything Tarim had said. And he believed that Tarim's words were true. Aside from the fact that the old man charged a fee for his black magic, he was renowned for trying to prevent people bringing misfortune upon their peers. Dilam himself had once heard that Tarim would simply accept, without question, a person's change of heart even if he had come initially with the intention of trying to destroy someone else

Dilam's problem was that he was unable to allow his inner light to shine. A black hatred had settled in his heart, preventing him from seeing his true self. His own words, spoken in front of Tarim just a short time before, came echoing back to him. "Come what may, let the future take care of itself!"

Dilam went back inside to face Tarim, his face even darker than before. He took several deep breaths as he took his seat before the old man.

"So, what have you decided, child?"

"I haven't changed my mind, Grandpa. I'll take full responsibility for everything."

"Fine. So be it."

Tarim stood up and left the room, returning after a few minutes carrying a small cup filled with water and a sheet of unbleached cloth. He spread the cloth on the table and Dilam noticed that there was a sewing needle threaded with cotton in one section. He was taken aback by the simple objects that would effect the magic.

Grandfather Tarim sat down. His breath became labored. Beads of sweat forming on his brow sparkled in the lamplight. He held up the needle by the thread, swinging it in a circle above the water in the cup. As the swinging stopped, the needle continued to spin. Tarim waited for it to stop, then he dropped it into the middle of the cup. The water seemed to boil, and he quickly covered the cup with the cloth. A moment later they heard the sound of flowing water. Tarim turned back the cloth to reveal the cup again; the needle had disappeared.

"Your missive has departed," said Tarim. The tension in his face began to relax. He mopped his sweating brow with the hem of his shirt. Dilam felt incapable of freeing himself from a stupor that had overtaken him. He was startled to hear, once more, the sound of flowing water in the cloth-covered cup. As Tarim lifted the cloth once more, Dilam's eyes widened. The threaded needle was visible again, sparkling in the water that was gradually turning red. Coagulated blood on the thread was slowly dissolving, spreading evenly through the liquid.

"It's been done," Tarim said as he cleared up his tools. "Don't forget, child. All of this is entirely your responsibility. If you return to Warubosok tomorrow, you'll be able to witness the burial of your foe's corpse."

The expression on Dilam's face revealed a combination of satisfaction and horror. He could not bring himself to speak. He could feel sweat trickling down the back of his neck. Seeing Dilam, pale and trembling before him, Tarim smiled. The old man had witnessed this time and again in his guests.

"So that you don't keep trembling like that, there's only one thing to do. You must try as hard as possible to place righteousness in your heart. You must be convinced that your enemy brought disaster upon himself through his own actions; let this conviction grow strong inside you.

Unable to hide his feeling of shock, Dilam retreated to his room. There he found Marsusi lying on the mat on the floor, looking up at him.

"All done?" asked Marsusi, smiling.

Dilam responded with a flat, empty look.

"Are there still motorboats going down the channel to Cilacap? I have to get home quickly," said Dilam. Observing his distracted friend, Marsusi could feel doubts rising within him. He had listened to the entire conversation between Dilam and Tarim, a conversation that had made the hairs on the back of his neck stand on end. Marsusi felt sure that his friend, like himself, was haunted by bad thoughts.

The two men were silent, withdrawing into their respective thoughts. Dilam stretched out on his back, his arms behind his head. His eyes gazed upwards, beyond the ceiling, as he imagined his enemy suddenly coughing up blood. He could envisage the commotion which would ensue. The man's wife and children screaming, calling to their neighbors for help. Crying, loud and continuous. The confused voices of men and women and finally, the figure of a corpse lying on a platform, covered with a shroud from head to toe.

He could see people who at first had been seized by panic calming down and sitting together. Dilam imagined hearing the conversation as they speculated the cause of the tragedy. No doubt, the gossip would turn to the possibility of a spell. Dilam started feeling more and more nervous as he thought again about what he had seen slowly dissolving in the cup of clear water.

Marsusi sat with his back against the wall, his legs stretched out in front of him. Smoke billowed from the cigarette in his mouth. He paid no outward attention to the distraught Dilam. However, it was Dilam who was actually occupying his thoughts.

Marsusi was sure that Dilam was a farmer, and that he belonged to the type of community that had always been considered a symbol of the simplicity, honesty, even wholesomeness found in humanity. He wondered how this simple farmer had found the boldness to spill the blood—even indirectly, through a method that defied conventional explanation—of a fellow farmer. Marsusi learned a simple lesson from this: that the need for vengeance could be powerful enough to destroy one's humanity, including the humanity between two villagers connected by their simple lifestyle.

Marsusi was shocked to realize how close he had become to being just like Dilam. Here he sat in the same room, harboring the very same intentions. If Dilam had murdered the owner of the rice field who had poisoned his water buffaloes, then what was different about Marsusi's desire to carry out the same deed toward a young village woman who had humiliated him.

Marsusi's vision began to blur. He imagined Srintil clutching her chest as she coughed up fresh blood, splinters and nails, her eyes open horribly wide. He imagined a funeral bier being carried to the cemetery, accompanied by the crying inhabitants of Paruk.

Marsusi shook his head. He swallowed, stubbing his cigarette on the floor. Experiencing a similar initial reaction to that of Dilam, Marsusi also wanted to go home immediately, but the image of Srintil, the way she had looked at him when she rejected him, rose again in his mind. The muscles of his jaw grew hard. At that moment he heard a voice. Tarim was calling him

Like a man who had lost his resolve, Marsusi stood up slowly. Dilam watched him from his prone position. His eyes held hidden meaning, as if the villagers from Warubosok were sending a message to him. Unfortunately, the oil lamp was not bright enough to reflect the meaning in his eyes. Marsusi heard the voice calling again. He crossed through the front hall and opened the door leading to the back room.

"Please sit down," said Tarim calmly, but with concern. "Now, tell me why you have come here."

After coughing nervously several times, Marsusi told the story of his experience in Paruk about two weeks earlier. His voice, controlled and devoid of emotion, drew the attention of his host. Tarim was used to people speaking with hate, spite, with resentment. Yet, such malice was not apparent when Marsusi spoke.

Suddenly, Tarim smiled, interrupting Marsusi's explanation. "Are you talking about Srintil, young man?"

"Yes. Do you know her?"

"Yes, I do. She's a ronggeng who can make a man want to explode with desire. I once watched her perform. And she humiliated a handsome man like you?"

Marsusi was overcome with embarrassment.

Tarim laughed. "No, it's not pleasant to be made a fool of, especially by a beautiful ronggeng. So, what do you want from me?"

"Naturally, I want to pay her back, somehow. I know for sure that she accepted all the men who came to her before I did, with a little money or one or two grams of gold. But she rejected me, even though I offered her a gold necklace with a diamond pendant. What else can it be called but the greatest insult? But…"

"But?"

"I've changed my mind."

"And ….?"

"Oh, just let her go."

Marsusi smiled indifferently, but Tarim guffawed.

"Because, when Srintil glances at you, when she moves her head in dance, your heart melts? Because, when she flicks her scarf, you become distracted, correct?"

Tarim continued to laugh even harder. His distended stomach jiggled. His dull lips drew back. He looked exactly like Semar, no doubt about it.

"Everyone should be like you," he then declared. "There's no need to feel embarrassed about changing your mind when you realize that your intentions were not good. Why is it that people come here to take vengeance, sometimes only because they feel jealous toward their peers? They think that after they take vengeance on someone the matter will be finished. But they are mistaken. In taking vengeance, they actually open up a whole set of new problems, often long-standing and far more serious. In this world, my son, nothing stands alone. No deed can be independent of consequences. Good deeds result in good consequences, bad results in bad.

"Even more strange than this, my son, is that people, knowing full well that their deeds may have evil consequences, are still willing to take their chances."

Marsusi listened to Tarim's sermon with rapt attention, not only because he felt there was truth in what the old man said, but also because he detected inconsistencies. A specialist in black magic sermonizing about the standards of noble character. The strangeness of the situation transformed into a questioning look on his face and in his eyes. This was not lost on Tarim.

"As for me. I can be compared to a gunsmith. A gunsmith knows that a gun has only one purpose: to take lives. If there were no gunsmiths, the corpses we bury would likely be people who died of natural causes. And that would be good.

"My life is similar to that of the gunsmith. I'm just Tarim. I can't change the course of my life. I can't avoid who I am."

Marsusi nodded his assent. "Yes. Well, fortunately, at least I have succeeded in changing my plans." But he was surprised when Tarim laughed at him, and regarded him with an ironic expression.

"You are indeed fortunate. Yet what you have done is only that: just made a change in your plans. Following through with that won't be easy, my son. Can you truthfully say that you've succeeded in wiping away your malice so that your thoughts are clean and pure? I don't believe so."

Tarim stared long and penetratingly at his guest's face. Marsusi felt annoyed, but could do nothing except question what lay in the man's heart.

"Think about it. Right now you acknowledge that you've forgiven Srintil, the ronggeng of Paruk. But how would you feel if you saw her applauded by a hundred men during a performance? And how would you feel if you found out one day that Srintil had become the mistress of a man whose rank in life was lower than yours? Isn't it true that your desire to take revenge on her would return?"

Marsusi felt cowered by Tarim's questions, and the look from his eyes, from someone with complete self-confidence.

"I'm an old man. It may be that I have a better grasp of your problem and know best what you should now do."

"You mean I wasn't wrong to come here."

"No, you weren't. In fact I would advise you to take revenge for the pain you have endured but you must be just. You were humiliated, weren't you?"

Marsusi nodded his head like a small child.

"So take revenge by humiliating her in turn. Only in this way can you free yourself from the malice you feel. You might even be able to forget Srintil forever. Take revenge that is just, do to her what she did to you: humiliate her. But don't injure her or endanger her life."

"I understand. But may I ask you something?"

"Of course."

"If the person who humiliated me wasn't Srintil, would you still advise me the same way?"

Tarim's face grew tense. If the person facing him hadn't been the manager of a plantation, he would have probably exploded in anger. Only because he was aware of his rank and status, had Marsusi felt bold enough to ask the question of this man so well versed in esoteric knowledge. Tarim's understanding deepened. His fat lips split into a grin.

"I have to speak honestly. Srintil does not belong just to her parents or her relatives. She doesn't even belong just to Paruk Village. She belongs to all people. To you, and to me as well. So, to bring too much misfortune upon her would result in consequences more terrible than we could imagine. It would be very bad, especially for you. Believe me!"

Marsusi had to admit to himself that he was defeated, but he felt relieved. He continued to nod his head vigorously as he listened to Tarim's guidance.

During the evening an offshore breeze had begun to blow. Although there were thousands of mosquitoes buzzing around him as he lay on the mat, Marsusi slept soundly until morning. The only thing that disturbed him from time to time was Dilam who slept restlessly, muttering occasionally in his sleep.

News quickly spread through Paruk that, on the night of the Independence Day Celebrations, Srintil would resume her role as a ronggeng and perform. Two days before the festivities, people were already busy preparing. Children asked their parents for money to buy snacks. Food vendors found funds for additional ingredients to cater for the expected crowds. So, too, did the lottery ticket seller who always went around seeking opportunities for sales whenever people gathered together.

Nyai Kartareja quickly repaired her relationship with Srintil, first by admitting that she had acted wrongly in the incident involving Marsusi several weeks earlier. She also changed her attitude towards the young woman, no longer speaking to her like the child she had adopted a long time ago. Nyai Kartareja now called her "young lady", and used polite forms of speech when she referred directly to her, a sign that she recognized Srintil's adulthood and her autonomy.

Nyai Kartareja treated Srintil as if she were about to become a bride, keeping the young girl in seclusion, and treating her body with traditional cosmetic herbs to maintain the youthfulness of her skin. Each night before Srintil retired, Nyai Kartareja gave her peppercorns to chew to keep her voice clear and pure. She washed Srintil's clothes with special soap. Nyai Kartareja no longer used soot and papaya sap as eye liner. She also no longer required Srintil to chew betel before the performance. Simbar's stall at the Dawuan market now stocked lipstick, makeup, and other items for her.

While his wife took care of Srintil, Kartareja prepared the calung. He urged the musicians to put on their best performance. All instruments were inspected and, if necessary, repaired. A man who claimed to be a member of the committee came to the village and gave Kartareja some lyrics for the songs they would perform. Because Kartareja was illiterate, the man read them out to him. It turned out that the dukun knew all the songs but, here and there, certain words or sentences had been changed. Kartareja thought it odd that words like "proletariat" and "revolution" had been slipped into the lyrics: words that sounded unfamiliar to him. But he did not ask any questions. For him, it was virtuous to obey the orders of the wealthy or those who were in authority.

Sakarya was the only person who was not completely enthralled by the happiness which permeated the village. His cautious attitude arose out of a simple belief that everything came in balanced pairs of opposites. This included happiness. Its mate most surely was sorrow. In the course of his long life, Sakarya had learned that nothing was ever far from its mate. People always chose what brought fortune and avoided what brought misfortune but, he believed, one must be always aware of the connection. In Sakarya's mind, this meant that one should always be careful. He believed that he must maintain a balance and not go to extremes.

Sakarya did not, therefore, join in the enthusiasm of the other villagers. His preparations for Srintil's return to the stage tended more towards the spiritual side. He laid down more offerings at Ki Secamenggala's grave, often stayed awake all night, and ate and drank less. He told Srintil to avoid eating salt on her Javanese birthday: according to the recurring thirty five-day cycle of her birth date.

The August 17 Independence Day Celebration festivities began with a morning ceremony at the Dawuan fair grounds. Cloth banners were stretched between trees and in the fields where the people were gathering. The surge of thousands of heads created a picture, like the view of a tobacco field swept by a breeze. A thousand hands lifted high to the accompaniment of roaring shouts, comparable only to a thunderstorm in a leafless teakwood forest.

People giving speeches expended all their energy, their necks straining. Agitation, propaganda and slogans burned throughout the field as a thousand fists were raised with the cacophony of drums. Those in the audience stood tall with a self-confidence forged out of the speakers' rhetoric. The overflowing sense of enthusiasm permeated the members of the audience, giving them the strength to withstand the torment of the increasingly hot sun.

Carried away by the euphoria of the crowd, young girls, usually shy, lost their inhibitions and behaved more like the boys. They, too, raised their clenched fists and screamed. The jubilation peaked when an effigy made of corn husks, wearing a rimless hat and a pair of sunglasses, was burned by the masses. "The enemy of the people has turned to dust!" screamed a young man, his glistening eyes red with the outburst of emotion.

Sakum, in the audience, carried one of his children on his shoulders.

He stood beneath a tree, a speck lost in the confusion of humanity. For the first time in his life, Sakum cursed his blindness. He found that he could not read the situation or the voices he heard around him. He could always see joy in a spirited ronggeng performance, although not with his eyes. He could also see panic among people during a windstorm. Or the anxiety of his children when lightning struck. He could also sense the happiness in their faces when they received servings of rice larger than their own fists.

But he didn't despair. Through the throbbing pulse of the child perched on his shoulder, he tried to follow and determine the meaning of the jubilation going on around him. When his child's pulse raced, Sakum focused on his other senses. Sometimes, too, he tapped into the eyes of the child.

"What do you see?" he'd ask.

"Red, Daddy, I see red."

"Red, Daddy, I see red."

"What's red?"

"Everything. People have red hats. Banners are red. Oh, there's also black, green, and yellow. Wow, it's great!"

"Who's giving the speech?"

"I don't know."

"Well, let's get closer."

"But I'm hot, Dad, and thirsty."

"Well I don't have any more money, to buy you something to drink."

"Before we left, I saw Srintil give you some money."

Sakum gave in. His son climbed down from his shoulder. They walked through the crowd, the child pulling his father to the drinks vendor. Sakum also bought a drink for himself. After he had paid and received his change, Sakum squatted down. His agile young son returned to his perch on his father's shoulders.

"Okay, point me toward the *kuda kepang* dancers."

"'Scuse us, 'scuse us," called his son from Sakum's shoulders. The dense crowd of people moved aside to open a way. Almost all of them knew the blind man. But Sakum's son, just six years old, knew how to take advantage of his father's blindness. He didn't lead his father to the group of hobby-horse performers, but toward the balloon vendors in the corner of the field. Although he knew that he could never own such an amazing plaything, the boy wanted at least to see one up close.

"Son of a bitch! Where are you taking me?" Sakum asked sharply.

"Closer to the hobby-horse performers" he answered.

"Bullshit! We're not near them. That smell is most likely the balloon seller inflating balloons with gas, right?"

The boy laughed and then turned his father's head.

"'Scuse us, 'scuse us."

The ceremony ended with a parade. Cheers and raised fists filled every corner of the district seat. Two or three children fainted, overcome by the hot sun, but the crowd's enthusiasm wasn't diminished in the least.

Towards noon, the celebrating subsided. Dawuan became quiet; even the market was quieter than usual. Along with other villagers, Sakum went home, but he was no longer carrying his son on his shoulders. Now his child became his guide along the road. In the blackness that dominated his world, Sakum tried to understand the festivities in which he had participated that day. Everyone knew that this year's Independence Day celebrations were livelier than usual. Far livelier than in previous years.

But as much as he thought about it, Sakum could find no meaning in the jubilation that he had witnessed that day. He had heard it said, without really understanding, that the festivities celebrated the day of independence, not independence itself. At the same time, the concept of independence was, for him, meaningless.

It was his belief that life must be endured with submission, with or without what people called "freedom."

Supposing that Sakum or the other villagers of Paruk did understand the meaning behind the festivities, what would that have given them? Perhaps it was better that he and his fellow villagers did not understand the significance of that day or its history. The party speeches, the party symbols, the banners that decorated the field in Dawuan: would an understanding of what they meant help the people of Paruk? And it wasn't because they were illiterate that they did not understand; it was something else. In the traditional kind of life they led, the villagers were interlinked by a sense of solidarity and a sense of equality that rarely went beyond the village limits. National politics of even the simplest kind had never taken root in this isolated hamlet. Paruk's way of life was a tradition that was based on inherited bonds of blood. The solidarity of the villagers was centered on the dome over a grave on a small hill in the middle of the village: the grave of Ki Secamenggala. Paruk was a sovereign state unto itself whose sovereignty was maintained by the village elders.

On one occasion, a party organizer came to the village and handed out party posters. On them were pictures of what the man called the "downtrodden proletariat".

At first Sakarya had been interested, because people who came to the village often mentioned the word "proletariat", which he interpreted the word to mean "subjects". Everyone in Paruk thought of themselves as subjects, but he became confused when the man began to speak of "the miserable proletariat being victims of the evil oppressors".

"Who are these 'victims of the oppressors'," he asked the man.

"You yourself, and all the inhabitants of this village," the man answered. "Your blood is being sucked dry so that all that's left is what you see now: misery! On top of this you can add ignorance and all kinds of disease. It's time for you to stand up with us."

"Wait a minute. You say we're oppressed. Are you sure? We don't feel oppressed. Honestly! We've always lived here peacefully."

"That's just it. You're not aware of your own oppression. Since the time of your ancestors, the oppressors have been working their evil. Their methods have become part of history. Look at the consequences of the evil right here. Everyone's starving! Everyone's ignorant and sickly. Children are suffering from worms and scabies. Your children live without hope."

"But who are these 'oppressors'?"

"The imperialists, capitalists, colonialists, and their lackeys. There's no mistaking them."

"I'm confused, sir. We've never met those people. What you say seems strange. For a long time, this hamlet has been called Paruk and we like living here. It is a reality that we've accepted. We don't think about whether there's something better than that reality. You've made a big mistake if you think you're going to hear us complain. Maybe we are ignorant, and poor, and sick, but that is our business. You don't have to bother thinking about us. Strange, isn't it? We don't feel any different than usual, so why is someone else so bothered?"

"Aren't you the one who's strange, not knowing or not wanting to know history?"

"So now it's history. What do you mean, sir?"

"History is very powerful. You can reject it or you can fight it. But you will be crushed by it if you remain silent in ignorance. Just wait!"

"We here believe that the most powerful force is the venerable one who decided that we live here and who determined the way we live."

So, Paruk Village remained Paruk Village, even though in 1964 the outside world was jubilating. Speeches everywhere. Party symbols everywhere, and parades everywhere. Paruk remained calm, watched over by a grave on top of a small hill in its center.

Sakarya, the elder of the little hamlet, might have been the only person there who never stopped reading natural omens. From them he gathered that the days ahead would be savage. Days when people left their places of employment to gather in open fields. Days when roads would be filled with humanity, raising clenched fists and screaming shrilly. All of this reminded Sakarya of a coconut tree being blown by wind. As the wind blew, it would lean to the south. When the wind stopped, the tree didn't simply return to its upright position. Instead, it first swung back to the north. For Sakarya, the jubilation outside of the village was a strong wind that was sweeping through their lives. Like the coconut tree, before their lives found their former calm, something else would happen first.

Yet that something was not within the ken of anyone in Paruk, not even Sakarya. Sakarya had always paid close attention to the rhythm and equilibrium of the world. As a result, he had learned that, if something extraordinary happened, it must be paid for with an equal amount of destruction. "Don't laugh too hard lest later you will be filled with tears of sorrow," he often said to the village children.

That evening, almost everyone in the village accompanied Srintil as she left to perform at the Independence Day celebrations in Dawuan. This was the first appearance of the Paruk ronggeng at an official function, a matter that carried special significance for them.

The enthusiasm of the small town of Dawuan focused on a soccer field near the office of the sub district head. A wide stage, about a meter high, stood in one of the corners. Dawuan did not have electricity but that night there were plenty of neon lights around the stage. The noise of the generators was, strangely enough, a symbol of pride for the people. No one was bothered by it; after all, it was the source of power for the amazing neon lights. For many of the people swarming around the field, bright lights that needed no oil was an unusual phenomena.

The group from Paruk was welcomed with blazing lights and beaming faces. The committee received the musicians with their calung instruments. They were placed behind the stage, but Srintil, along with Nyai Kartareja, was invited to sit with the functionary ladies of Dawuan.

Srintil found that she felt completely restored as a mature ronggeng. The electric atmosphere made her entire body come alive; her skin and eyes glowed with life. Perhaps, at that moment, the spirit of ronggeng truly and completely possessed her. Her bearing and form radiated an authority and enchantment that was almost supernatural. She sat calmly, full of self-confidence. The steady look in her eyes radiated a power to incapacitate, to hold a person under its spell.

Srintil at eighteen was a woman who had already experienced the pain that came with "the opening of the mosquito netting". She had also felt the bitterness of being rejected by the man she loved. At that young age Srintil had also already experienced relations with about two dozen men. And long before that, in the place of her birth, she had been brought up in an environment of deep-rooted poverty. Such a bitter history would be likely to make her rumpled, shy, and lacking in self-confidence. But at that moment, Srintil sat as an equal among the most highly-ranked women in Dawuan.

The neon light revealed what had happened to Srintil to make her the special person she was. The influence of her background the misery of her past, could best be represented in a metaphor. Goat shit, as revolting as it might be, can also provide fertilizer for aromatic tobacco leaves when the soil is barren. Srintil had not been ruined by her background. On the contrary, she had risen above her background to become what she was. The results were obvious that night under the light of the neon lamps. Srintil was the center of attention, and in complete control of the situation.

"That's the dancer from Paruk Village, isn't it?" whispered the wife of the sub-district head to the woman next to her, the wife of the district chief.

"Yes, that's her."

"This is the first time I've actually seen her."

"So, do you think she's beautiful?"

The wife of the sub-district head felt uneasy, but she hid her feelings behind a bland smile. In all honesty, she had to admit that the ronggeng from Paruk was definitely superior to herself in many ways. More beautiful than she had been, even when she was the same age. Surreptitiously, she stole a look at the seats in the front row which were filled with men. She felt more uneasy when she realized that almost every single man was looking at Srintil, including her husband.

The wife of the district chief smiled. Her smile was wholehearted because, for her, Srintil's beauty didn't matter. No one, not even a beautiful ronggeng, was going to break up her home. Her husband was old and impotent.

"Don't you think her hair is tied up too high?"

"Yes, but that's intentional, better to show off her neck."

"And her lace blouse, it looks like it's made from rags."

"That hardly matters. She's going to take it off later, anyway. Besides, look under the blouse. You can see that her shoulders are perfectly formed. What's more, she's going to bare those shoulders."

The wife of the sub-district head muttered under her breath, then excused herself and moved next to the wife of the police commander.

Again, the wife of the district chief smiled, this time a smile of victory. "Who said that it was unfortunate to have an impotent husband?" She said to herself.

The sub-district chief's wife began whispered to the wife of the police commander: "Although she's pretty, she's a bit of a bumpkin, isn't she?"

"Indeed. It's quite inappropriate really. I'd like to know who or what man, rather, placed her in our midst."

"You're absolutely right. I'm going to ask my husband to order someone to have her moved elsewhere."

She began to stand up.

At the same moment, Srintil stood up and looked straight at the two whispering ladies, with a strange smile on her face. The smile of a queen. The sub-district head's wife stopped in her tracks. The wife of the police commander pretended to open her handbag. And, from her more distant seat, the wife of the district chief laughed out loud. This awkward situation continued for about half a minute, while Srintil's eyes, radiating softness, yet powerful in their gaze, muted the enthusiasm of the women around her. The awkwardness only ended when Nyai Kartareja pulled on Srintil's hand to sit down again.

Srintil sat down, but the smile remained on her face. It was the smile of a young performer who was aware that her ability to entertain was her most prized possession. The atmosphere among the women reverberated like thunder. The face of the wife of the sub-district head was bright red. This was the first time she had been put down by another woman and, to her disquiet, by a woman who, in her view, was no better than a whore. She was seething inside, but a strange power seemed to paralyze her. She remained fixed in her chair, defeated by the smile and eyes of a rural girl. It seemed that a mere smile and glance could hurt her far more seriously than the slap of a hand.

The uneasiness felt by the women dissipated a little once the program began. As had happened in the morning, the evening ceremony began with speeches accompanied by shouts of support from the clamorous crowd. More than a thousand fists pounded the air, ready to destroy the enemy. The rhetoric of the speaker described the so-called enemy so cleverly that the crowds could envisage a devil of great evil, who had to be annihilated without delay. The annihilation was metaphorically carried out and the enemy torn apart by the enthusiastic masses. Although all of this happened through words and raised fists, the audience seemed satisfied. The speaker stepped down from the stage to thunderous applause.

The entertainment program was due to begin. The master of ceremonies, a man with owl-like eyes, appeared on stage. He spoke enthusiastically about the ongoing revolution, which demanded the utmost dedication, including that of artists. Although most audience members already knew it, the man explained that traditional keroncong music represented the strength of this political position, the self-defense group another position, and the ronggeng yet another. The three, he said, had to unite, together as one to crush the enemy through artistic service.

"And the ronggeng troupe of Paruk," he said, adding special emphasis to each word, "is made up of proletarian artists! A proletariat so powerful, so undefeatable that they can still sing and dance even after centuries of oppression. Shortly, Srintil and her friends will appear on stage. But make no mistake. Whatever they perform can be seen as nothing else but a demand for freedom. Freedom from the oppression of imperialists, capitalists, and colonialists along with their lackeys. For freedom!"

From one corner of the field, noisy cheering could be heard. The audience became aware that the jubilation was carefully regulated by command, and that there also was an attempt to make the ronggeng troupe appear to have a more dominant role in the celebrations than the other troupes. In the spot next to the stage where they had gathered, Sakarya glanced sharply at Kartareja. The two did not comprehend the words of the master of ceremonies, much less their significance. But they felt that something was wrong. In their experience, a ronggeng needed no lengthy introduction before performing.

"I'm worried," said Sakarya.

"Why?" Kartareja asked.

"Maybe this is a mistake. It doesn't seem right. Did you hear what the master of ceremonies said?"

"I did," answered Kartareja. "But what can we do? It's out of our control."

"They wouldn't let me burn incense. And there are other regulations. I don't like this. Anything could happen."

"You're right. They don't know how hard we worked to coax Srintil into dancing again. She wants to dance now, but they don't seem to appreciate the rules that go with a ronggeng performance."

"I have to leave."

"Leave? Where are you going?"

"Outside. I'm leaving you in charge of the troupe."

Kartareja understood. His colleague had to commune with the spirit of Ki Secamenggala. He couldn't possibly do that in the middle of the crowd.

The keroncong musical performance began. The melancholy tones of the music roused the audience's sentiments. A neatly-groomed young man sporting a bowtie sang a traditional song. Many people were deeply moved and were carried along on a wave of nostalgia. Srintil looked straight at the young man, her heart singing. As she listened, she gradually became aware of murmurs coming from the crowd. Suddenly a voice rang out.

"Get off the stage! Get off! We don't like your imperialist nonsense. Get off the stage!"

The young man obviously heard the catcalls, but ignored the interruption from the corner of the field. He signaled his musicians and skillfully changed songs. The strains of a different song reverberated across the field, a rural song that ruled the national air waves in 1964. The enthusiasm and happiness of the audience was once again fired up. Many stood up to clap or to sing along. The atmosphere was fired with joy.

Strangely, Srintil didn't appear to join in the change of mood, but not because she wasn't moved by the circumstances; in her heart she felt an outburst of happiness that could only be enjoyed in silence.

"His name is Murdo, Tri Murdo, the son of a school supervisor here in Dawuan," Nyai Kartareja whispered. Only a smart madam like her could have grasped what was going on in Srintil's thoughts. She had also made it her business to know all the important information regarding the men of that region "He went to school in Yogya. In my opinion, he's a handsome young man. What do you think?"

Srintil pushed away Nyai Kartareja's hands, indicating that she wanted the old woman to stop talking. She felt embarrassed. And it showed in her face to such an extent that Nyai Kartareja laughed.

Before the music ended, someone asked Nyai Kartareja to prepare the ronggeng troupe as it was almost time for its performance.

Nyai Kartareja took Srintil to a room where she could change her clothes. Unlike several years ago, everything now fitted Srintil perfectly. All of the natural assets of her body were at the peak of their development. When she removed her blouse and camisole, she looked like a goddess. Her neck balanced her perfectly-formed shoulders. Her gold necklace, rings, and three bracelets sparkled, affirming the youthfulness of her skin. The large diamond studs in her ears reflected light off the faceted stones every time she moved her head.

A large number of people had pushed their way in to look at Srintil getting dressed. Nyai Kartareja ordered the children to leave. With the adults, she pretended to feel reluctant about their being there but, in reality, she was happy to show off the beauty of her adopted child.

Srintil looked at herself in a small mirror she held. "Yes. This is who I really am; the person I should be. I am a ronggeng and nothing else!"

When she left them room, accompanied by Nyai Kartareja, Srintil became the focus of hundreds of pairs of eyes. A man walked in front of her to make a path though the mob, leading Srintil directly to the stage where the keroncong instruments had been replaced by the calung. The man gave Sakum a pair of sunglasses which he at first refused since blindness was a part of his life that he accepted without any embarrassment whatsoever. But after he was told that he would look more handsome wearing them, he changed his mind and put them on.

Srintil climbed the stairs to the stage to the accompaniment of thunderous applause. From one section of the audience she heard a chorus of voices shouting political slogans. "Long live the people's arts!" She appeared as calm as the white clouds which moved across the sky at the end of the dry season. For a moment, she was startled by the vast, brilliantly lit stage. She was used to performing in an area covered only by a grass mat, softly illuminated by a gas lantern. The audience witnessed the true professional as she quickly regained control of herself. As she turned toward the audience, her lips pulled into a small smile, a slight indentation at each corner. Her eyes sparkled like gemstones. Proudly and completely collected, Srintil acknowledged her audience without lowering her sense of self-worth.

Then, silence. Everyone watched as she seated herself to face her musicians. The troupe from Paruk followed its usual procedures, pausing for a moment of silence before beginning the performance. No one knew what was occupying Srintil's thoughts. She was fully aware that she was the center of attention of more than a thousand pair of eyes. There was the wife of the sub-district head, Mr This, Mr That, and all the citizens of Dawuan. Yet Srintil felt there were no differences among them. For her, they were all the same. They were the eyes of Rasus. Srintil would show him that she had so much more to offer so that, although he had joined the army, he would realize that he didn't have the right to diminish who she was.

One did not have to have a profound knowledge to say that ronggeng dancing is usually but a crude imitation of *gambyong*, a dance which was performed to arouse desire in people from aristocratic circles. As it developed over the years, ronggeng also drew from other places and other dances which were imitated in a raw, folk style. Sometimes the dances were connected without rhyme or reason, so that one would think on seeing a performance that the swaying and swinging of the ronggeng were nothing more than spontaneous movements, their meaning superficial and tending only toward the erotic.

Those who had watched Srintil's development as a ronggeng would not be able to point out any profound changes in her style of dance: except on this particular night. Sakum was the first to notice. Sakum heard the scrapping of Srintil's feet on the stage. He felt the flapping of her dance scarf, and he heard the trembling of her voice. Everything had changed. Srintil seemed to be dancing in anger. If Sakum had eyes to see, he'd have noticed how Srintil raised her arms higher than usual, so that her white underarms showed. She shook her shoulders more boldly. When she turned her head, she looked, not at her audience, but upwards, as if challenging the stars above her.

The smile of a ronggeng, has never had any other meaning than that of a flower in attracting bees or butterflies. A ronggeng wooed without words, enticed with the power of magic. But that night, there was no possibility that Srintil's smile could be read as wooing or enticing. Her slight smile only showed a spirit full of dignity, an aloof flirtatiousness that was more off-putting than enticing.

If Srintil was determined to lower Rasus's thousand eyes, she succeeded in her efforts. While she danced, she imagined Rasus cowering, powerless and full of regret, wondering how he could have had the heart to make her suffer so. What sort of person was Rasus, Srintil was thinking as she commanded the stage. "Here, a thousand eyes have fallen under my spell. There's the sub-district head, the district chief; there's Tri Murdo, and all the others. They're frozen in their seats, wearing their hearts on their sleeves, allowing me to play with their feelings."

Srintil continued dancing with astounding fervor. Her skin was glistening with beads of perspiration. In the fifth number, when an instrumental piece was played to provide her an opportunity to rest, she continued to swing and to sway. People would have said that she was spurred on by the unusual atmosphere. Or, that it was all the spectators crowding around the stage, including the VIPs of Dawuan among the audience. No one understood that Srintil was releasing the pent-up anger that lay just below her consciousness. No one was aware of that.

No one, except Sakum. The blind man was accustomed to using his intuition. He recognized the danger signals and wanted to stop her. With his elbow, he nudged Kartareja who was sitting next to him on the stage.

Kartareja quickly understood what Sakum wanted, but wasn't bold enough to take action. So Sakum took the initiative. He dropped out of the rhythmic meter, playing a special pattern of tones. This was the agreed-upon method when the musicians wanted to talk to the ronggeng. But Srintil continued to dance. Only after three more pieces did she obey Sakum's signal.

The cessation of the music created an awkward and empty silence. The vacuum was filled moments later by whispering that developed into a generalized buzzing throughout the field. People had the chance to relax from the tension of sitting still so long. A moment later, they heard a loud voice. "Keep going, keep going! Long live Srintil! Long live the people's arts!"

"You have to rest, young lady. Don't force yourself. It's not good for you," Sakum instructed.

Srintil sat down with her legs folded to one side, hiding her face with the end of her scarf. It looked as though she was using the scarf to wipe the perspiration off her face but, after a few minutes she was still hiding behind it. The people sitting next to her could see that her face had become pale. Her breathing grew labored. Nyai Kartareja quickly grasped that the situation had become critical and stepped onto the stage.

"What's the matter?"

"I'm dizzy, Nyai. Oh, God. I can't breathe."

Nyai Kartareja held Srintil in her arms. She understood that this was a serious problem. Srintil could no longer hold herself up. Srintil fell, sprawled on the floor of the stage. Nyai Kartareja shrieked, causing the people around to panic. Within moments the stage filled with people, curious to see what had happened. One person among them knew what had to be done as soon as he realized that Srintil had fainted. He loosened all the tight binding clothes on her body, then prepared himself to resuscitate her. Yet before he began, Srintil had already begun to regain consciousness. She gasped as if she had been drowning, and for a moment appeared confused. Her eyes rolled. She sat up quickly when she realized that Tri Mundo, the man with the bowtie, was standing above her with his legs straddling her body. She blushed when her eyes met his.

Confusion reigned for some time. Although people had urged Srintil to leave the stage, she had quickly regained her composure and said that she felt fine. Those around her couldn't believe that there was nothing wrong with her. Yet she insisted that she didn't need any help, just a little time to adjust her clothes and prepare herself to dance again.

Only one person knew exactly what had happened. Marsusi, wearing dark clothing, stood unseen in the shadows. In his right hand, he clenched a small bottle about the size of his little finger.

When he had stopped the mouth of the bottle with his thumb, the uproar on stage had begun. Srintil could not breathe. But one moment of commotion was not enough to satisfy the resentment he felt toward Srintil. Patiently, Marsusi waited for another chance.

Fifteen minutes later, Srintil returned to become the center of attention as she commanded the stage. She danced as if she floated on air, energetically and freely. Sometimes like a *beranjangan*, bird with trembling wings and beak. Sometimes like the white egret that flies like a kite, gliding along the air currents. Even Srintil's voice, emanating from the loudspeakers, gave the impression of being more alive.

For a moment, the spectators were carried along by the rhythms of her dance. They followed every movement of their darling of the stage with their eyes, with their minds, and with every beat of their hearts. The wives of the sub-district head and the police commander watched bitterly. The wife of the district chief, on the other hand, was joyful because she saw her husband straddling his chair, full of desire, just like a powerful man should be. The spectators were entranced, but were startled again when they saw Srintil stop and stand motionless on the stage. Her arms, extended high, grew stiff. Her open mouth did not close for several long moments. The music stopped at the same time. Kartareja jumped forward, catching Srintil's body as she collapsed backwards.

Once again, commotion. People leapt onto the stage, including the district chief. His wife, however, restrained herself.

Tri Murdo, who had been watching from a front row seat, was at Srintil's side in seconds. "What did I say? Srintil shouldn't have danced again," he said.

Security guards removed those members of the audience who had come onto the stage while Tri Murdo and Nyai Kartareja attempted to revive Srintil. They removed her tight camisole. Srintil's face was blue, her breathing had stopped, but Tri Murdo was sure that her heart was still beating. He stood, his legs wide apart, directly over

Srintil's belly, moving the ronggeng's arms up and down, in an attempt to create artificial respiration. Srintil's lungs suddenly filled with air, and she drew a deep breath. Gasping for air, she opened her mouth like a fish. She stared wide-eyed seeing that her sash and camisole had been opened. Over her body for a second time stood the young man wearing the bowtie.

She sat up. Tri Murdo stepped to the side. People tried to lift her, but she refused their help. Nyai Kartareja guided her down the stage stairs. When the situation calmed down a bit, the MC shouted over the chaos that the evening's program had drawn to a close. The audience responded by shouting as one and raising their clenched hands in the air as they dispersed. Most of them would have had a suspicion of what had probably happened to the ronggeng. An evil spell was a familiar concept to the people of Dawuan. Only a few of them would have thought that Srintil might have been struck down by epilepsy or some other kind of illness.

If Marsusi had thought he could damage Srintil's reputation by engineering the incident on stage, he was sorely mistaken. Probably only he, along with the wife of the sub-district head and the police commander, felt satisfied by what had happened. Thousands of others felt sympathy toward the ronggeng of Paruk. Marsusi had injured the mourning dove which belonged to the public. It was fortunate for Marsusi that nobody knew what he had done.

Except for Kartareja.

Moments after Srintil regained consciousness, Kartareja slipped into the throng of spectators. He wanted to find out who was responsible. It wasn't easy to look for one person among the thousands of spectators. But Kartareja knew a simple method. He had to look for a person with an expression and movements that were different from all the other spectators. Kartareja saw a well-built man wearing black clothes and a turban hurrying away from the area.

"Wait a minute, young man," he called. The man glanced back at him. Kartareja's eyes widened when he saw his face, and at first he doubted his conviction that this was the culprit.

"Oh, it's you? Have you been watching the performance with the district chief? Why aren't you with him?"

"Well, sometimes a person just wants to be alone," answered Marsusi calmly. Kartareja smiled. Marsusi smiled in return. In the silence of those few moments, they had already communicated at a deep level, but an unavoidable awkwardness sprung up. Marsusi offered a cigarette to Kartareja and lit it for him.

"The performance tonight had a few problems," declared Marsusi.

"Yeah, I know. I understand how you feel. The important thing is that all debts are now paid."

"Hmm, yeah."

"Yes."

"And her …"

"Who?"

"Your ward!"

"Srintil?"

Marsusi did not answer. His broad smile was immediately understood by Kartareja.

"Oh, that's a simple matter, especially for you. If you still want her, the only question now is how patient you can be."

"I still need to know... Oh, never mind. What I mean is that your ronggeng certainly can be irritating!"

The two chuckled together.

Marsusi threw the small magical bottle to the ground, smashing it. The debt was paid. There would be no more humiliation.

The two men parted company, smiling in mutual understanding.

By one o'clock in the morning, the group from Paruk had still not left the area. They were enjoying hot coffee prepared for them by the committee. Srintil had changed out of her ronggeng outfit and sat surrounded by several men who felt fortunate to be able to be near the queen of the stage. She looked around for the man with the bowtie. Tri Murdo was still there, but was about to leave with his keroncong orchestra. When he came to take his leave, he acted as if nothing had happened. Srintil swallowed. The district chief stood up and sang a verse from a traditional song, tembang pucung, praising the ronggeng dancer, his hands clapping the rhythm:

Sengkang ceplik, cunduk jungkat sarwi wungu
Pupur lelamatan
Nganggo rimong plangi kuning
Gandanira kaya sekar dhedhompolan

Adorned with ear studs shaped like the hibiscus flower,
Crowned by a purple comb,
Her face powdered with a light color,
Wearing a scarf of bright yellow,
Her scent a bouquet of roses.

His wife clapped her hands, encouraging her husband. Other people clapped as well and sang another traditional song, one as old as Paruk Village. Srintil laughed and laughed. And with her laughter, her beauty shone out, in her eyes, in her bright and clear skin, and in the freshness of her mouth. Srintil glanced at the district chief's wife when her husband pinched her cheek. His wife was even happier. "Who would ever think my husband is impotent?" she thought.

Srintil almost didn't go home that night. The district chief and his wife tried to persuade her to spend the night at their home in Dawuan, but Kartareja was reluctant to agree to the plan.

"Please forgive us, sir. We cannot transgress a village tradition. This is *Pahing* of the five-day market week and *Ahad*, or Sunday, and by tradition we must, without exception, all sleep in our own homes in the village."

Sometime later, from far off, a moving light from a torch crossing the dikes that bordered the rice fields could be seen making its way toward Paruk. The flame left a trail of undulating black smoke in the air. The village people were walking back to their place of birth. No one spoke. Except for the sound of a calung instrument rattling as it was carried on someone's shoulders, there was silence. The villagers' feet were wet from the dew on the grass. The torchlight created illumination for a performance of another kind. A night bird chased an insect in the sky. A grasshopper flew directly into the fire of the torch. And Sakum screamed when he stepped on a frog.

Ahead of the procession, the village lay like a giant, sleeping water buffalo. Above it were the southern stars, with an occasional shooting star briefly lightening the sky. The sound of the night owl reverberated from its perch above the cemetery, as if welcoming the inhabitants home.

4

The black horse was foaming at the mouth. Every step he took created a soft whap-whap, as his testicles rubbed against his flanks. He had been pulling the wagon with its driver and passenger for more than thirty kilometers. Sentika, the only passenger on the wagon, was a man of some sixty years. His body was solid, his face open and calm. His shirt and the loose pants that came over his knees were black. His head was covered by a turban of neatly-wrapped cloth, and his lips were red from chewing betel. Sentika was a relic of the past who lived in the neighboring mountainous region.

"Your horse looks tired," said Sentika to Sartam, his driver. "Over there, up the road is a food stall. Let's rest for a while."

"It's not just my horse that would like to rest, sir."

"You must be hungry, too. I have a bitter taste in my mouth. Chewing betel while lurching along in your wagon isn't the most enjoyable experience."

Sartam stopped the wagon under the shade of a tree. The horse whinnied at another horse nearby, a female. Sartam fed the horse some grass and a mixture of rice and bran. Sentika strolled leisurely over to the food stall. By the time Sartam joined him, he had already rolled himself another cud of betel. He placed it in his mouth and set his molars to work.

"Is it far to Dawuan?" Sentika asked the woman at the stall.

"Oh, you're heading for Dawuan? It's a long way, about half a day from here."

"From Dawuan, I want to go on to Paruk Village. Do you know how to get there?"

"I've never been to Paruk, but I've often heard of it. Paruk is famous for its ronggeng. You want to hire a ronggeng?"

"Something like that."

"Where are you from?"

"Alaswangkal."

"Alaswangkal? And you rode that wagon all the way from there?"

"I'm an old timer, not used to riding buses."

"So that horse and wagon belong to you?"

"I'm renting 'em. This here's the owner," answered Sentika nodding toward Sartam who smiled, thinking of the large amount of money he would soon receive for the use of his horse and wagon. Sartam knew that Sentika owned a cassava plantation that was almost as expansive as the entire mountainous area of Alaswangkal. Two or three tapioca factories depended on the harvest of his plantation. Knowing this, Sartam did not hesitate in choosing the best dish offered at the food stall. Sentika would pay for it.

After he had eaten his fill, Sartam returned to his horse and wagon, and sat down for a smoke. The cigarette, hanging from his mouth, continued to billow smoke, even as he dozed off. He awoke with a start when Sentika clapped a hand on his shoulder.

"Wake up! You're like a python. When your stomach's full you go to sleep. Come on, let's go!"

The woman at the food stall was right in her predictions. It was approaching midday by the time Sentika and his horse-drawn wagon reached Dawuan. After asking directions from someone on the side of the road, they continued their journey towards Paruk. The wagon stopped at the end of the dike leading to the village. Sartam could now rest for an extended period; he had to wait with the wagon while Sentika walked on alone to the village.

Sentika walked at a steady pace despite the intensity of the sun, beating down on his head. Even after a half-day's journey, he did not give an impression of weariness. His legs were strong from a lifetime of ascending and descending the slopes of Alaswangkal, and he was accustomed to walking long distances.

At the outskirts of Paruk, a child indicated to him where Srintil lived. Since the incident with Marsusi, she had lived at the house of her grandfather, Sakarya.

Nyai Sakarya and her husband met the stranger as he approached.

"My name is Sentika, and I'm from Alaswangkal. Am I correct in assuming this is the home of the ronggeng Srintil?"

"Yes, that's right," answered Sakarya.

"Good. I've come a long way to see you because I have a business matter to discuss with you."

"Of course. It's about hiring a ronggeng, right?"

"What else? But there's something else…"

"One moment."

Sakarya told his wife to call Kartareja. After a moment, Srintil emerged holding Goder. Sentika examined her at length, his lips moving without saying a word. She was every bit as beautiful as he had been led to believe. But why was she holding a baby? He continued to watch her until Srintil looked down, embarrassed by his steadfast gaze.

"This is our granddaughter, Srintil. The baby isn't hers. It's a neighbor's child."

"I wasn't wrong..."

"Excuse me?"

"I wasn't wrong to come here."

"No. So, when did you want to have your event? Oh, here is Kartareja, the ronggeng trainer here in Paruk here," said Sakarya, introducing his colleague.

"I would like to propose two alternatives: On *Manis* Thursday, the first day of the five-day market week, or *Pon* Sunday, the third day of the five-day week."

"It so happens both days are open," said Kartareja, pulling up a chair. "But Thursday would be better."

"That's up to you."

"How many nights?"

Sentika was silent.

Sakarya turned his head toward Srintil. "Srintil, make some drinks. The gentleman has had a long journey."

"How many nights?" Sakarya repeated.

Sentika pulled out a small box of betel chew. "Actually, it's like this," he finally said. "I need Srintil for something else, not just to perform as a ronggeng."

Silence.

"What do you mean?" asked the two old men in unison.

"I want to begin with a story."

"Go ahead."

"I have had fourteen children, two of whom were boys. One of the boys died when he was small. That left Waras, who is now my only son and favorite child. Now Waras is seventeen years old."

"Go on."

"A long time ago I made a vow that if Waras grew up to be a healthy adult, I would sponsor a performance on his behalf with the best ronggeng in the district." He paused. "And that I would hire a beautiful *gowok* for him."

Sakarya and Kartareja looked at each other.

"Don't worry," Sentika added. "I'm prepared to pay a fee that won't disappoint you."

Kartareja spoke for himself and Sakarya: "That's not the problem. We've heard about the practice of *gowokan*, but we don't know much about it as there is no such tradition here."

"I understand. In my area too, gowokan has been abandoned. And if it weren't for my vow, I wouldn't go through with it. You understand that, don't you?"

"Yes, but please explain further."

Srintil sat next to her grandmother, listening to Sentika's explanation. The man from Alaswangkal was not used to talking at length. Words did not come easily to him. But, his listeners learned from him that a gowok was a woman hired by a father for his son when he reached a marriageable age.

A gowok provided lessons for the young man regarding matters of married life. These ranged from learning what was needed in a kitchen to how to treat one's wife with respect and love. While she was a gowok, the woman stayed alone with the young man and kept her own kitchen. The period of training was usually just a few days, at the most a week.

The general understanding was that the most important duty of the gowok was to prepare a young man so that he would not disgrace himself on his honeymoon. Related to this was the delicate problem that arose if a young man refused to part with his gowok, even when he had a potential bride already picked out for him by his parents. The gowok's position was always tenuous because, customarily, she was a widow or divorcee, or a woman who otherwise offered herself for the task. Although there were in fact men who volunteered their wives as gowok, such cases occurred only in very rare circumstances.

"So, as well as performing, I'm asking that Srintil stay for a few days to keep my son company. As for the fee, I repeat, you won't have any need to worry."

Sakarya and Kartareja again exchanged glances, but Srintil doubled up in laughter. "That's ridiculous," she said, looking at her grandfather for affirmation.

Sentika smiled warmly at Srintil. "You think it's ridiculous? Fine. But you, young beauty, you'd be willing to be a gowok for my son, wouldn't you?"

Srintil laughed again. "I don't know. What do you think?" she asked Nyai Kartareja.

"It's up to you. But I'd like to know more about the fee."

"But I've never been a gowok."

"So, you'd have a new experience," interrupted Sentika, reaching into his pocket.

"This money here is an advance for a performance and for your work as a gowok. You can have it all if you're willing to do both."

Perhaps if the villagers had known who Sentika really was, they would not have been shocked by the amount of money he put on the table: a stack of bills as thick as his finger. Next to it he placed a gold ring with a design known as woven thread. The ring was as thick as a betel flower. Srintil sat staring in astonishment. Unaware of what she was saying, she mumbled, "Has your son been circumcised?"

"He was circumcised by a circumcision specialist, but not yet by you!"

Everyone laughed except Srintil, who felt embarrassed by the remark. Doubts were emerging about the idea of acting both as a ronggeng and a gowok. The matter of dancing as a ronggeng was no problem to her, but to be a gowok? Srintil had sworn to herself that she would never again service any man who believed there was nothing more to the deal than a simple buying and selling of flesh, a transaction in which she once had no say about whatsoever. She was willing to give herself to a man, but only one she whom herself chose.

Everyone in Paruk knew that such thoughts diverged from custom, and so did Srintil. But at the age of eighteen, Srintil knew that a divergence like this had to happen if she wanted to have a say in her own fate.

Sentika looked around the room. "So, I guess none of you know what to say. He spat a red gob on the hard dirt floor. "But I await your answer, especially yours, young lady. You may not be aware of it, but I have to leave soon so that I won't be on the road at night. Alaswangkal is a long way away and my horse and wagon have been waiting for a long time."

Everyone looked at Srintil. This, too, was a divergence from what had happened previously, when Kartareja or Sakarya took the initiative and made decisions without checking with her first. Now Srintil's authority prohibited anyone from even making suggestions. Suddenly, Srintil's eyes shone, her expression full of confidence.

"I'll come to Alaswangkal on Thursday to dance. We'll see then whether I'm prepared to be a gowok for your son. That's as much as I'm willing to commit myself to right now."

As she finished speaking, Srintil stood up to leave the room. She kissed Goder, who was whimpering in his sling. Sentika quickly spat out the remnants of the betel chew in his mouth.

"Wait a minute, young beauty, not so fast. I'm an old man. Of course I understand your feelings, but sit down for a moment. I'm not finished yet."

Srintil softened her stance. She sat down next to her grandmother.

"Please listen to me, young lady. I'm pleased that you're prepared to dance as at my home. As for becoming a gowok, I agree with you. Leave the decision until you come to Alaswangkal. But take the money I've offered and go ahead and wear the ring. It's no loss to me to give it to you. And it doesn't matter whether you will or will not be a gowok."

Srintil sat passively as he approached her and took her hand. In the blink of an eye, he had placed the money and the ring in her palm. He closed her hand around the valuables.

Sentika left Paruk feeling satisfied, even though the goals which had brought him to the hamlet had been only partially fulfilled. He would still have to find a woman as a reserve in case Srintil refused to be a gowok. Maybe he wasn't so different from other men, after all, he thought to himself, so impressed had he been by the flower of Paruk, he would rather grant her wishes than see her angry or disappointed.

With the sun now low in the sky, creating long shadows, Sentika quickened his pace, realizing that he wouldn't arrive home until after nightfall. It doesn't matter, he thought. I have found the most beautiful ronggeng I've ever seen in my life and she is going to dance at my home!

During the week before the scheduled performance in Alaswangkal little of note occurred in Paruk. Srintil became even closer to Goder, as Tampi was pregnant again. The air was growing cooler. The dry season came again to the village as it had since time began, a change the village always welcomed. Crabs dug their holes deeper into the dikes separating the wet rice fields so that they could find adequate moisture in the earth. Snails withdrew into their shells, sealing the opening with a mucous that, when hardened, prevented any moisture from escaping. The snail and other similar animals would hibernate until the rainy season returned.

All the water birds had abandoned the village. Not a single bluwak was left to be seen. The trinil and hahayaman had disappeared even earlier, heading for the swamps at the mouth of the Serayu and Citanduy rivers. Their kingdoms, now only fields of dried mud, had become the domain of quail and branjangan. These birds built nests from grass or paddy stalks which had been dried to a crisp by the intense sun.

While the quails called to one another from behind the clumps of dried grass, the *branjangan* chased one another with giddy joy high in the sky. Their warbles were imitations of the calls of almost every kind of bird. Sometimes they sang like the *kutilang,* sometimes like the starling, the *podang*, even the *cucakrawa*. Perhaps the only bird the branjangan could not imitate was the crow.

In Paruk and the surrounding area, the lushness of the leaves of the trees and bushes had begun to fade. The banyan tree over the cemetery shed thousands of yellowed leaves when the wind blew. Young leaves of the banana and taro trees became thinner and drier. Groves of bamboo withered. Nature had taught all of them that to survive they had to conserve moisture during the dry season. The only exceptions were the mango and bungur trees. Unlike other plants, both of these began to flower with the approach of the dry season.

Early in the morning of the day of the performance in Alaswangkal, Srintil and the ronggeng troupe set out from Paruk. From Dawuan they took a bus that was going as far as the district seat. The calung xylophones and the drums were piled up on the roof. The other passengers, who were mostly either dozing or feeling nauseous from the exhaust fumes that filled the bus, suddenly brightened when they saw Srintil and her entourage. Most of them knew who Srintil was, and a few began to chatter excitedly. Several of them stood in their seats to get a better view of the ronggeng, wondering whether she was still as beautiful as ever. They were happy just to catch a glimpse of her, knowing that to gain her services, in any sense of the term, would require a great deal of money.

The chatter would have continued had Srintil reacted to it, but she said nothing at all. She refused even to look at those who were making crude remarks. If she turned her head, it was only to speak to Nyai Kartareja who was sitting next to her. Even this was carried out with dignity and poise. A new element had emerged in the relationship between Srintil and Nyai Kartareja. For six years Srintil, as her adopted child, had been completely submissive to Nyai Kartareja. Now, it seemed that the older woman had withdrawn, yielding the rank and status to her charge.

After two hours on the bus, they came to a secluded region in the middle of a teak forest where the troupe from Paruk disembarked. A man wearing Javanese style trousers approached Kartareja and introduced himself.

"My name is Mertanakim. I was sent by Mr Sentika to meet you."

"Thank you for meeting us," Kartareja answered. "Is there anyone to help us carry our things?"

"These men will help you," he replied, as several men picked up the instruments and bags. "Just follow me."

"Is it far?"

"About two hours walk at most," Mertanakim replied.

The porters walked in front and soon drew far ahead, leaving the troupe lagging behind. The path was narrow and rough, steep in parts and quite rocky. Along the track, they were constantly passed by people carrying cassava going in the opposite direction. The men carried their loads directly on their shoulders or backs, while the women used cloth shoulder slings, with their suspended burdens resting against their lower backs. Mertanakim told them that the porters all worked for Mr Sentika. They carried the cassava from Alaswangkal to a pick-up point at the edge the highway. From there the cassava was transported to a tapioca factory by horse-drawn cart or truck.

For at least half an hour, the visitors did not see a single dwelling. The path was bordered by teak forest and cassava plants. At various intervals footbridges made of coconut tree trunk led off from the path into the forest. Srintil could only wonder where they went. Near a sharp turn in the path, they came across a small food stall where they stopped for a rest. Although far from any settlement, the little stall seemed to be thriving, with a regular clientele in the passing porters who bought tamarind water sweetened with palm sugar and fermented cassava.

Srintil drank two glasses of tamarind water, sweating from every pore on her body. Two men stood up to offer her a chair.

Mertanakim, chastised those porters who remained sitting. "Hey, get up everyone. These are guests from Paruk Village."

Five men, all porters wearing traditional Javanese shorts, stood up immediately. They gathered outside, around their loads of cassava, but their eyes remained focused on the little food stall, and on Srintil as she massaged the calves of her tired legs. They were mountain men in every sense, and Srintil was the most beautiful woman they had ever seen. The event they had long been waiting for was to be held later that evening: the ronggeng performance at Sentika's house. The excitement they were feeling was reflected in their faces.

"Is it still far, Kartareja?" asked Sakum, who always found walking in unfamiliar terrain difficult.

"It's still a ways," Mertanakim answered. "But don't get discouraged. Our boss has prepared a special welcome for you."

They continued their journey and, although the heat from the sun grew more intense, it was alleviated by a cool mountain breeze. They walked in single file, led by Mertanakim. When they reached the ridge of a hill, they could see an expansive vista beneath and around them: mountain slopes either green with cassava plants or red where the tubers had already been harvested. Far off they could see a desolate teak forest. Here and there, stiff *wangkal* trees dotted the landscape. They could see the narrow trail winding around the hills, sometimes lost in the dense foliage. The solitude of the mountains was disturbed only by the *kacer* bird, chirping from its hiding place in the clumps of bushes growing on the slopes of the steep ravines.

They could see one or two dwellings with roofs of ash-colored grass. Separate pens for the goats had roofs covered by vines, squash, and gourd. Small children came out of their houses, all naked. Men also emerged, with machetes strapped to their backs, wearing their weapons with obvious pride. Even some of the young boys, although naked, had machetes strapped to their backs. Children and adults alike stared at the newcomers, and whispered among themselves. Like the porters, they, too, seemed happy with the prospect of seeing the ronggeng performance.

It was almost noon when the visiting troupe reached the hamlet of Alaswangkal. Srintil was surprised to see that the settlement consisted of just a few clusters of grass huts, each group separated from the others by broad grassy fields. Had she come this far from Paruk to perform in one of these dingy huts?

But her disappointment quickly faded when Mertanakim pointed to a spot further ahead.

"We're almost there. That's the home of Sentika, my boss who employs everyone around here."

The house Mertanakim was pointing at was still some way off. All they could see from where they stood was a large yard bounded by tall leafy trees. The yard, covered by loose gravel, looked neat and well-kept.

As they drew closer, they got a better view of the house. The entrance to the yard was a stone gateway. Although not particularly well constructed, it created a substantial impression. The house itself consisted of three main structures with tile roofs adorned by zinc carvings. The walls were teakwood, sparkling with new varnish. The yard was extensive, with smaller, more simply-built houses to the left and right of the main building, in which they could see stacks of dried cassava.

As she stood under the trees in the middle of the yard, Srintil thought to herself: this is a true home, a house that gives the impression of being aesthetically in harmony with nature. A house that does not try to master the trees and rocks that surround it. She saw two birds flying in and out of the verandah. In the fork of a bough of one tree, she spotted a honeybee hutch made from coconut shells. Hanging from the highest palms of a coconut tree near the house, were weaverbirds' nests. Although the manyar birds were rather fussy, their boisterous singing was not unpleasant to Srintil's ear. The sounds of birds in freedom were the sounds of nature.

Sentika appeared at the front door with his wife. His face was full of life, his jaws continuously moving as he chewed betel. Nyai Sentika's eyes fixed on Srintil who, although tired, still radiated beauty.

"My dear friends from Paruk. Come in. We've been waiting for you. We were worried that you wouldn't want to come to our isolated shack."

"Oh, my poor beautiful young lady," said Nyai Sentika, grasping Srintil's hand. "Please forgive us for forcing you to walk so far. Oh dear, my child, young beauty, please come in."

The warm welcome and open friendliness rendered the seven people from Paruk speechless, the enthusiasm of the hosts muting even Kartareja. They could only smile and laugh. Their smiles indicated a feeling of respect, a humbleness, now that they saw Sentika as a man of true wealth and power. Sentika lived like a minor king in this mountain village. As they entered his home, the Paruk villagers instinctively walked with a slight stoop, like palace servants. All, that is, except for Srintil. Her demeanor was exactly the same as always. While she indeed acknowledged that Sentika possessed considerable status and wealth, she did not feel she had to bow before the most powerful man of Alaswangkal.

Kartareja sat across from Sentika at a large round table. His wife sat with Nyai Sentika on a raised platform at the side of the expansive living room. Sakum and the other three musicians sat around the table. Srintil, however, did not wish to sit down. With considerable grace and dignity, she requested a room so that she could rest. Kartareja felt rather annoyed at her behavior. For him, being a guest meant being prepared to do the host's bidding.

"Of course my child, we've prepared a place for you. The servant will show you."

Mertanakim had not misled them. Sentika had indeed prepared a grand welcome for the Paruk troupe. Servants brought out coffee and *dodol* rice taffy, layer cake, and sticky rice. Cigarettes were distributed, a pack for each person. Bananas, other local fruits, and fresh coconut meat were offered. And, since it was lunch time, hot food was also served. Special rice from dry rice fields, with dishes made from vegetables, coconut milk, and chicken curry were set out on the table with a spicy sauce, and raw tiny chili peppers on the side. The Paruk villagers weren't used to such luxury.

After lunch, Sentika and Kartareja remained sitting on the verandah while Sakum and his three colleagues went off to rest. Between the host and the head of the ronggeng troupe, there were several matters to discuss.

"I'd like to organize social dancing with the ronggeng," said Sentika, opening up the discussion. "What do you think?"

"Oh, really? In my opinion, a ronggeng performance and social dancing should always go together. Without social dancing, the ronggeng tradition loses its attraction. However, these last few years, there's been an official prohibition against social dancing."

"But I'm determined to have it anyway. I guarantee there won't be any problems. Alaswangkal is a long way from any other village. I can take care of the village chief here. The social dancing is to be especially for Waras, my son. What do you say?"

"If that's what you want, you already know what my answer is."

"And I've bought a case of alcohol from the city."

"Well, it'll be a lively event tonight."

"But there's one more thing. And this is the most important. Is Srintil prepared to be a gowok? I'd be sorely disappointed if she has come all the way here only to dance."

Kartareja smiled, but responded cautiously.

"You'll have to forgive me. You see, although we've come this distance, I still can't give you a definite answer. You must speak directly to Srintil. No one knows what she is thinking."

"Really?"

"Yes. I don't even know. Since arriving in Alaswangkal, Srintil may have made up her mind. Perhaps she will decide that she wants to be become a gowok after seeing your son.

Sentika, at a loss for words, said nothing further. He had already arranged for a substitute in case Srintil refused to take on the role of a gowok. But this woman was absolutely no match for Srintil. And she would certainly lend no prestige to Sentika.

Meanwhile, in her room, Srintil wasn't interested in resting. The thing that was on her mind was how she might steal a look at her host's young son. This was necessary before she could make a decision about whether or not to agree to serve as a gowok. Should Sentika's son turn out to be greedy or bossy like Marsusi, or disfigured with empty sockets for eyes, like Sakum, then she would certainly refuse. On the other hand, if Waras looked like that man with the bowtie, Tri Murdo, or, if the boy was really seventeen, as Sentika claimed, that alone would make the experience interesting. The idea of carrying out the role of a gowok was something quite new for Srintil, and to service a boy younger than herself was even more novel. Two completely new experiences. If nothing else, Srintil felt challenged.

But she was growing impatient peeking out of her window. She still hadn't seen Waras. Earlier, when she had gone to the well outside, she had looked at every young man who could possibly have been Sentika's son. Her candidate, however, was not among them. She only saw members of the household staff, as well as some more well-dressed young women wearing ear studs and large necklaces. The latter were most certainly Sentika's daughters.

But Srintil didn't have to wait too long. Nyai Kartareja rushed into her room and urged her to go to the window.

"I've seen him," she said.

"Where was he?"

"In a moment you'll be able to see him from the window."

"Are you sure it's him?"

"Absolutely. I was behind the house with some women when a young boy approached from the direction of the forest. They told me that he was Waras, their employer's son."

"What did you think of him?"

"Look for yourself. I couldn't see him clearly. There!"

Outside, about twenty meters from the window, Srintil saw a young boy approaching, accompanied by a small child. Her first impression shattered Srintil's earlier fantasies. Waras was tall and thin. And he appeared even taller because he was wearing a singlet and knee-length trousers. His hair was cut in what was known as *polka* style, as if a bowl had been placed on his head and everything beneath it shaved, giving the impression that his head and neck had been stretched upwards. His shoulders were thin and narrow, his arms looked like a pair of bamboo reeds, pale yellow and without any muscle tone. And it appeared that, as his legs had grown, they had only increased in length without growing thicker, like those of a stork.

As he drew closer, Srintil could see him more clearly. She found it hard to believe that Waras was seventeen years old; his face looked far younger. There was no sign yet of masculinity. Srintil was so engrossed that she almost didn't see what it was that the boy was holding so lovingly. A baby oriole. In Paruk, Srintil often saw people keeping baby birds as pets, but usually only children ten years old or thereabouts, not long-legged teenagers like Waras. When she saw Waras feed a grasshopper to the bird, Srintil turned around. She stood silently staring at Nyai Kartareja. Her lips began to quiver and she exploded in laughter.

"Not so loud, young lady!"

Srintil continued laughing, burying her face in Nyai Kartareja's lap. The wife of the dukun pushed Srintil's face into her legs so that her laughter would not be heard outside.

Finally, Srintil stood up. Wiping her eyes, she spoke softly. "Nyai, teach me now what it means to be a gowok."

"So you want to be a gowok? But I can't teach you. I've never been one."

"Just teach me whatever you know."

"Wait a minute, young lady. Why now? What made you decide to become a gowok?"

Now not only Srintil laughed out loud, but Nyai Kartareja as well. Both laughed until they cried, and for a few moments they forgot that they were guests in someone else's home. Nyai Kartareja blurted out: "Once, when you undertook *bukak klambu*, you had to endure a forced honeymoon. Now is your chance to do the same thing to the male species!"

It seemed to the visitors that dusk fell more quickly in Alaswangkal than in Paruk, the hills to the west extinguishing the rays of sunlight earlier than they were accustomed to. Thousands of weaverbirds started chirping, growing more and more boisterous then slowly subsiding into silence. Dozens of chickens around the hamlet sought a place to roost in the bushes or in the shed where firewood was stored. Sometimes there were quarrels over the best places. In the growing stillness, the buzzing of honey bees could be heard. A crow screamed as it was attacked by a pair of *keket* birds. Then, silence. The darkening sky began to display an adornment of twinkling stars. Unlike in Paruk, the dusky sky of Alaswangkal was filled with fruit bats flying together in a single direction. They would fly to a particular area and attack a banyan or fruit-bearing tree and drink from the bamboo tubes that had been attached to the coconut trees to collect sap.

Sentika's house was brilliantly lit by three propane gas lights. The broad verandah with its stone tile floor had been prepared as the stage for the ronggeng dance. Tables were set up along the sides so that about twenty square meters of open space remained in the middle. There, a soft, fine mat made from pandanus leaves had been laid out.

The first spectators to arrive were the village women and children. Being the richest man in the district, Sentika had often sponsored ronggeng performances. But this was the first time that the ronggeng was Srintil from Paruk, and her fame had spread far beyond Dawuan.

As the evening grew darker, more and more torches began to move toward Sentika's house. All visitors brought a sense of joy and excitement. The children would be satisfied just to watch. The men came either expecting to feel aroused with passion or with nostalgia for past passions. The women would experience a strange feeling of pride. They were happy to see a ronggeng like Srintil show women's natural power over men. For the village women, the only time they could experience men being manipulated by the female sex, and not the other way around as was the usual state of affairs, was during a performance of ronggeng.

The front yard of Sentika's house quickly filled with spectators. In a spot in the middle where there was no overhanging foliage, incense was burning. Although the dry season had obviously arrived, Kartareja was not prepared to take any risks and had done what he always did to prevent rain.

In contrast to the bustle outside, one part of Sentika's house remained subdued. Here, Srintil was being introduced to Waras. On learning that she was willing to become a gowok for his son, Sentika had brought the two together. This meeting was witnessed by almost all of Sentika's extended family. Srintil was impressed by their honest, open friendliness. It was as if she had been accepted as a family member.

After a few moments, and without any apparent feeling of awkwardness, Srintil asked to speak with Waras alone. No one objected. On the contrary, Sentika and his children felt proud, and saw this as a sign that Srintil wished to become more intimate with Waras.

Alone, however, the two found themselves plunged into an awkward silence.

"I'm going to call you *kakang*, older brother, even though I'm older than you," said Srintil, opening the conversation.

Waras, already disturbed at suddenly being left alone with Srintil, seemed even more confused. But then he smiled, the smile of a child.

Srintil smiled back.

"So you don't mind if I call you *kang*?"

"Why do you want to do that?"

"I just want to."

"So, what should I call you?"

"Srintil. My name is Srintil. That's all."

"Okay. That's easy."

"It is easy. And, *kang*, do you like dancing?"

"You mean, watching dancing?"

"No. I mean dancing with a woman."

"I can't dance. But Daddy can dance really well. You should dance with my dad. I'll watch. Yeah!"

"Oh, no. You have to dance. It's easy."

"My dad can dance. Why do I have to?"

"If you dance, you'll get a reward."

"A reward?"

"Yes. I'll give you a reward after the performance. I'll spend some time with you."

"Spend some time with me? I already have friends. I spend time with lots of them. They help me look for grasshoppers to feed my bird."

"But, those are childish friends. What I mean is that, later, when you go to bed, I'll stay with you."

"But if you do that, where will Mommy sleep? There isn't enough room for three of us. Oh, I know, we'll roll out a mat on the floor then we can all sleep on it. I'll be in the middle, with mommy and you on either side. That'd be great, wouldn't it?"

Srintil didn't laugh, despite feeling amused at his response. She could see that some major trauma, be it genetic, psychological, or physical, had retarded Waras's development. If it wasn't a genetic factor, then whatever had happened had certainly occurred some time ago. Srintil could see the effect on the boy's posture and behavior. No, she could not laugh. She swallowed, moved by compassion. She held his hand, his arm thin as a reed. She felt as if she were holding the arm of a small child, soft and lacking in muscle tone.

"No, tonight it will just be the two of us. You and I. I'll hum a song to help you sleep. Your mommy doesn't sing to you, does she?"

"No, but she does stroke my head."

"I can do that."

"Mommy fans my face."

"I'm good at that too."

"Would, you go with me when I go out back to pee?"

"Of course."

"And if I want to play before I go to sleep?"

"That would be great."

"Hurray! You're really nice. I like you."

Waras stood up and hugged Srintil, pulling her close and kissing her. Srintil was passive. Amused. There was nothing sexual about it.

From a hidden spot, Sentika and his wife saw what their son did, and their hopes soared. Their eyes were moist with tears. What they had hoped for all this time had finally happened. Waras had kissed a woman. He had held a ronggeng in his arms, a sign that he might at last be interested in the opposite sex. Indeed, it could have been a sign, although not necessarily so. Nevertheless, for Sentika and his wife, it was enough for now. Nyai Sentika's joy overflowed. She called out to her four daughters, all of whom were already married.

"Come here! Look at your little brother. He's kissing a ronggeng!"

At eight o'clock Sakum and his friends sat ready at their instruments. Because they had been so well treated by their host, the entire ronggeng troupe was in fine form. Srintil was getting dressed, assisted by Nyai Kartareja. Sentika's daughters watched the ronggeng as she prepared herself, their hearts full of admiration. Outside, the noise level from the spectators began to rise. Those in back of the crowd shouted for the ones in front to squat or sit down. Children and women were pushed aside.

Sentika appeared in the empty space in the middle of the verandah. He told the spectators about the celebration and asked that they become witnesses that night. By watching the ronggeng performance, they would witness that Sentika had fulfilled the vow he had made on behalf of his son.

Waras, for his part, sat alone at the front, his shirt pockets stuffed with money. Waras looked happy, displaying the expression he usually showed when he was playing with his baby oriole.

As practiced hands began playing the calung instruments, the mood of the spectators became more lively. Sakum, in peak form, instantly drew the attention of every spectator. His empty eyes, his adept hands, and his foolish and hilarious calls brought noisy applause. A pack of cigarettes from the middle of the densely packed audience flew through the air toward the musicians. The first pack was followed by others, and several even came from a group of female spectators.

The audience grew silent as Srintil emerged. Jostling spectators calmed down and waited with anticipation. Srintil was a picture of elegance. She was at the very peak of her physical and emotional development, in full bloom, and she quickly seized everyone's attention. For several long moments she stood there, her lips parted into a slight smile and her eyes radiating the cool clear light of morning dew. She formed an image which combined authority and beauty. In those brief moments, she made it obvious to her public that the master of that evening's performance was neither Sentika nor his son, but Srintil herself.

She stepped forward and sat down elegantly in front of the musicians as they played, raising her face as if to convince the audience of its beauty. She began to sing, her clear voice flowing, weaving a melody into the calung music. The audience exploded into applause. A profound joy gripped the soul of every person present.

When she had decided to become a gowok for Waras, Srintil had been fully aware of the crucial role she had been taken on. She had to have the power to take on several roles for a boy who hardly could be thought of as masculine, and who had obviously grown up with a major handicap. This realization was the instinct of a true ronggeng. And it emerged powerfully during her performance and colored one of her dance movements, interpretable only by those souls sensitive toward surges of the spirit.

Hundreds of eyes watched Srintil perform. The most important people of Alaswangkal sat near the stage, including the village chief. But Srintil felt she was dancing for one person only, a young boy who compelled Srintil to act sometimes as his mother, sometimes as his younger sister, and sometimes as his playmate. At one point Srintil's voice became soft and her face calm, a mother embracing and stroking her child. At another, her voice filled with energy, her movements became athletic, a mother teaching her child to walk. And at yet another point in the performance, she smiled at Waras, her movements seductive, as if she wanted to arouse the desire of the boy from Alaswangkal.

Deep inside, Waras could feel a stirring of enthusiasm. Sitting next to the stage, he was beaming, his eyes bright. But when Srintil danced close to him and bent her face to his, Waras did not react in the way the spectators had hoped, especially his mother and father. Waras did not kiss Srintil. Rather, he put his two hands on her cheeks. Even this rather dissatisfying vignette did not escape the perceptive instincts of the blind Sakum. At the exact moment Waras's hands touched Srintil's cheek, Sakum pointedly vocalized; "Siusssss!!" And the audience whistled and cheered. Waras then clapped his hands in joy, and jumped up and down like a baby lamb after draining its mother's teat.

The troupe played set after set. Alaswangkal, usually quietly hidden behind forests of teak and fields of cassava, came alive with calung music and the cheers of its citizens watching Srintil dance. Their host had ordered his servants to serve large jugs filled with rice gin. After only half an hour, several of the men were already drunk, shouting incessantly. The village chief became restless, his senses confused by the gin. Suddenly, the hollow-cheeked old man stood up and staggered to the center of the stage. Standing with his legs wide apart and his arms open, he began to dance, inviting Srintil to join him. He sang a traditional song, but his words were disjointed and slurred, and his voice sluggish. His face was burning red with lust and alcohol.

At first Srintil thought that the chief's appearance on stage would upset Waras. But no. Waras clapped his hands to inspire the village chief, shouting with glee when he saw the man's hand groping Srintil's chest, ostensibly to place money down the front of her camisole. Finally Waras stood up. With his fists full of money, he imitated the village chief. At the appropriate moment, without missing a beat, Sakum vocalized: "Scesssss!"

The festivities at Sentika's house finally ended after the cocks began to crow and dawn began to break. Srintil had danced and sung for more than seven hours. During that time, she had accommodated the men who wanted to dance; many of them had been satisfied only after she had sat on their laps. Two or three times she had retreated to her room to straighten her clothes, especially those covering her chest. Equally often, she had had to reapply powder to her face, particularly to her cheeks when she was most often touched.

As the rays of the sun began to brush over the hills and sweep the morning mist away, Srintil was sound asleep in her room. By this time, the home of the cassava merchant was bustling with servants busy clearing up after the evening's festivities. Sentika's daughters were still there, enjoying the novelty of having a ronggeng staying at their parents' home, and fully aware that, beginning that day, Srintil was to be a gowok. What Waras would do with a gowok was a subject of considerable interest and speculation amongst his relatives.

Waras awoke, as usual, to the sound of his pet baby birds cheeping. But on this occasion he wasn't interested in feeding the baby orioles. As soon as he got out of bed, he went looking for his mother who was busy in the kitchen:

"Where is she?"

"Who?"

"The one that danced last night. The one whose front I put money down. Where is she? She didn't go home, did she?"

Nyai Sentika's shoulders slumped with relief. The fact that he had asked for Srintil indicated to her that Waras was a real man, healthy in mind and body. Her eyes became moist.

"She's still sleeping. Do you like Srintil?'

"Yes, I do. She's pretty, isn't she?"

"Do you know what it means to be pretty?"

"Yeah. Her skin is soft and her mouth is red like the mouth of the baby oriole. And she has nice eyes."

"Yes."

"I'll go and wake her up. I'll ask her if she wants to play."

"No, don't do that. Wait until she wakes up herself."

Waras' face fell with disappointment and he grumbled to himself.

"You should go and wash yourself. Srintil won't want to play with a person who hasn't washed and dressed properly."

"Really?"

"Yes, really. Go on, off to the well."

Waras skipped off. People watched him with amusement. It was a tragic joke. Only Nyai Sentika held out any real hope behind her restrained smile.

At eight o'clock, Srintil opened her eyes to find Nyai Sentika sitting quietly near her bed. Without any sign of embarrassment, Srintil got up and straightened her clothes, in disarray after she had fallen into bed without undressing the previous night. Her long black hair had come down, and she quickly tied it up as best she could without the assistance of a mirror. Every movement was followed by Nyai Sentika, who never tired of admiring the ronggeng's vivaciousness.

"So, you've woken now, young lady?"

"Yes, Nyai. Is it late?"

"Not very. About eight or so. Nyai Kartareja and the troupe have already left for home. Everything's taken care of."

Srintil smiled vaguely, while Nyai Sentika smiled with a sense of satisfaction. She told Srintil that she and her husband intended to absent themselves for a while. Her husband did, in fact, intend to leave the area for several days, but Nyai Sentika just wanted to get out of the house and stay in hiding at one of the neighbors' homes. Her daughters would be leaving for their homes later that morning or early in the afternoon.

"We should have prepared a house especially for you and Waras, but we felt that it would be better if we just let you stay in this house together. You can sleep in any of the bedrooms, except for my room, of course. And so I put my son in your hands. Ah, such as he is. Actually, I should be embarrassed, but…" she couldn't continue the thought. "The important thing is that I believe in you."

"Hey! She's awake!" declared Waras, suddenly appearing in the doorway. He was wearing a brand new shirt and his pockets were full of change. A pair of long skinny legs emerged beneath his black knee-length pants.

"What'd she say? Does she want to play with me?"

"Of course I do," Srintil announced before Nyai Sentika could answer. "Later, we'll play to our hearts' content. But I want to bathe first. You wait for me here."

"Don't be long."

"Okay."

"Then you'll dress up like last night?"

"Yes."

But Waras did not want to wait. He followed Srintil to the well, skipping along with joy. The well was located in a small valley behind the house. Waras drew water from the well to fill the wooden tank so that Srintil could use a dipper and splash water on herself to bathe. He filled the tank until it overflowed.

"Go ahead and bathe. I'll stay right here."

"You'll stay here?"

"Yeah."

"No, don't stay."

"My mom lets me watch when she washes herself."

"She does?"

"Yeah. Hey! Last night I put money down the front of your blouse. Let me see if it's still there?"

"I've already put the money away. It's not there anymore."

"Really? But I still want to see."

"No."

"You said we were friends. You were just tricking me, weren't you?"

"Of course not."

"So, how come you won't let me see your chest?"

Srintil could hardly keep herself from laughing. She squatted in front of Waras and opened her camisole, revealing her breasts completely.

"See, there's no money here, okay?"

"Yeah. I believe you now. But my mom's tits are thin and flabby. How come yours aren't?"

This time Srintil could not come up with an answer. So she scooped some water with her hands and splashed him. The virgin boy shrieked with delight. He had no other understanding apart from the fact that a game he liked had begun. He drew water from the well and poured it directly over Srintil. The game soon turned chaotic, water splashing everywhere. Many people spied on the two at play, well-hidden so they couldn't be seen. Some smiled with pleasure, amused at the antics. Most of them, however, smiled sadly, feeling only pity.

That day Sentika's home was like a magical forest from a children's story as a pair of childish creatures played, their pleasure arising from a purity, an innocence possessed only by kittens, cubs, and pups. It was Srintil who always took the initiative. At first she invited Waras to play "marriage". Srintil dressed up like a bride, beautiful beyond words. Waras wore his father's traditional headdress. They sat together as if they were the bride and groom in a Javanese wedding ceremony.

"In the story, you become my husband. And I become your wife," said Srintil. "And now that I've become your wife, I'd like some money to go shopping."

And so forth. Later, Srintil asked Waras to chop some firewood for the wood stove. Waras attacked this chore with a fervor that could hardly be likened to play. His body was covered with sweat and his hands became blistered from the ax handle. However, his labor only produced an embarrassingly small number of tiny splinters. Meanwhile, Srintil went out behind the house carrying a small basket. She picked cassava shoots and *kecipir* leaves. Who would have thought that this woman, who seemed to know all about matters of the kitchen, was a ronggeng. All that village people knew was there was an art to picking vegetables and an art to holding baskets. Srintil executed both tasks expertly and elegantly. She had the flexible manner of a real housewife, an attractiveness that manifested itself as she put her heart and soul into playing her role as a gowok.

Yet there was more to it than that. Her desire to represent the world of women honed her sense of responsibility toward this boy who was unable to become a man. This sense of responsibility instinctively turned into a self-awareness out of which emerged a complete image of womanhood. Srintil picked the shoots of the young cassava so delicately that the plant hardly trembled. She carried her basket with grace: a synthesis of delicate hands and sinuous hips. A perfect combination that was captivating, pliant, and attractive.

After playing house for almost half the day, Srintil called Waras, who was still outside chopping wood, to dinner. She had prepared plain white rice with several dishes on the side: fried tempeh, a spicy sauce and vegetables in hot sauce. After setting the table, Srintil had prepared a pinch of tobacco she'd found in a cabinet, a gesture toward the adult male world of smoking.

Waras entered, his face gleaming with perspiration and his hands filthy. Srintil drew water from a large jug with a dipper, for him to wash his hands.

"We've played 'marriage', and 'house'. What are we going to play next?" Waras asked, his mouth full of rice.

Srintil thought a moment. The baby oriole cheeped in its cage.

"Next is 'sleeping together'. You're tired from chopping wood and I'm tired from my work in the kitchen. So, the next thing we do is sleep together. That will be fun, won't it?"

"Yeah, but not just yet. I have to find a grasshopper for my bird."

"Don't go out. I want to sleep. I want to sleep with you."

Waras raised his head for a moment, then returned to eating a handful of rice. "So, you like playing sleeping together? Is it your favorite game?"

Srintil responded with a smile, her eyes gazing at him sleepily. It was a suggestive look designed to evoke the most primitive feelings of a man, a look that would normally bring a man's nerves to a quivering standstill and tease his heart to beat faster and more heavily. Srintil, an emissary from the realm of femininity, who instinctively and totally understood the prime function of her existence, knew full well how to arouse men with a mere look.

But Waras just sat stupefied for a moment. In some vague way he could understand that Srintil's smile was not like the smile of his mother. The look in her eyes made him feel strange. It brought about the soft twitching of a basic instinct he had never even known existed until that moment. Even within his limitations, Waras saw something in Srintil's eyes that was new to him.

"I once captured a mourning dove at night," he said suddenly. "I used a torch to see it. Have you ever seen mourning doves sleeping? They sleep in pairs, close together."

"So they do."

"In the middle of the day, they sometimes fly one on top of the other. I see it all the time. My friends once caught a pair of starlings that were doing that. They fell from the top of a tree all the way to the ground. They were like stuck together.

"Goats are like that too. And chickens! Have you ever seen monkeys doing it?"

"No, never."

"It's great. Really fun to watch."

Waras continued to describe the sexual habits of the various animals that he had seen. He spoke quickly, but without any sense of excitement. Srintil listened patiently, believing that eventually he would talk about the sexual practices of his own species. Yet such a topic never came up in his ramblings. Waras seemed to be talking about something that couldn't possibly happen among human beings, about a world far removed from his own being.

Nevertheless, Srintil did succeed in taking Waras into the bedroom, inviting him to play "sleeping together". The concept of sleep for Waras was simple. For him it meant lying down next to his mother, in a fetal position. His right arm would be buried in her armpit and his left hand would fidget with the cloth of her bra. Or, he might squeeze and pull her nipple. And this is what he did with Srintil.

At first, Srintil felt that what was expected to happen, would indeed happen and she waited with a willingness that was virtually unconditional and completely selfless. Yet her waiting was in vain. Waras stopped playing with her bra and started whimpering softly like a baby. Eventually his movements lessened. His eyes closed, and he began to snore. Waras was deep in the dreams of a little boy.

Srintil got up, moving softly so as not to awaken him. She stood and watched the sleeping boy, cursing the cause of his incompleteness. She wondered what had caused him to exist yet not really exist in the world. She was not willing to accept that what had happened to him was the will of the Creator. As a ronggeng, Srintil believed that night is mated to day and cool air to hot fire. Srintil was the Feminine and, as such, felt cheated when faced with the absence of the Masculine.

Srintil's understanding was that everything in the world had its mate, an understanding that was deeply rooted in her belief system and was not easily shaken. As long as she believed in her femininity, she believed that Waras possessed masculinity. A gowok was an artist in the management of the masculine primal instinct. If this was lost, then she had to find it. Srintil reminded herself that this was the reason for her coming to Alaswangkal. Yet, there was more to it than that. Without even being employed as a gowok, Srintil would have done this for her own personal reasons, reasons that couldn't be understood by other women, not even, perhaps, the woman who had given birth to Waras.

The following night, after the commotion of the weaver birds nesting in the coconut trees had long subsided, and when their voices had been replaced by the cries of bats fighting over the fruit trees, and the moon had emerged over the hills, Srintil took a bolder approach. She gently guided the conversation, asking Waras to demonstrate how monkeys mated, with her acting the role of the female. At first, Waras seemed confused, and then flatly refused.

"Those are monkeys that do that. We can't do something like that. Momma says that it's obscene. It's not nice. And I've never seen people act the way monkeys do. Have you?"

Srintil, considering carefully how to responded, slowly nodded her head. Waras gazed at her in utter amazement. Srintil tried to explain, but the expression on his face told her that he was convinced that men and women could not possibly engage in such activities. Srintil had to accept the fact that Waras was lost to the world of men and that she was unable to bring out his masculinity.

She resigned herself to a feeling of deep disappointment, not because her own personal needs were left unsatisfied, but because, for this particular man, her femininity had no meaning, something she had never imagined would happen to her.

That night, Waras compared her again to his mother. Breast full, not flabby. Her cheeks taut, arms and legs lithe, and her body warmer. Her breath fresh, like a baby. That night he fell asleep earlier and more deeply. He had never once asked why they had been left alone, just the two of them, in that large house. He had forgotten about his mother and anyone else who, until then, had cared for him.

That night, Srintil was aware that someone was outside the bedroom door. In the almost total stillness, she could hear soft breathing. She realized that she had to do something. So she started moving her legs rhythmically. Then she pinched Waras's nose briefly and released it. Waras gasped for breath, and Srintil moaned.

Hearing the sounds, the two people outside of bedroom hugged one another in deep satisfaction. Nyai Sentika and her husband tiptoed away, fully believing that their son was now a real man, that there was nothing wrong with him. Possibly the rhythmic movements Srintil had made with her legs reminded the aging couple of their youth, and they went off to find a place where they could experience their nostalgia together.

The fourth and last day dawned. Early in the morning, Srintil said goodbye to Sentika and his wife. It was a deeply emotional parting. Nyai Sentika and her daughters wept, as did Srintil. Nyai Sentika hugged her, and stroked her back as if she were her own child. Waras, still asleep, wasn't even aware of her departure.

As the thin fog began to dissipate, burned away by the sun, Srintil descended the hill, leaving Alaswangkal behind her. Mertanakim followed, assigned by his employer to accompany the ronggeng back to Paruk. In her hand Srintil carried a cloth purse filled with money. But all this money could not expel the heartache she felt in returning home a complete failure in her estimation. She would never forget Waras and the sadness she felt for his enduring calamity. She would have felt worse if she had known that Waras had cried pitifully, wailing and rolling on the ground when he learned that she had left him. That she had returned to her secluded world: to Paruk.

5

No one in Paruk owned a calendar. And even if anyone did, no one would have been able to read that the year was 1964. Paruk was feeling proud of its beautiful ronggeng dancer, a young woman just eighteen years old. The little hamlet had achieved a fame it had never known in its entire history.

Whenever the Paruk ronggeng troupe performed, hundreds of people gathered to watch. They never seemed to tire of hearing calung music and Banyumas songs. For Srintil, performing was still very special for her. She was the essence of freshness and passion. Watching her, even recalling her performances, had the effect of freeing people from the tedium of their everyday life. And whether they admitted it or not, the ronggeng performances had become a necessity for each and every person. For the men in particular, Srintil was a fantasy, a soaring butterfly that many wanted to capture.

Several homes had broken up as a result of the husbands attempting to possess Srintil, or to take her as a wife. Many young men had felt compelled to sell their possessions to become a worthy suitor, worthy even of holding her hand. And none of them cared whether Srintil was truly beautiful or just seemed pretty because of an illusion created by the practice, known as *susuk,* of inserting slivers of gold or a small diamond under the skin behind an eyebrow or lip, or in the buttocks.

In Paruk, however, Srintil did not present a danger to domestic tranquility. None of the married woman there felt threatened by her beauty. Perhaps they felt that they still had blood ties with her, being descendants of a common ancestor. Or, perhaps they were conscious of being connected by common, uniquely local, customs, and social norms. It was not unusual for a pregnant woman, or a woman who had recently given birth, to tell her husband to ask a special favor from Srintil. A midwife often gave similar advice to the husband. "Be careful not to have sex with your wife before a hundred days has passed after the birth. Ask Srintil to help you if you can't hold out."

For such primordial reasons, Srintil usually gave herself willingly, but the relationships never went any further. No local man felt bold enough to become close to her, not just because she was quite wealthy by Paruk standards, or because she seemed far superior to the average villager there, but mainly because she possessed a personal dignity that set her apart. Unlike any previous ronggeng, Srintil could not be bought with money alone. Some people noticed that she would only service the men she liked. Others thought that she only accepted men with pretty wives. And if the man was not of an adventurous nature, she would often take the initiative by teasing him.

In 1964 Paruk was very much as it had always been: crude, diseased, and its inhabitants ignorant. The only small changes that were apparent involved Srintil, Sakarya, and Kartareja. Their homes were now whitewashed and even sported glass windows. Kartareja and Sakarya owned propane gas lanterns. Other than that, the village was the same as it had been for several generations. In fact, over recent years, it had probably become even gloomier. The tiny hamlet could not avoid the economic decline which had been affecting the whole nation for some time.

Not only did Paruk not have the wherewithal to understand the nation's economic plight, nature was testing its inhabitants as well. Banana and coconut trees began to droop, leaves started falling, and the bamboo groves were withering. The broad wet rice fields surrounding the village had become dry and barren due to an unusually hotter and longer dry season. On one occasion it rained, and the rice fields turned green and lush. The people thought that there would be a crop and that they could find work helping harvest the rice. But rats and a plague of insects beat them to it. Even wild pigs joined in to dash their hopes.

In the village, the people were able to cope with the effects of the drought and put off starvation for a time. They knew how to cook various kinds of normally inedible wild foods in a special way so that they were not poisoned by tubers, or their tongues were not paralyzed by wild taro. Oddly enough, they refused to eat the flesh of rats, even though at that time the practice was advocated in government propaganda, and the eating of rat satay was demonstrated at public rallies and meetings.

Normally, during times of food shortage, ronggeng performances were rarely given, as people gave priority to obtaining rice over entertaining themselves. Srintil would remain at home for months, waiting for a good harvest, or for the moment when parents wishing to circumcise or marry off their child had the money to pay for a celebration. During these periods she had to endure long periods of boredom.

However, in 1964, when famine was spreading like wildfire throughout the country, the ronggeng of Paruk found herself performing more often than ever. Not at places where people held ritual celebrations, but at public meetings, held both in the daytime and at night.

At these rallies, the members of the ronggeng troupe became acquainted with Bakar, a man from Dawuan who was a very clever orator and always gave fiery speeches. Although he was gray-haired, he had an enthusiasm for life that belied his age.

In Srintil's eyes, Bakar was a perfect father figure. He was friendly, and seemed to understand many things, including her personal feelings. His fatherly role was not only apparent from the generous amount of money he always paid her, but also evidenced in his cool disinterest regarding erotically-oriented matters. Bakar presented Srintil and her troupe with the gift of a complete sound system, the first electronic equipment to enter Paruk Village, and it became a source of great pride among its inhabitants.

In their naivety, the villagers instantly accepted Bakar as a wise man, one who could lead and protect them. Whenever he came to the village, the orator was treated with great respect. Following his orders, each entrance to the village was adorned with party symbols, and a sign was erected in front of Kartareja's house. No one in the village could read the words on the sign, but they believed that the writing had something to do with the ronggeng tradition. No one had objected. No one, that is, except Sakarya.

On one occasion Sakarya asked Kartareja about what was happening.

"Do you remember the time the group played for the Independence Day celebration last year?"

"Yes, of course. Why?"

"That's when we were first called a troupe of proletariat musicians, even though we never publicized any kind of name like that. At that performance, I wasn't allowed to set out any offerings or burn incense. The person who called us 'folk musicians' and told me not to make offerings was this man, Bakar, I'm sure of it. Now he's coming here all the time. What do you make of it all?"

"I don't know. What do you think?"

"I don't know. We've never experienced anything like this before. A ronggeng was always just a ronggeng. We never needed a name or a sign. Paruk was just Paruk: without posters of political slogans at every entrance. Oh, Kartareja. What do we do about this?"

Kartareja was silent.

"And," continued Sakarya, "what are we going to do if we're not allowed to make offerings anymore! That is the worst kind of transgression against our traditional laws. Kartareja, I'm terrified of the consequences."

Kartareja was still silent, but he felt the same.

"I understand. Unfortunately, it all comes down to Bakar, and he's been good to us. We're indebted to him. Maybe we should break off our ties with him. Can you think of how we might do that?"

Now it was Sakarya's turn to be silent. To break off relations with someone was something almost unheard of. If it did happen, there had to be a legitimate excuse, an argument for example. But Bakar had not created a dispute. He had only prohibited Sakarya from burning incense and setting out offerings when a performance of ronggeng was about to begin. And this always happened outside the village. On the other hand, he had come to the hamlet with a fatherly attitude, giving them a sound system, even presented the musicians with complete outfits. Srintil had received a batik wrap-around skirt and a bright red dance scarf.

"Maybe," said Kartareja.

"We don't really need to worry about the signs and posters," Kartareja posed. It's the same everywhere else. I think it's just the times. If that's what the times call for, then maybe we should submit to them?"

"Maybe. Who can refuse the demands of the times? But the matter of offerings involves everyone in the village as well as our ancestor, Ki Secamenggala. Whatever the times may be, we cannot change these customs. We are not permitted to do this!"

"There's a way out of this though. What about this. Before we leave for a performance, let's make the offerings here first. Or at the grave of Ki Secamenggala. I think that would do just as well."

Sakarya was not entirely satisfied with Kartareja's answer. Being the village elder, a position he had inherited through his forefathers, was not a simple matter for him. Deep inside, he was unwilling to accept change, and he wanted to see Paruk remain as it had always been, especially in the way its inhabitants honored the spirit of their ancestor. But he felt too old to worry about such weighty matters.

He was well aware that he had reached an age where many of his wishes simply remained wishes. He no longer had the drive to turn them into reality. In the end, he accepted Kartareja's proposal.

Wherever Bakar went, his speeches were filled with propaganda which was incomprehensible to the simple people from Paruk. He spoke about the struggles of the downtrodden masses in regaining their rights, matters which the villagers would always find impossible to understood, even if they were explained a thousand times to them. The people from Paruk believed that life followed a predetermined course that could not be changed; a story in a book that could not be altered because the ink had long since dried. Thus to them, there was no point in struggling. And the concept of rights was contradictory to their fatalistic attitude of simply accepting what life offers.

However, it seemed that Bakar had worked out a solution to deal with the people of Paruk. In the village he never spoke about issues like "struggles" and "rights". All he wanted was to use Srintil and her troupe as a means to draw the masses and, at the same, to put him in a position of authority. He had achieved this goal at relatively little cost: the purchase of a sound system, some new clothes, and the adoption of a paternalistic attitude. He had even succeeded in adapting the lyrics of the traditional songs sung by the ronggeng to include political slogans.

Thus, the ronggeng troupe of Paruk had unwittingly become a part of the propaganda rallies organized by Bakar and his people. The rallies, packed with people, always turned into noisy, unruly affairs. It was not important to Bakar whether the people came to see him or Srintil. What was important was that large masses of people were gathered together and that he had the opportunity to manipulate their emotions. And it was not only emotions he sought to manipulate. A man like Bakar, with his head full of theories, was well aware that more complex issues, such as political ideologies, were difficult for simple villagers to understand. Most of these people did not possess the intellectual means to grasp ideological concepts.

If there was a basic ideology among the villagers, it would be along the lines of the messianic belief that they were awaiting the arrival of Ratu Adil, the Just King. Aware of this basic belief system, Bakar used it successfully in his dealings with the village people. His group took on the role of messengers from Ratu Adil, promising delivery of justice, through promoting ideas like the equal distribution of land, regardless of rank or position.

Srintil did not understand the need for political rallies, speeches, and parades. In particular, she didn't understand the purpose of the rallies which preceded her dance performances. All she really understood was that she, a simple child of life and nature, was the most important element of Paruk Village. She lived according to the basic belief that her life followed the lines of a blueprint, the blueprint of a ronggeng.

She had pursued the trajectory of her life willingly. She had become a ronggeng, accepting it as her duty in life. She possessed the ability to manipulate a primitive human instinct: that of sexual desire. This provided her with a role which freed her from the usual social norms and ethics. That was her world, her world view. Believing this, Srintil was aware that something was missing when she performed at the rallies. She was unable to say what it was exactly, but her instincts told her that her presence was somehow being trivialized. A ronggeng was femininity, a woman who danced, sang, and willingly serviced masculinity. She had to be independent and unaffected in that role. But, as long as she followed Bakar, she was unsure of why and for whom she performed.

While her insights were naïve, Srintil continued to believe that her ronggeng performances at the rallies were just a kind of supplement. They were lively, but different. Noisy, but somehow empty of meaning. Even the texts of many of the songs had been changed. The spectators were always worked up into a wild frenzy which she could not understand, and this sometimes terrified her. Even the blind Sakum was affected by the change, she noticed. The calung player had lost his characteristic spontaneity, no longer calling out or making amusing vocalizations at the precise moments the ronggeng thrust or swayed her hips. Sakum, with his heightened sensitivity and perceptiveness, was well aware of the aridness of a ronggeng performance in the context of such rallies.

Srintil frequently wondered why all these new thoughts had come to her only at the time Bakar's favors had accumulated to a point where she could not avoid feeling deeply indebted to the man. Once, she wanted to try refusing to perform at an event but, when Bakar's envoy came to pick her up, she found she was unable to say anything. She could not bring herself to say no.

By the end of 1964, Srintil, now closely associated with Bakar and his followers, had become popularly known as the "Ronggeng of the Proletariat". Her previous title, "Ronggeng of Paruk Village" was all but forgotten.

Srintil found that the less frequently she heard the name of her village the more she missed it. Paruk, a village without a public address system or political symbols, was real to her, despite its being miserable and crude. It had no need for the commotion and noise of rallies.

Her longing for the world she had known reached a peak after an experience that shook her to the core, and she discovered another side of Bakar. One night, after a rally in which she had danced, hundreds of the spectators went berserk. As if possessed, they rampaged through rice paddies, plundering the ripening crops. The situation became violent as the owners arrived to protect their fields. By the time the police had arrived, seven bodies lay on the ground covered in blood.

This first brawl was followed by a second a month later, and another the following month. During the third riot, the situation was particularly tense. It took place in the daytime, and involved hundreds of aggressors fighting the owners of fields. A full-scale war of hoes and sickles was avoided only because of the timely arrival of the police.

The horror of what was happening brought Srintil to a decision, and Sakarya was in full agreement with her. The two of them went to Bakar's home in Dawuan to tell him how the situation was affecting them all.

"Bakar," said Sakarya. "We Paruk villagers do not want to be involved in riots. If this goes on, you will bring about our downfall. We can't bear violence and can no longer participate in your political rallies."

"You see, sir," interrupted Srintil. "People will associate us with the unrest in the paddy fields."

"You shouldn't be swayed by such sentimental feelings," Bakar told them. "What's happening is just a form of mass action, a reaction by the poor who have long suffered injustice. They have sweated working the paddy fields owned by a few, but have never benefited from their labor, except to receive just enough to subsist, sometimes less than that. All they are doing now is demanding what's rightfully theirs."

"With violence like that which occurred the other day?"

"With whatever it takes."

"So you agree with what these ruffians are doing?"

"I can't prohibit a mass action which is part of the struggle for justice."

"Then, enough said! We don't want to be a part of this kind of business any longer, so please do not do anything more on behalf of the people of Paruk. We don't want to be involved in any kind of unrest."

"Wait a minute, Sakarya," replied Bakar, with a smile. "I happen to know that what took place in the fields around here is nothing unusual for Paruk villagers. Do you think I'm not aware of what your ancestor did in the past?"

Sakarya was astounded. He never thought he'd hear such words from Bakar: contemptuous remarks regarding Paruk's forefather, whose descendants held him in sacred esteem. It was true that Ki Secamenggala had been a criminal and the leader of a gang of robbers that had murdered many people. Nevertheless, Ki Secamenggala was the man to whom all the inhabitants of Paruk were related by blood and whom they now revered.

"Bakar. I am offended by your remarks. You don't know who Ki Secamenggala was. You might have forgotten that our ancestor did not die in the act of robbery or some other criminal act. He died peacefully in a quiet place in Paruk, an old man full of regrets. Among his final words, he forbade his descendants from doing anything that might hurt someone, particularly acting violently."

"Is that so?"

"Yes, and from this moment, I am forbidding the ronggeng troupe from participating in any political rallies."

"I don't want to be associated with all this fighting," Srintil added.

Bakar thought for a moment, slowly nodding his head. His expression relaxed.

"Fine. I guess all of you need some rest anyway."

"And we'd like you to take back your party posters and the sign.

"Let's not go that far. Leave the posters up. I won't take them down, and I don't want anyone to remove them. If anyone does, there will be trouble from my men. You don't want any problems in the village, do you?"

Srintil and her grandfather returned home feeling partly relieved, believing that they had extricated themselves from a relationship that had been difficult to avoid from the start. In this late period of his life, Sakarya did not wish to see changes in his ancestral village. While there still was the outstanding matter of the political posters and the sign, he felt he could accept this in exchange for the sound system that Bakar had given to the village.

Back in Paruk, Goder, now two years old and able to walk, had become ever more receptive of Srintil's motherly love. No one from outside the village would have thought that their relationship was based only on a woman's basic instinct and a baby's pure heart. Goder, always naked, was as round as an eggplant and as healthy as a young sprout. Living with Srintil, he received more gifts than any other baby in Paruk. He owned all the toys that could be purchased in the Dawuan market. Srintil even went so far as buying goats and butchering a chicken in his name. The year before, she had purchased a plot of wet rice field in Goder's name.

People said that Srintil spoiled Goder so much because she worried that his real mother, Tampi, would take him back. This may have been the reason. But Srintil believed that the things she did for Goder could not be measured against the happiness she felt in being able to hold him close to her every day. Goder was her hope for the future should her fate be like that of most ronggeng: to live her old age in loneliness because of her barren womb.

For some weeks, the calung instruments that usually accompanied the ronggeng were kept in storage. Paruk was cut off from the political rallies and parades, the turmoil of which affected the surrounding villages. By taking the attitude that they did not want to know anything and by remaining aloof the people of Paruk believed that they could preserve the original character of their village.

However, the calm in the village didn't last long. One day, Sakarya discovered to his horror that the gravesite of Ki Secamenggala had been vandalized, an act that struck the village to its very core.

Within moments of the discovery, the whole village population had climbed the hill in the cemetery. Children were led or carried by their mothers. The blind Sakum followed his son's footsteps. Everyone came with feelings of sadness and boundless rage. Two old women wept hysterically.

"This is surely Bakar's doing. That son of a bitch! The scoundrel!" cursed Sakarya, his voice hoarse. "That bastard is annoyed because we don't want to associate with him anymore. The son of a bitch!"

"We won't put up with this!" yelled Kartareja. "Beloved Grandfather, may the persons that wrecked your grave die of yaws, or be covered with sores. May they all die of syphilis!"

"Hey, Darkim!" called out Sakarya to one of the village boys. "Tear down and burn all the political party posters. Tear down the sign too, the one in front of Kartareja's house."

As Darkim descended the hill in the cemetery to carry out Sakarya's orders, another boy suddenly appeared from behind some bushes holding a cone-shaped farmer's hat made of bamboo, the type of hat worn by farmers in the region. It was painted green and had writing on it that nobody could decipher.

"I found this behind the bushes. No one here owns anything like this. It must belong to the scoundrels that vandalized the gravesite."

The villagers grew silent, tense. All eyes focused on the green painted hat and, while no one was able to read the letters on it, they all knew one thing for certain. Bakar's people never wore hats like that.

Sakarya's shoulders slumped and he sighed heavily. The village elder walked around the ruins of the gravesite, his arms folded.

"Go home, my children. Get your tools. We'll repair the tomb immediately."

News of the destruction of Ki Secamenggala's tomb quickly spread through the district, even though no one from Paruk related anything about the sacrilege outside the confines of the hamlet. And word spread that the vandals had worn green hats. In 1965, everyone knew that the members of the land owners' organization, whenever they paraded or gathered in rallies, wore such hats.

Never before had the people of Paruk felt so deeply insulted. The hamlet was gloomy and quiet with restrained rage. The inhabitants were all of one mind, ready to pay back with interest the insult they had received. Revenge was only postponed because they couldn't determine the names of the perpetrators.

Reporting the matter to the police only added frustration and disappointment to their feelings of outrage. After five days the police still could not provide any clues as to the identity of the vandals. They made it worse by forbidding the villagers from taking any action themselves in response to what had happened.

Eventually, the people of Paruk found a way to vent their anger: not by swinging machetes or beating the heads of people wearing green hats, but by accepting Bakar's invitation to return to the propaganda rallies. Srintil resumed dancing with extraordinary enthusiasm. She no longer cared whether her performances were in accordance with the true spirit of the ronggeng tradition. By dancing more boldly and more defiantly, she felt she was retaliating against the people with green hats, and acting on behalf of Paruk Village and the spirit of Ki Secamenggala whose tomb had been vandalized. Sakum rediscovered his characteristic style, calling out provocatively at precisely the right moments in the dance. The blind calung player even joined in the shrill cheers of the audience when, in his speeches, Bakar attacked the group who wore green hats.

The unprecedented anger that enveloped the village filled the ronggeng dancer with boundless energy. Towards the end of September, 1965, Srintil performed constantly for two weeks at the Dawuan town square during evening rallies organized by Bakar's people. Two weeks of festivities, marked by social rebellion. Social dancing with the ronggeng had been officially banned by the government but, at those evening rallies during September 1965, this regulation was openly and capriciously flaunted. Anyone could get up on the stage and dance or kiss Srintil to his heart's content.

This continued into the beginning of October. It was a period which none of the villagers could fathom. Suddenly, however, the evening rallies were banned without any announcement. Dawuan, and especially the usually busy market, grew increasingly subdued with each day that followed. People became silent, waiting uneasily.

The confusion that was overwhelming Paruk spread well beyond the village. It began with rumors, news that in Jakarta, a fabled land for the people of Paruk, there had been murders. The murderers were said to be people like Bakar. And the victims were government officials. At first the people of Paruk rejected the rumors.

"It's just hearsay," said Sakarya. "Whoever brought this news obviously did not witness it himself."

Then one night, Bakar and three of his friends appeared in the village. Sakarya and Kartareja questioned them about the rumors but only received terse answers. Bakar seemed to have lost his characteristic calm.

"There's nothing to worry about. Just keep calm."

"You, yourself, seem nervous," noted Sakarya. "What is actually going on?"

"In Jakarta, military people are killing one another."

"Civil war?"

"Yeah."

"Will it reach us here?"

"It could."

"What should we do?"

"Stay calm, I say. You don't know anything. My friends and I will stay here for a few days. But you must keep your mouths shut. Don't go around talking if you'd rather not be the target of a bullet."

Bakar stayed at Sakarya's house for three days, during which time he and his friends went outside only to go to the toilet, and even that was done at night. A week after he had left, news reached the village that his house had been burned down, as well as the homes of his followers. The police or the military had them all in custody.

"More than ever, I don't understand what is going on," Kartareja confided in Sakarya. "The news from outside is becoming more and more terrifying. To be honest, I'm worried that Paruk will be associated with the name of Bakar. If that's the case, what will happen?"

The question hung in the air unanswered. The people waiting for Sakarya to say something slowly came to the realization that the village elder was in a state of anxiety. As a respected elder, he knew that he was expected to provide an answer. It was only for that reason he finally spoke, in a trembling voice.

"I repeat what I said before. Everything we do in our lives must be within the bounds of appropriateness, because safety lies between two extremes. What we've been witnessing is a kind of life that is at one of these extremes, one that is not natural and has gone beyond acceptable limits. Such a life won't return to a balanced state without us first experiencing the consequences of its unnaturalness. My children, my grandchildren, we too have lost our way.

The villagers listened with their heads bowed. Sakarya spoke using simple words and concepts so that nobody could fail to grasp the meaning of his words. Silence enveloped the gathering. The calls of owls could be heard in the sky. The people were used to hearing the sound of the owls, but on this occasion they felt it was a subtle message from the cemetery, a message they couldn't comprehend, and that made them all feel small and helpless.

"What should we do?" asked Srintil, breaking the silence.

"We can do nothing but submit to our fate, remember who created us, and be vigilant. I ask the young people to stay on guard, and make rounds of the village every night. The older people should prepare offerings. Next Friday we will tidy the grave of Ki Secamenggala and hold a ritual feast. We must give offerings to try to avert the calamities that may descend upon our lives."

The nights at the beginning of the dry season in 1966 were very cold, and there was widespread anxiety amongst the people. Wild dogs roamed the area, savage, aroused by the smell of blood and corpses that had not been buried properly. The southeasterly breeze carried the smell of rotting carrion. The stillness of the nights was broken by the sounds of the heavy footfalls of boots and the occasional reports of gunshots. In the early hours of the mornings, a comet streaked across the heavens, its head a shining point of light: a powerful omen for the villagers.

The night before the Paruk villagers had held their ritual feast, dozens of men stealthily approached and surrounded the isolated hamlet. Their presence was discovered by the young men keeping watch. Paruk Village woke up to protect itself. All the men took out their wooden slit gongs and beat them, an age-old method of announcing an emergency. The women participated by striking whatever objects they could find. The children screamed in terror. The intruders beat a hasty retreat from the cacophony of sounds.

The next day the villagers gathered at Sakarya's house. The expressions on their simple faces revealed their fear. Sakarya couldn't help weeping. Before him were gathered the flesh and blood of Ki Secamenggala, seeking protection. They were like baby chicks running to find safety from the attack of an eagle under the wing of the mother hen. The women were wiping tears from their eyes. Children were clinging onto the arms of their mothers, their clear eyes wide with fear and curiosity. The men were silent.

"I'm going to the police station!" said Srintil suddenly. "I want to ask them what we have done wrong."

"I agree," declared Kartareja. "We only give ronggeng performances. We never once stole rice from anyone's fields. I'll go with you Srintil."

"Don't go, my granddaughter. Stay here. Don't go anywhere," wept Nyai Sakarya.

"We know we have done nothing wrong. We must seek protection. The police have to protect us. We're innocent."

Kartareja's words did little to inspire hope or confidence. Only Nyai Sakarya tried to dissuade her granddaughter from going to the police, but in the end she had to give in to Srintil's insistence.

"I know them all, Grandmother, including the commander," she said.

As Srintil and Kartareja left, all eyes followed them. The villagers' last hope left with them.

Paruk waited.

A horse-cart driver saw Srintil and Kartareja walking along the dike and approaching the main road, but he didn't stop his cart and offer them a ride as he usually did. People they encountered returning from the Dawuan market did not greet them as they passed. They walked with their heads down, avoiding people's eyes. Dawuan market showed no regard for the ronggeng who had once been so warmly embraced. The vendors looked coldly at her as she passed on her way to the police station.

Outside the station, Kartareja stopped in confusion, doubts crowding his mind.

Srintil didn't hesitate. "Come on. Those that do no wrong need not be afraid."

In the station, not only the police but also the military were there. Immediately recognizing Srintil and Kartareja, they glanced uneasily at one another, unsure of how to react to the entrance of two people known to have been associated with Bakar. The police commander and a military officer invited Srintil and Kartareja in. The others stood there stiffly.

"We have come here to ask for your help, sir," said Srintil boldly. "Last night several men came and surrounded out homes. Clearly, they meant us harm. We wish to ask for protection because we feel we have done nothing against the law. If we are accused of anything, then, please sir, tell us what it is that we have done wrong."

The police commander was obviously nervous, his hands fidgeted and his eyes were unable meet Srintil's, even though he was acquainted with her already. He stood up and went into another room, followed by the military officer. The two armed men spoke softly together.

"They came of their own free will. What do you think?"

"Are you sure their names are on the list?"

"Here, look," said the police commander, opening his already dog-eared notebook.

"I think it's just a coincidence. At least it saves us the trouble of going to get them."

"So, that's what we'll do?"

"That's the way it has to be. We have no choice."

The commander came out again, his face hard, officious. He looked straight ahead, towards the front reception area.

"We will look into the matter of men surrounding Paruk Village but, aside from that, there is something else. Both your names are on a list of people we are required to arrest. This is a command from my superiors, and I must carry out my duty."

Srintil tried to concentrate on what the commander was saying. She heard his words but found them difficult to comprehend. When the reality of what he was saying began to vaguely penetrate her mind, her soul rejected it harshly. The process required enormous effort. Her heart began to beat more quickly and she could feel her blood pounding in her brain and nerve centers. Her face became pale as it drained of blood. Her hands and feet broke out in a cold sweat. She stuttered as she fought to regain control of herself.

"Arrest? We're under arrest?"

Srintil tried to smile in a last ditch effort to reject the reality of what was happening, but the smile stopped with a trembling of lips, like someone about to weep. Slowly her face turned into a mask with an expression devoid of emotion. As two uniformed men led her off to the holding cell behind the office, she walked like a robot, incapable of thought processes and without spirit.

Throughout the day, the people of Paruk waited for Srintil and Kartareja to return. They stood around in groups in and around Sakarya's house. No one left to go work or to do household chores. Above them, a hawk circled in the sky searching for prey. A mother hen cackled to its baby chicks, gathering them under the protection of her wings.

The village was almost deserted. Even the children had lost their enthusiasm to play after seeing the depressed faces of their parents. The only sound to be heard was the bleating of goats who had not been let out of their stables all day. A child cried because its mother had not lit the fire in the hearth.

The sun moved to the western sky, yet the two people they awaited still had not returned. The faces became gloomier, and they began to sigh heavily. In the tense silence, a child shouted out. Somebody was coming. Some of the men went outside, hope welling up in their hearts. But that hope lasted only momentarily, then turned into fear. It wasn't Srintil and Kartareja approaching the village, but five uniformed men wearing heavy boots and holding rifles. They were more than enough to make the villagers turn pale in terror, wiping out any feelings of courage and self-confidence they may have had.

Paruk would be represented by Sakarya. The old man shut his eyes tightly for a moment, looking within himself to read the message that flashed into his brain. Yes, he must surrender to the demands of the times. It was an era that was manifested by the five rifles and five steely visages standing in front of him. If one was to live, one had to assume the role of a wayang puppet in a story whose plot has already been determined. This belief didn't leave Sakarya for even a moment. To attempt to protect himself against an unhappy fate when the times were against him would be useless. Sakarya had lost not just his nerve; he believed that the power of the times couldn't possibly be matched by the strength of the will of one individual.

He found strength, however, within the depths of his soul to maintain a state of calm. His face reflected a feeling of both acceptance and innocence, ready to receive whatever might come, whatever treatment might be meted out. Being calm in such moments is as important as adopting a polite attitude in a situation of powerlessness. That afternoon, due to their ignorance and poverty, the people of Paruk Village were helpless to act as Sakarya, Nyai Kartareja, Sakum, and two other people were led off by the security officials, to join Srintil and Kartareja in jail. Only the tears and sobs of women could be heard. A haunting fear rendered the village even more lusterless and dejected. Paruk without Srintil, Sakarya, and Kartareja was a village without a ronggeng. A village with no status whatsoever.

This, however, was just the start. The real fate to be borne by the village happened two days later. Early in the morning, as the eastern sky was adorned with the glory of the shooting star, the village was in flames. Paruk was burning. Flames engulfing the zinc roof of Kartareja's home rose into the sky, and thick black smoke towered over the village like a gigantic tree. Sakum's dilapidated home withstood the tumultuous flames for only a few minutes before it turned to ashes. The wails and howls of the people could be heard over the crackling bursts of burning bamboo. Panic gripped the hearts of the people, accompanied by feelings of utter defenselessness.

One woman fled, carrying her baby under her arm and screaming for her other children. An old man stood with his arms wrapped around the trunk of a tree only a few steps from the approaching flames, his grip so strong that others had to force him to let go. But when they had succeeded in prizing him off the tree, they discovered that he was already dead, his body quite stiff.

The chaos abated only when all the women had succeeded in finding their children. The men, suddenly remembering their slit gongs, began beating them together with an insane zealousness. The reverberating thunder brought people in the areas surrounding Paruk out of their homes. They could see a towering fire in the middle of the wet rice fields. They could hear the wails and shrieks of the people watching their world being destroyed in front of their very eyes.

Officials who came to Paruk afterwards found only the few shacks that had not been engulfed by the flames and the carcasses of five goats which had burned to death because the owner had not been able to open the gate to the pen. The officials didn't stay long amidst the remains. They faced too many eyes that demanded some sort of accountability on behalf of humanity. And they were unable to offer anything.

Many opinions were batted around regarding the reason behind the burning of Paruk. One was that the village had received its just fate. The Great Director had a taste for playing out His game in this universe, but Paruk, whether knowingly or not, had ignored Him. Another observed that the dialectical law in political turbulence often dictated irony in history and humanity, and that the destruction of Paruk was only one small way of proving this. Others believed that what had happened was a simple case of revenge by land owners, angry because of the theft of rice from their fields over several seasons. They knew that the people who had stolen their rice were Bakar's followers, and that they had all been arrested. Paruk had become implicated because its ronggeng had often appeared with Bakar during his propaganda meetings. This view discounted the possibility of religious or political sentiments being involved because Paruk had never been able, in its entire history, to grasp political ideologies of any kind.

The simplest theory, though, was that what had happened was no more than a mere trick involving the green bamboo hat. The people of Paruk didn't realize that Bakar was the person who vandalized the grave of Ki Secamenggala. By leaving a green hat behind, he had deceived the villagers, who then directed their anger at the group represented by the green hat, and returned to support Bakar with their ronggeng troupe. Everything could have turned out differently had the ronggeng of Paruk stayed away from Bakar and his followers.

Much later, when the grass began to grow again around the charred village, people began to ask about the fate of the person who had played such a major role in their lives: Srintil. Where was she and what had become of her?

That the upheaval in Srintil's life had actually just begun the day she was first jailed, is narrated elsewhere. That story begins with the story of a beautiful ronggeng, twenty years old, who was physically imprisoned and held psychologically captive within the walls of history, walls that had risen out of selfish greed and misadventure.

To enable us to open the pages of that story, specific conditions must be met. One of these is the passage of time, which has the power to dissolve all sentimentality. The conditions also demand a maturity of character and a certain degree of honesty in the reader which would provide the courage to acknowledge historical truth. Only if these conditions are met, can the story of Srintil be told. If they are not met, the story will disappear forever to become a part of the secret that surrounds Paruk.

III

The Rainbow's Arc

1

A small town in a remote corner of Central Java, February, 1966. More than six months of oppressive darkness. Apart from security personnel such as the police, the armed forces, or paramilitary officials, nobody ventured outside after the sun sank beneath the horizon. Sounds of occasional gunfire sporadically echoed in the distance. Every so often, there was the roar of an arriving or departing truck followed by the heavy steps of booted feet. The nights were often shattered by the howls of roaming wild dogs inflamed by the smell of blood and rotting flesh. Corpses, by the hundreds, drifted lazily down the rivers and streams. Hundreds more were buried in shallow mass graves, others left lying in open fields.

In this small, remote town in the dead of night, a dim light could be seen emanating from a house with concrete walls. The windows and doors were all secured with sturdy metal bars and, in a ghostly silence, in the guardhouse in the front yard, several soldiers wearing red scarves stood guard, rifles and machine guns at the ready. Every fifteen minutes, two of them patrolled the perimeter of the house.

The walled house was an emergency prison camp, holding almost two hundred people, many of them women. Because of the extremely limited space, the prisoners had to remain standing, packed together like bundled kindling wood. The air reeked of the stench of humankind. Sweat. The floor was slimy with urine and shit. The walls had turned moist with condensation from sweat and humidity. Despite these appalling conditions, several of the women, no longer having the strength to stand, sat on the floor leaning against the wall with their legs folded up as tightly as possible. There was little communication among the two hundred prisoners, only occasional soft whispering and the momentary exchange of glances. Some of the prisoners remained awake, while others dozed off even as they stood, no longer able to withstand the physical exhaustion and lack of sleep.

In those eyes that were still open were inscribed images and entire stories of the collapse and destruction of human dignity. They held pictures of a human civilization that, ironically, had wiped out humanity itself. The eyes winced in unison at the sound of gunfire in the distance. What were they thinking? Perhaps they thought that the gunfire was the source of power representing the authority that now shackled them. And if every gunshot was being aimed at a particular human target, who would be the next one to fall headlong with his chest or head shattered by a piercing bullet? The eyes squeezed shut.

A crude power was now controlling history: a history that had always been either violently defended or seized. The captives in that emergency prison camp were those that had been defeated; they had failed in the struggle to seize command of their country's history. They had been conquered physically as well as ideologically, and their utter defeat was manifest in the various forms of personal hardships they now endured. The consequences of their ideological defeat were not immediately apparent, but evidence of their personal downfall was already obvious. Terrorized, they did not know what they would face in the days that followed, or even in the moments ahead. And they pondered the sporadic gunfire they heard in the distance.

These defeated people could only hang onto a faint hope that the revolution which they knew could devour its own children would not now turn against each and every one of them. Otherwise, they could only hope for a miracle as they marked time with the beats of their own hearts. They had absolutely no idea what would happen from moment to moment, and they knew nothing of what was going on in the world outside of the prison camp.

They did not know why a truck arrived regularly at the camp and carried off several of the prisoners. Were their fellow prisoners being taken to more permanent facilities? Were they being interrogated at some security command center? Or was there a connection between those prisoners being taken away and the sounds of gunfire that pierced the stillness of the night?

Among the tightly crowded prisoners, a woman could be heard sobbing softly. She had briefly dozed off while standing, and her thoughts had momentarily left the cruel reality of that night, returning to her life of yesterday. She had dreamt she was back home with her children, her husband, and the rest of her family. But the beautiful dream had lasted only a brief moment, and she had awoken to find herself still crushed in with a group of prisoners in a room smelling of sweat, urine and excrement.

A soldier peering at the prisoners from the outside turned his eyes away. Private Rasus stepped away from the window. He could no longer stand to watch the scene inside, all those defeated people. They were being treated like trash. Human trash.

Rasus walked dejectedly toward the guardhouse. He had lost the jaunty look of a soldier, despite his uniform and the loaded rifle on his shoulder. The sight of the room filled with prisoners had shaken him profoundly. Before joining his colleagues, he stopped in the shadow of the guardhouse deep in thought. He was thinking about his birthplace, Paruk.

The roar of the engine of a truck arriving shattered the evening silence, and the ensuing scene became increasingly bizarre as it unfolded. The truck stopped in front of the guardhouse. Two young men in black uniforms and two paramilitary officials stepped down.

They reported to the guardhouse, and the two officials hurriedly made their way to the prison house. The bar was lifted and the door opened. The weak and weary prisoners were suddenly aroused from their sleep and lethargy. Those pressed against the door were pushed out by the crush of humanity inside, but were quickly shoved back inside by the paramilitary officials. Jostling one another, the prisoners stood on tiptoes to see what was happening outside the door, each entertaining the hope that he or she could leave the room which was unbearably hot and claustrophobic.

The prisoners listened carefully as a paramilitary official called names. Those whose names were called responded, startled. Some replied with a clear shout, believing that there was hope they would be freed. Others swallowed in dread before answering in a faltering and choked voice. The latter group had already made the connection between the prisoners being taken away and the sounds of gunshots in the distance. Seven prisoners were called, all men, and they listlessly made their way toward the door. After they were brought out, the officials attempted to close the door. At the last moment, a female prisoner managed to break through the crowd and slip outside. She pleaded with the officials.

"I want to come along, sir. I want to come along. If they're leaving, why can't I go too? Please, sir, I don't even understand why I'm being held here with the others."

"I'm only following orders. You aren't allowed to come along. Perhaps later. Go on, get back inside. Go on!"

"Let me go, sir. Let me go, too. I'm…"

"Get back in! Go!"

The woman stood for a moment transfixed, then she fell to the ground at the feet of the paramilitary official. The men were startled, but the scene that followed was even more astonishing. The woman stood up and ran to the back of the truck. The soldiers and paramilitary officials watched, but, knowing that resolve is an element that emerges only when there is some turmoil, they didn't want to make matters worse.

"Very well," said the paramilitary official, relenting. "Take her with the others. What's her name?"

Nobody answered.

"Who is she?" repeated the official.

Silence. Then, a soft voice from among the seven male prisoners could be heard.

"Darsinah."

"Darsinah?"

The prisoners were ordered into the back of the truck. The seven men were told to place their hands behind their backs. Their thumbs were tied together with strong twine made from canvas. Darsinah's eyes widened with fear. Her instincts had suddenly told her what she could expect to experience in the very near future. But she no longer had the strength to cry. The engine of the truck roared into life and the wheels began to turn. The vehicle lurched, a monstrous horror creeping away into the night, its belly full.

The grim irony of this tragedy was not lost on Rasus. Groups of prisoners carried off during the night was something he had witnessed again and again. Scenes like this had become commonplace over the past several days, but this was different. In her naivety and stupidity, Darsinah had asked to join the seven prisoners who would shortly face the bullets of history. Without realizing it, she had chosen to speed up her own doom, a terrible way of dying that she couldn't possibly have desired.

Unseen, Rasus stood behind the guardhouse and shut his eyes tightly. The image of Srintil appeared before him. Srintil, the renowned ronggeng who had once belonged to Paruk. According to the rumors Rasus had heard, Srintil had often danced at communist propaganda meetings. Would her fate be the same as that of Darsinah: first held prisoner and later to meet her end under a hail of bullets? Rasus tried to stop himself thinking, turmoil bursting in his chest. He started as he heard the voice of a comrade calling out to him from within the guardhouse. His coffee was ready. Ah, coffee. At least that might momentarily quell the anxiety overwhelming this son of Paruk.

When Paruk was burned to the ground in early 1966, almost all the twenty-three houses there had been left in ashes. At the time, many people thought that the future of the little hamlet was doomed. All those hoping to survive would have had to leave because their possessions—their rice paddies, their dried cassava, their goats, their chickens—had been destroyed by the fire. Those who continued to live on that mound of ashes would have only been choosing a way to die: through starvation or by being forced to eat potentially poisonous wild tubers and cassava plants, the only food available.

In the past there had been a universal belief that, come what may, Paruk would always be Paruk. It had had plenty of experience with the upheavals of life and the most primitive conditions of existence. It never complained. Paruk had survived with a self-awareness that was admirable. It had already been tested by numerous cases of food poisoning, by its inescapable destitution, and by its perpetual ignorance.

But that disastrous inferno in the wake of the political upheaval of 1965 had all but completely destroyed the village. It had been the most terrifying experience in the lives of its inhabitants. During the first few days after the fire the village was silent, paralyzed. Families gathered near what was left of their houses, squatting, the only sounds being the sighing and weeping of women. There was no food or shelter. Then, one evening they began building little shacks with frames made of cassava stalks covered with grass and banana palm leaves. Starvation had become a real possibility; no one outside the village had offered help to these people who had been overwhelmed by disaster. But the villagers had found some cassava growing in the surrounding area which kept them alive.

The village regained its first breath of life when Sakarya, the hamlet's elder, was released from detention after being held for two weeks by the security forces. Later, Kartareja and his wife, as well as Sakum and the other calung musicians were also released on parole. They were required to report every day to the army base in Dawuan. But Srintil had not yet returned. Every villager was aware of this, but no one had the courage to say it out loud. Srintil had not returned to Paruk, and no one knew where she was or what had happened to her.

Why Srintil had not yet returned was a just one minor blip in the historical narrative of Paruk. In the monstrous fire that had turned almost every house to ashes, not only were homes destroyed; the soul of the village had also been annihilated. Every bewildered inhabitant had to question his or her own existence and look at the possibilities for the future. A difficult predicament was oppressing the slow-witted villagers. Eyebrows were furrowed, heads bowed in fear and anxiety when their eyes met those of any outsiders. And resignation. That was the last capability of Paruk. Resignation in absolute silence, so that the village was virtually mute.

Even when the inhabitants started working together to build new shacks for one other, few words were spoken. Bamboo was cut into lengths and coconut palms plaited to become roofs and walls. By the second month after the fire, a few rough shacks stood on earth that still held dead coals and powdery ashes. Paruk again possessed shelters against the hot sun and falling rain.

But how was the village to resume the heartbeat of normal life while it remained in the grip of silence? In the laughter of its children? In the sounds of mortars used for pounding dried cassava? Or in the billowing smoke from the kitchens of its people? No. The heartbeat of Paruk probably began with the popping sounds of legume pods bursting to spread their seeds after being heated by the sun, with the squeak of bamboo stalks rubbing together in a gentle breeze, and with a pair of *brondol* birds busily carrying dried grass to their nest behind the stems of the thick areca plant. Or perhaps it began with a spring of water at the base of the trees, a gushing stream that wasn't at all interested in the calamities that had struck the people who parted its waters to enjoy its coolness. The spring continued to gush out, arcing through the air like living crystal, then breaking on black moss-covered stones. Thousands of drops of water splattered in every direction, capturing the rays of the sun as they pierced the leafy foliage, refracting the light in a misty rainbow.

Whatever brought it about, Paruk was finally able to draw its first breath of life. Its ability to recover might be compared to humble lichen growing on a rock. The lichen exists on almost nothing and seems to die off in the dry season, growing dry and peeling away from its host. But, even in its apparent death-like state, the lichen still carries the energy of life: small spores wrapped in pods have the power to continue their life cycle as soon as a drop of water or any humidity in the air touches them. Paruk was like a kind of lichen, created to fulfill its destiny of life in the most minimal conditions. Paruk still *exists* even without one smile, much less laughter, among its children. It still *exists* even while its people no longer know the point of its existence.

One home had been left standing after Paruk burned. This small house was entirely surrounded by a bamboo grove and received sunlight only in the middle of the day. An ancient woman, stooped with age, lived in the house. Her name and the name of her long dead husband had been forgotten by the villagers. The old women was simply called "Nenek Rasus", the grandmother of Rasus.

For several days, Nenek Rasus had not had the strength to get up from her sleeping mat. Everyone knew that the old woman was close to death. Some said that what was happening to her was nature's course: because of her old age she was approaching her last days. Others, however, were of the opinion that Nenek Rasus should have been strong enough to dodder around and ask for food from her family and friends in the village. They believed that what had brought about her weakened state was the harsh reality that her one and only grandson never came to visit her, even during these difficult times.

When she had the strength to speak, Nenek Rasus often called out for her grandson. She desperately hoped that someone would tell him to come home. Everyone knew what she wanted, but nobody felt able to fulfill her request. Not even Sakarya, the village elder. No one in Paruk could possibly contact a soldier, even for a dying woman. Their situation simply did not allow it. Circumstances only gave them enough liberty to breathe the air or to walk around with their heads bowed. A Paruk villager in the aftermath of the fire was fully aware of his or her place in the scheme of things. Be fatalistic, don't cause a fuss. If a villager was dying, then she should just die, be buried, and be done with it.

Only Nenek Rasus herself continued to try communicating with her grandson, perhaps through the final pulses of blood coursing through her veins. When her lips were moving, she may have been appealing to the supreme power of God to convey her message to her grandson, wherever he might be.

When people experience a great shock to their sense of order and values, when anxiety and uncertainty reign, and when the ties that hold them to life itself are at stake, they seek a place of calm, a place where the soul can once again find peace. They also seek security in belief in certain concepts and institutions. Such institutions could be a mother, always ready to offer comfort. They could be a grove of bamboo where one was born. They could take on the form of a perpetually gushing spring of water or the musty old lap of a grandmother. One institution could be a combination of all these things; nurturing a child from the moment of his birth and teaching him the meaning of his existence. It is such concepts and institutions people hold dear and to which they remain loyal.

At the time his grandmother lay dying, Rasus was serving a tour of duty in an area of Central Java almost two hundred kilometers from Paruk. Sometimes he felt bad because it had been almost four years since he had last visited his grandmother, which was when he had entrusted the care of the old woman to the people in the village. But most of his feelings of guilt had abated, perhaps because of his busy life as a soldier or because he was determined to let life in Paruk take its own course. Paruk could get along with its cursing and swearing, with its calung music, and with its beautiful ronggeng named Srintil. Rasus did not want to disturb the autonomy of his birthplace that was now so distant from him.

The turmoil of 1965 changed Rasus's attitude toward his home village. In his mind's eye he could clearly visualize his grandmother's little house, almost entirely surrounded by the grove of bamboo. His ears could hear the cries of children playing and flying kites made of dried leaves, and the buzzing of dung beetles that flew over the dewy wet rice fields in the early morning. As days went on, the images of Paruk increasingly filled his mind, and the old hamlet tugged at his heartstrings. Its pull became stronger whenever he remembered the rumors he had heard that Paruk had been drawn into the communist propaganda meetings held in the area. He hoped and prayed that his village had not suffered as a result. For some reason, Rasus found that he could not calm the anxieties he felt. And the image of his grandmother, too, often intruded upon his thoughts.

If Rasus had not been a soldier on active duty, he would have immediately submitted a request for leave. But with the upheaval of the previous months, all leaves of absence had been canceled for an indefinite period. To find out what had happened in his birthplace, Rasus was compelled to write letters. He wrote to Sergeant—formerly, Corporal—Pujo, who had been, for a long while, Rasus's one and only friend. Sergeant Pujo now commanded a barracks in the territory surrounding Dawuan, the town near Paruk.

Sergeant Pujo's response was immediate and brief: a telegram notifying Rasus that his grandmother was mortally ill. But there was no request for Rasus to return home. Rasus understood why. Sergeant Pujo didn't have the authority to direct a soldier who was not under his command. Rasus accepted the bitter fact that, in the light of the current situation, an old woman's death had to be considered insignificant. The cursory tone of Sergeant Pujo's telegram was proof of that.

Nonetheless, despite the tight security situation, Rasus hoped that there would still be some room for indulgence for a personal crisis. With the telegram from Sergeant Pujo in his hand, he sought an appointment with the commander of his unit, and requested leave from duty so he could pay his final respects to his dying grandmother. The commander gave him a very hard time, but eventually, if reluctantly, granted him compassionate leave.

Taking the first available bus, Rasus left for Paruk. About four in the afternoon, he arrived in Dawuan. He was met by an assistant to Sergeant Pujo who asked him to stop by the barracks before continuing on to Paruk.

"I know that you want to see your grandmother as quickly as possible but, before you do, please give me a moment to fulfill my own duty with respect to you," said Sergeant Pujo, his manner official, almost stiff.

"Of course, Sergeant. Please go ahead."

"First, I must ask that you surrender your rifle as well as the machete on your hip."

Rasus did what Sergeant Pujo asked without saying a word. The two sat down in a more relaxed manner.

"Your grandmother is still alive. I received confirmation from paroled Paruk villagers who reported in this morning."

"Thank goodness. I've been worried that I'd be too late. My thanks to you, Sergeant. The telegram you sent has given me the opportunity to stay with my grandmother during her final moments."

"I have one request. We're both soldiers and, as such, we are required to be resolute: resolute no matter what we face.

Rasus could sense a hidden message in the sergeant's words. And he had also just learned that there were Paruk villagers on parole. He wanted to know more, but Sergeant Pujo did not give him an opportunity for questions.

"So, go ahead and continue your journey to Paruk. But don't forget, you're a soldier."

"Very well, Sergeant."

Paruk was waiting for its son to return home, a wait with even more significance since the fire that had all but engulfed the little hamlet and transformed it into a pensive, almost ailing place. All the principles of life that had formed the character of Paruk, carried from generation to generation, now teetered on the edge of collapse. Paruk had suffered such a profound loss of confidence that its people were confused about how they should receive their son.

That son was now walking with long, purposeful strides toward the leafy grove of bamboo where he had been brought into the world. The closer he got to the thicket that was Paruk, the faster he walked. Suddenly he found himself disoriented by the strange emptiness around him. He stopped and peered ahead. Where was Sakum's home? It was usually visible from the nearest corner of the dike that framed the wet rice field surrounding the village. And where was the gleam of the sun reflecting off the tin roof of Kartareja's house?

His pace slackened, the feeling of desolation tightening its grip on him with every step. There were no children roaming the fields, nor could he hear their shouts. Oh! Rasus stood frozen, his brow furrowed. He struggled to interpret and come to terms with the scene that opened before him. The houses of his people had been transformed into little hovels hardly different from the makeshift shanties thrown together by farmers to get out of the hot sun when working in the fields. Paruk, what brought you to this? What disaster had struck?

Rasus's shoulders suddenly slumped. An obvious answer had presented itself to him, explaining everything. His intuition was quick enough to draw a connection between the current political situation and its implications for the village. He recalled the rumors he had heard that Paruk had been swept along by the savagery of the political propaganda activities in the recent past, and had no need to ask further questions about what had happened. A lump of bitterness entered and then congealed in the depths of his heart.

Feeling as though he was being carried aloft, as if his feet no longer touched the ground, he entered the village precinct. Two small children, unaware of his arrival until he had almost stumbled over them, fled in panic. They dashed into the open door of a shack to hide inside, their faces ashen with fear. Women peered out through holes in walls that were made from plaited coconut leaves. They did not have the courage to show themselves, even after seeing that the soldier in front of them was Rasus, a member of their own clan.

Paruk was trapped in an identity crisis. Because it felt that history had pushed it into the realm of everlasting disgrace, the little hamlet yearned for the help of its favorite son. Paruk wanted to hide its face behind Rasus, now that he had become a soldier. But no one was sure what his attitude would be: sympathy toward the burned-down village, or perhaps the opposite. In its innocence, Paruk had already learned from history that blood relatives might be deaf and mute when life is in turmoil as a result of a collapse of the social order.

Groups of men and woman were gathered at the home of Nenek Rasus, standing around and whispering, when they saw their favorite son come home. On their faces was fear. Rasus noted the ash and cinders on the ground, the tiny hovels, and the children who ran off in fear. All of this spoke volumes of the disaster that had befallen the village. Any questions he may have had were answered fully—in detail, critically and completely—by the behavior of the people gathered in his grandmother's home. They were living monuments, inscribed without words, their looks narrating with profound efficiency the cruel treatment the village had suffered. When he looked into the blind eyes of Sakum, Rasus could read the story of the inferno that had burned down his people's homes; he felt the overwhelming fear and panic his fellow villagers had endured when he gazed at the wrinkled face of Sakarya, and he could hear in his mind the shrill screams of terror when he saw the tears on the anxious faces of the women and children.

Rasus felt that if he took another step closer he would dissolve into the devastation of his people. He could not bear to continue looking at Sakarya, Kartareja, or the others. And he did not have the strength to witness the tears streaming down the gaunt and pallid faces of the women. He faltered. The resoluteness that Sergeant Pujo had asked of him prevented him from collapsing altogether, but he could not stop his tears from falling when he saw his grandmother.

"*Nek*, I'm here. It's me, Rasus."

The old, worn out woman lying beneath the faded batik cloth did not react.

"*Laa ilaaha illallaah*."

Rasus sat on the edge of the sleeping mat. A faint pulse was still evident in the vein on the old woman's neck, and her chest moved slightly. Yet, Rasus sensed that his grandmother no longer had the strength to communicate with anyone. While there was still life in her body, it seemed that her soul had already left.

It took five or six minutes for Rasus to come to terms with where he was and in what circumstances he found himself. A heavy sigh signaled that he had succeeded in regaining control over the feelings that had initially overwhelmed him. After gently stroking his grandmother's face, he stood up and turned around. He looked around at the faces of the villagers: faces full of guilt, begging for forgiveness from the world. Paruk had yet to recognize the reality of its situation: forgiveness would come only after a great deal of time. But Paruk was having great difficulty believing the world would ever provide absolution, without which the little hamlet would be utterly destroyed, engulfed by history. Its destruction was already etched on the faces of its people.

Rasus not only noticed this; he too felt destroyed; He felt that he was in an even more difficult situation: he was the son of Paruk but, as a soldier, he had to have a much broader perspective, one that went far beyond the interests and lives of his people.

Before anything was said, Rasus offered his hand to Sakarya, Kartareja, and the other people around him. He spoke heavily but calmly.

"*Sedulur-sedulur*. Are you well?"

Silence. No one could answer directly. They could only swallow and lower their heads, deeply moved by the way Rasus had addressed them: *sedulur*. Rasus still thought of them as family. Using such a term to refer to one's fellow villagers was customary in rural Java but, for a group of people that had survived the devastating fire, it held very special meaning. Sakarya coughed. His lips trembled, but he could not bring himself to speak.

Finally, Sakarya was able to respond, affectionately referring to Rasus as if he were his own blood relative. "Yes, my grandchild. We, your kith and kin, are all safe: for what it's worth."

"Thank God for that," Rasus sighed.

"And we are happy that you've come home. Here is your grandmother, as you can see. It's fortunate that you're not too late."

"Yes, it is," Rasus replied.

"We've been waiting for many days. Your grandmother is very old. Will you be staying to the very end?"

"I hope to, although I'm not sure. I have only been given three days leave."

"You can only stay three days?" asked Sakum. He stood up, his hollow eye sockets blinking.

"Hey, Sakum! It's not proper for you to be so familiar with a soldier!"

"Oh yeah. I forgot. I should say 'sir'. Rasus is, of course, so handsome now. Are you married, sir?"

"No, not yet."

"That's fortunate. Srintil is still alone. But no one knows where she is. Do you know?"

Rasus was unable to hide his surprise. He had sworn to himself that he would not speak about any of the villagers who had been arrested because he could not bear to think about what might have happened to them. He had assumed that they had all been released and returned to the village. Now he learned that the woman who had always had a special place in his heart was the one villager still being held under arrest.

"I don't know. I don't know where she is being held," answered Rasus, shaking his head.

"The poor girl. Who can help Srintil, if you can't, sir? Well, go and find her. Bring her back here and make her your wife. That would be the proper thing to do."

"Sakum, that's enough. This isn't any of your business," interrupted Sakarya. "Anyway, do you think it's polite to speak of such things while Nenek Rasus is so seriously ill?"

That night almost the entire village population gathered at the home of Nenek Rasus. While they all knew of her condition, her grandson's return—after being gone for almost four years—was another matter altogether. Not least of all, they wanted to see what Rasus had made of himself. Did he still retain allegiance to his village and the blood descendants of Ki Secamenggala? After the disgrace Paruk had suffered as a result of being associated with communist ringleaders of the 1965 debacle, the village longed for a new guardian: a guardian that could offer the little hamlet some security as well as some pride, no matter how small. Rasus was the person the villagers most desired for this role if he indeed still felt a basic allegiance toward them. They now looked for evidence of this allegiance.

Rasus greeted his fellow villagers with a smile, his eyes glowing. But not because he realized he was being scrutinized. He pinched the cheeks of babies in the arms of their mothers. He even took one child from its mother, rocked it in his arms, and kissed it. In doing this, he felt he was inhaling the past: smelling the odor of Paruk, the bosom of his own mother. His heart trembled with the intensity of the affinity he felt for his people and his concern over what had happened. Fate had brought a fire that had almost destroyed the village. Fate had also made the little hamlet so timid that the rustling of a lizard crawling on dead leaves frightened the people, not to mention the footfall of booted men. Paruk now faced the gaze of outsiders with cast-down eyes and feared everything because it no longer believed in itself.

For the first time in months, smiles could be seen on the faces of some of the villagers. Their hearts felt a glimmer of hope when they learned that Rasus had not changed, that he remained the son of Paruk, that he still wanted to kiss their rancid-smelling babies. His eyes were clear and pure, not like the accusing eyes of an outsider. Oh, imagine how devastating it would have been if Rasus, had like an outsider, regarded Paruk villagers as no longer a part of humanity.

However, the smiles had not yet turned into laughter and joy. Everyone realized that Rasus had his own troubles. The villagers were satisfied at this stage that he had greeted them with warmth, using kin terms that reflected their status and position, referring to each as "uncle", "older brother", "aunty", and so forth. Afterwards, they left him to his vigil at the bedside of his grandmother.

By midnight, just a few people still remained at the house. Rasus sat with Sakarya, Kartareja, and Sakum, frequently getting up to sit at his grandmother's side. Two women were fast asleep together on a bench. Kartareja was leaning back with his eyes closed, and Sakum sat with his head resting on his knees. Only Sakarya was still awake. They were all weary from staying up for several nights to watch over Nenek Rasus. Finally, even Sakarya dozed off in his chair.

Suddenly, Rasus's nostrils quivered. He could smell something. It was not the smell of a moldy old fabric, nor the smoke of incense. Something else. The smell of death. Rasus bent down to look more closely at his grandmother. She was still breathing. But from her slow exhalations he could smell death. He looked over at Sakarya. Asleep. They were all asleep. Feelings of solitude and emptiness slowly crept over him, embracing him from all directions. He felt himself suspended in a vacuum.

The smell of death. It was a smell that originated in the processes which transformed loosely connected organic tissue. The life of Nenek Rasus was ending, not as result of damaged organs within her body, but because her physiology had reached the limits of its endurance. Like an engine running out of fuel, her body released the last of its energy with choked and sporadic movements. Rasus saw his grandmother's breathing suddenly speed up, her eyes abruptly open wide, and her mouth fall agape: her face turned into a terrifying and revolting visage. A spasm that began in her stomach quickly moved up to her chest and abruptly stopped in her throat. Nenek Rasus looked as if she was going to cough, but only vomited a bit of liquid. That was the last exertion her tired old body could muster. No energy remained to close her eyes or shut her mouth. Life had been embraced by death, humanity perfectly dissolved into eternity. A unique form shaped out of seventy years of life in

Paruk Village was gone, becoming part of the dust of the universe. Her soul had returned to the Great Creator.

"*Innalillahi wa inna ilaihi roji'un,*" Rasus murmured. He ran his hand over her face to close her eyes, and lifted her lifeless jaw to close her mouth. He drew up the sheet to cover her body. Then he stood up thoughtfully, his arms folded. The silence pressed in on him more heavily. He could sense a miraculous connection, full of secrets, between his own body and the body stretched out before him. A link in the chain forming a line of descent had been broken, and the next link was Rasus himself. The heartbeat of his grandmother had ceased, but the hereditary pulse of life continued. Rasus believed that he could now feel this pulse more strongly within his chest. He was overwrought by emotion, and tears flowed from his eyes.

It had taken just a minute or two to bring Rasus to this understanding of his own existence, but it seemed like an eternity. On hearing the call of an owl, Rasus felt that he had returned to the everyday world. Silence. In front of him was the corpse of his grandmother, covered with a sheet. Behind him, two women slept huddled together on a wooden bench. Sakarya, Kartareja, and Sakum were all there too, sleeping in their respective chairs. A firefly was flying aimlessly around the room. He heard the rustling of a field mouse outside and, again, the owl's echoing call. Sakarya woke up, wiping his face with both his hands, and saw Rasus standing deep in thought next to the bed. He frowned, grasping the meaning of the situation.

"How is she?" he asked, standing up.

"She's gone," answered Rasus calmly.

"You didn't wake me up:"

"It happened too fast. It's okay. She's gone."

Sakarya bowed his head, his shoulders drooping. Softly he moved to the sleeping mat. Paying his respects, he pulled down the sheet to reveal the face of the late Nenek Rasus. Sakarya had seen on many occasions the image of death on a face, an image without life and without spirit. Without the breath of life, a body is only a monument made from an organic tissue: so very different to the body of a sleeping person. A corpse constitutes the observable process in which a person's identity is freed from that same person, a process of disintegration in the ongoing struggle for existence. Sakarya could only comprehend death through a poem traditionally sung whenever a Paruk villager died, which he recited over the body of the old woman:

Wenang sami ngawruhana pati,
Wong ngagesang tan wurung palastra,
Yèn mati ngendi parané,
Saéngga manuk mabur, mesat saking kurunganeki,
Ngendi parané bénjing, aja nanti kliru,
Upama wong anèng dunya, asesanjan mangsa wurunga yèn mulih,
Maring nagri kamulyan.

Let us try to understand the essence of death,
Every creature must die,
He soul to fly,
Like a bird freed from its cage,
Where will the future take us? Let us not lose our way.
As with all humanity in this world, out time is so brief and we shall return,
To rest in eternity.

Rasus had never really thought about the lessons contained in the poem. If nothing else, he could comprehend that there were relevant concepts in it about the reality of death. There were lines that said humanity lives with the inevitability of death, and that the journey of life ends in the land of glory, at the mercy of God. Rasus didn't really know the belief system that Sakarya used to interpret the words of the poem. He was aware though that, strangely enough, the source of Sakarya's reference was actually a belief system that he himself now followed, one which said that everything originates in God, and to God everything will eventually return.

In the morning when the dew had evaporated, the citizens of Paruk accompanied the body of Nenek Rasus to her grave. Everyone was there. A long procession followed the path that led up the hill to the graveyard. They marched in silence, like a line of ants. The death of Nenek Rasus was the first loss they had suffered since the major fire that had engulfed the village four months earlier, a loss that now brought them all closer together. In the extraordinary destruction of its very being, Paruk could now only make the most primitive and passive efforts to maintain its place in the world. People who didn't understand the annihilation of the soul of the village might have said that the people walking in procession up the hill to the cemetery were simply mourning the death of a relative. People who didn't know what the villagers had experienced couldn't see that the people accompanying the body were deeply troubled, and could only be comforted by a strengthening of the tie that held them together, legitimizing their solidarity through sorrow and grief. The death of Nenek Rasus was the first opportunity they had had to demonstrate their anguish, which could not be adequately expressed through tears.

After the burial, the people, still hushed, descended from the cemetery. Only Rasus and Sakarya remained. The two squatted, facing the mound of earth that covered the body of Nenek Rasus. In silence the men listened to the calls of birds, the sounds of fruits and seeds striking the leaves as they fell from the trees, and the buzzing of bees as they settled upon the flowers. Rasus squeezed a brittle clod of earth in his hand. Sakarya hesitated; he seemed to be waiting for an appropriate moment to speak.

"Your grandmother was several years younger than I am," he finally said. "I believe that my days will end before very long, too."

Rasus raised his head.

"My child, like your grandmother, I want to have my grandchild with me when I die but I am worried that Srintil will not return before I pass away. This is my burden, a matter that's in my thoughts day and night. Can you help me, my child?"

Startled, Rasus looked up at Sakarya's face, then looked away again.

"Help in what way?"

"Well, it's difficult to say. I want to ask your help in bringing Srintil back. I know that might not be possible, but, at least could you find out where Srintil is. I have to know what happened to her, if she's still alive, and what her circumstances are now. Or if she's dead and, if so, where she's buried."

Rasus felt his throat tightening. The pain that Paruk had endured had been caused by two different wounds, both of which he now felt acutely. The first wound was the torching of the village, along with the disgrace of its people. The second wound was the reality that Srintil had not yet returned. Srintil, who represented so much for Paruk, had disappeared. And the uncertainty of her fate could only be interpreted by the villagers as an uncertainty of the fate of the village itself. Rasus realized that this continuing ambiguity was a graver threat to Paruk than even the food poisonings that had struck its citizens in the past, and more frightening than the great fire that had reduced the hamlet to ashes four months ago. Rasus felt his throat tightening again.

"What do you say, my child?"

"Well. I'll do everything I can, but I can't guarantee that my attempts to find out what has happened to Srintil will come to anything. You know that these are still dangerous and sensitive times."

Sakarya exhaled slowly, a small hint of joy on his face. "As long as you're willing to try, my heart is strengthened. But, there's one more thing I want to talk to you about."

"What's that?"

"This is strictly confidential, and only you should know about it. It's about the gold jewelry that belongs to Srintil. I was able to rescue it from the fire. Do you want to take it all now, and give it to Srintil when she returns?"

"Is it a lot?"

"A great deal. More than two hundred grams."

"Oh, no. I don't feel that I should take it. Where is it right now?"

"My wife is keeping it."

"Just leave it with her. It's enough that I know about it."

"I'm worried about us being so old. What if we should die while you're away?"

"If that's a problem, hide the jewelry in a place only we know about."

"Good idea. I'll bury Srintil's things here in the cemetery next to the monument for Ki Secamenggala. I'm sure it will be safe here."

"Very well. I will guard this secret with my life."

The frown on Sakarya's face disappeared as he watched Rasus stand up and walk towards a tree, break off a branch and plant it in the ground next to his grandmother's gravestone. A tree would grow and witness that the earth of Paruk had been given back a part of its essence: the body of Nenek Rasus.

On the way back to the village, Rasus could not bring himself to speak; no words could express his feelings. He could not articulate what he had recently experienced: his birthplace transformed into a hamlet of tiny shacks, his people—even the children—no longer able to smile, his grandmother just buried, and the uncertainty of Srintil's fate. Was she dead or alive? Where was she? All of this was troubling for Paruk, for Sakarya and, most of all, for Rasus.

He felt even more uneasy when the time came for him to leave. But not just because he was unsure about being able to fulfill his obligation in finding out what had happened to Srintil; his position as a soldier made the task especially delicate. He felt uneasy mainly because he knew that the hopes of Paruk rested entirely on his shoulders.

Rasus did not feel it necessary to hide the tears in his eyes when the men, women, and children of Paruk gathered together to see him off. Their lifeless expressions and vacant eyes moved him to compassion, and to hope that Paruk could one day be restored to life: to breathe the air, drink the water, and walk the earth.

Once again, Rasus left the little hamlet of his birth. This time, though, he did not have the strength to smile; his brow was furrowed and his heart heavy.

At the officers' base for Territorial Mass Resistance Duty, Rasus met Sergeant Pujo for a second time. Suddenly, without fully realizing what he was doing, Rasus asked the sergeant about Srintil.

"Excuse me, Sergeant…" he began anxiously.

"Yes?" asked Pujo, looking at him nervously.

"Sergeant, I need to know what happened to Srintil. She's the only person from Paruk who has not yet returned. Do you know anything about what has happened to her or where she might be?"

Pujo's face changed. The atmosphere became charged with tension, suddenly losing any sense of familiarity, and becoming official. Pujo stood up and paced around the room, his head bowed. It was obvious that he was reluctant to give an answer, but finally he said that, as far as he knew, Srintil was being held in the town of Eling-eling. Rasus was struck by his manner: formal, even stiff, with absolutely no hint of compassion.

"Officially, I am not allowed to discuss anything regarding Srintil. What do you intend to do with this information?"

Rasus swallowed, and smiled foolishly.

"I might check on her since that's what I promised to do."

"What? Go and see her? Are you serious?"

"Yes. You know how important Srintil has been to me. All people from Paruk are closely linked."

"I understand that but, as your friend, I want to remind you of the situation. Think carefully about what you're going to do."

Rasus felt his heart tremble. He fully realized the significance of Pujo's words. Three incidents which he saw as possible outcomes from his search for Srintil sprang to mind. A soldier from his unit had had a bad experience when he tried to help another soldier implicated in security matters. The soldier had tried to bring along some of his friend's personal belongings on the truck which was transporting him to jail. In the end, the soldier was jailed along with his friend.

The second incident involved a soldier who, dressed as a civilian, was hitchhiking and had stopped a truck which, unknown to him, was carrying prisoners. He was taken directly to prison along with the other captives, despite his protestations that he was a soldier.

The third incident was similar to the situation in which Rasus found himself. A soldier had gone home to his village and discovered that many of his friends and family had died as a result of mass rioting. He had lost his head and said things in anger. When he returned to his barracks, a report of his outburst had preceded him, sent by his village chief. Nobody could help him when he was arrested and dishonorably discharged.

"And one more thing, Rasus! What I told you concerning the whereabouts of Srintil is strictly confidential. Don't tell anyone you got that information from me. I'll make it bad for you, if you do. I'll make sure that you're imprisoned and dishonorably discharged!"

Rasus looked at the face of his friend of many years. It took him no longer than a moment to see that the Pujo of the past was no longer behind the eyes of the person before him. Savagery boiled behind those eyes. Rasus stood up and saluted rapidly. Without another word he left the base.

He walked out, his thoughts in turmoil. When he reached the edge of the road, he still had no idea what he should do, but then he remembered how his commandant had punched him, splitting his lip, and kicked him in the head, knocking him out briefly. That was the price he had had to pay to get permission to go to Paruk. If he had to pay that price again to find Srintil, he would gladly pay it. Ten minutes later, Rasus was on a bus speeding toward the town of Eling-eling.

In the bus, he pondered his situation. He realized that his willingness to look for Srintil, his willingness to try to free the ronggeng, was driven by none other than a desire to please Sakarya as well as to confirm his loyalty to Paruk: even though he knew that a task such as this was like trying to lever the weight of history with a palm leaf. Aside from the weight of his task, the personal risk was great. To be accused of being a perpetrator of the cause of the 1965 debacle was akin to lifelong stigmatization. Defeat in the realm of politics was the ultimate defeat in life, and the consequences also implicated friends and family. That was the arrogance of history Rasus had to face.

Throughout the hour-long ride, Rasus was completely lost in his thoughts. He continued to ponder, even as the last passengers got off the bus.

"We're here, sir," the conductor announced. "Do you want to get off, or are you planning on returning to Dawuan?"

Startled from his thoughts, Rasus looked around him, then got off the bus. A pedicab almost ran him down as he crossed the street. He stood and squinted into the distance to the south. He could see a large building with a zinc-sheeted roof. At one time, that structure had been part of a coconut palm oil processing plant. Now the building was filled with hundreds, perhaps thousands, of prisoners from the area surrounding Eling-eling.

Rasus started walking towards the building. The closer he got to his goal, the slower his steps became. He stopped about fifty meters from the gate to the old plant. The various faces of Paruk emerged one after another in his thoughts. The face of Sakum remained in his mind the longest. It was Sakum who had bluntly told him to bring Srintil back to Paruk and marry her. Sakum's words rang in Rasus's ears: "I've never forgotten how much in love you two were." Then Sakarya emerged. If the people of Paruk had made Srintil a symbol of their lives, she was even more important to Sakarya. She was his granddaughter, and he had raised her ever since her parents' death. For Sakarya, Srintil was the tie that bound him to life. Then, Sergeant Pujo's face appeared, and Rasus heard his words: "Think one more time before you continue with your plans!"

Unaware of how long he had been standing on the side of the road, Rasus suddenly noticed a jeep passing. The top was down and the contents of the vehicle were clearly visible: two soldiers, three women and a large pile of vegetables. Rasus sprang into action, and he followed the jeep as it turned to enter the gate to the prison. His confusion had dissipated the moment he had caught sight of one of the women in the jeep and recognized her as Srintil.

A guard stopped Rasus as he tried to slip in the gate.

"Hey! Where are you going? Report first!"

"I'm sorry. I'm coming, corporal." Rasus changed direction and headed for the guardhouse.

It was only about twenty steps from the gate to the guardhouse and, in the space of that short journey, Rasus came up with a perfect excuse for being there.

"I'm Private Rasus, and I would like to meet the commander of this prison over a personal matter. I am a former assistant. I was once the commander's household servant."

"You're a former servant of the commander?" a guard asked, holding back a smile.

"Yes, but now I'm a soldier."

"So, you've been promoted."

There was an explosion of laughter in the guardhouse. Another miracle in the workings of mankind, the workings of time. A potentially frightening situation defused by a little humor.

Rasus showed the guards his identification and leave papers. He was ordered to open his bag of belongings which were hanging from the handle of the army knife he wore on his hip. A guard went off to notify the commander, returning several minutes later.

"Since you're his former servant, the commander will see you immediately," said the guard, smiling. "Go ahead he's waiting."

Rasus saluted the guards and walked briskly to the commander's office. The commander looked up in amazement as Rasus opened the door. Before the officer could say anything, Rasus sprang to attention and saluted.

"I am Private Rasus. I am prepared to be punished because I lied when I said that I was once your household servant. I have actually come to see a prisoner."

"Sit!"

"Yes, sir!"

The commander did not seem to be interested in asking questions immediately. He drummed his fingers on his desk, looking Rasus up and down. The private was nervous, and the back of his neck felt cold, as if chilled by an icy breeze. However, had he known what the captain was thinking, he would not have been worried at all. The captain was moved by the courage of the private before him. He was the image of a soldier that would make any officer proud.

"Who do you want to see?"

"Srintil, Captain."

"Who?"

"Srintil, from Paruk."

"Are you a relative?"

"Yes, Captain. A distant relative, and I also come from Paruk."

"Oh, I know. Srintil the ronggeng dancer, right?"

"Yes, sir."

The captain was silent. A slight smile crossed his face, very slight. Rasus had absolutely no idea of what it might mean.

"Very well," the captain said, causing Rasus's heart to race. "However, I want you to wash my car first. Report to me when you're finished!"

"Yes, sir!"

Rasus was surprised by the unexpected order. Nevertheless, he found out from some other soldiers where the captain's car was. The guards watched in amusement as he began his task.

In his office, the captain ordered his adjutant to get Srintil's dossier file. This wasn't the first time the officer had studied the report on the ronggeng of Paruk. This prisoner was something of a problem because of her youth and beauty. All the men flirted with her. The soldiers under his command often lost their sense of strict discipline when they came into contact with her.

However, the captain was not particularly bothered by the behavior of his men. What disturbed him was that the disposition orders in Srintil's dossier indicated that the ronggeng was to be held indefinitely, whereas he knew that Srintil should actually be released on parole. More than once, he had felt frustrated that he did not have the authority to simply override such orders. Sometimes he thought of his wife who, although no longer young, maintained a gentle but tenacious hold over his heart. Such a wife need never worry about her husband's behavior even if he were a warden with a thousand prisoners like Srintil.

But, perhaps no man is actually so decent. Perhaps when a man appears to be virtuous, he simply hasn't had the chance to behave like an animal. When order breaks down and society is in chaos, there are rifts through which potential violence can break. Perhaps such tendencies toward violence arise out of animal instincts. Only those that continue to maintain self-control in such times can preserve their humanity.

The captain leaned back in his armchair and let out a long sigh. Rasus knocked and entered.

"Sir! I have finished cleaning your car!"

"Sit!"

"Yes, sir!"

"Now tell me your reason for wanting to see Srintil. Is it that you don't like it that she's imprisoned?"

Rasus was silent.

"Are you in love with her?"

Rasus remained silent.

"Answer me!"

"Sir! I can't give you an answer!"

"Damn! So why did you come here?"

"To see Srintil."

Mortir stood up suddenly, leaned forward and raised his hand to strike.

He couldn't say why he stopped short of slapping the private. It is likely that, at the last moment, he saw something in the eyes of the son of Paruk, a ray of light that radiated purity. If purity is the pilot of true life guided directly by God's love, then it continues to exist despite powerful forces that conflict with basic human sentiments. It exists in each and every human heart. Rasus's inner purity had revealed itself, which, in turn, awoke the same purity, residing in the captain's heart.

The captain realized that it was very difficult for Rasus to answer his questions with words. If one human being wanted to join with another, what would be the motive? Only one's inner purity could answer that question. Because our purity can free us from the power of politics, profit, and ambition. Purity will only speak for basic human feelings.

"Private Rasus!"

"Yes, sir!"

"You may see Srintil for ten minutes. You must write down what you plan to talk about and submit it to my adjutant. Here's some paper. Now, go to the waiting room."

"Yes, sir!"

On the walls of the prison waiting room were signs reading: "Whatever you see and hear in these facilities is to be kept to yourself." Rasus read the signs, and the arrogance of the words struck him; words that were so reflective of the times, times of deepening suspicion and the breakdown of trust among peers. If communal ties rooted in fundamental human aspirations are considered so lofty as to be within the idealism of moralists, Rasus wondered, then where are the more worldly ties, such as family, friendship, and nation? The cramped waiting room spoke too much about the stunting and wilting of these ties.

A gray-haired woman and three small children were also in the waiting room. From the way they talked to one another, he gathered that the woman was the children's grandmother. He wanted to chat with them, but there was something about the children's eyes that made him hesitate. Their eyes were young, but they revealed that something had been destroyed there. Three pairs of eyes as clear as morning dew looked at Rasus with a profound fear. Was this because of the uniform he wore?

"Are you waiting for someone, ma'am?"

"Yes, sir. Well, no. I was, but now I'm not, sir."

"What do you mean?"

"I came here to meet my son, the father of these children, but I've just been told that he's been moved to Semarang. The children, however, don't want to leave until they see their father. So, I'm sitting here for a while until they realize there's nothing else we can do."

Rasus looked at the faces of the children. The oldest, a girl of about ten years, lowered her gaze and wiped the tears from her eyes. The two younger children struggled to climb up on their grandmother's lap. He turned his face away, lacking the strength to look at the hurt behind those clear eyes.

"Are you waiting for someone, sir?"

Before he could respond, he heard the sounds of approaching footsteps. Every step caused his heart to constrict. The door opened, and Srintil stood at the threshold. She was somewhat thin, but she wore a fine blouse and skirt. Her hair was combed and, to Rasus's surprise, he could see that she had applied rouge to her cheeks. Rasus attempted to stand up, but found he couldn't move. They stared at one another transfixed, mouths open. The only movement was the tears falling from Srintil's eyes, drawing two straight lines down her cheeks.

The knot that had gripped Srintil's heart for so many months suddenly loosened. From the time she had first realized that she was being held as a political prisoner, she had felt certain that Rasus would be able to do something to help her. Rasus was her kin from Paruk, the man she had known since they were children and who had always been willing to stand by her. Rasus was a soldier and, most importantly, he of all people would believe that Srintil was not a communist. Srintil did not even understand what it meant to be a communist. She had believed that, with the will of Rasus, her freedom would be a simple matter.

When the person on whom she had pinned all her hopes appeared in front of her, it would be expected that she would pour out her feelings. This expectation assumed that this was still the same Srintil of several months ago. But the person Rasus saw was only a façade, a shadow of the former Srintil. Other than her physical form, Srintil had lost everything, lost herself. She didn't know how it was with the other prisoners, but she had often asked herself what the point of her existence was. In the space of only a few months, through the attitudes and behavior of the people around her, through their looks, and through their words, she had come to believe that she was a source of disgrace to humanity. Without her disgrace, life would surely be better and more tolerable for others. Since she still existed, Srintil thought, it was only because disgrace is one facet of this life and her place was within it, just as fecal matter must reside in the guts of humanity.

Amidst such a crisis in her self-confidence, Srintil could not believe that there would still be anyone who felt any concern over her fate, even Rasus. So, when he appeared, Srintil reasoned that his presence in the prison had nothing to do with her. She drew back when Rasus moved to approach her, covering her face with her hands, and sobbing as he drew closer.

Rasus moved slowly. He felt unsteady, and unsure of what to do. He wanted to guide Srintil to a chair and sit her down, but he was nervous. His mouth felt as though it was clamped shut; he didn't know what to say. Finally, he sat down again to wait for Srintil to regain her composure, but was astonished when a soldier entered and told him that his time was up.

"I...we haven't had a chance to speak yet."

"Those are the rules. Your time is up."

"Yes, but..."

"You're not here as a soldier. Now, leave!"

Rasus's face betrayed his reluctance. Mouth open, he looked desperately from Srintil to the soldier and back again. He couldn't understand why Srintil did not speak out to help him stay. Was she no longer a person with interests to defend, no matter how fragile these might be?

"Get out!"

Rasus was overcome by confusion. Hesitantly, he walked toward the door. He turned back to pick up the piece of paper on which he had been ordered to write what he and Srintil had discussed. The sheet of paper was still blank, in contrast to his face which betrayed his confusion.

He surrendered the paper to the captain's adjutant, his hands shaking. The corporal looked at the sheet in surprise.

"What's this? You were told to write down whatever was said between you and the prisoner. This paper is empty."

"We didn't have a chance to say a word, corporal."

"That's not possible! Ten minutes without a word? Write it down, right here!"

"What do you want me to write, corporal? We honestly didn't have a chance to say anything."

There was the sound of a sharp slap. Rasus staggered back from the force of the blow, then stood at attention. A second blow made him stagger again. He stood up again, this time not with the perfect posture of a soldier, but to let fly with his fists at the adjutant's jaw. Exploding into action like a raging lion, Rasus pummeled the man with the strength of his fists and the might of his spirit. The corporal fell back, scattering the tables and chairs in the room. Fortunately for him, he ended up in the arms of the commander who had, unannounced, entered the room.

"That's enough! Private Rasus, you are ordered to leave these premises!"

"Yes, sir!"

Rasus saluted, his ears still ringing from the adjutant's slaps. He turned toward the door, but his steps were slow, deliberate. Seeing the desks in disarray and papers scattered all over the place, he put everything in order before leaving. The commander watched him closely, both hands still on his adjutant's shoulders.

Outside, the sun beat down on Rasus's face, enhancing the fiery rage he was feeling. He stopped in front of the guardhouse with his feet planted wide, his hands clenched and trembling. His voice was hoarse as he challenged the guards.

"I'm Private Rasus, and I'm ready to fight anyone who calls me a servant. We're all men, all soldiers. Who's next?"

The three soldiers stood up as one, taken aback by this sudden challenge. But, unlike Rasus, they were not angry. They even felt compassion, moved by the tears trickling down his cheeks. One of them leaned his rifle against the wall and picked up Rasus's bag of belongings. He hung the bag on the hip of the trembling soldier and spoke, gently.

"We're sorry. Now, goodbye."

Rasus stood to attention and saluted. The three guards watched him as he left, deeply moved.

2

When the woven palm-leaves were first fixed to the roofs of Paruk homes, they were a rich dark green color. But after only one day of sunlight, they turned ashen and the plaiting began to loosen. The color continued to change, turning brown as the leaves grew brittle and dry. In the daytime, the people could see the sky from inside their huts. During the evening, the children counted the stars in the sky as they lay in bed and looked up through the roof.

When the rainy season arrived, Sakarya suggested that the people add a layer of reeds onto their roofs to seal them against downpours. Reed was the most suitable material because it absorbed the heat beating down onto the roofs and also sealed heat within the home when the air outside grew cold and dry. Sleeping on a mat below a reed roof was a natural pleasure that no child of Paruk could possibly forget.

The dry season followed the rainy season. It disappeared and returned again the following year. The reed roofs that protected the houses were now more than two years old, and were beginning to rot. A pair of brondol birds were diligently stealing individual reeds from the roof of Sakum's hut to make a nest high up in a nearby tree. In this manner, Paruk village retained its grip on life. The roots of the grass growing on top of Sakum's home were slowly and inexorably absorbing the decaying reed roof. Yet the blind Sakum continued to survive because Paruk itself clung to life. While Sakum hadn't yet done anything about replacing his roof, others were more diligent. Sakarya had even enlarged his shack, now supported by eight beams. He had replaced a wall with bamboo plaiting and built a trellis in front, also from bamboo. Paruk spread slowly like the roots of the reed plant, following the spaces in the rocky ground. Despite the absence of the singing of the ronggeng or the percussive sounds of the calung ensemble, the air was again filled with laughter of children as they looked for nuts that had fallen from a nearby *ketapang* tree, breaking open the hard shell and savoring the soft white meat inside.

The villagers were still afraid of the sight of men wearing heavy boots, and reluctant to meet the eyes of outsiders. Although the village was still considered guilty of immorality, the children were nevertheless just children. They soon forgot the fire that had engulfed their homes after the 1965 upheaval. They roamed the empty gardens, looking for anything that could be eaten, seeking tubers, banana blossoms, and fruit, digging up grasshoppers and crickets from the ground or climbing the branches of trees to pick ripe fruit, eggs from birds' nests, and even larvae from ant nests. In their own way, the children of Paruk also managed to survive.

One little girl was watching over her two younger brothers and couldn't go with her friends to forage in the empty gardens. As she sat with her young brothers near the outskirts of the village, she looked across the expanse of the wet rice fields and noticed a figure moving rapidly along the dikes that separated the fields. As the figure drew closer and closer, she determined that it was a woman. The woman was in such a hurry that she stumbled and fell several times, getting up to run again each time. Her wrap-around kain was raised high to expose her legs as she ran, her body leaning forward with her arms partially extended for balance. The little girl was too young to remember the name of the person who was approaching, but when the distance between her and the running woman was reduced to only one section of paddy field, she recognized the person as someone who was well known in Paruk.

Srintil was nearly out of breath. When she finally reached the village precinct, she collapsed, her small bag which contained a couple of changes of clothing tossed to the side. She fell on her face to kiss the earth, her cries halting the activities of the children foraging nearby. They stood silently watching the weeping woman trying to hug the ground. Moments later, a few of the adults from the village appeared. Nyai Sakarya, the first to realize who it was, lunged towards the limp figure on the ground.

"Oh, my God! My God! Srintil is back. Srintil, my beautiful grandchild! You're alive! Thank goodness, thank goodness. You're alive!"

The exhausted Srintil was embraced by three crying women. Too weary to get up by herself, she was helped to her feet. But she immediately cried out when, seeing through her tears, that the village had changed radically. Her weeping intensified as she hid her face in the lap of her grandmother.

The villagers once again slumped their heavily burdened shoulders, and their eyes filled with tears. After the years of uncertainty that had seared their hearts, Srintil had been returned to them. Srintil, their protective charm, had come home to the bosom of her homeland. Paruk was relieved, but at the same time its people suffered because the return of its child reminded them of a past sorrow: the harsh accusation that they were somehow implicated in the tragic debacle of 1965. What kind of sorrow had made Paruk feel as if it no longer had the right to feel and see the sun, the earth, and sky? What kind of sorrow had made the villagers feel as if even the lizards laughed at them in contempt? And what kind of sorrow had made them feel as though they were only excrement in the eyes of humanity?

The whole village gathered at Sakarya's house, seeking confirmation that its most valued member had returned. Some of the women sobbed, while the children looked on in confusion. Most, however, were silent. Sakarya paced around his living room with his arms folded. For him, the return of Srintil had special personal significance: he no longer had to worry about dying without knowing the fate of his beloved granddaughter.

Srintil sat next to her grandmother. With swollen eyes she gazed at her entire family, person by person. When she saw Goder, standing unsteadily, supported by Tampi, her face transformed. Her eyes glistened, the eyes of a devoted mother who had been forcefully separated from her child. Now mother and child found themselves face to face. But Goder was too young to understand the emotion behind the tears of the person staring at him, and he hid behind Tampi. He cried noisily when Srintil picked him up, hugged him tightly and kissed him. Some of the women looked away, unable to bear the sight of Goder rejecting his adopted mother's love.

In the days that followed, the villagers were keen to know what had happened to Srintil during the two years of her disappearance. They wanted to know what her daily life had been like, even the minute details, yearning to find out about her extraordinary experiences. Such a desire was not unusual, since within each villager was a tendency to enjoy sensational matters to some degree. In this case though, perhaps, for the sake of getting at the truth, people simply wanted the complete and honest story of her experience.

It was not possible, though, for even the most skilled biographer to write about this period of Srintil's life. In the first place, no one had been willing to talk about her whereabouts or circumstances during those two years. Secondly, in absolute and utter desperation, Srintil had resolved to say nothing to anyone about what she had endured. And it was unlikely that she would ever publish her memoirs, as she could neither read nor write.

In the end, one had to believe in the power of time, that the sophisticated knowledge stored within its gullet could hold all the secrets of history. Some people might say that to surrender to the mystery of time is a form of weakness and abject despair. These people could never be satisfied with the idea that two years of Srintil's life could simply be erased from all record, to remain an historical unknown. The past is the past, and the role of history as teacher to humanity should never be disregarded. Wisdom and knowledge in life is tempered by histories that are constituted by deeds of heroism and human decency as well as acts of betrayals and human depravity.

In any case, history never stops creating narratives. If history didn't create narratives on plaques or in books, then it would create them elsewhere. In a biography, for example, history creates a narrative of a personal life. The gentle and relaxed experiences of a life cannot possibly be narrated realistically. But harsh and bitter experiences are etched deeply onto a person's soul, reflected in his or her attitudes and behavior. Such experiences usually have a profound impact on a person's sense of self.

Why, for example, did Srintil begin running headlong toward the dikes leading to the village the moment she stepped out the jeep that had driven her to the rice fields? Without looking back, she had taken off like a sparrow hunted by a hawk, falling down and getting up as she ran, finally collapsing only when she reached the boundaries of her hometown.

And why, in the first few days after her return, did she remain silent? Why did she appear so exhausted and her expression seem far older than her actual age of twenty-three years? It wasn't until the second week that she began to leave her house, though she was still listless, her gait slow and her eyes always cast toward the ground.

One day, she walked to Tampi's home. As soon as her emotions had settled, she had begun to feel a desperate desire for Goder. She had never once felt that Goder was no longer her adopted child, even though she had been away from this four-year-old boy for so long.

However, Goder no longer recognized her, hiding his head in his mother's lap when Srintil knelt down to touch him. At first, she kept encouraging him and trying to draw him to her. But he still avoided her. Finally, despairing, she stood up, wiping the tears from her eyes.

"Tampi, did you teach Goder to hate me? she asked, sobbing.

"No, not at all," replied Tampi, quite ill at ease.

Srintil continued crying, covering her face with her hands and trying to hold back her sobs. This was Srintil, but it could have been any woman, feeling a profound longing when she reaches out her hand and her love is rejected by her child. Goder's behavior caused her to ask herself, "Have I become so worthless that even a small child does not want accept my extended hand?"

"Mommy? Why is she crying, Mommy?" asked Goder suddenly.

"Because you're naughty. You won't let her pick you up," answered Tampi.

"Who is she, Mommy?"

"Oh, my child! She's also your mommy. You have two mommies, me and her."

Goder's eyes widened. Clear and unblinking, his eyes turned toward the still crying Srintil.

"Is she really also my mommy?"

"She is."

"Why hasn't she ever come to our house?"

"She just came back from a long trip."

"Far away?"

"Very far."

"Did she bring me any presents?"

"Oh, I forgot, my child," said Srintil, her voice hoarse. "But I have some money. What would you like?"

Goder hesitated. His clear eyes looked up. Two pairs of eyes, one pair clear and bright, the other dull and lifeless, each searching for meaning in the other. With his clear eyes Goder grasped the truth, the heart of a young child being sensitive to such matters. Perhaps the breast of the woman before him, from which he had long ago drawn milk, once again bound these two hearts together. Bit by bit, the gap between them broke down until Goder no longer felt uncomfortable with the idea that this woman, who had returned from a long journey, was indeed his second mother.

Srintil, gazing into the eyes of the child, saw a pure world, one far purer than her own world: the world of adults. She felt as if she had endured a long and difficult journey that had exhausted her body and soul, only to arrive at a point of ambivalence in her life. And in the eyes of Goder, she saw a world which was calm and untainted. With a sense of disappointment and even jealousy, Srintil admitted to herself that Goder's world was not her world. But would there be any objection to her taking shelter in his world even for a moment, joining him to rest from her weariness?

There were no objections; Goder eventually brightened, full of friendliness. The door to his world opened for the woman who had once breastfed him, and now craved a small place of refuge within his heart.

"What would you like, my child?" Srintil repeated smiling, her first smile since returning from exile. As the child approached her, she squatted down so that her face was close to his.

"I want, uh… What should I ask for, Mommy?" Goder looked at Tampi.

"Well, whatever you like. What do you want?"

"I want some lollies."

"That's all? What about some bean cakes, too?"

"Yes, bean cakes, too. Do you have lots of money?"

"Lots," answered Srintil decisively.

"Well, then, I want a balloon."

"Fine, my boy. Now let's go home; my money is in my house."

Srintil held her arms wide open. She felt alive again as Goder stood up and ran to her. She felt extraordinarily refreshed to be accepted into the small but meaningful world of the little boy. This small world was actually now in her arms. She hugged him, picked him up, and carried him home, her steps confident. As she passed a hibiscus bush, a flower dropped from its stalk, spinning as it fell soundlessly. Yellow, except for a dark red tint at the base of its sepals. Ahead of her, a hen escorted its chicks, which scattered as she approached. Above her, a *celeret* bird flew from tree to tree. And she continued on her way, holding Goder close to her breast.

Like a swimmer carried along by the wave of a sudden storm, Srintil felt as though she was drifting in a situation she couldn't fully understand. Just as the swimmer would cling to a plank of wood to keep afloat, she clung to the hope that she could survive after being drawn into the current of the times, an event which had turned her into the scum of humanity. The opportunity to enter the world of a small child enabled her to savor the pure beginnings of human nature. She sold a gold bracelet to pay for her daily necessities and some gifts for Goder. Many people wondered why she showered so much love and attention on Tampi's child. Srintil wasn't concerned what other people thought. On the contrary, she wondered to herself why people were unable to understand her craving for peace of mind. Why they didn't understand that she could only find it through the eyes of a laughing child. Only the chuckling Goder had the power to make her forget that miserable period of her life which she had so recently put behind her.

Rumors of Srintil's return spread all the way to the Dawuan market, thanks to the gossip of Nyai Kartareja. The market people finally saw the truth behind the rumors when Srintil appeared one morning with Goder in her arms. Realizing they were experiencing an extraordinary event, they responded to her arrival by giving her their complete attention. But they remained quiet. The caprice of the times demanded new norms of behavior, and expressing enthusiasm for the arrival of a political exile was not appropriate.

Srintil, too, was sensitive to the circumstances. She would not even have gone to the market had it not been for Goder's demand for a treat. She would never even have left Paruk at all if she weren't required to report at the Dawuan police station every two weeks.

No one noticed that Srintil's lips trembled or that her legs were shaky when she found herself in the middle of the market. No one realized that she felt everyone's eyes piercing her heart like splinters of bamboo. Even Babah Gemuk, the Chinese merchant, who began to chat to her, wasn't able to sense the sorrow in her soul.

"Ah, you the ronggeng of Paruk, aren't you? Eh, we no see you long time. You still pretty, yah. So, I have many good things for you. How about purse, sandal or hairnet?"

"No thanks," Srintil replied, cold sweat running down the nape of her neck.

"Well, you no wear face powder. Yah! Okay, pretty girl without facial powder. You soon lose beauty. So, I have powder used by people in Hong Kong. How about some lipstick from Japan? Very cheap. Perhaps I come sleep in Paruk. He-he-he."

Babah Gemuk moved to touch Srintil's shoulder, but stopped when Srintil suddenly stood stock-still. She looked coldly at him, then turned her eyes towards Goder.

The market people, especially the women, noticed the changes in Srintil's appearance. Her knot of hair was loose, worn, as most women wore their hair, modestly low to hide the nape of her neck. In the past, Srintil had knotted her hair high up on her head so that her nape, a characteristic aspect of her beauty, was exposed. Her blouse was now cut long, hanging well over her hips, and her skirt was loose fitting like that of a farm girl, so that when she walked her calves remained covered. But what impressed them most was the difference in her demeanor. Her eyes avoided all contact, her expression was frozen, and she never smiled.

Srintil stayed at the market only as long as was necessary to buy snacks for Goder. Many eyes followed her as she left the market place. A woman selling betel chew sighed, as if she had a heavy weight on her heart.

"I wanted to give her betel and areca nuts," she said to another woman nearby. "Her lips were so pale. A betel leaf would have made her lips rosier, and that would have been right for her."

"So, why didn't you do it?"

"I don't know. In the past I used to always do that when Srintil came here. But now I feel like it's improper."

"I know what you mean. I feel the same way. Actually, I wanted to ask her a bit about how she had managed. But, for some reason I just didn't have the nerve. My lips felt as if they were sealed shut."

"And, did you notice? None of the men said anything to her, except for Babah Gemuk. They weren't like their usual selves, joking all the time and chattering when she comes by. So, what's going on?"

"Do you feel sorry for her?"

The other woman frowned as she considered. Her answer was so soft it barely left her mouth.

"I don't know, what do you think? Is it wrong for us to feel pity for someone like her?"

"I don't know. Yeah, it probably is, in this case. For women whose husbands had Srintil as a mistress, the matter is simple: those women would feel little sympathy toward her. That's proper. On the other hand… Oh, never mind."

The two women suddenly busied themselves with their merchandise as market officials arrived to distribute contribution tickets. They hurriedly opened their purses and surrendered several bank notes to the officials who gave them a yellow-colored ticket in return. Dawuan market again grew busy, but the people there were aware that the woman who had once sexually charged the atmosphere there had returned with her soul torn, her behavior completely changed. So shattered was Srintil's image that the people found it impossible to be open and natural to the recently released political prisoner.

In 1969 Paruk was a still immersed in ignorance and poverty. Three years after being consumed by fire, the village had become an even more isolated place and had lost many of its unique characteristics. It no longer boasted the sounds of the calung or the songs of the ronggeng. The grave of Ki Secamenggala, traditionally a sacred place for generations of villagers, was abandoned and unkempt. The music of the calung, the songs of the ronggeng, and the prayers recited over the ancestral grave were practices which were no longer considered appropriate to the times. Only Sakarya secretly visited the gravestone at the top of the hill in the cemetery.

But Sakarya himself was experiencing feelings of utter defeat, convinced that his role in life was without meaning. He couldn't understand the reason for the existence of the village if it no longer held calung performances and no longer sang ronggeng songs. Among the greater public, these traditional forms of music now aroused feelings of deep hatred, sitting uncomfortably with the abiding charge that the villagers were guilty of playing a part in the nation's recent period of chaos. Thus accused, Paruk was not allowed any happiness. It could only remain silent and bow to the whims of history.

As he sat musing under a tree near the gravesite dome of Ki Secamenggala, Sakarya came to the conclusion that Paruk no longer needed a traditional village elder. The more he thought about it, the more convinced he became, and without realizing it, this conviction gnawed away at his will to live.

One day, Sakarya placed a stone next to the gravesite dome. He told Kartareja that he wished to be buried under that stone when he died. In doing so, he had planted the suggestion of his demise in his own mind and, indeed, death soon followed. Sakarya died feeling a failure, and the only thing that could have possibly raised his spirits was the fact that Srintil was close by as he took his final breath.

Sakarya's death increased the feeling of fragility of the village. Srintil, too, lost a shelter that, although tattered, had provided her with at least one place of refuge. In the absence of such a refuge, the presence of Goder in her life took on even greater meaning. Goder offered her another world, a child's world of innocence and tranquility: pure and without profit, greed, lust, or sexual desire. In the child's eyes, she saw nothing of the 1965 debacle, no accusations or indictments of any kind leveled against her. Goder never once sneered or looked at her with contempt. For Srintil, he represented a world that accepted her completely and honestly, and she felt happy to immerse herself in it.

One had only to observe Srintil as she smiled watching Goder trying to catch a dragonfly, or see her beaming face as she watched the child bravely stand up to a fierce chicken to realize that a soul that had the power to be happy was a soul that had begun to grasp the joy of living. Srintil was at last regaining an understanding of the significance of life that could become the seeds of her self-worth.

Five or six months after her return home from exile, Srintil's eyes began to show signs of renewed life; her skin grew ruddy, her face came alive. Little by little, the bitter experience of the past receded into her subconscious. And, although that bitterness could become a potential handicap, the image of physical rejuvenation began to emerge like a betel leaf showered by rain.

At twenty-three years of age, Srintil's nature was sufficiently robust that, despite the experience she had endured, she retained her youthful appearance. But why was there always a part of humanity that felt little concern for a person's sorrow? And why was Srintil not aware that her recovery was being awaited by someone else?

One morning Nyai Kartareja left Paruk on a secret mission. From the Dawuan market, she took a horse-drawn cart to Wanakeling, reaching her destination just as the sun was beginning to set. The owner of the house, a middle-aged man, had just returned from work and was talking to his daughter. Seeing Nyai Kartareja arrive, he asked his daughter to leave them so they could speak in private.

"Please come in," Marsusi said, receiving her with joy.

"Thank you. You look happy. Are you so sure that I'm bringing good news?"

"If you weren't bringing good news, why would you travel so far to come here?"

"You have a point there."

"So. Now, talk. But, please, keep your voice down."

"What can I say if you already know the reason for my coming here?"

"So, Srintil has returned to her previous self?" Marsusi asked.

"Yes, sir. The only problem is, I believe, you need to come to Paruk."

"To Paruk? Do you really think that I need to go to there?"

"Why not, sir? You're a widower now. I don't think it's so strange for a widower to visit a single woman."

"Sure. But what about the times? No, madam. If I'm to meet Srintil, I want to meet her outside the village. And I'd like you to make the arrangements. Wherever you want, just not in Paruk."

"That could be difficult, sir. Very difficult."

"Yet, I'm sure you can do it. Look over there, madam."

Marsusi pointed to a motorcycle parked in his back yard: not an old Harley Davidson left over from the war, but a brand new Vespa.

"Tell Srintil that, if she wants that motorcycle, she can have it. I'm serious."

Nyai Kartareja's expression revealed the admiration she felt. How appropriate, she thought. She recalled that, when he had heard about Srintil's return, he had politely enquired about her circumstances.

Marsusi, you yourself have brought up the subject of the changed times. I can no longer always do just what I want. I don't think I can get Srintil to leave Paruk."

"So you came all this way just to report that she can smile and is in good health again?"

"No, of course not. I'll try to persuade her to do what you want. I'm ready to help you in any way I can, except to take Srintil out of Paruk. That, I can't do."

"But, there's simply no way I would go to your village."

Nyai Kartareja shook her head. "Wait a minute! I've just remembered something. On the first and fifteenth of every month, Srintil goes to report to the Dawuan police station. This could be an opportunity for you to meet her. What do you think?"

Marsusi didn't answer. But his expression relaxed, revealing that he considered that the stalemate had been broken. He seemed animated as he handed money to Nyai Kartareja when she took her leave.

During the inferno that had consumed Paruk, many of the trees and shrubs which were seared by the flames had subsequently withered and died. An areca tree behind Srintil's home survived, and after several months of struggle started springing into life. The burnt red palms had dropped and been replaced by fresh green leaves. New sheathes cracked open, spilling palm blossoms in scattered patterns of white. Older blossoms turned into stems that drooped, heavy with areca nut. Amid the luxuriance of the branches, the rustlings of two small birds building a nest could often be heard. Blade by blade, they stole reeds from the roofs of people's homes, arranging them to create their own little world hidden in the branches of the tree.

The work of the two busy little birds was occasionally interrupted by minor scuffles between the two; sometimes they chased one another and mated; other times they flew far away, crossing the broad expanse of the rice fields that surrounded the village as they hunted for seeds. They would return with gullets full and continue their work on the nest until dusk.

Srintil had been watching the activities of the two birds for several days. While playing with Goder outside, she often sat and looked up toward the areca tree. She saw the tiny world that been created there as a peaceful one, without bitterness, without fear and worry. But, in fact, that was not the reality. One afternoon, she noticed a crow land at the top of the tree. The big black bird tore up the nest of the two little birds, searching for their eggs or young. The two small birds escaped, and could only watch from afar as their world was completely destroyed by the crow. Srintil stood up in alarm, feeling a sudden need to find Goder, but encountered Nyai Kartareja beside her.

"What's the matter? You seem startled."

"It's nothing. I just wanted to find Goder."

"He's playing with his whirly-gig. Let him be. I need to talk to you. It's important."

Srintil looked at Nyai Kartareja warily.

"Important?"

"Yes, important."

"But, on the first of the month I reported to the Dawuan police. And on the fifteenth, I'll go again. I haven't forgotten."

"What I want to talk to you about has nothing to do with your reporting to the police."

"So, I haven't done anything wrong? It's not about me doing anything wrong?"

"No. No!"

Srintil was breathless with fear. Nyai Kartareja gave her a moment to calm herself, patiently waiting for the blood to return to the young woman's ashen face. She couldn't help but feel pity for Srintil when she realized how very frail her psyche had become.

"I just want to talk about my situation. In the past, I suffered, but not the way I'm suffering now. In the past, to tell you the truth, I was always able to follow your wishes. But now, young lady, it's a matter of whether there will be food on my table. So, I have a proposal: In return for the help I gave you in the past, I would like you to give me the opportunity to join you in a better life."

"Join…me?" asked Srintil looking at Nyai Kartareja long and searchingly. "Join me in a decent life? How could that be possible when I don't have any income whatsoever myself?"

"But, my dear, your situation is not the same as mine. You're still young, and who can deny your beauty? No matter where, no matter when, a beautiful woman is always better off than an ugly woman, isn't that right?"

"What are you saying?" Srintil asked.

"Just this,young lady. You just said that you have no income. So, how about doing something so that you have an income once again. This would be easy for you; it's only a matter of whether you are willing to or not."

"Speak plainly, Ma'am."

"Very well. The other day, I met someone who would really like to invite you to, shall we say, find occasional relief with him from the troubles of everyday life. You remember Marsusi, don't you?"

A fog suddenly formed before Srintil's eyes, turning the world around her into a spinning haze. She felt as if mole crickets had crawled into each of her ears and were singing as loudly as they could, creating a buzzing whine that drowned out all conversation. Her face grew ashen and her pale lips began to tremble. Beads of sweat formed on her skin. Her chest heaved as she tried to control the struggling emotions within her—emotions of profound regret and outrage, sadness and fury—and her expression gradually changed from ashen dread to full-blooded anger.

"My God! This is too much!" Srintil screamed. "You're telling me to go back to what I did in the past? Haven't you paid attention to the times? Haven't you seen what my situation is? Oh God…"

"Be patient, young lady. Listen to what I am saying first. Nobody is misunderstanding your situation, but are you going to put your own interests above the basic needs of the people in Paruk, people who need to eat and can only follow your wishes?"

"I really don't know what you mean. The people here can live independently of my circumstances. They are used to eating tubers, even banana stalks. Go and do that, and don't ask me to return to my past life. You only endured two weeks of imprisonment. I went through two years! That's enough for me. No more!"

"Now, hold on, young lady. Marsusi is now a widower. He said he is prepared to give you a Vespa, if you want it. Who knows? Perhaps he intends to ask you to become his wife. Think about this calmly."

"We both know Marsusi's position. Do you really think that a man like him would want to marry a former prisoner?"

"That may well be a consideration. But, just think about it. Marsusi and other men may want to marry you or perhaps just get together with you for a little diversion. They all know who you are, don't they?"

"Oh God, they do. And they are right. All the blame lies with me. This means that I have to know my place. People are demanding that I change my behavior because they didn't like what I was doing before. Now, to do the same thing again is the same as being a criminal. You know what could happen if people thought I was doing something that is considered criminal?"

Nyai Kartareja shut her lips tightly and walked away, leaving Srintil brushing tears from her eyes. None other than a fellow villager had planted seeds of doubt, which would erode the health and happiness that had begun to return to her heart. She watched the woman's receding form with sadness and deep disappointment.

Oh, Nyai Kartareja, Srintil thought, people say that when you were young, you too were a ronggeng like me. The difference is that you didn't make much money. Nevertheless, just like me, you experienced male lust since the time of your first menstruation. And I know the men of Paruk, I know men from other places: even men

I encountered during my imprisonment. We both understand men. These days, I ask in my heart of hearts, isn't the bitterness I have had to endure the result of knowing too much about men? Isn't it all because I thought I represented femininity and therefore had to serve the needs of masculinity, even the most primitive needs? Isn't it because I was a ronggeng, that I was exiled and imprisoned?

Srintil continued to muse: It seems that you aren't even a little bothered by questions like these. You're a foolish old woman. Do you care so little about my emotional pain that you could suggest the return of men into my life? Haven't you even noticed the changes in me? Oh Lord, God…

"Are you crying, Mommy? Why are you crying?"

The clear high voice came from behind her. Srintil carefully wiped away her tears before turning and looking at Goder, his face questioning.

"Are you crying? Was someone bad to you?"

"Oh, no, my baby. I'm not crying."

"Yes, you are. Who was being bad?"

Oh, those clear brown eyes! Must I tell you? Must I taint your purity by admitting that my life has been full of sin? No. Your world is too pure and I will not introduce the sins of life to you because I have too much at stake in your innocence where I find my only solace.

With enormous effort, she restrained her tears and took the child in her arms. A bamboo door squeaked as Srintil and Goder disappeared behind it. The grass hut grew quiet. Inside, two extremely different worlds coexisted.

At times the vast wet rice fields surrounding Paruk gave hope for a good harvest, but the ocean of ripening paddy held an irony which had passed from generation to generation. Paruk had never once fully participated in a harvest because, only one or two of the villagers owned any rice fields, and these were only a few square meters in size. Every harvest, the villagers had only been able to participate as field laborers, the workers who harvested the paddy by hand. It didn't occur to any of the children that they should ask their parents why they were all poor, why they didn't possess even the smallest rice field. They didn't really understand. The children only knew that the harvest always brought a time of happiness. For the little girls, of particular delight was to go to the rice fields to gather empty paddy stalks to make reed flutes. The unique, sweet sounds of these flutes could be amplified by adding to the end a flared bell made from a coconut leaf. The surging tones blended with the sound of the wind sweeping through the trees, and the flowing music combined with the waving sea of paddy, in a carpet of reddish yellow, golden and soft green.

While children elsewhere had already been introduced to factory-made toys, the little girls of Paruk remained most familiar with the reed flute. They knew how to get the best tones out of a dark green stalk of paddy. They also knew that to get a more distinct tone, they had to soak the flute for a while in water. And if they blew into the flute in a breathy way, the sound would come and go like the moon disappearing and emerging from behind the clouds.

A man stood in the shade of a tree at the side of the road that led to the Dawuan market. He could clearly see Paruk in the distance. The sounds of a reed flute reached his ears, along with the cries of the beranjangan and ciplak birds. The beranjangan, high up in the sky, sang in perfect imitation of several other birds. It could remain in the sky for hours, chattering away, the only danger it faced being the attack of a hawk. At the same time, the male *ciplak* flew in circles, its cries directed at a nearby female. It would make a steep dive back to earth once the female revealed her location.

It was not clear whether the man standing beneath the tree was concentrating on the musical strains of the reed flute or the revelry in the sky above the carpet of ripening paddies. What was clear was that Marsusi was keeping a constant watch on a point on the dikes that bordered the village. He was waiting for Srintil to emerge as she left to report to the Dawuan police. His presence under the tree was the result of a decision he had made after a violent inner struggle.

Marsusi was acutely aware of the current social situation where accusing fingers were pointed at men who tried to pursue intimate relationships with former female prisoners. He understood that his plan to woo Srintil was fraught with the danger of his being publicly ridiculed at the very least, or losing his job as an important official for the Wanakeling plantation, at worst. But Marsusi, now a widower, could not get the ronggeng of Paruk out of his mind. His thoughts kept returning to her graceful neck, her soft glances and her sweet smile. The fact that he was now a single man made his fantasies even more vivid.

Two days earlier, he had acted on his decision. He had gone to the constable to whom Srintil reported: not to the police station, but to the constable's home. The two were already acquainted as they were both government bureaucrats, and also, everyone in Dawuan knew Marsusi because he was one of the first men in the area to own a motorcycle.

"What a surprise to have you come to my home," Darman, the constable, said to him. "Are you offering me those old rubber trees that you want cut down? If that's what you've come about, believe me, I can't afford them. I just don't have the money."

"If you really do need some firewood, that's okay. I'll have a truckload sent to you tomorrow," answered Marsusi.

"Go on. I was just joking."

"But I'm not. Tomorrow, I'll deliver a truckload of firewood for you, and at no charge."

"Really, I was just joking."

"Whatever, but I was serious."

"What can I say?"

"Well, I hope you can help me. Otherwise, I wouldn't be here right now."

"So, what would you like me to do for you?"

The atmosphere, which had at first been stiff and awkward, thawed, and the two men found themselves relaxed and more at ease. Nevertheless, Marsusi took a moment to reply to Darman's question. He pulled out a cigarette for his host and one for himself. Billows of smoke soon surrounded the two, a symbol of the privacy of the conversation between them.

"It's like this," Marsusi said in a low voice. "I need some information regarding Srintil."

Darman leaned forward, eyes wide. "Srintil?"

"That's right. How long do you think Srintil will have to report to you as a parolee?"

"Why are you asking this?"

"To be honest, this is related to the fact that I'm now a widower."

"So, why Srintil?"

Darman's words were terse, but inside he was wondering why, when everyone else was making every effort to erase any evidence of connections to the people associated with the 1965 debacle, Marsusi seemed to be doing the exact opposite.

"To be honest, Darman, I feel rather embarrassed. But, whatever I do, I can't stop thinking about her."

"Very well, Marsusi. As long as you recognize that the situation could develop into something that may cause problems for you."

"Oh, I understand completely. I will also make sure that the consequences of anything I do will be my responsibility and mine alone. Now, can you tell me, when she will be free from parole obligations?"

"Usually the parole period is one year. Srintil has just finished about six months. Are you considering marrying her?"

"Very possibly. For the next six months I want to see how things develop. There, now you know it all. I hope that you'll be discrete and understanding when you see me courting her."

"Yes, but just remember…"

"Oh, by all means. I shall respect your reputation and status. On the one hand, I can't bear the thought of being considered an old man. But on the other hand, in matters of discretion, especially in relation to people who offer me help, believe me, I am indeed old and wise."

So, two days later, Marsusi stood under the tree at the edge of the main road leading to Dawuan. At first glance, it looked as if he was just standing there savoring the idea of the upcoming harvest. But if the birds flying nearby had understood human behavior, they might have noticed that he was quite nervous. All too often, he tossed away his cigarette before it was finished and then lit another immediately afterwards. He felt that he had been standing there for a year instead of only fifteen minutes.

He felt instantly relieved when he saw a small dot in the distance moving around the outskirts of the village. The dot moved along one of the narrow dikes leading to the main road, drawing closer to the place where he stood. As it approached, it took on the shape of a woman. If that woman had smooth and clear skin, it would be Srintil, Marsusi told himself. He grew increasingly restless, but his expression and smile remained vague. Srintil had emerged without a child in tow. This would not have been the case, if it hadn't been for the efforts of Nyai Kartareja, working on Marsusi's behalf.

Grasshoppers and dragonflies flew in front of her as she walked, and the lower half of her body seemed to be immersed in the sea of paddy. A ciplak bird cried as it circled in the sky above, fretting about its mate, which was hatching a brood of eggs in a nest not far from the dike she traversed. A hahayaman, startled by her approach, flew off into the distance, shitting in panic.

When Srintil was just one paddy field away, Marsusi was able to confirm her identity. At that stage, Srintil had not yet recognized the man standing under the tree. She only began to really grasp the situation when she had almost reached the main road. Realizing who it was, she suddenly stopped. Apprehensively, Marsusi began walking towards her.

"You're a bit late. Darman has been waiting a long time and he asked me to meet you to get you there more quickly. Come on, let's go."

Srintil stood stock still in the middle of the carpet of undulating rice paddy, her mouth open and her eyebrows furrowed, reflecting the tension within her. Her expression grew increasingly distressed as Marsusi advanced several more steps and beckoned to her.

"Come on, you're already late. I'll give you a ride so you can get there quickly."

"I'd…I'd rather just walk by myself," she answered haltingly.

"Come on now, don't turn down my offer. That wouldn't be wise, especially since you're going to be late. Let's go."

The people of Paruk, Srintil included, knew little about the workings of the bureaucracy. In their view, everyone connected with the state was aristocracy. And all aristocracy was the same: an arm of the state authority. Any aristocrat could speak on behalf of the state, whether he was a security guard, a police officer, or a minor civil servant working for the Department of Agriculture, like Marsusi. When the state became the most dominant force in the lives of the people, villagers like Srintil could not possibly understand the difference between police, armed forces, and agricultural officials. All of these represented an arm of authority and, confronted with this, Srintil could only bow her head in submission, especially since Marsusi's words carried an implicit threat. Nervously she followed him, her gaze directed at her feet, wet from the morning dew on the grass growing along the dikes. Kick-starting his motorcycle to life, Marsusi said in a friendly voice.

"Please, get on."

Srintil slowly drew a long breath before finally giving in. She sat behind him, stiff and awkward, not used to riding on a motorcycle.

Perhaps, too, she was unconsciously trying to avoid being close to him.

They covered the distance to the police station in just a few minutes. Yet for Srintil it seemed like an eternity. During the short ride she noticed several people gazing in amazement, obviously saying to one another, "Srintil sure has gall to go gallivanting around the countryside with men on their motorcycles. Isn't she worried about getting arrested again?" Everyone had assumed that she would slink about in shame, filled with remorse. It was clear from their disapproving looks, that they viewed her behavior as reckless and disrespectful. She was acting in direct contradiction to the norms and standards of the times.

Srintil did not realize that the great suffering in her heart was caused only by the drama playing out in her own mind. Nevertheless, people hadn't forgotten how she had been queen of the stage at the propaganda rallies where spectators had been turned into a raging mob that looted paddy fields, without regard for the rights of owners. They had also not forgotten that, at several of these incidents, farmers had been killed trying to defend their property. Srintil could not possibly extricate herself from the moral dilemma that these incidents had created. Social norms and values had been turned upside down by men like Bakar, during the month of September, 1965. On every face, Srintil could see the story of Bakar, killed by a vengeful mob. A man associated with the ronggeng of Paruk.

Is history made only by a certain general whose name is synonymous with power? Not necessarily. But Srintil did not know that. She did not know either that history is also created out of everyday human compassion. But compassion never comes from raging mobs, never arises out of state bureaucracy. Human compassion remains resolute and steadfast, persistently giving voice to social justice. The plea for compassion can perhaps be heard in the whimpers of a hungry baby crying at its mother's barren breasts. Perhaps, too, in the tears of some of the women at the Dawuan market, who were moved with pity at Srintil's misfortune in being given a burden far too heavy for her frail shoulders. Historical evidence of compassion manifests itself through the wisdom of a simple people who often quote the traditional expression, "*Aja dumeh maring wong sing lagi kanggonan luput*," don't look with contempt upon people ensnared in wrongdoing.

No. Srintil was not aware of all this. She was certain of only one thing, that the role she must now play in life was that of social disgrace. How long she would have to play this role, she didn't know. That was a secret perhaps located somewhere in the vagaries of the present, within the unfolding story of time itself. And, if the present moment demanded that she carry the burden of history on her shoulders, Srintil could only submit. For this child of Paruk, the burden of history meant crawling before her social superiors, filled with remorse. It meant she could not walk with her head held high, that she must seek the approval of her superiors before even smiling.

Since her release from prison six months earlier, Srintil had had her thumbprint taken eleven times by the constable, Darman. Although she had faced this representative of the state authority on several occasions, she still quaked in fear every time she saw him. Nevertheless, men like Darman are not machines. After a few times, he began to tease her and joke with her. When he guided her hand to stamp her thumbprint to the report, his hands were not completely innocent, lingering over her smooth skin. But on the day Srintil arrived with Marsusi, Darman was a model of officious formality: perhaps because Marsusi had been true to his word and had already delivered the promised truckload of firewood to his home.

After providing the required thumbprint, Srintil meekly took her leave. She bowed low to the two government bureaucrats, her face a raw reflection of the humiliation she was feeling. As she walked to the door, Marsusi stopped her.

"Wait, I'll take you back."

"Thank you, sir, but I usually return home alone."

"It would be better if you go along with Marsusi," interjected Darman. "Go ahead. I'm sure his new Vespa is a pleasant ride."

Srintil felt trapped, like an animal surrounded by a mob. Then, perhaps because of the firewood, Darman spoke more decisively.

"If I were to order you to ride with Marsusi, would you still refuse?"

Her trapped look became a mask of utter terror. Srintil stood transfixed, only moving after Darman gestured toward the door with a movement of his chin. Marsusi followed her out, like a soldier after a victorious battle. As on the previous ride, Srintil sat stiffly on the back of the motorcycle. As they drove off, her body became a distinctly separate part of a moving totality. She leaned her torso backwards, her hands at her sides like someone unable to find a comfortable position. She kept her eyes cast down, watching the ground rushing by at an unbelievable pace beneath her.

Marsusi's plan, after leaving the police office, had been to take Srintil to a hotel behind the market place, and there have his way with her, despite all the risks this entailed. However, as he approached a three-way intersection, a new thought occurred to him, and he made a sudden decision. He turned onto a narrow road that led to the Wanakeling plantation. Since he already had the object of his desire in his grasp, he thought, why not take it home?

Srintil, who had believed that she was being escorted to the dikes that lead to Paruk, immediately noticed the change in direction. Her mouth moved, but she could barely give voice to her words.

"Uh, where are you going, sir?"

"Relax, we're going to my home."

"Your home?"

"To Wanakeling. Where else?"

"Sir…?"

"Relax. I'm not kidnapping you. We're just dropping by Wanakeling for a moment. Later, I'll take you back to your village."

"But I don't want to go there. I want to go home."

"Listen to me. I want to talk to you, and I'm not to be fooled with. Nyai Kartareja said something about this, didn't she?"

"But I don't want to."

Srintil began to thrash about in her seat so violently that the motorcycle began to wobble.

"Stop! I want to get off!"

"Stop thrashing about. You'll fall off."

"I don't want to go with you. Stop!"

"Wait a minute. You haven't heard what I want to say to you yet."

Several times, Srintil attempted to leap off the motorbike, but at the last minute, hesitated. The gravel on the mountain road raced past beneath her, like the teeth of innumerable saws, ready to slice into anything that fell upon its surface. Finally, she gave up, thinking, "Oh, God, what more must I endure?"

The mountain road they were traveling on entered a teak forest. The trees stood close together, the large ones standing proudly over the smaller ones below. Branches grew in all directions to catch every ray of sunshine, leaving the ferns below to live in shade.

Why is it that a great desire or major plan can be thwarted by a small factor that might never have been entered into the equation? A powerful soldier might die in battle, not from an enemy bullet, but from the bite of a harmless looking but poisonous little snake. Marsusi's desire to carry Srintil to Wanakeling failed because his actions were guided by haste. As he drove over the ruts in the badly damaged road, the motorcycle seemed to leap about, its speed changing dramatically. At one point Srintil was catapulted off the seat of the bucking motorcycle at the very same time Marsusi suddenly accelerated. Srintil briefly floated in the air, then landed heavily on the ground, while Marsusi raced ahead on the bike, completely unaware of what had happened.

At first Srintil felt as if thousands of trees were spinning around her head. The spinning gradually slowed down and eventually stopped, and she made out the heaving outline of a forest. To her left she could see the motorcycle disappearing in the distance. Struggling to stand, she became aware of pain in her leg. There were abrasions and bleeding on her left ankle and knee. Her hands were stinging. Small bits of gravel were embedded in her palms. Beads of blood appeared wherever the small pebbles came off.

As soon as she felt calmer, she walked over to the side of the road. There was no one around. She quickly realized that she had to seize the opportunity that had inadvertently been presented to her. Marsusi would come back to look for her as soon as he became aware that she was no longer sitting behind him on the motorcycle. However, with her leg hurting so much, she knew that she could not possibly walk back to Paruk. Even if she were to start walking with perfectly healthy legs, Marsusi would surely catch up with her.

Staggering, she set off, with the aim of putting distance between herself and the road. After a short time she noticed a narrow trail leading into the forest. The trail was likely one used by the wood gatherers whose voices Srintil could hear nearby. A moment later, she saw two young men making their way down a hill toward her, each carrying a load of firewood. Another young man followed behind them carrying rolls of teak leaves. Upon seeing her, they stopped and stared in astonishment. Occasionally, women foraged for firewood and teak leaves in the forest, but the three young men had never seen anyone like Srintil there.

Srintil found herself sitting alone in the middle of the forest. In the silence she contemplated her circumstances. Around her were tall trees, all teak. And beneath the trees flourished innumerable small plants, ranging from mosses which blanketed stones and bark to several varieties of ferns covering the slopes of ravines, from groves of bamboo and wild sugarcane to creeping plants, the shoots of which formed a complex braid, as complex as that of the various roots creeping along the ground and penetrating the earth. When the wind blew, thousands of leaves rustled to create a musical sigh, every leaf swaying in unison. In those moments of contemplation, Srintil grasped the meaning of the perfect harmony of nature, a harmony reaching back thousands of years. Every young shoot groped towards life despite having to break through the complex weaving of equally sophisticated fellow plants, no root tip failing to reach the earth. A small banyan tree grew on top of a rotting tree trunk, and the spirit of harmony allowed the roots of the small tree to crawl along to the earth, its leaves arranged so that each one had a chance to be touched by rays of sunlight.

The wind blew again, this time accompanied by the sound of falling leaves. Srintil could hear a woodpecker hammering away in the distance, along with the faint sound of a woodcutter's axe. She turned her head towards the sound of the far-off woodcutter. She could hear his rough singing, giving voice to "Kutut Manggung," a traditional song. For no particular reason she started, not because she, too, knew the words to that song, but because she suddenly realized that what was expressed in those words was related to the restlessness within her soul.

"Gendhing Kutut Manggung," was a classical song of delicately expressed passion, its words full of esoteric descriptions of desire and basic human urges. It expressed the primitive instinct of lust, but lust according to civilized values that differentiated between human desire and the lust of animals, subtly describing the connection between humans and nature. Only adults could understand what was meant by the words *wis wayahé lingsir wengi, perkututé arsa muni*, or *perkututé nyaluk ngombé.* The lyrics painted a picture of physical desire between man and woman, conceptualized within a cosmic order where the motivation behind this physical relationship is the struggle to attain harmony in life. Yet the conceptualization of desire in the song also made allowances for human frailty. It described a civilized sexual relationship between a man and a woman, as well as being holy and sacred, as also full of playfulness and flirtation. The words contained a feeling of intimacy, couched in euphemistic language to avoid any sense of lewdness.

Although her understanding was somewhat superficial, Srintil knew about the conceptualization of desire expressed in the song. Nyai Kartareja had once explained the difference between two types of desire: that of "Kutut Manggung" and that of the ronggeng tradition. In the past, Srintil had been certain that the ronggeng version was superior because of its lack of moral standards. Its conceptual realm was masculinity in a general sense, not the masculinity of a particular male. As a result, she had believed that being a ronggeng was better than being a man's wife. But, the conceptualization and realization of desire in the style of a ronggeng had, in fact, turned out to be crude, loose, and raw, lacking in harmony. The ronggeng tradition had even led Srintil to prison for two years. During that time, she had almost lost her sense of identity and, even after being freed, her soul remained imprisoned. She realized at that moment in the forest that her spiritual imprisonment would end only when she let go of her role of representing femininity for a general, raw masculinity, and took on the role of representing femininity for a specific man, namely a husband.

The fragments of lyrics of the song were just audible above the soft rustling of the wind and the twittering of the birds. Srintil bowed her head, her thoughts full of beautiful fantasies about being a wife, a woman who was able and willing to devote herself to one man. Beautiful to Srintil, because she had never heard of a woman having to endure the bitterness of prison or being isolated in lifelong shame for having chosen to spend her life as a man's wife.

She raised her face and saw in the distance the sprouting petals of a newly blossoming sugar palm tree. Bright yellow, their freshness contrasted with the colors around. Srintil's eyes followed a hawk circling over the treetops, searching for prey. Her vision blurred and another image emerged: Rasus. Why was it, she wondered, that all those years ago, Rasus had disapproved of her becoming a ronggeng? Maybe it had been because he just wanted to protect his own interests. But maybe it was because he had been expressing basic human instinct, recognizing that the ronggeng tradition was not in harmony with the highest human ideals. Srintil covered her face with her hands. The answer to her question was in the bitter memory of her experience in prison, of the changing times that had brought down her self-esteem, and of the state authorities that had crushed human values.

A ray of sunlight penetrated the leafy canopy of the forest. The trees had already formed shadows in the east, and she had a strong, sudden urge to go home. People in Paruk were very likely worried, thinking that perhaps she had been detained once again. Goder was probably crying because the snacks he wanted hadn't arrived. But she was not sure which route she could take without encountering Marsusi. Meanwhile, her leg was throbbing with pain and she knew that she was at least seven kilometers from home.

She stood up and set off down the narrow trail towards the mountain road that divided the teak forest, unsure of what lay before her. Maybe she would meet Marsusi again or maybe she would collapse in exhaustion somewhere along the way. As she reached the first slope, she suddenly stopped. Before her, some distance away, she saw a man parking a motorcycle under the shade of a tree. He turned around and scanned the edge of the forest with his eyes. Srintil surmised that Marsusi must have spoken with the three woodcutters she had passed earlier. They would have directed him to the path that she was following.

When Marsusi spied a figure on the path, quickly moving away, he jumped from his motorcycle to give chase. The forest inspired Marsusi's primitive instincts to hunt. As he hurried after the disappearing figure, his heart beat more strongly, and from it emerged a male animal, keen to be king of the jungle. His face became savage; his skin grew damp with sweat. Although his lips were drawn into a tight smile, his eyes were hard. Marsusi was a man well adapted to hiking through the woods. His purposeful stride was accompanied by the sounds of dry leaves and small snails being crushed by his canvas shoes.

When he had realized that Srintil was no longer seated on the back of the motorcycle, conflicting thoughts passed through his mind. The first thing he imagined was that she had fallen and was seriously injured. This would be an embarrassment to him and would considerably complicate his position. But he felt he must find her to rectify his transgression. He figured he might even be able to stick to his first plan, with some adaptation if necessary.

But what actually presented itself was a different scenario. The three young men he met in the forest had testified that Srintil was not seriously injured, just limping as she walked. This presented a new situation to Marsusi: Srintil was attempting to flee from him. So it was not surprising that his sentiments, which at first had been filled with remorse and regret, now suddenly became enraged. If Srintil hadn't fled, his attitude would have softened and he would have apologized a thousand times over. But because she had attempted to run away from him, he was transformed into an eager hunter the instant he saw his prey moving ahead.

"Srintil! Wait! Where are you going?"

Although she was in considerable pain, Srintil continued, turning down a steep slope toward the road. An inner voice told her that she couldn't possibly move faster than Marsusi, and that any moment she would be caught. The voice also told her that there would be nothing to hinder Marsusi in carrying out whatever plan he had in mind. She wanted to put every effort she could towards getting out into the open before he caught up with her. She had to get to the road!

Marsusi, now completely transformed into a hunter, became further enraged when Srintil ignored his shout. His self-esteem was offended, and all his desires became focused on dominating Srintil in the solitude of the forest. However, he made a basic mistake. He had assumed that Srintil would move further into the forest, and he continued his ascent along the trail, hoping he could cut his quarry off at some point. From a high vantage point, he stopped to assess the situation, and was dismayed when he realized that the person in the swaying underbrush below was Srintil, who had left the path and was now charging toward the main road. He turned around and descended quickly, but he was too late: the distance between them was now too great.

By the time she reached the road, Srintil had expended all her resources, collapsing, exhausted, in the middle of the road. The sun and sky bore witness to her weeping. And to the wounds on her knee and ankle, now bleeding profusely.

Marsusi emerged two minutes later, a predator that had succeeded in overcoming his prey. Feeling proud because he considered that he had won, his walk was confident. But his pride suddenly shriveled as he saw at close range the exhausted appearance of his quarry. Srintil sat with her legs folded to one side, facing the sun setting in the west. Her skirt was tattered, hiked up to reveal her thighs. Marsusi's animal instincts flared, but quickly subsided when he saw the bleeding wounds on her leg.

Who had conquered whom? Did Marsusi conquer Srintil? Or was Marsusi overcome by his own humanity? Perhaps, according to hunting ethics, a true hunter loses his savagery when confronted by a helpless prey whimpering in pain, its blood forming a puddle on the rocks.

Marsusi stood before Srintil, stupefied. The waves of wildness reduced to small ripples, but they weren't completely stilled. He looked around, not wishing to be seen in a state of hesitation. They were alone except for a *tlimukan* bird flying across the open sky before disappearing into a gorge. The only sounds were the wind and two unseen prenjak birds chasing one another in the forest close by. Marsusi's expression showed his confusion, then it relaxed. The blood. He pulled out a handkerchief. He wanted to do something good, tender, to wipe the blood from Srintil's leg. But Srintil flinched, avoiding his touch, and wiped away the blood herself with the edge of her skirt.

"Srintil, please. I'll take you home to Paruk," said Marsusi, his voice husky. The half-minute waiting for her answer felt interminable to him.

"No. I just want to sit here. Do what you want with me here in the light of day."

Suddenly Srintil noticed a man approaching on a bicycle from the west. Marsusi was facing her and wasn't aware of him.

"You can see that my leg is injured. My whole body hurts. I couldn't do anything even if you wanted me to."

"I know. So, let me take you home. There's no way you can walk on your own."

"Please, just let me go home on my own."

The man riding the bicycle was carrying two rolls of teak leaves. He was astonished at the scene in front of him. He was more amazed when the woman sitting in the middle of the road called out to him.

"Hey, stop! Where're you going?"

"Well, I'm going home."

"Where's that?"

"I live in Pecikalan. You're from Paruk, aren't you?"

"What, do you know who I am?"

"Who wouldn't know you?"

"That's lucky. May I ask for your help?"

"Help with what?"

"Give me a ride to Paruk. You wouldn't be embarrassed to have me ride on the back of your bicycle, would you?"

"I don't know. I'm Partadasim."

"And I am Srintil, from Paruk. We're from the same district. You'll help me, won't you?"

"Sure, but I wouldn't be doing anything wrong, would I?"

"No, you wouldn't be doing anything wrong," interjected Marsusi, tongue-tied until that moment. "A Pecikalan villager has to help a Paruk villager."

"Yeah, sure. But why me? What about you? And what happened here, anyway?"

"Well, it was like this," Srintil began. "I was walking along when suddenly there was a water buffalo running on the road. I got frightened, and ran to the side of the road, where I fell. This gentleman was kind enough to help me until you came along."

"So, please take Srintil to Paruk," Marsusi pleaded. "I'll pay you for your trouble." He took out several notes.

Partadasim was astonished. "Hey, what's with this? I'm from Pecikalan."

"I know that. What's the matter?"

"I didn't ask for money. I'm quite happy to have the Paruk village ronggeng ride along with me. I've dreamt about her for a long time. But, are you sure that I wouldn't be doing anything wrong? If I'm with someone that was involved in…involved…. You'll take responsibility, won't you?"

"Of course. You can tell everyone that I asked you to take Srintil with you."

After considerable effort, Srintil managed to sit on the back of Partadasim's bicycle. With her legs half extended over the rolls of teak leaves, it felt a bit awkward, but it did ease the pain of her wounds.

A pair of brondol birds had already hatched several broods of eggs. Each time they wanted to hatch a new brood, they stole blades of grass from the roof of Sakum's house to patch up the nest. In this way their species continued to survive against the overwhelming odds. Despite the fact that hawks could strike the small birds at any time or place, and crows and green lizards delighted in stealing their eggs, since they had first begun building their nest, the pair had increased their numbers to become a community of four couples. Until nature confronted them with more prey, their numbers would continue to increase.

During the dry season there was no sustenance near their nests and this group of brondol birds had to seek food far away, leaving the village for places where grass and paddy might still be growing. They went in the face of danger, becoming a target for hawks whenever they flew over the extensive dry fields. They would leave early in the morning, and return when the sun was nearly overhead. In the afternoon, they departed again, returning home only when the sun began to set. As they were flying overhead, they passed a group of men wandering about in a field on the western side of the village. A car was parked on the side of the main road, some way off.

A small child saw the men first. From the edge of the village precinct, the child watched them with suspicion, and then ran off helter-skelter, screaming over and over, "Soldiers! Soldiers! They've already reached the rice fields. Soldiers!"

"Hey, what're you talking about, child?" asked Kartareja, anxiously.

"Soldiers, Grandpa. Look for yourself. They're already at the rice fields!"

Kartareja stood up stiffly, his legs shaking and his face pale. Perhaps Rasus had returned. But, if so, why were there so many of his comrades? But he didn't really believe that Rasus had returned. He walked unsteadily towards the spot the child indicated. "Haven't you made enough trouble? Aren't you done with your mischief?" asked Kartareja of every villager he saw on the way. In front of Srintil's house, he shouted loudly, "Srintil! Did you forget to report to the police?"

"What, Grandpa? Report?" answered Srintil emerging from her hut. "I'm no longer required to report. What's the matter?"

"Soldiers are coming. Think carefully, what have you done?"

Srintil's face turned pale and her lips trembled.

"No, Grandpa! I haven't done anything. Yesterday I went to the market to buy Goder some clothes."

"So, maybe you talked too much at the market."

"Oh no, Grandpa. I'm especially careful when I go there."

Kartareja was confused by the denials he received from everyone. The village was silent, everyone hiding in their little shacks. The blind Sakum, standing outside, was pulled inside by his children. Paruk seemed completely deserted, and only the rustling of a soft breeze could be heard.

Finally Kartareja gave up; he felt no need to hide himself. With Sakarya's death, he had become the village elder. He walked to the edge of the village to find out for himself who the soldiers were. He stared off into the distance and made out the shapes of men moving back and forth. There was one peering into an apparatus set up on a tripod, while another was holding a long pole in a vertical position. A third was taking detailed notes. Whatever they were doing, Kartareja was certain that they were not making their way toward the village. The movements of the men triggered a memory of something he had seen during the Dutch colonial period. He remembered officials doing something very similar to what he was seeing now: surveying land!

"That damn kid!" he hissed to himself. "They're not soldiers, They're government workers surveying the land."

"Hey, kids. Come on out. It's okay. Those aren't soldiers, and they're not coming here. Everyone come on out!"

Silence. At first, no one dared to come out of hiding, but after a few minutes, one or two people emerged cautiously in response to Kartareja's call. Gradually others came, and they gathered in groups at the edge of the village. The children clung to their mothers' skirts. Srintil came with Goder on her back.

Look, they're not soldiers. They're surveying land. I heard that an aqueduct would be passing through that field. An irrigation dam is being built on the hill over there.

Kartareja felt that this was a good opportunity to demonstrate his extensive experience in front of the villagers. He explained that the apparatus on the tripod was a spotting scope and that the person who looked into the telescope was known as a surveyor. However, he didn't know why the spotting scope always needed an umbrella over it. "Maybe that tool is a kind of talisman that can't be exposed to the heat of the sun."

"We used to call them *klasiring*," Sakum, then said, proud that he could help in elucidating something for his friends.

"Yes, klasiring was carried out to classify and measure the boundaries of land. Hey, where's the kid who yelled out that soldiers were coming?"

Kartareja looked around, but the child he sought was standing some distance away and didn't realize he was being called. He was completely engrossed, watching the men busy with the surveying equipment.

In the middle of the field, about a hundred meters away from where the villagers were standing, Bajus was directing his colleagues surveying the land and driving stakes into the ground. Tamir was at the theodolite, Kusen held the umbrella aloft, and Diding positioned the measuring pole. Others were assistants who placed stakes in to the ground. Their job was to mark the boundaries for a large aqueduct, using plans for a tertiary irrigation canal which had been conceived during the Japanese occupation but had never been built. Bajus and his colleagues had been sent from Jakarta to oversee the construction of a dam that would provide water for 2,500 hectares of rice fields mostly located in the county of Dawuan.

It was 10:30 in the morning. In the middle of the village, perhaps, the sun was not yet particularly hot, but in the middle of a rice field where there was no shelter, it was blistering. The heat came from above but also reflected off the ground. From a distance, the surface of the ground appeared to shimmer, ripples of heat on a boiling lake. Bajus saw the faces of his men reddening and their backs becoming wet with sweat. He ordered them to take a break.

"Come on, let's go to the car. We can go and find something to drink in Dawuan." Kusen, Diding, and the others followed his suggestion, but Tamir continued peering through the spotting scope of the theodolite. He was so engrossed that he didn't notice that he was no longer shaded by the umbrella.

"Tamir!" shouted Bajus. "Did you hear me?"

"Just a minute, sir. Come and see this. Amazing! You won't believe that something so lovely could be found in a place like this."

"What're you talking about, Tam?"

"Look for yourself, sir. Otherwise, you'll say I'm bullshitting."

Tamir moved back so that his boss could take his place. Bajus looked through the lens of the theodolite. The image, its point of focus set by Tamir, displayed the face of a young woman holding a baby on her hip.

"What do you think, sir? Fantastic, isn't she?"

"Yeah, yeah," answered Bajus, not moving from his position.

"What did I say!"

"Take a look at the map, find out the name of that hamlet."

"I already know," replied Kusan from the back. "It's Paruk."

"Paruk?"

"Yeah, why do you ask, Bajus?"

Bajus didn't reply, his attention focused on the face in the middle of the theodolite scope. He saw an image of classic Javanese beauty rarely found in the larger cities. The woman embodied a perfect balance of neck and shoulders, as well as perfection in the shape of her profile. A narrow scarf of delicate fabric, streaming out in the breeze, held her luxuriant hair together. This entire picture was of a youthfulness poised at the threshold of maturity.

For a brief instant her eyes looked straight into the lens of the spotting scope, but the subject of scrutiny could have no idea she was the focus of so much attention. Bajus looked into those eyes: eyes that had an extraordinary power of attraction, eyes from the world of womanhood. Yet, at the same time, he saw something sweep over the expression in those eyes. They were eyes of someone who had lost her self-esteem, beautiful eyes full of anxiety.

"Bajus!" shouted Tamir, grinning. "You wanted to take a rest, didn't you?"

"Yeah. Let's take a break."

"What'd you say? Okay?"

Bajus smiled distractedly, his mind still on the classic face refracted through the lens of the theodolite. Sometimes a man is moved by a woman simply because she exists outside of his everyday life, such as in this instance. Sometimes he submits to his natural instincts: the tendency to wander. Sometimes, too, a woman is in fact endowed with a particular superiority, placing her in the realm of male attention. By such standards, Srintil had not yet fallen from the eyes of people, at least not for the county of Dawuan or the surrounding areas.

The subject of Srintil immediately took precedence over all other topics in the conversation of the men under Bajus' supervision. All too often while they were working, the spotting scope of the theodolite was aimed, not on the measuring rod, but on the lines of people standing watching at the edge of the village. Its focus was always on the face of Srintil, although she never realized that she was the center of attention. No less so with Bajus, who could say little when his men used the theodolite for purposes other than what it was built for.

On the third day, while Bajus and his men were sitting at a food stall in Dawuan, sipping a drinking, Tamir made an impudent confession.

"What would you say if I told you that yesterday I went to Paruk to relieve myself?"

"What do you think you're doing there? Trying to meet that woman?" asked Bajus.

"Don't get pissed off. The main thing is that I got some important information. I found out her name: Srintil."

"Srintil? That's a strange name."

"No matter, eh? What's important is the person."

"And?"

"She's not married. So there!"

They all fell silent, as if the information from Tamir's lips needed special effort to process. Tamir grinned.

"Okay. If it's true that she's not married, what's it mean to you?"

"Ah, there's no news that means anything to you except for news of payday. But, who knows? Maybe Bajus is glad to hear my news."

"Quiet! I happen to be a bachelor to the core. And I happen to be the oldest of all of us here. But I sure don't have to be the target of such empty chatter."

But Bajus' expression did not reflect his playful words. His smile was forced and his eyes flashed.

"Wait a minute, 'Mir. You seem to know a lot, but where'd you get that information?" asked Kusen.

"Getting information is, in fact, my expertise, something you might very well doubt. But no matter. When I went to the village to ask for matches, an old woman helped me. She sure was friendly. She probably noticed that I was stealing looks at Srintil. And, as you know, old women love to chat."

Tamir, Diding, Kusen, and the others laughed. Only Bajus remained silent, the image of Srintil dominating his mind, as Tamir reported the conversation.

"Sounds like you are talking about Srintil," the owner of the foodstall said. "Pretty, isn't she?"

"You know her?"

"Everyone knows Srintil," she said."And it's not just because she's beautiful, but because she's a ronggeng dancer."

"Is she married?"

"No," she said.

"Well, I'm amazed. A woman like her without a husband."

"That's because she's a ronggeng."

"So what if I were to…"

"Why not? She's a ronggeng, isn't she? You all know what a ronggeng is, don't you?"

All the men laughed again. Only Bajus smiled weakly, scratching his head. He remained silent when Tamir stood up and walked over to an open area and began to dance. From the way he danced, it was apparent that he did indeed know what a ronggeng was. Children watching clapped their hands, and Tamir danced more animatedly in response. Returning to the table, he sat down next to Bajus.

"Sir, tonight I'm not going back to the hotel. Me and Diding are staying here."

"Huh? Why me?" interrupted Diding.

"Relax, I'll give you some money."

"You're not coming back with us to Eling-eling?"

"Just one night, sir. I'll work harder tomorrow morning, believe me, sir."

That night, an almost full moon was set against the dry season sky. Dark, dark blue, the sky looked as if it could swallow everything except light. The stars sparkled as if they were trying to free themselves from the grip of the darkness. Only the moon floated placidly, a moon all the more elegant because its brightness remained unconquerable by the dark.

At first glance, the sky above the rice fields looked like a universe abandoned. Yet upon closer observation, the night sky was full of life, just as it was during the day. The dynamics of a complex ecosystem continued through the darkness and apparent loneliness of the night. Millions of insects flew about, each one recapitulating the life cycle of its kind. Some would win their particular struggle to survive, and others would fail. They would win if they were able to find food and a mate, lose if they met up with a predator. The cave bat flew in sharp, twisting spirals to catch every insect it encountered. This fluttering creature competed with the extraordinarily nimble *cabak* night bird. With its wings extended and leaning forward, the cabak appeared as a dark elliptical shape when seen flying against the background of the moon's light.

Beneath the sky, three boys were stumbling through the rice fields with a flare. Sakum's children were searching for insects. They had captured several locusts and grasshoppers in a bamboo tube, along with crickets, but were looking for something specific. The *jangkrik sungu*, the horned cricket, was considered special. The males made a particularly piercing buzzing sound and were often kept as pets by children. Anyone who wanted a horned cricket without having to wander about in the dark to search could buy one from Sakum in the morning at the market. The locusts and grasshoppers which the children collected in the bamboo tube were fried in reused oil and salt the next day. An early morning breakfast of rice porridge was often served with fried locust. The villagers, never having learned about dietary health, fulfilled their nutritional needs through locusts and grasshoppers.

For most kids, the task of searching for crickets and locusts was nothing more than child's play, the world of games and toys. Not so for Sakum's children. The three boys fully realized that crickets and grasshoppers had to feed everyone in their household. They were working, not playing. Persistent and serious, they had little time to enjoy the beauty of the moon over their heads. Indeed, the boys never even noticed the two men passing by.

Tamir and Diding drew closer to the village. In Tamir's mind, Paruk at night was a place filled with an emptiness and wretchedness that begets prostitution. Of this, he was certain, absolutely certain. Feeling this way, he was unmoved as they entered the loneliness of the village, a place that seemed desiccated like long discarded rubbish. The only sounds were those of scores of crickets, coming from Sakum's shack. The other homes were completely silent. It was common to hear children crying in impoverished settlements such as this, but Paruk had produced no children since the debacle of 1965. The villagers had lost their will to reproduce.

"Is this a village of ghosts or a village of humans?" Diding asked. "Why does it seem like a graveyard?"

"Are you looking for a party? We'll get plenty of that back in the bars of Jakarta, "Tamir replied.

"The hardship of following a young man taken by a pretty face!"

"Enough, I said I would give you some money."

"Weasel!"

"Hey?"

"I'm a weasel. I'm always worried about not having all of my paycheck to take home. So, I'm willing to become your lapdog just to get a bit of money on the side."

The two men made their way to Nyai Kartareja's home. Her house differed little from the other shacks. An oil lamp hung inside with its wick trimmed to burn as low as possible. The polite announcement of their arrival by Tamir was not answered for a long time, but inside they could hear whispers. Nyai Kartareja was trying to determine the identity of the people who had come but, once she recognized the voice outside, she opened the door and set the oil lamp to burn brighter.

"Oh, it's you. Please, please come in. Well, some gentlemen have come to visit the humble shacks of Paruk."

"I hope we're not disturbing you."

"Not at all. And is this your friend?"

"Yes."

"Come in and sit down."

After they had sat down on the verandah, Nyai Kartareja went inside and spoke softly with her husband for a few minutes, then returned alone. Tamir lit a cigarette. Diding sat quietly. He didn't smoke, as he had to live as thriftily as possible to avoid squabbles with his wife when he returned home to Jakarta.

"Coming to Paruk on a night like this, I'm curious to know what you two are looking for," declared Nyai Kartareja affably. Tamir responded with a broad smile, a hint so effective in communicating his meaning that words were unnecessary to his host. Nyai Kartareja was, of course, an expert in the skill of soliciting prostitution.

Nyai Kartareja recalled what had happened when she had conveyed Marsusi's proposition to Srintil. She still felt irritated by it and she still didn't know what the problem had been. These guests were from Jakarta, young and reasonably good-looking. Her task now was finding a way to get Srintil together with the two young men. Inviting her over held little hope for success, since Srintil would most certainly refuse to come. Going to the ronggeng's house and telling her about the young men would also likely end in failure, as Srintil was likely reject any proposal to have them visit. Clearly, the best method was to surprise her.

"Well, I know what you want, so why don't we go to Srintil's house?"

"Is it far?"

"Just two houses from here."

Another grass shack. Tamir grew increasingly confident, but at the same time a question was nagging at him: why was Srintil living in such a place? Tamir was sure that even he could provide a more appropriate home for the right woman. With that, his thoughts soared and his heart sang.

Nyai Kartareja called out as she entered Srintil's house. There was a response from the bedroom. Srintil was watching over Goder as he fell asleep, softly hushing him into the realm of dreams. She stood up quietly, her hair tied back loosely.

"What is it?" she asked Nyai Kartareja while composing herself.

"You have guests. Two young men. Officials who have been measuring the land. They're waiting outside."

Silence. Srintil could hear a mosquito flying around her ear, along with the rasping sounds of crickets in Sakum's little hut. Goder stirred, but his eyes remained shut. Her shoulders slumped.

"Why did you bring them here?"

"I didn't invite them here. They came by themselves. What could I do, tell them to leave?"

"Oh, God… Ask them to go home."

"Hey, now don't be like that. It's not proper to kick your guests out before we've even had a chance to talk to them. Remember, young lady, these are officials from Jakarta. Shouldn't we act respectfully toward them?"

Realizing that the situation was opportune, Nyai Kartareja went outside, leaving Srintil to collect her thoughts. Intentionally raising her voice for Srintil's benefit, Nyai Kartareja invited Tamir and Diding inside. Srintil remained alone in her bedroom, brushing the tears from her eyes.

Once again Srintil regretted her lot as a woman whose existence offered her little control over her own life, a woman whose existence always depended on masculinity, whether she wanted it or not. She had been introduced to masculinity in its raw state through Rasus, Marsusi, and dozens of other men. She had been introduced to the impotence of Waras from Alaswangkal, and to the decency of the commander at the prison where she had been held. In Srintil's eyes, that man had had only one weakness. Why couldn't he have stopped those other officers who had often taken her from the prison to seek their pleasure? Through all these experiences Srintil had developed a great distrust toward masculinity. She had learned that in the nakedness of men there existed humanity with the instincts of a goat, the needs of a whining baby, and an awkwardness often simply arising out of feelings of inadequacy. In her mind, men wanted to be told that they are in control only because they had doubts over the purpose of their own existence.

Now this masculinity was emerging again in the bodies of the two young men from Jakarta. "God! I still don't know how to face men, even though for years I felt pride in being the guardian of their instincts," she chastised herself.

As if no longer restrained by her thoughts, Srintil slowly stood up. She looked at Goder's face, deep in sleep and peaceful. She put on a blouse over her revealing camisole, covering the upper part of her body. She changed her old skirt for a newer one. She stood there, confused for a moment, then crouched down. In a secret place on the ground, she dug a hole with her fingers and pulled out a small cloth bag from which she drew a necklace, bracelet, earrings, and a ring. Almost two hundred grams of gold to decorate her body.

But she still hesitated. By wearing her jewelry, Srintil had intended to demonstrate that she was not really poor, that it was not poverty that defined her grass shack from top to bottom. Perhaps, too, she wanted to find something to give her courage in facing the men. Gold. But weren't her actions inviting danger? Weren't the men outside her bedroom strangers? Srintil felt she didn't have the strength to think about it any longer. Wiping the tears from her eyes, she went out. Two faces looked up together. One looked down again in shyness, but that of Tamir continued to stare boldly at her.

Tamir's eyes remained steady and his expression struggled between lust and disbelief. His mouth fell open, and he didn't know whether to laugh or gape in incredulity. He wondered how there could be so much beauty in the midst of such misery. Then he asked himself why she was sparkling with gold, yet living beneath this roof of grass. His heart beat with indecision and he felt uneasy, wondering why such social graces were accompanied by such sad, glistening eyes.

"Welcome," said Srintil in a throaty voice. She sat down next to Nyai Kartareja who was feeling no small surprise to see Srintil wearing all of her jewelry, until now carefully hidden. Yet she smiled cheerfully, thinking that Srintil's appearance was proof of her enthusiasm.

"Well, here is the person you came to see," declared Nyai Kartareja. "Please, go ahead. I have things to do at home."

"Ma'am! You have to stay with me here," begged Srintil, reaching for the old woman's shoulder.

"What's the matter with you? You're acting like a little girl."

"I'm not kidding, ma'am. If you go, I'll come with you."

"Oh, very well. I just want to go to the toilet for a moment. I'll be right back."

"I mean it, ma'am!"

"I'm not a child. Believe me, young lady."

They heard the creak of a bamboo door being pushed open and swinging shut. Outside Nyai Kartareja stood close to the house, placing one ear close to the wall. She didn't want to miss one word that was being uttered inside.

With the old lady's departure, those inside the shack were suddenly overtaken by awkwardness. Diding continued looking down, and Tamir, usually adroit around women, was nervous. The opening words of conversation had yet to be spoken and were proving difficult to find. Srintil was silent intentionally, determined not to speak until Nyai Kartareja returned. For as long as five, even ten minutes, the old woman did not reappear. Tamir wanted to begin a conversation, but the wish was only reflected in his expression. His urges were diverted into the act of pulling out a cigarette and lighting it.

"So…so, you two young men wanted to meet me. Well, that's been taken care of, hasn't it?" blurted out Srintil, suddenly. The standoff was resolved. Diding raised his head slightly. Tamir smiled broadly, but he now had a new problem in answering Srintil. She had pre-empted him by referring to him as “young man”. Should he call her “ma’am”? Calling her “miss” was no longer appropriate. It was a psychological hindrance when associated with his reasons for coming to Paruk. She had trumped him, a small triumph for Srintil against the masculinity that had come to ambush her.

“Yes…yes,” answered Tamir, at a loss for words.

“But please forgive me for not being able to offer you anything, young man. Such are my circumstances: as you can see for yourself. Very different from life in the city, isn’t it?”

“Yes…yes. Oh, that’s okay. Uh… We heard that you’re a ronggeng. Do you still dance?”

Srintil was surprised that Tamir’s question made her heart pound the way it did. Her chest heaved as she spoke.

“Well, young man. That was a long time ago. I no longer dance as a ronggeng. I was once a ronggeng.”

“Not at all?”

“No.”

“Why not?”

“I just don’t.”

“But, uh, how about if… What I mean is, you know why I came here, don’t you?”

“Yes, I know.”

“Why don’t…”

“*No*, young man.”

Tamir fell back into his chair, completely stumped. He looked around indecisively and his nose flared.

No. The word kept resounding in his mind. No. For a young man from Jakarta, if a woman said “no” and only “no”, that presented a problem. It was different when “no” was preceded by other words. In that case, it represented a qualified response, a challenge to overcome.

"Uh, *Mbakyu,*" said Diding in a deliberate tone, using the honorific title that meant "elder sister". "We came here mainly just to meet you. Anything else is secondary."

"Yes, that's right," agreed Tamir quickly. The gullible Diding had unwittingly helped extricate him from the deadlock. "Diding is absolutely right, we mainly just wanted to meet you. One never knows, we might need help from someone here in Paruk. We will be working around here for another few days."

"But what could we possibly do for you? We don't have anything."

"Just a place to take shelter against the sun. In the middle of the field it gets incredibly hot."

"Oh, yes. That we can provide. Paruk has plenty of bamboo groves, jackfruit trees and shade trees. Please feel free to use them, feel free."

"Thank you, Mbakyu," answered Diding. Tamir just smiled, looking down and shaking his head. His inner groan was disguised within a long, drawn-out breath.

Walking back through the village, Tamir and Diding were greeted by an explosion of quails suddenly flying into the air. At the edge of the village the men passed Sakum's children on their way home. Frightened, the children ran off, their flare making a rumbling sound.

When they reached the middle of the field, Diding could no longer withhold his laughter. His morale rose while Tamir's mind was in chaos. Tamir could not say anything in the face of his friend's wisecracks.

"Eat shit and die, Mir. Spend the night in Paruk Village. Sure. Can do. But only at Nyai Kartareja's house!"

"Bastard!"

"But don't forget, Mir. You owe me money for this."

"Take it all, beggar!"

In the darkness of the night, guffaws could be heard from the middle of the rice fields. Defeat accompanied that journey in the dark. And the two young men from Jakarta had a problem they had not anticipated: where would they sleep that night?

3

Sakum's four sons were the happiest boys around despite living in the smallest shack in the village. The dry season provided them with ample opportunities to hunt for insects during the night, and as a result they often enjoyed rice porridge with a side dish of fried locusts and crickets. Sometimes they also hunted for cuckoos: large, fat birds that slept in the bean grass at night. Armed only with torches and an ability to move as stealthily as cats, they were able to catch three or four a night.

In the morning, when the other village children were still curled up in bed or squatting sleepily outside near puddles of urine, Sakum's sons had already roamed the village grounds. They searched for loose bamboo stalks to burn for firewood and collected *salam* fruit dropped by bats and flying squirrels and sucked out the juice. During the dry season, the village grounds also became a favorite place for them to play. The earth was dry, packed flat and hard, ideal for games. In places that were shady and moist, the surface of the ground was covered with a layer of soft yellow-green moss. Sakum's children were clever and alert, attuned to the meaning of natural signs that often remained obscure to everyone else. When the earth cracked along the borders of the grounds, they would dig it up and almost always find sprouts of edible mushrooms. If they saw bird droppings scattered on the ground, they knew that a turtle dove or morning dove was sleeping in the trees above. They would then prepare the tools to capture it: string for a snare or some sticky sap for a trap.

One morning, the boys were playing near the edge of the village while they were waiting for their father to return from selling crickets at the market. They had just finished hanging a bamboo swing on a horizontal branch of a tree. The swing creaked and made the branches of the tree sway. They shouted and laughed with sheer joy at their construction. Their revelry drew the attention of other children. Goder tugged at Srintil's hand, wanting to go and look. She followed him and sat down to watch as he joined Sakum's laughing offspring.

The swing continued creaking. The children took turns swinging one another. Sitting there, watching the children, Srintil thought of her grandfather, Sakarya, who had recently died. Once she had heard him say to the villagers that society doesn't follow a straight trajectory. Instead, it moves forward while, at the same time, swinging the same distance to the left and right. In contrast, reason never shifts from its position in the middle. If the swing to the right was black, for example, the swing to the left, in most matters, would be the reverse, white.

To the villagers, however, information like this was considered esoteric lore, not real knowledge. An understanding which didn't result in practical knowledge, which never came down to earth for them, nor could be put to good use. It simply remained forever wrapped up in abstract mysticism.

Paruk villagers, including Srintil herself, would never really understand that they were victims of a society which was reaching the apex of its swing to the left and beginning its reversal to the right. As that happened, there was a shift in values and a reversal in the order of things. Had the old values been able to survive or even prevail, the swing to the right could have been mitigated and Paruk would have been safe. Yet what had happened in 1965 was the downfall of past values and the old order. The new values, which had always been latent and full of potential, had arrived with a crash.

Perhaps Srintil would also never be able to understand that the extraordinary bewilderment she felt inside was related to the explosion of new values, which were coalescing around her. New values so passionately held that the voice of reason could no longer be heard. Many of the restraints over tendencies that went against reason were loosened. And these latent tendencies would run free once the reigns of control were relaxed.

Symptoms of this social change had penetrated even the most remote areas. Srintil didn't understand that the increasing number of radios in Dawuan or the arrival of Jakarta officials to build a dam were just early signs of the social upheaval taking place around her. The nation's doors, at first closed to outside economic assistance and most foreign cultural influences, were now being thrown wide open. National values, formulated according to passionate ideas regarding sovereignty and the preservation of culture and tradition, had subsided after a violent struggle with modernity. And time and again, reason was being disregarded.

"Mommy!" shouted Goder, bumping against Srintil's leg.

"What is it?" answered Srintil, startled.

"Make me a swing. I wanna have a swing."

"You're too small. You'll fall."

"Make me a swing!" Goder began to whine.

"I can't make a bamboo swing like that. But I could make you a cradle out of cloth and rock you back and forth."

"A cradle, Mommy? Okay, I wanna swing in a cradle. I want one."

"Very well. Let's go home and make you a cradle."

As Goder ran ahead, Srintil saw in him the image of life's sprouting promise. He hopped and skipped, sometimes returning to hug her thighs, then running ahead again, shouting with happiness. Srintil's face, clouded only a minute before, brightened. She felt fortunate because the young boy belonged to her, even though she had not given birth to him.

She was still quite a distance from her hut when she noticed a man standing in her front yard, waiting. As she drew nearer, she recognized him: the village administrator of Pecikalan whose jurisdiction included Paruk. In his hand he held a folded sheet of paper. Her steps faltered, her lips grew pale and her thoughts turned to the prison house in Eling-eling.

"What's is it, sir? A letter for me?"

"Yes…well, no. It's for Goder."

"Goder?"

"Yes. But you'll have to act as his representative. This has to do with property affected by the construction of a water conduit.

"Oh, that's right. I do own a small bit of land that I bought in Goder's name. What is it you want me to do?"

"You need to attend a meeting at the community hall this morning. It's to compensate affected owners. Here is the letter. But, why are you trembling?"

"Oh, it's nothing, nothing at all."

The village administrator smiled, and in return received the humble smile of someone who was obviously still feeling profound shame. The old administrator simply took pleasure in the smile of someone who was, nevertheless, very beautiful. Srintil, in turn, savored this simple act of human kindness, a pleasure she had not felt for a long time.

"Please hurry. People have already begun to arrive at the hall," said the administrator as he walked off.

"I'll be there shortly."

Goder had other ideas and was pulling on her hand. "Come on, Mommy. Make me a swing. Hurry."

"We can't make a swing right now. We have to go to the community hall."

Goder's lips began to tremble in disappointment and his eyes began to fill with tears. Srintil quickly scooped up the little boy and drew him to her breast. She kissed him tenderly.

"Don't cry, my child. We'll put on some new clothes and go to the community hall. You're the only child in the village to be invited because you're the only child that owns land."

"Are there snacks at the community hall?"

"No, but we can stop by the market. We'd better hurry and get dressed if we're not going to be late."

Other than going to the market, this was the first time Srintil had attended such a gathering of people. When she had danced as a ronggeng, men had gathered to watch, all bowed under her spell. Their feelings, their dreams, became the targets of her lilting songs and sensual movements. Her seductive eyes and the graceful movement of her head played with their hearts. And most of the important men gathering at the community hall had begged for her attention.

Now everything was reversed. When she sat down in the community hall, the women moved away from her. The kindly village administrator, who had earlier asked her to come, invited her to take a seat, while many of the men tried to appear strong and dashing, but fooled only themselves. Others just looked at her in a way that made her feel as if she were being stabbed through the heart by a sharp bamboo spear. But one man, a government official, looked at her with gentle eyes. Srintil recognized him as the man she had often seen surveying the land on the west side of the village.

She sat with Goder on her lap, her head down. Only the feeling of Goder's warm body calmed the emotions reeling inside her. Her clothing was deliberately simple; she had no wish to draw attention to herself. Her humble appearance was meant to represent her belated confession to a lifelong guilt. Perhaps it was a mute appeal for sympathetic understanding or a wordless request for a cessation of the stares that cut into her heart, and of the looks of soul-shattering scorn.

Bajus was sitting next to the chief administrator. The two had already met several times. The first time was when Bajus arrived to begin his survey of the land, which fell under the village's jurisdiction. Then, at the county seat when coincidentally both had business with the county supervisor, or Pak Camat as he was called. The third occasion was a social function at the home of the village chief. It was at this function that Bajus had candidly admitted that he was a bachelor, a smile on his face and his eyes beaming.

At that time the old chief of Pecikalan had tried to understand the meaning of Bajus's words and behavior. Here was a man who, without prompting, had made a particular point of saying he was a bachelor. His eyes shone, but his smile seemed to hide something. Everyone in the region still seemed to think according to the old ways, that there was only one pond where all water flows. In matters of sexual escapades, Paruk was the pond and Srintil its fish. Sure. Bajus and his friends were surveying the land right next to Paruk. Obviously he had seen the beautiful fish in this pond.

The chief of Pecikalan, although a fair age, was quite familiar with Srintil. Being the kind of traditional person he was, he believed in the ancient notion that minor authority figures were obliged to pay tribute to major authority figures. Tribute. If Bajus, who was considered a major authority figure as he came from Jakarta, claimed he was a bachelor, then the chief of Pecikalan knew what he wanted. And, following this value system, the chief had absolutely no reason to fault the man from Jakarta.

When all the landowners were present, the compensation process began. The chief preceded the process with a speech. Since a state system of authority like this one did not encourage queries or discussion regarding the amount of reimbursement, everyone remained silent when he told them that their compensation would be cut by so many percent to pay for community hall improvements, so many percent for security officers' uniforms, so many percent for agrarian administrative costs, and so many percent for other fees: cuts totaling forty percent. The landowners had all known of these cuts long before the meeting and were careful to remain quiet, as it had been whispered that only those involved in the 1965 turmoil would protest.

Srintil was actually not interested in hearing about this or that percent, nor was she interested in the amount she would receive on behalf of Goder. The only thing she wanted to do was get out of the meeting as quickly as possible and be free of the prying eyes of all those people. She wanted only to return to the village and hide in Goder's world. Yet, her name did not come up, even as the sun slipped towards the west. Eventually, she realized that her turn would be last. Of course, she thought to herself, of all the people who had come to the meeting, I'm the only former prisoner. Such was the contempt she had to endure in these changed times.

When only Srintil and Goder remained, the chief of Pecikalan ordered the disbursement officers to count up the income he had made from the forty percent surcharge on the state's payment to the landowners. Once again, this seemed a matter of course to Srintil. A former prisoner would not be treated like the others. She would receive different treatment. Perhaps the amount she was to receive would be cut even more drastically. Or maybe she would have to jump through endless bureaucratic hoops, face all kinds of rules and regulations. Everyone else assumed that such would be the case with her.

"Srintil," said the chief softly. The color drained from her face and she pressed Goder to her thumping heart. The chief, however, laughed out loud.

"Now, don't be afraid, young lady. Listen to me. We only want to talk to you. Bajus has come a long way from Jakarta. It is possible, I'm not really sure, that he might need a friend. Is that it, Bajus? Oh, I almost forgot. On his recommendation, I won't be cutting any of your reimbursement."

Bajus coughed. He turned to the chief of Pecikalan and signaled him. The old man stood up.

"So, I ask that you do what Pak Bajus asks. Indeed, whether you are required to or not, someone in your position should obey. Please, go ahead." With that, he walked out of the room.

Bajus coughed again. He smiled with embarrassment, and asked Srintil to move to a chair closer to him. He reached out and stroked Goder's cheek. His first words took Srintil by surprise.

"This isn't your child, is it?"

"No, sir," she replied, her eyes still downcast.

"I know a lot about you. Please, look at me. I just want to talk a bit."

"Yes, sir."

"Listen, about what the chief just said. Take what he said at face value. I really just want to get to know you. Don't worry, I'm not married and my intentions are honorable. What do you say?"

"But, sir…"

"What do you think?"

"I don't know, sir."

"You don't need to be so formal and call me sir."

"Srintil hesitated before speaking. "So, you know about me. But I'm afraid. You really shouldn't socialize with someone like me, a former prisoner."

"That's alright. Well, that's all for now. Tomorrow or the next day, I'd like to come to Paruk and visit you. Would that be okay?"

"Why?"

"Obviously, not to spend the night or anything like that. Honestly. What do you think?"

"That's fine, But I'm afraid of doing something wrong."

"I know you are and. I take full responsibility."

A small glimmer of courage emerged in Srintil's heart, like a tiny star appearing on the eastern horizon on a pitch-black night. Yet, she was not sure. She glanced briefly at Bajus's face. She saw friendliness and honesty, a sign that he acknowledged her place in society. But she also saw a smile, a man's smile, and it made her want to leave. Her experience with lustful men was a bitter memory for her, and yet her face brightened when Bajus reached out again and stroked Goder's cheek. This was not the behavior of a lecherous man, and any gesture of humanity, no matter how small, meant a great deal to her.

Once out of the community center, Srintil walked quickly. If it weren't for Goder demanding a treat, she would have returned home immediately. However, the child asked for a balloon and some ice cream, and so she stopped at a small store. After that, she continued her journey. Suddenly, she felt less inclined to please Goder who chattered on and on.

When she got home, she poured a glass of water and sat down on her bed in a state of confusion. Goder went out to play by himself in the backyard. The memory of her meeting with Bajus replayed in her mind with stark clarity. She still hardly believed that it had taken place less than an hour before: a meeting that was far more significant than the compensation money hidden behind her sash.

Oh Lord, what else will men do to me? Tomorrow or the next day, he will come to visit. What shall I do? Will Bajus come as a part of civil society or will he represent his own particular world? Who knows? Nevertheless, I can't believe that there is no ulterior motive to his visit. Suddenly, she realized that she had done something beyond her authority: she had passed judgment on someone by thinking he might have ulterior motives behind his actions.

Srintil quickly tried to dismiss her suspicions of Bajus and the purpose behind his proposed visit. At the same time, however, other notions surfaced, equally disturbing. Namely, that Bajus would come with completely honorable intentions, a bachelor who wanted to become acquainted with an unmarried woman. In other words, if he is not trying to initiate an affair with her, then his visit could have only one other meaning. Srintil felt repulsed by the momentary appearance of such idealistic thoughts.

She was pathetically frightened. Pathetic, because she could not free herself from the feeling that she was unworthy of being a recipient of honorable intentions.

"Oh, Lord, if I only weren't a former prisoner," she sobbed.

She fell backwards and rolled onto her side, her legs still dangling over the side of the bed. When that train of thought played itself out, she found that she couldn't break out of her ennui; visions of times past—a thousand memories—surfaced one after the other. Some were of the prison house in Eling-eling where she had officially been assigned kitchen duties. She recalled a gigantic clay pot, used to cook *kangkung*, a leafy vegetable, and *genjer*, an edible river plant, spiced only with salt as a side dish for *grontol*, boiled corn. She remembered the attitude of the other women at the prison towards her, jealous because she owned a nice towel and fragrant soap, and because she kept a hand mirror and face powder under her bed.

Then, an image of Bajus came to her mind. He was the first stranger to behave sincerely toward her. Only now could Srintil determine that what she wanted from life was sincerity, something she could accept as genuine and honest. Yet, why was this sincerity, arriving in the form of Bajus, so frightening?

The sun slipped further to the west. Wind currents created soft sighs as they slipped through the gaps of the grass roof of her house. She could hear the creaking of bamboo near Sakum's hut and Goder's laughter as he played with his balloon in the backyard. Srintil's body and spirit were tired, demanding sleep for just a moment. She fell into a dream, her ears filled with the joyous sound of calung playing. Before her, she saw thousands of pairs of eyes, looking at her with awe. She challenged them with a swaying and gyrating dance. Her song suggested vague erotic visions but, for some reason, the audience began to leave in an unruly fashion. Suddenly there were gunshots. She ran, leaving the stage behind her, and an iron hand gripped the back of her neck. She wanted to scream but the hand was choking her. She could only struggle. When she felt the hand loosen its grip, she gasped for breath, like a sheep about to be slaughtered.

Kartareja's voice entered her subconscious: "Hey! Taking a nap and talking in your sleep. Wake up. Your boy fell into the drainage ditch. Come on, wake up."

Srintil thrashed around. She sat upright in a daze, panting. Her eyes looked wildly about her, still seeing something terrifying. Her forehead and the back of her neck were wet with sweat.

"What is it, a nightmare? Well, well. How can someone who has just received money mutter so in her sleep? Goder fell into the ditch and I've cleaned his hands and feet.

Srintil, still dazed, only momentarily saw Nyai Kartareja holding Goder in her arms. Without saying a word, she got up and went into the kitchen where she ladled out some water from a large jar to rinse her face, and drank a glass of water.

"Now tell me. What were you dreaming about, being bitten by a snake?" asked Nyai Kartareja as she handed Goder over to Srintil.

"Never mind. It was just a bad dream."

"But these are safe times now. What is there to be afraid of?"

"He's going to come to visit. I'm afraid. I don't know what to do."

What are you talking about? "Who do you mean?"

"Bajus."

"The man who oversees those men surveying the land?"

Srintil nodded. Seeing that there was no pretense in the young woman's face, Nyai Kartareja realized that Srintil was facing serious doubts about herself.

"I don't understand. Why are you now afraid of every man that comes by? You rejected Marsusi. Tamir, too. Now you are afraid to face Bajus. I don't understand."

"I don't understand either. Saying no to Marsusi or Tamir was easy. But I'm not able to say it to Bajus. I don't know why. What should I do?"

"Why are you being like this?"

"I can see…I can feel that Bajus isn't just playing around…"

Nyai Kartareja studied Srintil's face closely, trying to read her expression. She could detect something there that was coming from the depths of the young woman's very soul. Little by little she began to grasp what Srintil was envisioning. It wasn't hard for Nyai Kartareja to draw her conclusions. She smiled, then nudged Srintil's shoulder.

"Well, sure. You're still young. You're only twenty-three years old and quite beautiful. It's certainly not strange that men desire you."

"And Bajus is still a bachelor."

"Well!"

"But I was a ronggeng. I'm not the kind of woman who could be a wife. People would never believe that someone like me could possibly become a decent wife. Nobody would ever believe that."

"That's not necessarily so, young lady. The proof is in Bajus. If he doesn't believe you could be a wife, why would he have honest intentions with you?"

"I don't know, but it could be that his faith in me hasn't yet been tested. I'm really scared that the time will come when that test results in bitter reality, in disillusionment. If it comes to that, everything will be for nothing. I would have to endure even more suffering."

"If I were you, I wouldn't think that far ahead. I would only think about how I might make use of such an opportunity Bajus is a bachelor and a government official. He lives far away and you could start a new life in a new place. And, as you said yourself, he doesn't seem to be just playing around. What more could you want?"

"I know, but what should I do?"

Nyai Kartareja was startled. To her, Srintil was a completely honest and open book. The old woman knew everything about her; she knew that Srintil had once had many men, scores of men, that she had liked. She knew that she had been a gowok. Nyai Kartareja was certain that to find an answer to Srintil's question was as easy as blinking her eyes.

"Look. You're beautiful. You have nice clothes and gold jewelry. Take a bath and wash your hair. Make yourself as beautiful as possible. Then make your guest court you. But, why should I, an old woman like myself, have to repeat the lessons I taught you ten years ago?"

Srintil looked away quickly. Nyai Kartareja's answer did nothing to dispel the doubts in her heart. It was a bitter reality: that this woman, who had grown old in Paruk village and had for so many years been her adoptive mother, was unable to reach the root of her complex situation. She groaned, and sighed heavily. Desperate to return to her thoughts in solitude and knowing the best way to get rid of the old woman, she gave her some money.

After Paruk had been burnt to the ground during the aftermath of 1965, what remained were really only bits and pieces. Where there had once been houses with tiled roofs and gaslights, there were now only huts with grass roofs lit at night by oil lanterns. There were no traditional songs, no calung playing, and no men visiting from far away. No man wanted to be associated with a ronggeng dancer who had recently been released from prison. Marsusi, perhaps, was an exception, but even he had not been as brazen as he once might have been.

Now the most backward village in the region, Paruk had once enjoyed independence, standing out in the world of calung music and ronggeng dancing. When the spirit of ronggeng had inspired

Srintil, everyone had been proud to be called a Paruk villager. Everything that happened since provided evidence of the truth of the words of the late Sakarya: that the changing times always move like a pendulum, a swing. After reaching its apex of pride, change swept the village to a period of complete reversal. Now the people of Paruk felt hard put to hold their heads up whenever they ventured outside the village, reluctant to do anything that might suggest they appeared to be proud. In everything they did they tried to give the impression that they were following the path of regret and guilt. They blamed themselves, not for being inadequate in the face of a disruption in the order of things, but for causing that disruption.

While most people in Paruk suffered under such feelings, Srintil felt she was implicated far more seriously. And this influenced her life profoundly. She hid in her little hut even though she was fully aware that she could build or buy a new home far more appropriate to her means. A bracelet or necklace would have been adequate to purchase a new wooden house with a tiled roof. But she didn't want to do this. The scorn of society demanded that every person in Paruk demonstrate remorse and frugality.

Sakum had once sung traditional songs at night. When every stomach in his household was full, he would sing joyous and sometimes humorous children's songs. If he was unable to find food on a particular day, he would sing a didactic song, which aroused feelings of loneliness that pierced the soul. Now the sounds emanating from his home could only be compared to those from a tobacco plantation or bushes growing near a river. Every night dozens of crickets sang, competing with each other to make the loudest sound. The small crickets made a dry piercing buzzing noise that was painful to the ears, while the larger ones emitted a deeper, more pleasant hum. All the while, Sakum and his children were cooped up and crowded together in the little hut, like baby chickens trying to get out of the rain by hiding under the porch of a house.

In her hut, not far away, Srintil often lay awake, although her eyes were shut. Once Goder had dozed off, she felt herself floating alone in a world without a place to stand. The thought of her tomorrows filled her with worry. Sometimes she wished to return to the whimpering state of infancy. Sometimes she wanted to croon popular songs like a teenage girl. But most often she longed to become a snail that could hide itself, whenever it wanted, in its shell. Slow and quiet, entirely self-involved, and completely unconcerned with its surroundings, the snail's primary concern would be safety and comfort.

One particular night, an owl hooted in the tree overlooking the long-abandoned grave of Ki Secamenggala. Its echoing call made Srintil feel even smaller and more insignificant. She lay under the cover of her bed-sheets, held hostage to her thoughts. More than ever, she wanted to become a snail, retracting herself in the labyrinth of her shell, to forget everything and just sleep. She could find no peace in her troubled heart. Her doubts and anxieties kept returning. Finally she gave up and got up, the bamboo fiber mattress of her bed creaking as she did so.

A memory just below her consciousness drew her to the adjoining room. She opened the door quietly and entered, stopping at the edge of the sleeping pallet. Her grandmother, Nyai Sakarya, was sound asleep. The old woman looked deflated and worn out.

"Granny," called Srintil, softly. For some reason her heart was suddenly overcome by helplessness. Tears fell from her eyes.

"Granny."

"Who is that? Srintil? What is it, my grandchild, my beauty?"

"I'd like to sleep here next to you."

"Okay, that's fine. You poor, poor thing. What's bothering you?

Srintil didn't answer, but lay down and made herself as small as possible as the frail and musty old woman held her. This made her feel a little better. She remembered twenty years back, to a time when she had often sought safety in her grandmother's lap when she felt sad and helpless. While Srintil knew full well that her grandmother could do nothing to help resolve her doubts and worries, the stroke of her hands on her hair could calm her anxieties. Nyai Sakarya didn't press the girl to express her feelings, as her repeated questions were answered only by sobs. The old woman knew full well that Srintil was deeply troubled. And because Srintil's troubles were located at the core of her private life, Nyai Sakarya felt that she could do little more than to stroke her hair. Eventually Srintil stopped sobbing. After several deep sighs, her breathing grew soft and regular, like somebody who had journeyed long under the hot sun and then reached the protection of a large shady tree. Refreshed and comforted for a short while, Srintil was freed from her worries. She drifted off to sleep, soothed by the soft caresses of her doting grandmother.

In the morning, the gardens and fields of the village were decorated by a mosaic pattern of leaves that had fallen during the night. The leaves of the jackfruit tree had fallen in shades of reddish yellow-brown. Those of the almond tree were red. In places that hadn't been exposed to direct sunlight, moss and various types of grass added a motif of soft green. Under the bamboo trees dead leaves were scattered, chocolate-colored and ochre. In the pale light of dawn this natural mosaic seemed especially vibrant. The fields of dead leaves glistened through the refraction of early morning dew. Occasionally, thin plumes of steam rose from the trunks of cut banana trees.

It is amazing that the heart can hold so many different emotions. While during the night Srintil had been gripped by doubt, in the morning her confused feelings had settled down. Perhaps she was not sure what to do in the long term, but her activity that morning at the back of her house made Nyai Kartareja smile. She was burning a bundle of rice stalks to make shampoo. Before she went to the fountain, Srintil walked over to Sakum's hut.

"Are you still selling crickets at the market?" she asked, watching Sakum organizing the bamboo tubes containing his merchandise.

"Why, yes. What else would I do, young lady? Luckily, I can always sell crickets!"

"Good. I'd like to ask your help. Could you please buy some sugar and good ground coffee for me? Also, some papayas and oranges. Could you do that for me?"

Sakum stood stock still for a moment. His two blind eyes moved beneath his lids. He had a unique sensitivity for grasping a change in circumstances. Once or twice on previous occasions Srintil had asked him to buy something at the market, but usually it was rice cakes or snacks for Goder. This time it was sugar, coffee, and fruit. Furthermore, Sakum could read the sound of Srintil's voice to its origins in her heart.

"Could you do that for me? Here's the money."

Of course I'll do it for you," answered Sakum, grinning. "So, you're expecting a guest? Who is it?"

"How do you know?"

"Since you were a little girl, you've known the way I am."

"That's true. There's someone who wants to visit me at my house."

"Is it Marsusi?"

"No. Somebody from Jakarta."

"From Jakarta? People at the market are saying that there are a lot of Jakarta government types around here. So, young lady, if you were still dancing ronggeng, that'd be something!"

"I'm no longer dancing. I'm too old."

"Obviously, someone like me can tell that you're no longer a ronggeng dancer. It's not because you're too old. You're still young. But I hear your voice every day and it's not the voice of a ronggeng. No doubt about it, Paruk is without a ronggeng."

Sakum's words carried a particular meaning and, at first, Srintil was shocked. Her eyes grew round and her eyebrows rose, demonstrating her serious efforts to comprehend the words of the blind man. She pondered what he had said as well as the meaning hidden behind his statement. Then she whispered into his ear.

"Is it really true that I'm no longer a ronggeng?"

"It's true! If you were forced to dance as a ronggeng, you wouldn't be able to. The spirit of ronggeng no longer resides within your body."

Srintil's shoulders fell and she exhaled a long breath of relief. Sakum's words were like a magical incantation that freed her from an overwhelmingly heavy moral burden. She couldn't hold back her tears.

"Are you crying?"

"No, I'm not crying."

"Don't lie to me. I can hear you. It's no use. Don't cry. Even crying won't bring back the spirit of ronggeng."

"You don't understand. I'm not crying because I'm sad. I'm crying with happiness."

"Well, okay. It's better to accept your fate. And be happy too that you're expecting a guest from Jakarta. Now, where's the money? I have to get going, before the morning gets old."

Srintil handed over the money and watched as the blind man left for the market. Although his eyes were useless, Sakum knew the way just as he knew things from feeling with the tips of his fingers. Srintil walked towards the fountain to bathe. She didn't hear the sounds of Sakum's children, shouting with pleasure as they played on their bamboo swing. She didn't hear the birds singing around her. In her mind, she only heard the sound of the zither of Wirsiter and Ciplak, the musicians who sang the traditional tune, "Asmara Dahana".

As she bathed, Sakum's words continued to resound in her ears: she was no longer a ronggeng. Oh Lord, how wonderful it was to hear such news. Sakum is the first person to say that I'm not a ronggeng. I'll prove it, so that later everyone will say the same thing.

At the fountain, Srintil began to prove to herself who she was now. When she had danced as a ronggeng, she had always bathed naked, undisturbed when young men spied on her. She used to pretend that she didn't know she was being watched, or even acted in ways to excite her hidden male audience. That was before. Now, she bathed modestly and discreetly, wrapped in a sheet that covered her body from her breasts to her legs.

Srintil wanted to become an ordinary woman, down to the minutest detail. She had thought about this for a long time, a very long time. Yet, it was at the fountain that she first acted on her thoughts, now that Sakum had told her that that spirit of ronggeng had left her.

Perhaps for some time Srintil had been re-examining her concept of femininity: a concept that she once held to be a kind of truth. She had once believed that femininity was on one side of the scale while masculinity was on the other. That was primary. Furthermore, she had believed that woman, as wife of a particular man was secondary. With this kind of understanding, Srintil had felt proud to be a ronggeng because such a woman was like cool water on the hot fires of masculinity. A ronggeng was the manager of masculine instincts, not just a woman that managed a man's instincts. Serving masculinity, seen this way, had far broader implications that just servicing a man. Thus, she had believed that the duties of a ronggeng were more noble that the duties of a wife.

However, she had eventually learned for herself life's bitter lessons about being a woman who belonged everyone. She had reversed her original understanding, and now believed that to become the wife of a particular man was essential in balancing out femininity and masculinity. Thus, she saw now that the duties of a wife were nobler than those of a ronggeng. And that morning Sakum had told her that she was no longer a ronggeng.

When she returned from the fountain, Srintil looked in on the still sleeping Goder then went into the kitchen. Beginning this morning, she decided that she would take over all the kitchen tasks that she had previously surrendered to her grandmother. To be a wife was to be a woman who knew how to work in the kitchen. She would therefore carry out such tasks with pleasure.

At the market, Sakum quickly drew attention to himself because he was buying such a large amount of fruit. The market people knew that he could afford to buy only so much with the little earnings he made from selling crickets. Usually he bought just a little coconut oil, a half bottle of kerosene, some cassava and a coconut. This time, however, he was buying oranges and papaya.

"You shopping so much!" Babah Gemuk called from his booth. You have much money now. You make money gambling?"

"What, gambling crickets?" Sakum jokingly returned.

"Gambling. What Paruk villager doesn't like gambling?"

"Not so. Paruk villagers don't have any money to gamble."

"So, how come you so much? Where you get the money?"

"Srintil gave me this money. Where would I possibly find money?"

"Eh, sure. Hey! Srintil long time no come to market. How she?"

"Didn't you know that Srintil recently came home from prison?"

"I know, I know. But now she at home. Tell her come here. I have many good tings. I have powder from Paris, lipstick from Hong Kong, purses from Singapore. Many good tings."

"And I have crickets from America!" answered Sakum. The market people joined in his laughter.

"I not kidding. Tell Srintil come here. She still pretty, no?"

"Beauty is one thing she has."

"Well, what I say. You tell her. If she come here, she get present from Babah Gemuk."

"Can't do that. Srintil is having a guest from Jakarta. These oranges and papayas I'm carrying are for Srintil to offer her guest."

Sakum continued walking through the market, carrying his heavy purchases. Babah Gemuk, distracted by a customer, had already forgotten their brief conversation, but several of the women began to gossip.

"How lucky it is to be so beautiful. Even after being imprisoned, after living in an isolated little hovel in Paruk, she can still find a young man interested in her. And Srintil's guest is even a man from Jakarta."

"Indeed. That's not your fate. How come your lips are floppy and your nose looks like a salak fruit?"

"Well, sure. Luckily, my husband is so stupid that I was able to have some kids."

"Your husband isn't stupid, he's just poor. If he had money, I bet he wouldn't be quite so happy to have you as his wife."

"So, what about your husband?"

"He's my husband at home. Elsewhere, I really don't know."

"Well, sure. I don't know what my husband does at home while I'm here at the market. But, I don't think about things like that. I don't want to worry myself sick."

"In the world we live in, there will always be women like Srintil."

"That's true. It must be nice to be a woman like that. Not having to work like a slave, yet getting money."

"You're jealous!"

"Sometimes, I am. Sometimes, I'm not. I'm jealous when I go through rough times and my husband acts up. But, I'm not jealous when I remember my ugly body. I'm lucky to have a husband at all!"

"But take a look at our neighbor, that woman over there selling material. Here, in the market, she's probably the prettiest and most elegant woman, and she's from a wealthy family. Her husband is worthless. The only thing he does is trap mourning doves. Sometimes he even uses her money to gamble. What do you say about women like her?"

"That's easy. Of course, she's stupid because she doesn't have the presence of mind to find a more suitable husband. For example, I would…"

"Do you think their families would stand for that?"

"If they wouldn't, then a woman like her just needs a man to father her children. Nothing else. But, no matter what, with a husband who's an asshole, you can do whatever you want!"

"What about a husband who is handsome and wealthy, but whose wife thinks she's royalty?"

"Then it's the woman who's an asshole!"

"So, who's morally right?"

"Morally right? Why, we are. We're ugly women but we still have husbands and children. And our husbands aren't unfaithful because they're too poor to fool around. That's right! We're lucky because we've accepted our lot in life."

"So, you aren't really jealous of Srintil."

"I guess not."

"You aren't going to complain that you have a nose like a salak fruit?"

"Hush!"

Their giggling filled one corner of the market. These were the sounds of simple women, full of patience and resignation, having accepted the world as they found it.

Rasus felt anxious about what to do with the three days leave each soldier in his battalion had been granted before being assigned to West Kalimantan. Of his comrades, those who were married had left to say goodbye to their wives and children, while the unmarried men had gone home to their parents to seek their blessings. Because Rasus no longer had any real family, he didn't know what to do.

In his mind, Rasus had created for himself a kind of symbolic family. He had convinced himself that the army was his family. His father was the Seventh Diponegoro Division of the Army, and his mother the PQR Battalion. His brothers were all the other soldiers, wearing their green uniforms and carrying a rifle and ammunition. Yet, as he watched them all leave for their respective homes, this carefully contrived symbolic family suddenly evaporated. The Seventh Diponegoro Division and its battalion were parents he had only met after joining the army. They brought no early memories, nothing about a childhood of laughter and tears. The army had never helped him build a kite of gadung leaves, and had never provided him with a sheltered place beneath the shade of a jackfruit tree to use as a playground.

His thoughts turned to his hometown. While he had no family there, Paruk still held memories for him. Yet the thought of going there made him hesitate. He was aware that the village of his birth was now more miserable than it had even been. If he returned there, he would not only find a place filled with the buzzing of flying dung beetles early in the morning and children infested with tape worms. He would not only see pinched, wan faces and hear obscene curses. Paruk in its present state would receive him with grass-thatched hovels, with silence, and with fear hidden behind the eyes of all his people.

However, Rasus could not forget that Paruk was the home of his mother. It represented his own history, and he came to the conclusion that this history could only be adequately reviewed while he had three days leave. So, it was to Paruk that he walked when he stepped off the Dawuan bus, longing for his tiny motherland. He needed to see the place of his birth once again, before he departed for West Kalimantan.

When he reached the long dike dividing the rice fields, he noticed a man walking a long way in front of him. Because the distance was so great, he couldn't make out who the person was at first, but as he got closer he recognized the tentative gait.

"Hey Sakum, wait!"

The blind man hesitated, searching his memory for the owner of the voice. He had not heard the sound of that voice for a long time.

"Sakum! Where have you been?"

"Is that you, Rasus?"

"That's right."

"Well, you've returned? I would've thought you had long forgotten us now that you're in the army."

"No way! Even a cat remembers the place of its birth."

"Well, I'm glad to hear that. You'll make everyone in Paruk happy by coming home. Especially now that Sakarya has died."

"He died? When was that?"

"Almost a hundred days ago."

Rasus shook his head sadly and, for a moment, could not bring himself to speak. Paruk, so miserable these days, had even lost its leading elder.

"And, did you know that Srintil is back?" continued Sakum.

"Oh, really? Thank heaven. How is she now?"

"How is she? Once, long ago, I told to you to take her as your wife. Well, it seems that Srintil is expecting a guest. I heard it's a man from Jakarta. She asked me to buy some oranges and papaya. I guess it is to offer to her guest later."

"Oh, really? So she often receives guests?"

"Never. I heard that she did have guests before on one occasion, also some men from Jakarta. But she refused to entertain them. This time, who knows? The point is, you should take her as your wife!"

Rasus just smiled, unable to respond to Sakum's words. He shook his head to clear his confused thoughts. Glancing at the bamboo tubes Sakum carried, he found a way to change the conversation.

"Do you sell crickets at the market?"

"I sure do. Lucky my boys are good at catching them. I don't know what we'd do without them. There's no more calung music. And no more ronggeng, either. Srintil is no longer a ronggeng. She won't ever be a ronggeng again. The spirit has left her. That's for sure. You'll see for yourself. Srintil's voice is no longer that of a ronggeng. Probably her behavior, too. I'm just not able to see for myself. These days I never hear her laugh, much less sing songs. Oh, nowadays nobody in Paruk would dare sing those songs."

Sakum went on talking as if he needed to tell Rasus about everything to do with Paruk and about Srintil. He even mentioned the disappearance of the keris that Rasus had given to Srintil long ago.

When Sakum mentioned the keris, a pang of nostalgia pierced Rasus' heart and caused him to fall silent.

"Hey! Why so quiet, soldier?"

"It's nothing. Come on, let's get going. I want to get to the village as quickly as possible."

Srintil had finished her work in her hut. She had cooked, but she really had no appetite. She had swept the grounds around the house and wiped down her simple dining table and chairs, some still with evidence of burns here and there. Her grandmother had gone to Tampi's home with Goder. Alone, she paced about aimlessly. She sat down, and then stood up again. Several times she examined her face in a small mirror. She wanted to make sure that she hadn't applied too much makeup and lipstick, that she couldn't be criticized for looking like a ronggeng. She tied up her hair to emulate the wife of the prison commander whom she had seen several times and thought was very pretty. She had always appeared appropriately matched with her military husband as they strolled side by side. Srintil also imitated the way the woman wore her wrap-around skirt: not tightly to emphasize the shape of her body, but neatly. She departed from her earlier style of wearing her skirt short to reveal her calves, which would be interpreted as an attempt to allure men.

As she paced about the room, Srintil kept glancing out her window towards the path that Sakum would follow coming home from the market. As the sun rose higher in the sky, she grew more anxious. Had the blind man fallen into a ditch? Or had he been run over as he walked along the road? She finally sat down and resigned herself to accept whatever might happen. At that moment, she heard a commotion outside; it was Sakum's children, shouting that their father had returned home. She stood up and looked out her window. Oh Lord, who was that soldier walking next to Sakum? The blood suddenly drained from her face and for a moment she saw stars. The first thought that came into her mind was that she would be imprisoned again. The soldier had come to arrest her.

Then her eyes opened wide as she realized the identity of the soldier who was befriending the children. It was Rasus.There was no mistake; the prodigal son had returned. She held her breath, and stood there without moving, her expression tense. Her eyes stared without blinking and her legs trembled. She sat down again, feeling weak, her cheeks stained by tears.

Srintil watched dispiritedly as Rasus walked by, only glancing momentarily in the direction of her shack. The bamboo trellis might have hampered his view her or was it that he did not want to see her?

Not far from her home, Rasus was ambushed by Nyai Kartareja and her husband, their display of affection demonstrating how much they had missed him. Nyai Kartareja kept patting his shoulder.

"You're looking more handsome than ever. Stop by our house for a moment."

"Where else would you go?" Kartareja added. "Your grandmother is dead. Even her shack is falling to pieces."

Rasus was shocked at their words, and his step immediately lost its bounce. But after a moment he smiled.

"I'll be back later. Right now, I want to see my grandmother's hut: my hut."

All eyes in the village followed as Rasus walked slowly towards and then stopped in front of his grandmother's shack. He didn't go in immediately, but stood and stared at it for a few moments. Rotting bamboo leaves covered the roof and a small banyan tree had begun to grow at the edge, its roots seemingly choking the entire tottering hut to death. The bamboo walls were full of holes and were coated here and there with green moss.

The door broke with a snap as he pushed it open. The interior of the hut was littered with debris, and he had to squint to keep the dirt and dust from obscuring his view. The floor was green with moss and full of holes made by nesting mole crickets. A millipede slowly crawled towards the rotting wooden center pole that had begun to break apart. Rasus entered, wiping the cobwebs from his face.

A distinct little world had ended here a long time ago and now there remained only remnants. A sleeping pallet that Rasus once used was also just a remnant. The leafy mattress was covered with small animal droppings, from the minute excreta of moths and crawling insects to the small turds of lizards and mice. Rasus attempted to sweep the filth off his old bed with his hat. His efforts made little difference, but he set his knapsack down and sat upon the bed, the frail bamboo frame creaking loudly under his weight.

Using his knapsack as a pillow, he lay on his back with his eyes closed, not wanting to see the decrepit state of the place where he had spent more than fifteen years of his life. He heard the soft rustle of a lizard scrabbling across the litter covered roof above. At the same moment there was a small commotion in the crossbeams as a mouse squeaked and tried to free itself from the jaws of a grass snake.

Rasus kept his eyes shut, perhaps because he wanted to keep from crying or because a thousand memories were crowding his mind. Perhaps, too, because images of Srintil were suddenly emerging in front of his eyes. When he had left his barracks the day before, he had never imagined he would see Srintil in Paruk, assuming that she was still in prison.

The children were surprised that a soldier would enter and lie down inside the abandoned shack. They came and stood around in the yard, whispering to one another, some of them peering in through the windows and cracks in the walls. Sakum's children, however, were proud to be able to tell the others who the soldier was. The younger children were astonished and found it hard to believe that Rasus was one of them, that he was actually a child of Paruk.

"So you see, the soldier in there is related to us. Once, this was his house," said Sakum's sons, their faces beaming.

The chattering of the children brought Rasus back to reality. Yes, the children. How sad that they don't even know who I am, he thought. He stood up and walked out smiling. The children started to flee when they saw him and only stopped when he called after them, "Come back, kids. I'd like to talk to you. Come back!"

Timidly they gathered around again. Rasus felt awkward, unsure of what to say to these naked little village kids.

"Uh, let's see. This time of year, what do you usually play?"

One small boy raised a palm leaf kite he was holding in his hand.

"That's right. During the dry season you all like fly kites, right?"

"Yes, sir."

Rasus counted the children. There were eight boys and three girls. He told the oldest of the boys to come forward and handed him some, money.

"Run over to Dawuan and buy eight kites with string. You girls, what do you like to play?"

No answer.

"Very well. You can play with rubber balls. Buy three rubber balls. Here's some money for them."

The yard outside the derelict old shack was immediately filled with unbounded happiness. Taking the money from Rasus' hand, the little girls ran off skipping. The boys hopped up and down with joy, knowing that soon each of them would own a real paper kite, not just a palm leaf one they usually made for themselves using string made out of the fibers from a banana tree. Rasus went into the hut and brought out his army knife from his knapsack.

"Come here, kids. I like to play, too. Watch."

Rasus looked around for something to use as a target. He threw his knife at a banana tree trunk and it went in up to the handle. The children's eyes grew wide and their mouths opened in astonishment. After a moment, they exploded into cheers. Rasus continued. He threw the knife after jumping up and somersaulting in the air. The children held their breath. They could hardly believe that this agile soldier was actually a Paruk villager. Finally, Rasus held his knife by the tip and let it drop straight down. At the last minute, he swung his leg and kicked the handle with his boot. Once again the knife struck the banana tree trunk, straight and true. This time the children were silent with admiration. They wanted him to continue, but his enthusiasm had suddenly dissipated and he gently refused. He had recalled a fellow soldier who had once played with a knife like that. The difference was that the target was not a banana tree but a man with his hands tied behind his back. Rasus closed his eyes to blot out the memory; the children around him were unaware of his thoughts.

In almost no time, Sakum's sons returned with eight kites with attached strings.

"Pass them out; each boy gets one."

Rasus took off his boots and shirt and herded the children to the dry fields on the north side of the little hamlet. The dry season winds, blowing from the southeast, carried the colored kites aloft. The happiness that was apparent there that day was something that not happened in Paruk in a long time. Rasus didn't follow the children into the field, but stood at the edge of the village grounds. His face beamed as he watched the children playing, watching his own memories of a childhood long ago.

Several adults came over and stood with him. They, too, were overwhelmed by a profound longing and sense of fellowship inspired by the children flying their kites. Eventually, almost everyone from the village came to the edge of the field. Their calm silence and the look in their eyes reflected a pride in the knowledge that Rasus continued to care about his people, evidenced by his fondness for the children.

Rasus turned his back on the field to chat with the villagers. He couldn't see Srintil among them and wanted to ask about her, but couldn't bring himself to utter her name. He could only conjecture that she was receiving her guest from Jakarta.

In fact, Srintil was still sitting alone in her hut. She reflected bitterly that her heart was breaking, torn apart by two forces moving in opposite directions. From behind the bamboo trellis, she watched the villagers walking over to meet Rasus. Moving her chair closer to the trellis, she could see that Rasus was surrounded. Of all the people of this hamlet, I'm the one who really has something deeply personal to discuss with him. I can only hope that he hasn't erased it from his heart. But, why am I just sitting here?

Several times she tried to free herself from the imaginary shackles that held her so that she could run to Rasus. But every time she made an effort to stand up, a feeling of dread forced her to collapse back on her chair. She realized that Sakum would have already told Rasus a great deal, and she was aware that today or tomorrow the man from Jakarta would come to visit her. In her frightened heart, Srintil knew that she had unintentionally created a distance between Rasus and herself, just at the very time they had the opportunity to become close again.

Why did moments in life often explode out of control when certain tensions reach a critical point? As with the dried pods of the legume bursting open to spread their seeds, the explosion occurs suddenly and nobody can ever predict the moment with any accuracy. Suddenly, a practical motivation mobilized Srintil into standing up. Who knows when this prodigal child will return to Paruk? I must meet with him, and right now!

She stood still for a moment. Her eyes glistened and her lips were closed to a straight line. Then she moved, almost running, towards the people standing in a group around the soldier. Several pairs of eyes watched her as she approached. A few people were on the point of speaking, but they all stopped short. All the villagers knew the history behind Srintil and Rasus. They not only knew about the nature of this relationship and how it came to be, they also understood its very essence. In the past, they had not wished for any form of intimacy to grow between the two because their marriage would have jeopardized the village's fundamental source of prestige: the ronggeng dancer.

But now, major changes had taken place. Paruk had been severely punished by the world and left in ruins. It had lost its self-esteem and pride; even its village elder had died in shame. After all they had undergone, the villagers had no other option than to pin their remaining hopes on Rasus. He was an army soldier and therefore close to state power. From the perspective of the villagers, the army and state power were one and the same thing. As a young soldier, Rasus thus represented their hope for protection and guidance. But he could only fulfill such hopes if he were to settle down in Paruk. The all-important key was his sense of loyalty to his little place of birth.

Everyone waited for a sign of loyalty to the village from Rasus. His attitude toward Srintil would constitute a kind of official signal from which they might gauge his feelings of empathy for his people as they endured this period of misery. Srintil could be the tie that would bind Rasus to them and make him their guardian and advocate.

It was clear that Rasus was not ready to face Srintil. He seemed nervous as he watched her walking towards him, her eyes downcast, and her mouth slightly opened. Suddenly, she changed direction and approached Tampi who was holding Goder. She took the child from Tampi's arms and hugged him tightly, holding back her tears with great effort.

Rasus, Srintil, and everyone else was aware of the meaning behind the situation. They all understood what the stakes were. They also all understood that Srintil represented the villagers in their desire to keep their favorite son from leaving his people again. Paruk desperately hoped its two children would once again find the sweet love they had known when they were youngsters. And the villagers strongly believed that Srintil was more than a fitting wife for Rasus.

In that sustained moment, a major village meeting took place in complete silence as the men dropped their shoulders and the women wiped the tears from their eyes. Rasus stood still while Srintil continued to sob quietly, holding Goder close to her chest. Paruk Village waited mutely as its fate hung in the balance. One by one, people began to move away, leaving Rasus and Srintil alone together. They wanted to support a process born out of hope by providing the two with some privacy. They yearned for this couple to have the capability and desire to preserve the village. From a distance they watched with rapt attention as Rasus finally moved, leading Srintil by the shoulder towards her home, neither of them speaking.

At the house, Rasus sat Srintil on her bed. He drew up a chair for himself and collapsed wearily. Srintil was still wiping her eyes. She was picture of perfect maturity, her fine hair framing her cheeks, just as it had done eight years earlier. At that time they had slept together for several nights at Rasus's grandmother's home. Srintil still remembered the morning she had woken up to find that Rasus had left her without saying goodbye.

Fragmented memories filling their hearts caused the two to sink deeper into silence. The silence would have continued far longer if Nyai Sakarya hadn't emerged from within the house.

"I heard that Rasus has come. Is it really you, young man?"

"Yes it is," Rasus said.

"My eyes aren't what they used to be. Is everything okay with you?"

"Well, let me put it this way. I'm healthy enough to be able to visit Paruk."

"You've certainly become a handsome young man now. Are you married?"

"Uh, no. I guess I haven't found my soul mate yet."

"No, that's not it, young man. You just haven't accepted your predestined fate. Since the time you were a small child you've had a soul mate. Paruk has given us all a sign that Srintil is your partner in life. Is it that you don't like your fate?"

"Granny!" Srintil screamed. She began to stand up to stop her grandmother from speaking any further, but she stopped midway, then sat down and began to sob. Shocked by the old woman's bluntness, Rasus found it difficult to grasp what she had said. He stared at her with astonishment, his eyes unblinking. He felt like a fly caught in a spider's web. No. More like a bird that had landed on a branch smeared with sticky resin. No, not that either. Like a child who had tiptoed across someone's garden to take a shortcut and avoid a more circuitous route, then been caught by the owner of the garden who had chased him with a friendly smile, pointing toward the path he should have taken.

"Oh, my grandchildren, I'm only conveying the intuition of an old woman. Indeed, the intuition that you two have already been matched by Paruk. But, please don't misunderstand me; there are many people who don't accept their destiny."

"Granny, please, that's enough. You're embarrassing me," said Srintil between sobs. "Why don't you just take Goder home to Tampi."

Nyai Sakarya acquiesced and took Goder from the Srintil's arms. The old woman's expression was perfectly calm and gave no evidence of the words she had just spoken, words that had caused the other two considerable anxiety. Rasus remained quiet, his eyes and expression suggesting that he felt stymied. He sat down nervously.

"Forgive my granny, okay?" Srintil said softly to Rasus. "She's very old and forgets that someone like me must know my place. Idle chatter like that is humiliating. I feel embarrassed in front of you."

Rasus shook his head without meaning anything specific. His vague smile indicated what he felt: at a loss for words. It may be that he was not completely aware of what he said when he spoke: "The problem is that, until now, I hadn't even thought about marriage or about whom I might marry. Not even about you, Srin. I only just learned that you'd returned when Sakum told me this morning."

"I never dreamed to presume that I'd be the reason for your coming back here. This, here, means nothing to you."

"Ah, Srin. You really needn't talk like that. Times have changed. Let's leave the past alone. We should be happy with the way things are. We're safe and we're back home, both of us. Now, Srin, I'd like to take my leave. I haven't bathed since yesterday afternoon.

"But..."

"I'll be around for another day and night."

"Wait. I have some oranges and papaya."

"Don't, don't. I know you have oranges and papaya. But I need to bathe now. At the fountain."

Srintil couldn't speak further. She watched Rasus go out the front door, the image of his broad shoulders etched into her heart.

"When will you come back?"

Rasus didn't answer, nor did he even look back.

There was a whirlwind in Srintil's breast, and she felt the stabbing pains of jagged edges striking her heart. Dear God, the world is full of people, yet why do I feel so alone? She went into her room and lay face down on the bed.

Rasus walked, his head down, toward his little run-down shack. In the front yard, he stood and gazed at the place he had lived in when he was a small child. He went inside after carefully opening the door so it wouldn't collapse. He took his toiletries from his knapsack and went out again to make his way to the fountain.

The area had not changed since the days he had bathed at the fountain every day as a small boy, when he had first become aware of the difference between the bodies of males and females. Just as before, during the dry season, the volume of water was small, but the water remained clear. A large, flat rock onto which the water poured had likely not shifted even a millimeter. The falling water was like an arcing crystal, breaking into thousands of tiny wet fragments that leapt in all directions. When the sun broke through a gap in the leafy overgrowth and fell upon the myriad of crystalline drops, its reflection became a rainbow of colors.

Unfortunately, Rasus was not in a receptive state of mind to enjoy the beauty of the fountain. He just wanted to refresh himself, to cleanse his body of the grime that was making him feel tired and dirty. When he returned to his little shack, he found Nyai Kartareja waiting for him. She had brought two bowls of food, one filled with rice and the other with side dishes.

"While you are home here in Paruk, you needn't worry about eating. This is from Srintil. She is the only person in the village who is able to serve cooked rice. Now don't be afraid, there's nothing to be worried about. I didn't add any love potions.

"If there were potions in the food, I'd still eat it. I'm really hungry."

"Srintil will stop crying if you eat. Please, go ahead. I'll get some water for you."

Rasus smiled, watching Nyai Kartareja's animated movements as she went outside, happy as a small child. He hung his towel on the stem of a banana tree in the front yard, changed his shirt and pants, and combed his hair. He spread a length of cloth on the ground near his sleeping pallet and knelt to perform his prayers.

Nyai Kartareja returned carrying not only a glass and teapot, but also peeled oranges and papaya.

I haven't put any spells on these either, and Srintil would be upset if she thought you didn't want to eat them.

"I'll eat the rice and side dishes with great enjoyment. But I'll eat the fruit with a humble heart."

"Oh, I know what you're thinking. Srintil bought the fruit for someone else. But, you see, she didn't know you were coming back. Had she known, she probably would have bought satay and lamb curry for you. Other people are insignificant to her; the visitor from Jakarta wouldn't have been invited if she had known you'd be here.

"You certainly have a way with words. Very well. Go to Srintil and give her my heartfelt thanks."

Rasus watched the village children playing happily with the kites, the first real toys they had ever received. He felt refreshed after his shower. His stomach was full and the happiness he witnessed in the children filled him with contentment. He smiled to see them jumping around with such evident joy. His eyes followed the twisting and turning kites in the sky. Whenever the wind subsided, the children would shout in unison, without any prompting,a childhood rhyme. Rasus's lips moved as he silently joined the chorus. When he realized what he was doing, he smiled to himself at the irony of the situation. As a soldier he was considered too far removed from the world of children to return to it.

He stood up and walked to the west, without any particular destination in mind. He could make out three distant points across the rice fields, moving toward the village. After a while, he identified the three points as human figures. He could see that the one in front wore a pith helmet, and the color of his shirt and pants was now clear. The figures behind both wore caps and jackets. In a flash, Rasus realized that the three were outsiders. At the same moment, he also determined that these were the men who would be visiting Srintil. Deep inside, he felt that some kind of social boundary been transgressed, that an imaginary line defining the identity of the village had been crossed. He felt the primitive urge of an animal whose private territorial space had been invaded by another creature. For a long while, he stood there, his eyes fixed upon the image in front of him. His breathing quickened as he became quite certain that the three men were headed for Srintil's house. His body swayed with a desire to move towards them, but he suddenly turned around and walked quickly, almost ran, in the other direction to the dry field where the children were playing. He grabbed the string of a kite from a child and began playing with it energetically. The movement of the kites rolling and pitching up in the sky emanated his turbulent feelings. The children cheered with joy. Rasus smiled, but it was the most difficult smile he had expressed in his twenty-six years.

Bajus arrived in the village with Tamir and Diding. By coming with his two companions, Bajus wanted to confirm his earlier claim to Srintil that his intention was only to socialize with her. Outside Srintil's door, Tamir announced their arrival, and was greeted by Nyai Sakarya. From her bedroom, Srintil could hear the conversation outside and became aware that her guests had arrived. She clutched her pillow tighter and tighter, so that her body became as if a part of the woven bamboo sleeping pallet. Nyai Sakarya's voice sounded like a racket in her ears.

"Hey, Srintil. Time to get up. Your guests have arrived."

Srintil just shifted her legs a little.

"Wake up, grandchild. Come on, they're sitting in the front room."

Srintil moaned softly as she rolled over and sat up on the edge of the bed. Her red eyes stared vacantly ahead. Without combing her hair, which was hanging over her face, she stood up and walked out of the bedroom, her movements as if animated by a force outside of her body. The three men greeted her with raised eyebrows. She was obviously not prepared to receive guests.

"Welcome, Bajus. And the same to you two," Srintil said hoarsely.

"Thanks, but you look very pale. Are you ill?" asked Bajus.

"I'm just feeling a bit under the weather. Perhaps I got a little sunstroke yesterday when I came home from the community center."

"But you're ill," said Bajus leaning back in his seat, with obvious disappointment.

"How about this for an idea?" Tamir suggested. "Let's all go to the doctor so that you can get some medicine."

Silence. Bajus nodded without enthusiasm. Tamir's words made Srintil feel anxious, aware that Bajus and his two friends had something planned for her.

"To tell you the truth, Srin, we wanted to invite you to go with us to Eling-eling. My car has plenty of room for the four of us.

"Oh, I don't know..."

"Just to get out for a bit. Maybe watch a movie, whatever you like. You believed what I said yesterday, don't you?"

"What do you mean? Oh, yes, I remember."

"No, I have no mischievous intentions. Not like Tamir when he came by a few days ago. That was rotten of him. But, when he's with me, he has to be a gentleman."

"That's true. Forgive me for being impolite the other day. I'm going to behave myself."

"Thank you. But you can see for yourself that there's no way I can go out."

"How about we go together to get you some medicine?"

"Please forgive me, but I don't take any drugs. I use only traditional medicines."

"So, we'll go to the traditional medicine seller."

"No. I'll buy something for myself tomorrow at the market. I really don't feel very well. If I go out, I'm afraid I might become really ill."

"Okay, Srintil has a point," said Bajus. "She really doesn't look well. So, we needn't go anywhere. Let's just stay here and chat a bit."

Tamir smiled wryly, his expression sheepish. Srintil gave a weak smile, only the corners of her lip drawing back slightly.

"Later, if you feel better, we can go somewhere. You'd like that, wouldn't you, Srin?"

"Well, I really don't know. I'm not feeling at all well. I should just stay quietly at home. I feel so ashamed!"

"I understand why you might feel that way, but you really needn't. What's more, you needn't feel afraid. Regarding my becoming acquainted with you, I pulled some strings to clear it with the police and local officials. Don't worry, I'm not going to create problems of any kind for you."

"So, now that Srintil is feeling so ill, are we going sit around and bother her with idle chatter?" said Tamir, laughing out loud.

"Of course not. But, since we're all friends, there's nothing wrong with us chatting for a little while."

However, the chitchat that Bajus hoped for did not proceed smoothly. For almost a half hour, Srintil simply listened without speaking. Her face remained wan and her eyes dull. Her three guests saw that she was truly ill. When they took their leave, Srintil accompanied them to the door and made no attempt at politeness except to smile weakly. Such small unconscious gestures supported Sakum's declaration that Srintil was no longer a ronggeng dancer. If she had been, she would have used her smile as a weapon to pierce the hearts of the men.

Rasus lit a small lantern he had found in the shack and had filled with oil he had got from a neighbor. The hut that had been dark since his grandmother had died several years ago was now filled with flickering light. That night, after eating at Kartareja's place, he went to visit Sakum. Only Sakum, his wife, and their smallest child were home. The other children were in the rice fields hunting for crickets and other bugs. There were no tables or chairs so they all sat on a sleeping pallet. Sakum puffed continuously on cigarettes and his head was enveloped in a cloud of smoke.

"So, soldier. Have you thought about what I said yesterday?" asked Sakum.

"Marriage?"

"Yeah. You've reached the right age. And it's Srintil we're talking about!"

Rasus sighed. Sakum's question presented him with a dilemma that had completely stymied him since he had first asked it. He felt he could neither provide a direct answer, nor could he simply brush it off.

He sighed again. "I just don't know."

Sakum's empty eyes blinked rapidly. He seemed unfazed by the thick smoke hanging around his face. "But you know that she's no longer a ronggeng dancer, don't you?"

A clear image of Srintil suddenly arose in Rasus's imagination. Srintil as she was now, her fully developed body and her clearly transformed identity. She was a Srintil who cried because she no longer knew who she was, a Srintil who seemed to seek the smallest, most unobtrusive place in life, and a Srintil who played a role in the formative history of Rasus himself. Her eyes had lost their challenging power: her bright sunlight had turned into a pale moonlight. Her smile was no longer an invitation to sexual desire. It was as if a wild bumblebee had been transformed into a domesticated butterfly.

"So, why the silence, soldier?" asked Sakum, interrupting his thoughts.

"I can't really talk about it."

"Can't talk about it! Why is that, soldier?"

"You see, in a few days, I leave for Kalimantan. And there's nothing I can do about that."

"But..."

"There's no 'but' about it. I might be away from Java for a long time. Perhaps for a year: perhaps two, three, or many years. Because of that..."

"Well, duty is duty, but you've got to feel some sympathy for us here in Paruk. Promise that someday in the future you'll marry Srintil. That alone would give her, and the rest of the people in the village, the strength to go on. Or am I mistaken in sensing that you still care for her?"

Rasus jerked back at these words, and the creak of the sleeping pallet made Sakum smile and wait patiently. For a long time Rasus only puffed and sighed. When he finally spoke his words leapt to another matter.

"I want to walk for a bit. There are several people whose homes I still have to visit."

"That's true. You should visit all the families here, but it's still early in the afternoon. Stay for a bit longer."

"Many thanks but I can't."

"Very well. You intend to visit Srintil, too, right?"

"Perhaps, a bit later."

"You must. Remember that things have changed, and you can't expect them to be like they were in the past. Srintil won't come to you late at night and slip into your bed to sleep with you."

A brief smile flashed across Rasus's face as he got up to leave. Then, the darkness swallowed both him and his smile. He moved easily in the dark, but his soul crept along blindly, groping about without a compass. He had intended to go to Darkin's house but changed his mind. He then thought to visit Kastaliput, but changed his mind about that too. Similarly, he decided not to visit Wiryadasim. In front of Srintil's house, he halted. He stood as silently as the banana trees in the yard. The points of starlight in the sky above were diffuse because of the new moon that would appear later in the night. Bats, which were barely visible in the gloom, flew toward the south. A quail flew in front of Rasus, uttering a mournful cry.

Inside Srintil's house, Srintil was talking to Goder: "Listen, my child. That's a *bencé*. You should be asleep."

"Why, Mommy?"

"Because when you hear a bencé, it means there is a thief in the night."

"What's a thief?"

"A bad man."

"Those men this afternoon, they weren't thieves, were they?"

"No, they were good men."

"And what about that other man?"

"The soldier?"

"Yeah. Is he a good man?"

"He's a good man too."

"Do you think I could be a soldier?"

"It would be grand if you became a soldier."

"You like soldiers, don't you, Mommy?"

Srintil swallowed, unable to answer.

The person standing outside in the dark listening to the conversation also swallowed. He held back a cough that had begun to tickle his throat. He watched as Srintil drew Goder close into her arms. Rasus moved slowly and silently away from the hut. The bencé quail flew overhead again, crying, and he hastened his steps home.

As the moon rose, chasing away the blackness of the night, Rasus lay sprawled restlessly on his bed. From where he lay, he could see the gloominess in the trees brightening, the towering green bamboo stalks bending in the cold, dry breeze. He realized the truth of Sakum's words, that Srintil would not come to his bed; that was something that could only have happened if she were still a ronggeng dancer. Indeed, even far into the night, she did not come to him. Rasus was relieved. He wanted to sleep. Drowsiness began to slow the beat of his pulse, but it abruptly left him again when he remembered Sakum's question: "Am I mistaken in sensing that you still care for Srintil?"

The small lantern hanging from a hook on a rotting wooden beam had only a few more drops of oil in it. The oil moistened a cloth wick and, seeping upwards passed through the metal cover to reach the bottom of the flame. Every molecule of the oil was seized by the heat, which then released the inner energy to become part of the fire. That flame was now the size of a grain of rice. The flickering light grew smaller, the tip disappearing little by little. The yellowish-red color of the flame slowly turned to blue, and in the middle a tiny ember glowed. Eventually, all the objects around the lantern began to lose their distinctive shape. The flame that had become a small blue point began to tremble and finally went out.

Rasus sighed deeply. The ramshackle hut was totally dark inside, not even touched by the moon's dim light. He was a prisoner within, restless because he was unable to keep his thoughts from straying. If he hadn't been stymied, his musings might have continued far longer. When the moon began its descent into the western sky, he finally closed his eyes. The night air was chilly and the lonely little hamlet was utterly quiet, seemingly without even the smallest sign of human life. There were only the sounds of dozens of crickets in Sakum's house and of mice chasing one another in the dried rubbish layers of the roof.

Rasus slept no more than two hours, with terrifying nightmares bringing him back to consciousness. His head ached when he tried to sit up. Dazed, he massaged his hot, stiff neck. Through the holes in the bamboo wall, which faced the east, he could see the sky beginning to glow. In the west, the moon was just touching the tops of the bamboo grove, growing wan, as if fearful of being caught by the sun. Rasus picked up his toiletries bag, went outside and made his way towards the fountain.

A dung beetle flew ahead, buzzing loudly. It seemed to him little different from the time long ago when he was a little boy. A scrub jay, perched on top of the fountain, twittered. A cave bat at the mouth of a knothole in a sengon tree crawled inside as he approached. Honeybees hummed around the flowering bungur tree. Steeling himself against the cold air, Rasus squatted under the fountain. He sneezed repeatedly as the water, cold as the dew, struck his hot forehead. When he had finished bathing, he returned to the hut, changed into his green fatigues and then spread out a length of cloth to pray and meditate. He wanted to find some assurance that his decision to leave Paruk immediately, in the early morning gloom, was the best thing to do for his own peace of mind.

With his boots tied and his belt buckled, he snatched his hat from where it hung at the corner of his bed. His knapsack hanging from his shoulder, Rasus left the little shanty. His brisk steps were directed towards Kartareja's house. He knocked on the closed door.

"Gramps, come out for a moment. It's Rasus; I want to take my leave."

"What? You want to leave now?"

Kartareja opened the door, but Rasus didn't enter. He was in a hurry and wanted to talk to Kartareja outside.

"I thought you were going to stay one more day. Why are you in such a rush? Do you have other things to attend to?"

"It's not that. I need to prepare for my departure from Java. So, I have to leave here as early in the morning as possible."

"Actually, I wanted to speak with you. Last night, I waited for you, but you never came by. It's about something which I want to keep between you and me."

"There's only the two of us right now."

"Yes, but this is important. Well, if this is the way you want it, then so be it. My boy, I wanted to ask you about your relationship with Srintil. Forgive me, young man. But this is something I need to find out from you."

Rasus dropped his shoulders and lowered his head. He seemed to have trouble finding the words to answer.

"Last night Sakum asked me about this. I couldn't answer him because I'm going far away and don't know when I'll be coming back. That's it. If there's a good man who wants Srintil, then please, help them both. But if a man only wants mischief with her, tell her that she shouldn't behave the way she did in the past. I forbid it."

Kartareja nodded, trying to comprehend Rasus's hurried words. What he really wanted, however, was an explanation. Yet, just as he was about to ask for one, Rasus extended his hand to say goodbye, turned abruptly and walked away. Kartareja could only follow him with his eyes, watching, as he grew smaller and less distinct in the early morning gloom. Finally, he vanished behind a grove of bamboo.

4

In the early 1970s, life in Dawuan county became transformed by the constant rumbling of large yellow-colored trucks and bulldozers of all types and sizes. The trucks were transporting earth stripped from the hills to fill low-lying areas that would provide access for the planned water channel. The bulldozers dug and smoothed the earth throughout the day and night, sometimes continuously for twenty-four hours. The people of Dawuan and surrounding areas had the opportunity to observe the workers, many of whom came from other regions of Indonesia: their clothes, behavior, and the ways they amused themselves. The locals even had their first opportunity to see a few foreigners from Japan and France who always drew considerable attention, especially from the children.

Dawuan was jubilant. The project workers often showed films in the town square at night, for free. Small kiosks, open throughout the day and night, sprang up everywhere. Contact between the villagers and the visiting city dwellers became intensive, especially among the younger workers and the local adolescents. As a result, city values began to influence the established, rural ones. The young people of Dawuan began to imitate the style, conduct, and dress of the workers. They also imitated the Jakartan dialect spoken by many of the project employees.

This influence also spread to Paruk. Children there were now playing with toy tractors, bulldozers, and dump trucks, all carved out of banana tree trunks. Nyai Kartareja opened a tiny foodstall to sell pecel and fresh coconut juice. During the day, many of the workers stopped by her kiosk, partly because of the pecel, but also because of a certain young woman in the village who was often the subject of their idle chatter.

More than occasionally, men from the project visited Srintil during the day as well as in the evening. To some extent, she was pleased about this. Through such visits, she was provided with the means to broadcast who she had become. Yet, it was Nyai Kartareja who could explain more fully how Srintil had changed. Srintil no longer wanted to participate in illicit affairs. She now had someone in her life about whom she felt serious: Bajus, a man of considerable status in the irrigation project.

At first, Srintil had felt uncomfortable about Nyai Kartareja's idle chatter. It was as if the old woman wanted to destroy her fantasy over a young man who she believed could never be vanquished from her imagination. No. Srintil had no wish for that fantasy to die, although she had no idea how to make it a reality. Let that fantasy be like a tuber, the *umbi gadung*, that seemed to dry up and die during the dry season. Or a kind of memory that always carried a particular softness each time she recalled it. Srintil had also received orders from Kartareja: she was permitted to have a relationship with a good man, but strictly forbidden to become involved with scoundrels. She respected the instructions, not only because of their content but also because she knew that they had actually come from Rasus. She respected them, but didn't really understand them. Perhaps Rasus wanted her to be claimed by a man who truly needed her as a wife. But what would happen if he were to return one day and find her still alone? Trying to answer this question always made her tremble. Sometimes she smiled to herself when she was alone, and other times she sighed with restrained feelings of apprehension.

Then Nyai Kartareja's gossip, such as it was, developed into reality. Bajus politely visited Srintil, his behavior steadfast and apparently lacking in ulterior motives. Sometimes he came with friends, and sometimes he invited Kartareja to accompany him. Everything was open and correct.

One day, after visiting her regularly for several weeks, he invited her to go for a ride outside the village, and no one even looked twice when they left. Together with little Goder, they presented the image of a happy family. When they saw the village chief of Pecikalan near the community center, the old man gave them a friendly smile. When local dignitaries in Dawuan saw them, they greeted them with friendly nods. For Srintil, it was like a drink of cool clear water after a long journey over dry rice fields during a drought. She felt that she had emerged at the surface after drowning in an ocean of human disgrace.

In Bajus's car, Srintil sat quietly, her eyes directed at the road ahead. Goder sitting on her lap, was also silent, anxious because this was his first experience of riding in a car. Srintil was quiet because she was conscious of the changing currents in her soul. Her eyes were red but she broke into a smile whenever Bajus spoke to her.

"We'll go to Eling-eling, just to drive around. Is that okay with you?"

"That's fine. No, wait. Don't go to Eling-eling."

"Why not?"

"Uh, no particular reason. I'm just afraid to go there."

"Does it make you think of the past?"

"Well, you must understand. I was in Eling-eling for two years as a prison inmate. I really don't want to be reminded of all that again."

"Okay. We'll go to the south coast then. It's been a long time since I've seen the ocean. What do you think?"

Srintil nodded and smiled. The south coast was far removed from Paruk. One or two people who lived there might know she had been a ronggeng dancer and a political prisoner but the possibility of being recognized there was remote compared to Eling-eling.

The further they drove from Dawuan, the more relaxed she felt. At first, she only spoke to Goder, pointing out things along the way to him. Then she broke into laughter when he asked if she would buy him a horse to pull a cart, like the one he had just seen. She laughed again when he asked whether the cage he saw being carried by a man at the edge of the road didn't perhaps contain a human head. Bajus grinned, and even once kidded Goder, telling him that "the large tin box being carried by that man is filled with snakes", as he pointed to a shrimp-cracker seller walking down the road. Goder opened his eyes wide in fear, and Srintil and Bajus laughed together.

When they reached the coast, Bajus chose an isolated place to park his jeep. It wasn't the best place to park, but he chose it because he wanted some privacy, away from the prying eyes of other visitors. Goder had never seen anything like the ocean before and it filled him with fear. He clung to Srintil, reluctant to let go.

Srintil stared out at the ocean framed by the sky. Waves followed one another and broke on the shore. Fishing boats bobbed up and down, carried aloft by the waves. Small creatures crawled along the beach where the sand met the water. These sights were all new to her. On the beach children and wives of fishermen were busily sorting fish according to type, placing jellyfish in separate containers. But none of them could draw Srintil's attention. Her eyes became the link to her inner soul, penetrating what had previously been narrow and limited. Her soul now fled, liberated, roaming to understand the blue sea, the blue sky, the green island of Nusakambangan off in the distance, and the rolling white-capped waves. Suddenly her instincts took control and became a wise teacher. They told her that there was great passion behind the profound harmony spread out before her. This great passion transcended all human aspirations because the greatness of humanity had to bow to the pure voice of the soul, to ideal and deed, and to will and action. And then Srintil in her own humanity felt this great passion without saying a word, opening the door to all fellow humans, so that each soul could enter and she could harmonize with it. She recognized, on the other hand, that each human—each soul—could go his or her own separate way, following a road of selfish vanity and egoism much too weak to bear the burden of social or even personal harmony.

As this point an inner clarity began to develop inside of her, but she was interrupted by someone calling from behind. She looked back, and at that moment the camera in Bajus's hand clicked. A perfect moment became fixed in time. The camera not only recorded a picture of a young woman, it also captured the image of someone free of emotional upheaval, a woman touched by a deep inner peace. Bajus grinned widely without realizing that, while he was an amateur, he had by sheer chance accomplished something only a few professional photographers could ever hope for. Later, he would be astonished to see the results of his own work. In terms of the conventional matters of lighting, composition, and even perspective, his photos were not very impressive. Yet, in communicating the language of the heart—a difficult achievement in photography—that one photo would be truly outstanding.

After they had enjoyed enough of the sun and the wind, Bajus invited Srintil and Goder to a shady spot near the car. There, he took more pictures: one of Srintil sitting on the bumper of the car and another of her sitting in the front seat with Goder on her lap. He then walked off to find a shop and returned with a bunch of *rambutan* fruit and three bottles of soda. He watched Srintil's fingers as she carefully peeled the rambutan, and her face as she swallowed the soft white fruit. His face betrayed a conflict of emotions, but he quickly concealed them by turning away, silently and bitterly cursing himself.

Just before the middle of the day, Bajus started up his jeep, ready to leave. Srintil had bought a few treats to take back to her friends and family—papaya and a bunch of bananas—but Bajus had insisted on paying for them. After leaving the beach area, Bajus turned off the road and entered the parking lot of a small hotel. For a moment, Srintil was startled, remembering that it was to such places that men had taken her when she was held in jail. If Bajus had such erotic ambitions now, she was ready to reject his advances.

"Let's get a bite to eat. This place has really good fried rice," he said, pointing to a food stall next to the hotel.

Bajus walked on ahead and didn't notice Srintil letting out a sigh of relief. She took Goder in her arms and followed him. Most of the chairs inside were already taken by customers, and Bajus was unable to sit at his favorite table.

"Do you like fried rice?"

"I do."

"Let's get three orders. What would you like to drink?"

"Anything."

"Some lemonade?"

Srintil nodded. A provocatively dressed waitress came and took Bajus's order. Srintil secretly watched the way Bajus interacted with the waitress who was obviously there as a kind of enticement, like a decoy used by hunters. She was pretty and seemed to be acquainted with him. Yet Srintil had to admit that he was flawless in his behavior; he only spoke as needed and his words were simple and direct.

The excitement that had infected the entire region of Dawuan had been going on for almost five months. Trucks and bulldozers had become common sight. The locals had become used to the behavior of the city dwellers who had come to work there. Some were still interested in seeing the Japanese and French visitors. On one occasion, the foreigners created an amusing scene at a food stall, when they tried eating pecel, the spicy dish of vegetables and peanut sauce. They were beside themselves in discomfort, their eyes streaming, after their tongues had been stung by the tiny hot peppers.

Paruk was electrified by the excitement. Not only did Nyai Kartareja have the opportunity to sell pecel, and rather successfully too, but all the men from the village had been able to find work. They were paid well to work as assistants to the stonemasons, as ditch diggers, or as laborers who covered new embankments with a layer of grass. All this busy activity in the county gave the impression that the turmoil of 1965 was fading into the past and a new era was slowly emerging.

Srintil felt this change through the reactions in the faces she saw from day to day. The glance of a stranger was no longer filled with distrust and fear. And her association with Bajus, who played an important role in the irrigation project, influenced the way people regarded her. The people in the sub-district could only view the world in a simple manner. Bajus was a project employee. The project was governmental. Thus, Bajus was a government man. If Bajus was with Srintil, then the people could see it only one way: Srintil was connected with the government. Whether or not she was actually a former prisoner, she was a part of the government. So, her presence was now viewed as a good thing.

To reinforce this, there were the photos in Srintil's house that gave testimony to who she was and what her circumstances were. People looked proudly at the picture that showed her sitting on the bumper Bajus's car and the one in which she appeared quite comfortable in the front seat of that same car, her pride apparent in the smile on her face.

But Srintil wasn't entirely content. Why was it that these photos were fixed to a wall of plaited bamboo under a roof of field grass? She felt that she would much rather have the photos displayed on a brick wall with white plaster or, at the very least, a wooden wall painted light blue. She recalled some idle chatter she had heard: that it was entirely appropriate for her to become a housewife in a family that owned an automobile. She thought of all the gold jewelry she owned. She had enough to live in a home of sturdy wood: even one with stone walls, if she wanted. As a former prisoner though, she was still afraid to show any form of vanity, even in the vaguest, most indirect way. She feared that people would say she was lacking in remorse, and that, as someone once implicated in major crimes against society, she didn't know her place.

However, the fear in her heart began to erode when she considered an authentic value in rural life: harmony. If she wanted a suitable home, she would have to create harmony between herself and the vagaries of time. In a flash of insight, Srintil heard a clear whisper: "It's no longer appropriate for you to hide yourself in a grass shack."

Believing that she has been instructed by the times, Srintil decided to consult Kartareja. She intentionally picked a moment when he was alone so that nobody could overhear their conversation.

"Grandpa, would it be wrong for me to want to buy a nicer home for myself? Would people become outraged if I were to take such a step?"

Kartareja couldn't answer straight away. He had spent considerable time trying to interpret the changing times, and now believed that there were no obstacles before Srintil. Perhaps, if Srintil weren't pretty, matters would be quite different. Beauty was not something to be denied and, in that regard, Srintil was a jewel. Thus, although she was a former prisoner, she should not be denied a decent house. Kartareja was not surprised when he realized his own existence was a sign that he should bless her desire for a new house.

Yet, he hid his disappointment as he thought to himself: why was it Bajus who had inspired Srintil's idea for a house? Why wasn't it Rasus? It was still the hope of Kartareja and the people of Paruk that their own son would be the one to take Srintil to a new life without fear and, at the same time, cleanse their hamlet of the scars caused by communist debacle of 1965.

"You're silent." Srintil commented. "Don't you approve?"

"Oh, it's nothing, nothing. I approve, my dear. I was wondering whether you had heard of anyone wishing to sell a house," said Kartareja, hiding his real feelings with considerable skill.

"No, I haven't. That's the problem. I'm asking for your approval and your help in finding a house."

"Me?"

"If not you, then who else?"

"Well then, the first thing we must do is to get the village chief's permission. We should proceed carefully. If the chief doesn't approve, then there's little I can do."

"I won't do anything without your permission. I just want to get out of that grass hut. It's humiliating when Bajus comes to visit."

"I understand your situation. Okay. Get your money together. I'll go and speak with the village chief."

The elderly village chief had actually been feeling somewhat embarrassed that someone of Bajus's status was coming into the miserable Paruk Village. And of the obvious connection of the isolated hamlet with his office. He approved Srintil's request, made through Kartareja. He never referred to Paruk's erstwhile link to the communist uprising. He even mentioned the names of several people he knew who wished to sell their homes, most of them being recipients of compensation for land used in the irrigation project who intended to build new homes.

In less than a month, Srintil had found a house to buy, one made of teak, which was being sold by a wealthy farmer from Dawuan. Moving to the new house involved everybody in the village, even the blind Sakum. Bajus sent some workmen to add some finishing touches. In less than six weeks everything was ready: for the first time in Paruk, there was a new teakwood house with brick walls and a cement floor, even boasting a latrine and a well.

Srintil decorated the interior with the best furniture she could buy in Dawuan. She also bought gas lanterns so that in the evenings her house was so well lit that people could always see the three photos on the wall of her front room.

At that time Srintil felt as if she had almost achieved a kind of equilibrium. When she smiled, a nice dimple formed at each corner of her lips. For once, she felt completely free of fear. A radiance began to show on her face, slowly but surely replacing her earlier nervousness and general sense of apprehension. While it could not be said that she was fully healed, the improvement in her demeanor could be seen every day. When people looked at the photos, Srintil could feel her heart soar with the branjangan birds twittering joyfully in the sky high over the dry fields near the village. Their eyes beheld a vast world far more expansive than her dreary, isolated hamlet. A world a million times bigger than the prison complex in Eling-eling. From high in the air, Srintil might easily see yellow and red hibiscus, as well as the purple kecipir flowers. The puffy cumulus clouds sent a Kecapi melody picked by the Wirsiter's fingers and the song "Asmara Dahana", with its clean tremolo rendered from Ciplak's vocal cords.

As her heart soared with the birds, Srintil also found herself a new existence within the essence of womanhood: but not the kind of femininity that is opposed to masculinity in the primitive sense, where women belong to all men. She felt that there was a certain kind of masculinity around her, masculinity that could transform her into a household female, a woman with a home. Further, she felt that such a man was not necessarily the kind of male that makes a strong impression on a woman's heart. He was not Rasus, but Bajus. No matter. Srintil had already learned a great deal, and knew by now that there were some hopes that would never be fulfilled.

And she could not deny the reality that Bajus was increasingly pushing Rasus aside in her heart. Bajus, who never saw anything about her that he disliked. Her experience in knowing this man from the government project gave her a sense of hope. During the entire time he had known her, he had never touched her body, never even referred to erotic matters, either directly or through inference. He had always remained polite and respectful, like a true gentleman. Furthermore, he had been of invaluable assistance in building her house. Srintil could draw only one conclusion: that Bajus was an honest and good man. He had nothing to do with the world of scoundrels she so desperately wished to leave behind.

But he had never talked to her about marriage: he had never mentioned the word, nor even alluded to the idea. A feeling of anticipation had attached itself to her heart, like a termite deeply lodged in wood. Sometimes she felt impatient for him to speak. But each time she felt this way, she snuffed her impatience with the wisdom of a village woman. Women are like fish traps: when they are set, they can only wait for the fish to come on their own. A fish trap would never chase after the fish, nor could it force the fish to enter.

Only the nosy Nyai Kartareja exposed her feelings on one occasion.

"So, your nice house is now built, and love has awakened. I want to ask you now, when do you think Paruk might have a big celebration?"

"Don't ask about such things," Srintil answered nervously, her cheeks turning red. "It's embarrassing. And I really don't know."

"Forgive me, young lady. I just wanted to know. Everybody around here wants to see you get married soon. That's natural, isn't it? After all, what else needs to be done? Everything is just right."

Srintil said nothing further, just bowed her head and remained silent. Suddenly she had the feeling that a piece of time had been lost, as if she had been a chaste virgin the previous night who, without an understanding of men, became awkward in dealing with them. Nyai Kartareja saw the anxiety on her face.

"Now, don't let yourself drift off into your thoughts. All desires must be followed through. You haven't neglected to meditate on your birthday, have you?"

Srintil was silent.

"Or to fast on Mondays and Thursdays?"

"That's not all that I've been doing," Srintil said to herself. "Every night I pray to God, hoping that soon there will be a man who will want to marry me. A man with whom I could prove with all my heart that who I am now is different from who I was before. A man that could make me into what I have long yearned to become: a housewife."

"Well, perhaps I could help. Usually in such matters, one needs a go-between, a mediator. I could do this if you want me to. We people of Paruk believe in striving for what we desire by using mantras and sorcery, and through effort. As for effort, you can do that by yourself. Sorcery would constitute those slivers of precious metals which still remain under your skin in various parts of your body. But the matter of mantras...ah. You can't do them without me."

"Don't starting talking about sorcery and love charms. Your charms have surely dropped out of my body because I've disregarded your taboos. And I don't wish to become married through mantras or charms. I want to marry like other people marry, that's all."

"Oh well. If that's what you want. Nevertheless, you can't dismiss the crucial role of a go-between. I'm getting pretty old, you know. When you feel anxious, like you do now, you need a mediator. I would like you to tell me when you think I or my husband should meet Bajus. We'll invite him to discuss the possibility of a marriage between you two. What do you think?"

"Please don't," said Srintil softly, after a long silence. "I must wait patiently. Perhaps Bajus's attention is focused on his work. I don't know. What's clear is that I'm too embarrassed."

Nyai Kartareja understood what she meant. It was a sense of shame that emerged whenever she, as a former political prisoner, wished to demonstrate that she was just a human being like everyone else. A sense of shame resulting out of fear that she might be accused of being a fish trap that chased after, instead of waiting for, the fish.

February 1971 was called *mangsa kasanga*: the ninth season within the traditional Javanese calendar. The weather was hot and oppressive. From time to time dry winds gusted so violently they tore the leaves off the trees, knocked down banana palms, and toppled young stalks of bamboo. In the fields, germinating rice paddies suffered strong winds that threatened the success of pollination. And, if rain fell, there was danger that the drops alone could damage the large, delicate grains.

In the village, a strong wind swept through the trees and groves of bamboo with a loud, rushing sound. The trees and bamboo stalks rubbed against one another, creaking loudly. Dried twigs and branches fell, scattering everywhere. Grass roofs were blown off people's houses. People began to feel itchy from the small dried bamboo fibers hurled airborne by the raging wind.

About four in the afternoon, the wind abated. While the children ran out into the fields to gather the dry wood that had fallen, Srintil and Nyai Kartareja prepared to leave for Dawuan. The previous day, Bajus had sent a request for Srintil to accompany him to a meeting with irrigation project officials at a hotel near Eling-eling, specifically mentioning that Goder should not be brought along. Since he was pressed for time, he had asked that Nyai Kartareja escort her as far as Dawuan where he wanted Srintil to wait for him.

Remembering how the prison commander's wife had looked on such occasions, Srintil asked Nyai Kartareja's to help her to dress. The old women not only knew how to pin up the hair of a ronggeng dancer, but also all about the hairstyle of a Javanese lady. Srintil had only a few pieces of jewelry left, but a pair of small earrings fitted beautifully in her ample earlobes.

The two women set off for Dawuan. From far off, they could see a Jeep parked alongside the main road near the end of the dike running along the rice field. Srintil hastened her step, greeting people she encountered with the briefest hello. The simple smiles they returned indicated they understood her haste. Nyai Kartareja was correct in her estimation that the village people were full of hope as they watched Srintil growing closer to Bajus.

At the end of the dike, Srintil was met by the smiling gaze of the well-dressed Bajus. She could only smile shyly at his attention.

"Are you sure you won't be embarrassed to bring me along to your meeting?" she asked softly.

"Uh, listen, Bajus," interrupted Nyai Kartareja. "She's free to go wherever she likes, isn't that right?"

"Indeed. Otherwise, why would I go to this trouble? What's more, there'll be some important people from Jakarta at this meeting."

"Did you hear that? You'll be meeting some important people. Of all the people in Paruk, even in Dawuan, you're the only one that has such good fortune."

Srintil bowed her head, embarrassed. Bajus held the door open for her and she remained silent as she climbed into the car. The engine growled into life and the vehicle moved off, leaving Nyai Kartareja standing by herself on the roadside. "Oh, Srintil. Child of Santayib and Sakarya. Who would have thought that this good fortune was to be your destiny, becoming involved with a man who owns a car."

In the speeding car, Bajus stole several looks at the woman beside him. He had considered stopping off at a beauty salon in Eling-eling to have her properly made over, but after seeing her, he could see that this was not at all necessary. Srintil was obviously able to make herself look elegant. He had, in fact, changed his thinking altogether. If a beautician applied city-style make up to her, she would most certainly lose her unique beauty. A cherry blossom is quite beautiful, he thought. So is a tulip. And city people understand this. But they would have to recognize that the hyacinth, too, possesses a distinctive charm. Srintil's unique beauty had no reference to the face on Western sculptures like Venus or the goddess Aphrodite; rather, it evoked the face of Pradnya Paramita, the embodiment of simplicity and naiveté.

"I need to stop by my place for a moment," said Bajus as they approached the town of Eling-eling. "I left a file there. I was in such a rush earlier."

Srintil smiled. "That's fine. I'd like to see your home."

Bajus lived alone in a house he had leased for two years. It was not overly large, but it clearly indicated his economic status. Srintil sat in the living room while he went into his bedroom. She felt a powerful urge to clean the floor which looked as if it had not been swept for several days. The potted plants hadn't been watered and the flowers had wilted. Srintil's imagination soared unrestrained. Yes, soon I will do everything for him. Bajus will see that even a former ronggeng dancer and political prisoner like me can be a good wife, and that I can be better than a woman who was never a ronggeng dancer or a prisoner. Yes. Someone like Bajus—a man who never behaved discourteously toward me as an unmarried woman, who helped me build my house, who often takes me along with him on drives, and who has done so much to raise my status in the eyes of the people—surely he is the best man to receive my whole-hearted commitment. Even if he were not an official in the irrigation project and didn't own a car, I'd still owe him my commitment for what he has done for me. The question now is, when will I officially become his wife?

"Daydreaming? Come on, let's go," said Bajus after observing her from the front door for several seconds without her realizing.

Startled, Srintil stood up abruptly and walked out ahead of him. She felt as if she had suddenly been touched by a profoundly significant dream. She gripped her clutch purse tightly and chided herself for her lofty fantasies.

"The meeting will probably go on until late at night. After that, there'll be a party," said Bajus as he backed the car out of the driveway. "There won't be any other women at the meeting. But at the party you won't be alone."

"Are the other women the wives of officials at the meeting?"

"Yes and no. The bachelors like me, who can't bring a wife, will bring their girlfriends or a date."

Srintil smiled.

"So what time will we head home?"

"That depends. Maybe not until early morning. Or we could spend the night there. Don't worry, we'll have separate rooms."

"I believe you. But let's go home, even if it means leaving before dawn."

"Well, let's see what happens later. If everything ends before morning, then fine."

They headed towards a resort town about a fifteen minute drive from Eling-eling. The towns nestled in the foothills of the northern mountain range, which enjoyed cool and refreshing air. Bajus turned into the grounds of a pleasant-looking resort villa where he had already reserved several rooms. In the living room, waiters had set out plates of fruit and cool drinks. While they showed Srintil her room and the bathroom, Bajus busied himself with his files and appointment book. He had brought a tape recorder and showed Srintil how to use it. He gave her some magazines, either forgetting or not really understanding that she was unable to read.

"While I'm at the meeting at the hotel across the road, you can rest here. If you need anything, just ask the waiters in the back room."

"How long will you be?"

"Most likely quite a long time. But I'll come back and look in on you whenever we take a break."

Srintil's face radiated happiness, and she smiled as she walked with him to the front terrace. She stood and gazed at the man who was beginning to become important to her, soft feelings sweeping through her heart. She watched him as he crossed the street and turned into the grounds of a large, opulent hotel, then disappeared behind a flower garden. A large cloth banner was spread out on the terrace in front of the hotel, but Srintil was unable to read what it said.

At around seven that evening Srintil saw more than a dozen cars pull in to the hotel across the road. She began to have doubts about whether she really should appear in the company of such important people. In the confines of her room, she sought confidence in the full-length mirror. She found only what she saw every day. She had often heard people say that she was pretty. How pretty did they mean? Was she pretty only by the standards of villagers, or was she pretty to important people like those attending the meeting? If so, fine. But if not, she felt that she would only become the target of ridicule.

Feeling anxious, she went out to the living room and sat down. There was a selection of fruit on the table, but she had no wish to eat or drink. Ah, she thought, might as well try some. She picked up a couple of the smaller fruits. She noticed the cassette tape recorder, but felt no desire to listen to music. She had never even touched such an apparatus. However, she did pick up a magazine and flick through it, glancing at the pictures of the women in it. In doing so, she obtained a general idea about female beauty and realized that she need not feel too humble.

In the conference room, Bajus was busy even before the meeting began, assisting with the placement of chairs and other conference items. It was important for him to make a good and friendly impression. As a second-level contractor, he knew very well that a friendly approach was absolutely essential. He didn't actually have an official role in the meeting but knew that, if he didn't want to be dropped from the work roster, he had to be diligent about attending meetings such as this one.

Later on, he wouldn't sit among the participants. His intention was to speak with a first-level contractor, a squared-jawed man who was one of the main players in the running of the meeting. He planned to ask this man if he would subcontract work to him. He had actually known the man for some time, a long time, and felt he was halfway towards achieving his goal. When he saw the man climbing out of car, he hurried out, greeting him with deference, insisting on carrying his bags.

"Did you just arrive from Jakarta, sir?"

"No, I arrived earlier and rested in Eling-eling. Are there many others here yet?"

"There are. You're among the last to arrive."

"That's good. I won't have to wait around. But the meeting hasn't begun yet, has it?"

"No, it hasn't, sir. It's just past seven now. I heard that it will start at seven-thirty."

Bajus escorted the square-jawed man to his chair, chatting to him about this and that. Recalling that Srintil would likely be hungry, he went outside and found a street vendor selling *satay* near the hotel's main gate. He asked the vendor to follow him across the street. Seeing them coming, Srintil came out of her room. Bajus greeted her, smiling.

"Are you finished?"

"Finished? I'm just about to get started. I've come because I thought you'd be hungry. I've ordered some chicken satay."

Bajus sat down, his head leaning back on the back of the chair and his fingers tapping on the arms.

"A friend of mine from Jakarta might come here later. After the meeting is over."

"Is he someone important?"

"Yes. He's wealthy and a nice guy. You'll see for yourself later."

"I feel shy."

"You don't need to be shy. As I said, he's a nice guy. You've known me for several months, and you don't need to feel shy in front of my friends."

"What's his name?"

"Blengur. Mr Blengur. He owns several cars, but whenever he comes out here, he comes by plane to Semarang. Ah, here's our satay. Let's eat now."

While Bajus ate with relish, Srintil found she had no appetite for the meal. Although she felt hungry, she could not take pleasure in the bits of roasted chicken mixed in warm rice cake and covered with peanut sauce. Her mind was full of conflict and uncertainty. She felt disappointed that Bajus had invited her to come to this place that felt so foreign to her. But she also felt glad about being invited because of the hope it held for her. She was not unaware of this hope growing within her breast whenever she thought about him. It was precious. So precious that she wanted to nurture it carefully.

Bajus explained, "If it weren't for Blengur I would never have had the opportunity to ride in an airplane: several times, in fact. Maybe one day the two of us will be invited to take an airplane to Jakarta. Wouldn't you like to ride in an airplane?"

Srintil was taken aback, unprepared to answer this strange question. She just looked up at him as he carried his plate back to the satay vendor. Maybe he didn't mean what he said. After all, he didn't continue with the topic, but took his leave, keen to return to the meeting.

"I'm sorry, I have to leave you again for a while. Don't worry, I'll be back as soon as the meeting is over."

Alone again, Srintil tried to put aside her feelings of uncertainty. Everything came down to pleasing Bajus, She didn't want to disappoint him, and wanted to make a good impression on Blengur or any other of his acquaintances. She had to try as much as she could to ignore any emerging feelings of humility and inferiority. She returned to her room to repair her make up.

Bajus sat nervously in the reception area close to the door of the meeting room. His carefully conceived plan was to catch Blengur immediately after the meeting. He worried that someone else—especially men from the hotel office—might beat him to the square-jawed man as he came through the door. He had flicked through the newspaper several times, but nothing in it had held his interest. From time to time he opened his diary to make sure that the proposal he had prepared for Blengur was still there. A friendly middle-aged woman approached him and chatted idly before revealing her true intentions: she was a procuress and wanted to know whether Bajus wanted the services of a young female escort. At first, Bajus refused politely. But when she persisted, he sharply told her to go away.

As it turned out, the meeting lasted less than two hours. Bajus stood up and peered into the conference room. He saw Blengur chatting with an important government official from Eling-eling. Impatient, he went inside. With the deference of a domestic servant, he picked up Blengur's briefcase and stood waiting. The two of them then walked out together.

"Why is everyone going home, sir?" asked Bajus, noticing several of the cars driving off from the parking lot. "Don't they have any other business here?"

"No, they don't. The Regent had no desire for a party. And I'm also not feeling up to a party tonight. I just want to rest."

"Is it okay if we speak for moment here, sir?"

"What's the problem?"

"The usual, sir. Who else can I go to for work if not you?"

"But this time, it's more difficult. In the meeting it was decided that I would only get the contract for 100 million: building an agricultural research building with housing for the staff, as well as seven bridges for villages cut off by the irrigation canals."

"Without an official bid, sir?"

"Don't act as if you don't know. The bidding was conducted at the meeting just now: personal bids made among friends helping one another. That's all."

"Excuse me, sir. If you still believe in me, I hope you'll give that work to me."

"That's the way you operate, isn't it?"

"The point is that you shouldn't have to deal with such small projects. This one is more my size, sir."

"Oh, very well. We'll split the profit of ten percent between the two of us. And you can arrange something for the locals, without reducing your own portion. But remember, the locals are important."

"I understand, sir."

"Good!"

"So, where are you spending the night sir?"

Blengur looked at Bajus in a way that communicated something only the two of them understood.

"You asked me for work and you're getting it. Now you're asking me where I intend to spend the night. Obviously, you don't know your place. I should be the one asking such questions."

"My apologies, sir," said Bajus, hurriedly, leafing through his diary. "Um, look at these, sir. What do you think?"

Blengur examined the two photos Bajus handed to him. He turned his head from side to side as if he was unable to believe that they were only two-dimensional representations. The pictures of the woman struck him immediately and profoundly, but he wasn't sure what it was about her that moved him. Her beauty was not particularly outstanding, yet she was by no means ordinary. The impression was of a beauty of an era long ago: a beauty of stillness, like a wildflower, without any awareness of its own exquisiteness.

A skilled professional, who was able to transform the natural essence of his subject into something extraordinary by capturing more than the figure as such, could have taken the photo. There was a depth of spirit that stood out in the face and, because of this, the subject of the photos seized Blengur's imagination. The woman was not really unusual by his standards. She was remarkable only because of his own psychological make-up and particular circumstances. He had failed in his own marriage and, unable to show any affection at home to his wife, he constantly yearned for a romantic and erotic relationship elsewhere. He was a man for whom base sexual urges were an important spice of life, and he lowered his moral and ethical conduct in the search of their fulfillment. He was the kind of man that tended to regard every woman he met as more beautiful than she actually was. For him, certain areas around the town of Elingeling, where the prostitutes worked, were exciting possibilities for erotic encounters. When he went to these places, he lost his ability to reason objectively. Thus, he was actually incapable of articulating with any accuracy what it was that was beautiful about the woman in the photographs he held in his hands.

"So, what do you think, sir?" asked Bajus, after waiting for some time for his reaction.

"Not bad. What's her name?"

"Her name is a bit unusual, sir. It's 'Srintil'"

"Srin…?"

"…Til. Srintil. But the name isn't as important as her looks. Don't you think so, sir?"

"She's used to going out with you, right?"

"Hold on, sir. I've known her for more than five months. I know a lot about her. She is from a small, very isolated village in the region of Dawuan. Paruk."

While Blengur continued to gaze at the photos, Bajus described Srintil and her situation at length. When he mentioned that she aspired to be a housewife, his voice took on a particular tone to emphasize his words.

"If that's the case, then how did you get her to come here with you? You lied to her, didn't you?"

"Yes, you could say that, sir. I've helped her out in several ways, including with the construction of her house. So, I believe that she misunderstands my motives. She believes that I intend to marry her, although I…"

"…although you can't possibly marry her," interrupted Blengur, grinning. He knew that Bajus had become impotent after an accident a few years ago when he was working on a project in Jatiluhur.

"That's right, sir. You know all about it."

"I'd like to meet her. Where is she now? In this hotel?"

"No. She's at the villa across the road."

Srintil was gazing at herself in the mirror when she heard footsteps on the terrace. She could feel her heart pounding as she walked out to open the door. Smiling shyly, she welcomed Bajus, who was followed by Blengur. Srintil felt the eyes of the stranger appraising her entire body, then a big, pudgy hand was extended out to her. She took the hand in her own with considerable reluctance.

"This is Blengur, the man I told you about, Srin."

"Yes," answered Srintil almost inaudibly. Blengur smiled.

The two men sat down, completely relaxed. Srintil agreed to sit down only after Bajus had invited her several times. She felt shy and bowed her head, feeling Blengur's unrelenting gaze upon her. Bajus went to stand up, but Blengur stopped him.

"I want to shower," he said. "Do you have any hot water here?"

"I'm sorry, sir. The bathrooms here are only the traditional tank of cold water and dipper."

"Who could bear bathing like that in this chilly weather? Very well. I'll go back to the hotel to shower and change my clothes. I have to speak with my chauffeur, too."

"But, you'll sleep here, right? I'll arrange a room for you."

"Okay."

Blengur left, and Bajus took a deep breath: but not a breath of relief, because he knew he had to convey something of great importance to Srintil. The languid and easy silence of the situation a moment ago was about to change into something more serious. Bajus was uneasy, and Srintil was aware of the change in his demeanor.

"Srin, listen to me. I want to talk to you about something important to me. Important because my professional life depends on it."

"What is it?"

"Well, I feel somewhat embarrassed to talk about the things I've done for you during the time we've known one another. Everything I have done was sincere and without reservation."

"I know that and I feel I owe you a great deal. I'd like to return your kindness, but you've never told me how I might do this."

Srintil's lips continued to move for a few more moments but her voice was no longer audible. Bajus leant back, not because he saw Srintil starting to cry, but because he understood precisely the meaning behind her words. With the language of her tears and emotional state, Srintil was asking for the opportunity to return his kindness with the commitment of marriage. Yet, Bajus knew full well that such a request was impossible to fulfill.

"It's just this, Srin," said Bajus, his voice heavy. "If you really want to pay me back for helping you, there is a way you can do this easily. Really easily. I would be more than happy if you would do what I'm about to ask you."

"Tell me. What would you have me do? If all this time you've been hiding the fact that you already have a wife, that's okay. I'll be your second wife, even a servant to your first wife and your children."

"Oh, it's not that. I don't have a wife. My request is quite simple."

"What is it?"

Bajus drew a deep breath and shook his head as if he were trying to shake dirt off of his face.

"Um, you've met Mr Blengur. Believe me, he's a nice man. I'm sure that if you asked him for anything, whatever the price, he would give it to you. He's going to stay the night here. Sleep with him, will you? Spend the night with him, Srin."

Srintil stiffened in shock, her eyes wide. Her mouth opened and her chest heaved rapidly. Her hands trembled.

"That's all I am asking, Srin. To make it easier, just think of Blengur as me. Maybe that's not necessary since he's actually much more capable than I am in everything. Will you do it?"

"No!!"

Srintil stood up unsteadily and ran to her room. She threw herself on the bed feeling as if she had been tossed behind an invisible partition. In one split second, her world of budding flowers had been transformed into a dry and desolate wasteland.

Oalah, Gusti Pangeran, oalah,
Biyung, kaniaya temen awakku...

O dear, Lord God, O dear, Mother,
I am truly suffering...

Sitting uneasily in the other room, Bajus could hear Srintil weeping. Why had his calculations fallen so far short of his goals? He understood why Srintil had rejected Tamir's advances. Tamir was just a low-paid laborer who behaved like a thickheaded fool. But Blengur? That he, of all people, would be rejected by a former ronggeng dancer and prostitute! That was a complete surprise.

Bajus began to panic. He worried that if he failed to please Blengur, the contract he had just been promised might slip from his grasp. He might even lose any subsequent chance for other jobs. He would have to start from scratch. Bajus decided to try Srintil one more time. This time, like it or not, she must agree to do what he asked.

He carefully opened the door and saw that she was still sobbing, her hunched shoulders shaking. Bajus sat down at the edge of the bed and spoke, like a father to his sulking daughter.

"Srin, I hope that you'll try to understand. Take pity on me and help me just this once. What will become of us if you don't help me? You will help, won't you, Srin?"

Srintil straightened her shoulders and sat up. She glanced briefly at Bajus with a hard, cold look and got up off the bed. She adjusted her hair that was falling over her face and picked up her handbag.

"Wait. Where are you going?"

Without a word, Srintil began walking out of the room. Bajus moved quickly and grabbed her by the wrist to prevent her from reaching the door. He pushed her down onto the bed. It was the first time he had ever been rough with her.

"Are you refusing? You can't! You're from Paruk and you need to remember your position. I've done so much for you. I've spent a lot of money on you!"

Bajus paced back and forth, careful to keep himself between Srintil and the door. Srintil sat stiffly, not reacting in any way to what he was saying. Suddenly, Bajus stamped his foot and walked out. From the outer room, he spoke harshly.

"As a Paruk villager, you should remember who you are. You were a PKI member, a communist sympathizer! If you don't do what I say, I'll have you returned to prison. Do you think I can't do it?"

He slammed the door violently and locked it.

Why do people believe that murder is only about ending bodily functions or brought about through the use of some sort of weapon? Why do they think violence just involves the shedding of blood and injuring the body? Because of these widely held beliefs, Bajus could not be accused of committing an extraordinarily violent act, even murder. But in the space of two or three seconds and with just a few words, he had succeeded in causing a human being to lose her humanity, even without seeing it happen or being aware of what he had done.

A moment after the door slammed shut, Srintil began to lose her mind in a process that stole her personality in its entirety. Like a sledgehammer to the head, the first strike shook the very foundations of her consciousness, those which held her current sense of reality: her dream to be the wife of Bajus was brutally reduced to an empty illusion. At that time, she was, nevertheless, able to feel the bitterness and sting of this disappointment. The second blow undermined the foundations of her consciousness further by forcing her into an impossible dilemma: because of who she had become, she was simply unable to carry out Bajus's order to have casual sex with a stranger. Her desire to leave her past behind her was too strong. Finally, the foundations of her consciousness were shattered completely when she felt the finger pointing at her, like the head of a spear, accusing her of being a communist, ready to drag her back to prison, a place that had been hell on earth for her.

In the space of just a few moments, Srintil became an empty shell. This empty shell, this shadow, might still be called Srintil or the ronggeng of Paruk. Of course, she would still be referred to as a human being. But what had previously distinguished her from lower organisms—her reason and her sense of self—simply vanished from that moment. Srintil no longer knew anything from any perspective whatsoever. She was no longer aware of herself, existing now only as an embodiment of living but useless flesh. The position of her body still portrayed a person in shock, just as she had appeared when Bajus slammed the door. But the expression on her face was empty, completely dead. Her eyes stared without blinking and her mouth gaped. A human soul no longer existed in her being.

Only a few steps from the door, Bajus sat nervously. His mind was elsewhere and he wasn't thinking about what was happening inside the room. He had no idea about the death taking place behind the door. His worries were about the reality of having to face Blengur. He simply couldn't imagine what would happen if he failed to provide pleasure to the man from Jakarta.

He noticed someone approaching the villa, but his panic subsided when he saw that it was not Blengur. This man was thinner and smaller. His chauffeur. Nevertheless, Bajus felt nervous as he met the man at the door.

"Mr Blengur asks that you come to the hotel," said the chauffeur.

"Just me?"

"He mentioned only you."

"Very well. I'll come immediately."

Bajus went back inside to check that Srintil's door was locked. Then he went outside and caught up with the chauffeur. Perhaps I could tell Blengur that Srintil is feeling ill. No. It might be safer to say that she has just begun her period.

With this crazy scheme in mind, Bajus felt calmer as he walked to Blengur's room.

"Come in," called Blengur hearing him knock. "Please have a seat."

Bajus was not prepared to be met with such friendliness. Blengur sat calmly, smoking a cigarette. Completely at ease. He didn't convey the image of the lusting man he had earlier. His eyes now appeared calm.

"Jus, I'm convinced that what you said is absolutely right."

"What is that, sir?"

"About Srintil."

"That she is beautiful and simple?"

"I don't mean that. I was impressed by the image of her face. It is the face of a fallen woman who now wishes to become a legitimate wife."

"That's right, sir."

"You know me, Jus. I'm the kind of man that enjoys a sexual encounter. But I don't feel right about this. I can't bring myself to use Srintil for my own pleasure."

"Sir?"

"It's true. I want you to give her the opportunity to fulfill her wish. There are plenty of women out there willing to get involved with me. They certainly wouldn't object to Srintil removing herself from such a life."

"So, what would you have me do?"

"Take her home, tonight. Here's some money for her. Tell her it's a gift from me."

Bajus eyed the fat envelope that Blengur held out to him. He hesitated.

"Okay, sir. Okay," he said nervously. He slid the envelope into his jacket pocket. "But, sir."

"What is it?"

"The project. Uh, what about the project?"

Blengur smiled.

"You really are just small change, aren't you? Of course, the project will go to you. Now go and check out. Take Srintil home."

Like a dandelion seed blown before the wind, Bajus fled Blengur's room and hurriedly made his way back to the villa across the street. He felt relieved and glowed with satisfaction. All the confusion that had suddenly ensnared him had now with equal abruptness disappeared with unimaginable ease.

Inside the hotel room, Bajus called out: "It's all over, Srin. If you want to go home, you can. I'll take you right now." He proceeded to the bedroom.

"Srin, here's some money from Blengur. It's a gift, not payment..."

Srintil sat motionless on the bed. The hair on the back of Bajus' neck stood up. People might feel terror at being faced with a corpse, but the terror in encountering the living dead is much greater. Bajus immediately saw that there was something very wrong with Srintil. Her expression was empty. Her eyes didn't blink and her mouth gaped. He staggered backwards, and the envelope he was holding fell to the floor. In his shock, he couldn't come to grips with the fact that a person's life is as frail as the skin of a garlic clove. Just a few minutes earlier, Srintil had been complete, possessing the charm of a beautiful young woman. A charm that had even struck the heart of the impotent Bajus. But that charm no longer existed. Nor did her beauty. The only humanity that was left was a shell with the name Srintil. The rest was just flesh, a creature without a mind.

Bajus backed away, his thoughts in turmoil, unable to grasp the gravity of what he saw before him. As his terror gradually subsided, he thought about Srintil's state of mind before and after he had locked her in her room, and it began to dawn on him that he himself was the cause of her drastic and terrifying transformation.

As he slowly began to collect his thoughts, his shoulders relaxed and his breathing returned to normal. He continued to gaze at the living statue before him. He stepped forward.

"Srin, what's the matter?"

There was no answer, not even the vaguest sign of response. He picked up the envelope on the floor and held it out to her hand, which was poised in the air. Her hand didn't move. He bent down to look into her eyes. There he only saw black round pupils without expression or expressiveness, a form of death within life. Panic-stricken, he went out to search for assistance, for someone who might help him cope with this terrible situation. Perhaps Blengur. But on the terrace he hesitated. He went back inside. He hands groped in his pocket and he felt the keys to his car. Yes. Now, he knew what he would do. He would take Srintil home right away.

"Forgive me, Srin. Forgive me, okay? We're going home now."

Srintil turned her head, moving slightly. She didn't look into Bajus's eyes, didn't even see him. Her eyes didn't move; it was as if they had died within the sockets. Bajus took her hand and helped her off the bed, relieved that she complied with his wishes. Srintil walked as if she could see nothing, in spite of her wide-open, unblinking eyes. Bajus felt as if he were guiding a person who was partially paralyzed and blind.

When I was small, I often went out with my friends in the evening to watch wayang performances. Wayang kulit, a small world grounded in the trunk of a banana tree laid at the base of a white screen, its sun the flickering light of the oil lamp. The performances provided me with insights into life. The puppeteers taught me fundamental values that, at the time, I believed were absolute truths. These values became so deeply established in my mind that, whenever I watched a performance, I could feel that I was a child of Amarta: the kingdom of the Pendawa brothers, the five hero brothers in the epic *Mahabharata.* I was filled with disappointment whenever, in the numerous wars that took place on the banana tree trunk, the kingdom of Amarta was defeated by its enemies. I once wept when I was watching a performance of the story of Abimanyu, a warrior of Amarta, who died with his body pierced by arrows.

The values I obtained from the world of wayang may still have still been deeply embedded in my mind when I joined the army. Perhaps without being conscious of it, I saw myself as a kind of Bima or Gatotkaca, the two most courageous warriors and soldiers of Amarta. I admired these two characters: Gatotkaca would pluck the heads off the bodies of his enemies using only his finger, while Bima stamped his opponents into bloody dust. Their enemies were the people of Astina and other evil kingdoms. In my view, dashing soldiers were those who were brave and powerful like these characters.

Oddly enough, when I shot and killed the two thieves in Paruk so long long ago, the event had weighed heavily on my soul. I will never forget that incident which, in fact, had inspired me to join the army. I will also never forget that I swore never again to cut a person's life short, even that of a dangerous criminal.

Perhaps it was because of this vow that I had often felt inner conflict when I was stationed in Central Java immediately after the upheaval of 1965. I often had to fire mortar shells on bunkers that were probably filled with human beings. Fortunately, I never saw with my own eyes the people who fell, cowering under the onslaught of bombs that I had fired. But, I once found myself in a critical situation where I had only two choices, to kill or be killed. I chose the former. My opponent was a young man swinging a machete. He was the one that collapsed in death because my bayonet was faster than his machete. I saw him just before he died, gasping for breath, his eyes wide and staring, his chest torn open by my bayonet. Aside from the political motivations that drove him to join the rebels, he was just a man like myself. And I murdered him.

I have been directly involved in at least three killings. Despite being a soldier, I pray to God never again to be put in a situation in which I had to take more lives. Of course, some might say that this is the attitude of a coward, especially in the context of the military. But I don't want to be accused of this because my horror of killing isn't just a feeling arising from rationalization. It emerged as a natural tendency that had been present throughout my life. And as a result, it became clear to me that I wasn't really cut out to be a soldier.

On the other hand, during the two years I was in the military, I was a Gatotkaca facing situations that often departed from the military principles I learned from wayang stories. Gatotkaca twisted, then plucked off the heads of his enemies, all of whom came from other lands. They were foreigners. But the people I faced in battle were my brothers, my own kin: the robbers I killed in Paruk, the young man whose chest I tore open with my bayonet. And in West Kalimantan I killed a man as well. I even talked with him before he died.

In an ambush in which I was involved, a group of rebels entered a trap. The majority had fallen under a hail of bullets but a few had fled. One of the fugitives hid quite close to me, only a few meters from the muzzle of my rifle, intending to return fire at the spot where most of my infantry were located. But he fell from a shot I fired at him. When the situation calmed down, I approached him, a man with long hair. He hadn't yet died and his eyes gazed at me. His mouth moved and I heard a hoarse voice. What made me pause was the fact that the man I had just brought down spoke in my own local dialect, my mother tongue.

"You're from Java, aren't you?" he gasped.

"Yes. Why"

"I'm going to die here. Please, let my parents in Java know about my death."

He mentioned a name, the region, and an area in the district around Eling-eling.

The thing that troubles my soul more than anything else is this destruction of military principles. In the end, I felt I could no longer be a Gatotkaca. Maybe this was the fault of those puppeteers I had watched years earlier. Why didn't they ever show stories in which Gatotkaca kills soldiers from Amarta, soldiers who deserted him or rebelled against his political ideology?

But in matters of queasiness about drawing blood and killing, I was not alone. A friend of mine had lost his mind after a particularly difficult experience. He had been allocated the task of executing rebels who had been captured alive. Usually the prisoners walked in an orderly fashion and everything proceeded to plan. But on one occasion, one rebel, who was shot and whose body had been thrown into a mass grave, suddenly stood up and pounced. My friend was able to incapacitate his attacker only because the man was already mortally wounded. But, as a result of this experience, he lost his mind and remains locked up, a danger to himself and others.

Whenever I have thoughts that I'm no longer fit to be in the army, the reason is not because of the circumstances of my insane friend. Nor is it only because I have a weak heart and don't like to see blood and death. It's far more than that. Paruk never provided me with the psychological wherewithal in the use of a gun. Paruk only taught me about social cooperation and harmony, skills rooted in common courtesy. It may be that these themes were the final wishes of my ancestor Ki Secamenggala. He was, of course, known as a *bromocorah*, a career criminal, but in his last days he realized that the natural tendency toward cooperation and harmony was far more important for spiritual peace than violence. If this is true, my blood is truly the blood of Paruk and the military is not the place for me.

In any case, I was overjoyed when I heard rumors that my battalion would be pulling out of West Kalimantan and returning to Java. I saw that my friends were happy too. There were some who kissed the photos of their wives and children or their girlfriends. Others shouted and cheered with joy because they would soon be able to rejoin their soccer teams. Only one man was in a state of befuddlement, and that was my insane friend. Despite my feelings of pleasure, I too was unable to do anything other than contemplate my circumstances. I had no wife or children, not even a girlfriend. I only had Paruk and I hoped it was still faithfully maintaining the small tilting shack in which I grew up as a sprout of humanity.

While friends started to collect souvenirs to take back to Java, I preferred to stay in the barracks. One of my friends told me with great excitement that he had acquired a traditional Borneo sword and an Iban Dayak tribal shield. Another friend caught an albino monkey, a truly amazing animal with a small body, about the size of a musk shrew, and huge eyes in proportion to its body.

So, why did the increasingly old and dirty village of Paruk continue to call to me to come home? Why? Sometimes I fault myself for being too sentimental, especially over a little crumbling shack that may have even collapsed by now. People could easily have said that I couldn't forget Paruk because of a certain women there, a woman named Srintil. Others might argue that I was constituted from the same stuff as Paruk, which is why I always felt the pull of my home village. I admit to the accuracy of these answers, but I'm not satisfied with them either. I still continue to ask myself why I always think about Paruk.

For a long time, I wandered far and wide through my musings before I found a satisfactory answer. The answer came together with the realization that, until that moment, I had been wrong in my attitude toward my hometown. I had loved Paruk by just letting it sleep, with its smutty dreams, muttering its curses and obscenities. I had let the dung beetles buzz freely, let sores and scabs cover the arms and legs of the children of my people, and let them fill themselves only with cassava instead of a proper diet. I had neglectfully let my little homeland remain blind and deaf to God's merciful love, a real love that could become the basic motivation for the existence of the village and everything in it. From the beginning, I was convinced that my attitude toward Paruk had been correct: leaving my homeland according to its way was the same as leaving moss or weeds to grow freely, or like a tolerance toward the mongoose which keeps stealing chickens to save its kind from extinction.

For the sake of the Great Creator, I could no longer compare my little homeland to a mongoose or to moss. It was a place of humanity, filled with life and spirit. Yet, I saw with my own eyes how in that place humanity life, reason and spirit had only reached a primitive level. And if it was true that I loved Paruk, why did I remain quiet and let the people of my clan grow feral, destined to fail in life, leaving them to the indignity of being left behind by natural selection?

I used to think that leaving Paruk Village to its own devices was wise. Now, with the insight I discovered by myself, my thoughts turned around: leaving Paruk to its obscenities, vagrancy and ignorance contradicted the purpose of its own humanity. The people of my clan numbered no more than seventy souls. Shepherding them shouldn't be an overly difficult job. Even for me, a task like this would be easy compared to the duties of a soldier who has to spill blood. And, more fundamental than everything else, if Paruk village is to be raised up out of filth and garbage, who else would take on such a responsibility?

I had no desire to argue that I was the primary candidate to take on the burden of such a responsibility. The best candidate would have been someone who represented the proper authorities, but I had to realize that government authorities, at either the national or regional levels, were unlikely to drop other pressing issues to address the problems facing a small hamlet like Paruk. At the time, the authorities were dealing with so many problems that the district chief of Pecikalan, for example, could only feel embarrassment at having Paruk within his jurisdiction. As long as I could remember, I had never seen the local government actually do anything to improve the quality of life for the people of my place of birth.

Under these circumstances, I felt that fate pointed at me. I was the most appropriate person to take on the moral responsibility of helping the people of Paruk. This could be a satisfying job because I would do it on behalf of my birth mother. I would take great pleasure in carrying out such a duty without thinking about the decrepit little shack that was once my home, without thinking about Srintil, even without relating it to patriotic sentiments.

My heart sang at this profound realization. My life was obviously insignificant compared to the enormity and breadth of human life in its totality. Yet, even within the insignificance of my own life, I believed I had found meaning. While it wasn't bright and shiny, it was valuable. I now had an answer when I asked myself about the purpose of my simple existence. To encourage Paruk to find harmony in relation to the will of God was to invite people there to cleanse themselves of the filth, the drinking of ciu, the foul language, and the illicit sex. And, most importantly, I would introduce them to our True God for whom they must learn to behave as best they can. They must be able to read texts as well as to understand nature. They must be able not only to follow their feelings, but use their reason as well. And they must believe that misery should not under any circumstances be a measurement of pride and self-worth.

My lofty ideas floated along until they finally butted up against bitter reality. If I wanted to become a good shepherd, I would have to live among my flock. This meant I had to free myself from military duty and, as a result, lose my only source of income. How would I support myself? I owned nothing in Paruk except for my old home and the plot of land on which it stood. How could I possibly do anything for my little homeland when I couldn't even feed myself?

Perhaps, I thought, I could postpone my plans until I reached the age of forty. At that point, I would no longer be with the active troops and could request transfer to the District Military Command. But I was more than twelve years from the age of forty.

Until I returned to Java, my thoughts continued to cast about for a solution. My unit was given a leave time in shifts, and I intentionally chose the final shift. I wanted to let my friends first satisfy their longing to see their wives and children, or their lovers. I only had Paruk, and I figured it would wait patiently until my friends returned to barracks. And, even when my turn for leave finally came through, I did not immediately leave for Paruk.

I wanted to see Dawuan with its new irrigation system. I wanted, too, to see Srintil, to find out how her relationship with the project manager was going. And I wanted to start putting into place my new ideas for my little homeland. But I waited until the third day before I went home.

By the time I arrived in Dawuan, it was eleven at night because I had lingered, watching a movie in Eling-eling. I considered borrowing a bicycle from Sergeant Pujo at the Dawuan Command, but dropped the idea because I felt I had no compelling reason to hurry.

The night was pitch black and only the twinkling stars were visible in the sky. The ground was somewhat muddy, perhaps it had rained earlier that day. It was very quiet. The numerous vendors that usually remained open far into the night to serve the project employees working overtime were all gone. The only people I saw in the streets were watchmen in their guard booths. And it grew even quieter when I began to walk along the dike that headed directly to Paruk.

Only the sound of my steps and the light of my small flashlight accompanied me. I heard water splattering in the channels, a sign that the irrigation pipes and dikes were already working. Then I heard snatches of sounds in the distance, a voice. What? The singing of a ronggeng? I walked a few more steps, then stopped. The sound clearly came from my little village; I could see its dark silhouette. No doubt about it. It was the song, "Eling-Eling Banyumasan," with its characteristic lyrics:

Dhongkèl gélang daning bung alang-alang
Wis sakjegé wong lanang gedhé gorohé
Lisus kali kedhung jero banyu mili
Meneng sotèn atiné bolar-balèran
Wakul kayu ceponé wadhah pengaron
Kapanané, kapanané ketemu padha dhèwèkan.

Digging for weeds, finding grass sprouts
Men have always been the biggest liars
A deep whirlpool in a river stream
Absolutely silent with a racing heart
A wooden rice basket as a water jug
When on when will we meet, just the two of us.

Oh, Paruk. Although there were changes, I knew exactly to whom that voice belonged. Oh, my little homeland. Are you still stuck in filth, falling asleep to songs of lust? And you, Srintil. Nobody has the right to stop you from being a ronggeng. Nobody can do that. Not even I. I only want to ask you in all honesty: haven't you received enough bitterness as a result of following the ronggeng tradition? We are both children of Paruk and we both love this place because, like any mother, it cannot be evil. Yet, as a mother to us, Paruk has been stupid from the very beginning. It has never understood what was good and bad for its children. Srintil, you don't have to do what Paruk tells you!

I began walking again with a growing feeling of sorrow. The singing continued; this time it was a humorous song.

Klinthang-klinthung pasar kéwan kidul gunung
Tipar lor Sugihan, Jatisalu Pasar Manis
Terus ngétan anjog maring Pesanggrahan

Klinthang-klinthung ana mantri mikul calung
Mampir gubug randha, urut senthong dilongoki
Mbok menawa Nini Randha nggodhog wédang

Klinthang-klinthung, at the animal market south of the
mountain
Just north of Sugihan, Jatisalu Pasar Manis
Then, east until Pesanggrahan

Klinthong-klinthung, there are musicians carrying calung xylophones
Stop by the widow's hut, look into the bedrooms
Most likely Grandma will put on a kettle of water

Then I heard a laugh. It was Srintil, guffawing.

I was startled, realizing that it was almost midnight. Srintil singing and laughing all alone in the stillness of the night? I quickened my pace as I approached the village precinct and went directly to her house. Entering the front yard, I was astonished to see that the house had been transformed, now large with stone walls. I heard her laugh again. A strange laugh.

I shouted out as I knocked on the front door, "*kula nuwun, kula nuwun,*" announcing myself.

"Who is it?" I heard Nyai Sakarya calling.

"It's me, Rasus."

I entered as soon as the door opened. Nyai Sakarya was standing there, shivering, her face pale. Her eyes were full of tears and her mouth trembled.

"Oh, God, Rasus. Why have you waited so long to come home?"

"What's the matter?"

Nyai Sakarya just pointed to the door to the front room, secured shut from the outside with a wooden bar. My intuition told me that Srintil was inside. I pounded on the door, but the lock was strong. I drew out my dagger and ripped out chunks as big as my finger. It broke. I pulled at the wooden bar. The door opened and the smell of excrement immediately assaulted my nostrils.

Inside I saw a person I had known almost since birth. Someone who had once held a central place in my life. The person I had once seen as a reflection of my own mother. My mother, the woman who had given birth to me.

I felt all my muscles go slack. What my eyes beheld was too difficult to absorb; I was devoid of understanding, realization. I saw Srintil, completely disheveled, wearing drawstring shorts and a tattered chemise. She was sitting in something, perhaps her own excrement. She glanced at me momentarily, then began to talk to herself. The small lantern in the room illuminated the scene of a human wreckage, a person who had once been the sweetheart of the village.

I didn't have the strength to do anything, not even to open my mouth. This was not the first time I had experienced something that had shaken the very foundations of my soul. Rather, because I was somewhat faint-hearted, my life had been filled with such disturbing moments. Nevertheless, this scene was far more terrifying than anything I had experienced in the past, worse that the time I witnessed a man dying. I couldn't see that there was anything left of Srintil's humanity; she had been reduced to the level of a beast. This seemed to me a thousand times worse than death because, at the very least, the deaths I had witnessed had been of human beings.

Gentle hands urged me outside again. Unaware of what I was doing, I submitted and walked out. Only later I became conscious that I was outside of the room. *"Laa ilhaaha illallaah!* Oh God!" I cried.

"You've returned to your senses. Thank goodness. You're back," said Nyai Sakarya, her voice sounding to me as though it was spoken from a distance.

"Speak, my child. And be patient. We're enduring disaster yet again," continued Kartareja.

I gulped down a glass of water someone offered me. I realized that people from the village were crowding around me. Sakum was groping his way inside. I seized his hand and pulled him so that he sat down next to me. Nyai Kartareja and Tampi were crying. Goder was there too, perhaps the person this disaster affected more than anyone else. He was only four years old, and he whimpered for the woman who had become a mother to him.

Kartareja related the whole story.

"Srintil lost her mind when Bajus told her he couldn't marry her. That's what he told me when he brought her home."

"Did anyone ask him why he couldn't marry her?"

"I asked him about that. It turns out that Bajus is impotent as a result of an accident in Jatiluhur. If that's the case, there's little we can do about it," replied Kartareja.

"It's true that Bajus is gentle. Srintil once said that, in the months she had been with him, he never once tried to touch her," continued Nyai Kartareja. "He only seemed to want to marry Srintil. Nothing else."

"But he's still at fault," I said. "His excessive kindness would have had special meaning for Srintil, or any other woman."

"Yeah. But how can we demand accountability for something like that?"

I stood up and kicked at the floor. I wanted to hit this man Bajus. But such behavior was all for nothing. There was truth in Kartareja's words: this was not something for which we could easily demand accountability. Anything I did would only make matters worse.

"Well, then, has anyone done anything to try to help Srintil?"

"Well, I've had three different elders come here," replied Nyai Kartareja. "Srintil was bathed and purified, she was given an exorcism since it's possible she might have become possessed by an evil spirit. But she's only become worse. She has torn up almost all of her clothes. She destroyed the mirror over her makeup table. Last week she tried to strangle Goder. Luckily we saw her before she killed the child."

"That's why we were forced to lock her in her room. And because we're afraid that she might try to hang herself with a wrap-around skirt, we dressed her in a pair of shorts. It's safer this way."

"Did you report this to district chief?"

"We did," answered Kartareja. "He told us to take Srintil to hospital. But I'm not sure how to arrange this. I asked the chief for someone to help us, but he said he can't spare anyone at the moment because they're planning for an election."

Far into the night, just a few people remained in the house: me, Kartareja and his wife, and Nyai Sakarya. We told Nyai Sakarya she should go to bed. She had stayed up for several nights watching over her granddaughter, and I heard that only Tampi and Nyai Kartareja had been willing and able to help her. In her room, Srintil continued singing, occasionally stopping to talk or mutter to herself. Every now and then she would burst into sudden laughter and long giggles. I went back into her room, hoping to communicate with her, but I was facing extreme difficulty accepting what I saw before me.

Oh, Paruk. I once swore that I would never forgive you for seizing Srintil from me and turning her into a ronggeng. I gave her up to you because my needs regarding her were personal. Oh, Paruk. Because of your ignorance, all that remained of Srintil now was this living corpse. Because of your ignorance, you aren't even able to realize that that you're responsible for this utter destruction. Paruk! Your foolishness, your squalor, your indecency has wiped out in one moment the enchantment of your child and smeared it with disgust, with horror.

"Srin," I said, approaching her slowly. I gently placed my hand on her shoulder. "Look here. You know who I am, don't you?"

Srintil looked at me. I used to see a reflection of myself in her eyes, but could detect none of this now, not even the smallest evidence. It was difficult to believe that the person in front of me actually was her.

"You know who I am, don't you?" I repeated.

"Rasus, Crazy Rasus, and you want to take me back to prison?"

"Oh, no."

"But you did once come to me in prison?"

"Yes."

"Call Sakum. Get all the calung musicians. We'll dance. You want to dance, don't you?"

Before I could say anything, Srintil stood up, her body reeking of urine. She began to turn and sway.

Kembangé, kembang térong
Kepéngin cemérong-cérong
Arep nembung akèh wong

Blossom, eggplant blossom
I feel like being bad
I want it from any lad

I went out of the room again, feeling worse. Picking up my knapsack, I told Kartareja that I was going to sleep at my own place. Nyai Sakarya lent me a lantern, and I went outside.

Under the dim light of the moon, I couldn't see how far my shack leaned and I opened the door without any hesitation. I set my knapsack down on the bamboo sleeping platform and went outside again with a towel. Holding the lantern in my hand, I walked to the fountain to wash.

A waning moon was in the middle of the western sky. The rainy season had started, bringing with it thousands of mosquitoes. I couldn't sleep because of the mosquitoes, because of Srintil, and because of the firm realization that I was a true child of Paruk. I was its legal heir and, being so, had the right and the responsibility to stand up against ignorance among my own people. I had the right to prevent the birth of any new ronggeng in Paruk as long as this tradition constituted an attribute of human desire for those unaware of the transcendent desire for God. And I believed that it is love for God that must be central. I would never again leave

Paruk to its own devices. The worst disasters had fallen here, and I felt infuriated that it was Srintil who carried the burden.

I prayed. I prayed for Paruk and for its people to be able to emerge from the darkness of their ignorance. Weeping, I begged God to give Srintil strength and to restore her to humanity.

Early in the morning, by the time the sun first appeared on the horizon, I was already dressed. I wore a white, long-sleeved shirt and a pair of gray pants. My affiliation with the army was still apparent in the boots I wore and in my short haircut. I knocked on Kartareja's door and asked his wife to bathe Srintil and dress her appropriately. I planned to take her to a nearby army hospital, which had a ward for the mentally insane. Oh, God, I had to witness again how Srintil had lost her humanity. She was so wild that it took the strength of three men to take her to the well to bathe. I was forced to help when the situation became untenable. She struggled violently.

"Come on, just let me bathe you," urged Nyai Kartareja. "Look, Srintil, the soldier is here."

Srintil looked at me and calmed down. She then smiled crazily.

"Rasus, you are so handsome."

"And you're beautiful."

"Do you want to get married?"

Everyone fell silent, looking at me.

"Of course I do."

"I want to be a bride. Will you bathe me?"

"Sure. Let's go to the well. Come on, let's go take a bath."

Srintil giggled as I poured water over her body with a bucket. Nyai Kartareja and Tampi scrubbed her down and shampooed her hair. She continued giggling. Luckily it was only giggling, and Tampi and Nyai Kartareja could wash her unimpeded. After her bath, they quickly dried her with a towel. I went off to the front of the house to wait for them to finish dressing her. I could hear minor struggles and bouts of Srintil's laughter. I could tell, however, that everything was proceeding well enough.

Sakum came by, walking unsteadily. Somehow he knew that I was sitting on the front porch.

"Oh, soldier. See where we are now. What did I once tell you? If you had followed my advice, Srintil would not have come to this. But it's too late now, Soldier. Now, I would never think of suggesting that you marry her. You would, of course, be too embarrassed to have a wife who wasn't sane. Isn't that right?"

I remained silent and swallowed hard. I wasn't even able to look into Sakum's empty eyes. Suddenly I felt very much like the essence of Paruk stupidity, after my violent feelings the previous night. Sakum's simple words showed me that the way to break through the ignorance in my little homeland was within my grasp. In other words, not all of Paruk should have to take responsibility for Srintil's situation. It should be me alone. I could feel my heart pounding.

As I was mulling over Sakum's questions, Nyai Sakarya appeared. She was carrying a thick envelope.

"My child, this money belongs to Srintil. Bajus gave it to her when he brought her home. Nobody dared touch it. If you are planning to take Srintil to the hospital, use this money."

"This money was a gift from Bajus, that project manager?" I asked.

"Yes."

I took the envelope from Nyai Kartareja and threw it on the table. Its contents of brand new five thousand rupiah bills scattered on the floor. Strangely, no one was drawn to the money. They all watched my face.

"I'll have Srintil treated using my own money," I said flatly, decisively.

Srintil came out. Nyai Kartareja was at her side, carefully holding onto both her shoulders. Wearing a skirt and a nice blouse, she looked more like the Srintil of earlier times. The difference wasn't just that she was thin, extremely thin. It was her dead eyes, her wild expression and her face, which was devoid of humanity. I stood up and invited her to leave right away, but she refused to move from the front door. She demanded a flower to adorn her hair. Tampi dashed out to the side of the house and returned carrying two ylang-ylang buds that were already turning yellow. Their fragrance spread through the room like smoke. But Srintil grabbed them and threw them in Tampi's face. Then it was Sakum's son's turn. At the outskirts of the village he picked up several flowers that had fallen from a bungur tree. Again Srintil refused the gift. She crushed the flowers and threw the petals at Nyai Sakarya. Suddenly she picked up the hem of her skirt and ran off. Like a wild animal. I followed her from a distance. Beneath a bungur tree she squatted down, picked up a fresh bud and fastened it to her knot of hair.

"There, like this. Pretty, isn't it?"

"Yes. Now, let's go. It's getting late."

"I'm going to get married, aren't I?"

"That's right."

"Don't lie to me. Are you lying to me?"

"No. I want to get married, too."

Srintil whined, and continued to whine as she walked along, her hands sometimes swinging back and forth, sometimes reaching up to touch a nearby leaf. I went back to Nyai Kartareja and collected her handbag. The eyes of Paruk watched me: I saw eyes that reflected hope, eyes that shed tears, and others that expressed feelings I couldn't understand.

I hadn't planned for Srintil to walk in front of me, but she did so, and with direction and purpose. Oh, God! Now I truly do understand. A human being devoid of reason walking in front of me is an omen meant specifically for me. Yes, God. You don't place any importance on the reality of Paruk, but You have decided on a dialectical punishment for her. Floating like a dried leaf blown by the wind was someone who had suffered the punishment of the personal dialectics of time. My intuition told me that I should come to her aid, helping her find the strength to bring her form into harmony with your wishes.

As we walked along the dikes that connected Paruk with the outside world, Srintil stopped several times. At one stage she wanted to sit down, but I quickly took her hand. People working in the rice fields looked at us with the eyes of strangers. It was obvious that they regarded Srintil now as something that existed outside of their understanding. People coming from the opposite direction quickly moved off to the side as we passed. Children ran away.

When we reached the front of the market in Dawuan, Srintil became agitated. She wanted to push through the people watching us and go into the marketplace. Suddenly remembering a village belief that once an insane person goes into a market, it would be difficult for that person to recover, I quickly stopped her. Putting my arms around her, I carried her to the bus terminal. The market people, who had once doted on her, had become voyeurs. And they were afraid, as if Srintil were a rabid mongrel dog, ready to bite them all.

At first the bus driver refused to take us. He didn't want any disturbance in the bus, he said. With a sour look on his face, he reluctantly gave in when I pushed my military identification card close to his eyes.

Srintil was docile while we were in the bus, but as soon as we got off, she tried to run away. She screamed and shouted, accusing me of trying to return her to prison. Indeed, the large house with the tin roof that had held her for two years could be seen from the bus stop. I couldn't handle her by myself so I asked two pedicab drivers to help me. Weeping inside, I tied her hands with a handkerchief and held her as we rode in a pedicab.

The journey from Paruk had taken a total of two hours and I found it extremely stressful. The tension that gripped my heart was reaching a peak when the pedicab stopped at the gate to the army hospital. I asked a civilian worker in the guardhouse to help me with Srintil. We entered the building and went directly to the ward for the mentally insane. Oh, God! Because she struggled, Srintil was immediately put in a room with an iron door. When a staff member locked the huge bolt on the door, my tears flowed freely.

The ward chief of staff asked me for her details and personal data. I told him everything, adding that I would be responsible for paying the costs of her treatment. But, when he asked about my relationship to her, I fell silent, unsure of what to say.

"Is she your wife?"

"No. I'm not married."

"Your sister?"

"No. Just a relative."

"Just a relative?"

I remained silent and nodded. A whirlwind was spinning wildly in my head. This whirlwind changed into a terrifying cyclone when I heard Srintil screaming from her room: or, more precisely, her prison. She called out the names of people from Paruk, one by one, and I heard my name called more times than anyone else's. I felt, at that moment, that my existence represented the soul of my little homeland. I represented the shattered heart of a mother hearing her child screaming out at the moment of death, a sound far more horrifying than the utter silence that always follows death.

In a daze, I could see the hospital official smiling at me. Oh, it wasn't his fault. He couldn't understand the extraordinary grief that was shaking the very core of my soul. He remarked flippantly.

"What a pity. Truly a pity. The moment I saw her, I thought how beautiful she would be if she were healthy and whole. But, forgive me, sir. She's not your wife and not your sister. Is the patient perhaps your fiancée?"

"Yes!"

Clarity. Suddenly everything became clear and easy. Oh, relief! Relief. The vanity, the hypocrisy, that had been standing arrogantly in front of me dissolved with the utterance of one brief word. Everything became light and airy, like wisps of grass. I could hear the softest whispers in my heart. I could see the pearls of wisdom within the most secluded reaches of my soul.

Nobody would have understood the motivation behind the decision I made at that moment. Some would say it was because of my profound love that I decided I wanted to marry Srintil even though she was in a mental state which was devoid of humanity. That would be the most natural and reasonable assumption. But this assumption was superficial and too simple. When I said the word "yes", I was not acting out of sentimentality. I wasn't being romantic or emotional. The word "yes" represented the clarity in my soul. It communicated a basic aspect of my total being, something I had long been searching for: a sense of harmony within the larger scheme of things. That clarity of thought was not far from the very tip of a greater realization, formed like pyramid, its lines parallel with the lines that connect my own existence with the existence of God. I had made the decision rationally, reasonably and calmly: as calm as the stream of a river when it touches the deep waters of the ocean. I said yes, she was to be my wife.

It was dark before I returned to Paruk. I stood alone outside. Around me was my small, suffering homeland. With the disaster that had struck Srintil, Paruk had grown increasingly ill. Around me was a village asleep, its people silent in their grass shacks, a village that had never had the wherewithal to understand the greater purpose of life. My little homeland had never really tried to develop its ability to reason and, as a result, it never knew that it could prevent the ringworms and lice from infesting its children, as well as the ignorance that perpetuated misery from generation to generation. Because it had never tried to develop its ability to reason, my village had never tried to find harmony with God. Like my mother, it remained asleep dreaming its naïve dreams: naïveté that gave birth to the tradition of ronggeng dancers. By itself, ronggeng would not be wrong if it were in line with the larger scheme of things. However, the ronggeng tradition that had developed in Paruk was one that exploited primitive desire. And because of that, it did not enjoy God's mercy.

For a while I stood musing over the concept of the ancient, yet still naïve Paruk. The sky above was clear. A mysterious fog rolled in and created a kind of arcing rainbow around the moon. Sakarya had often told me that a rainbow encircling the moon represents an omen of difficult times to come. The people of Paruk had always believed his words. But I think Sakarya would have understood my different interpretation. This moon encircled by a rainbow, I believed, was an omen meant for me alone. It meant that I should see this small, isolated hamlet as a place where I might find meaning in life. I realized that I would have to help Paruk find itself again. I could help it find peace through the Almighty whose mercy is without bounds.

Translator's Endnote

The rich detail of Ahmad Tohari's narration, his lavish and knowledgeable description of local ecology, and the vivid imagery in his depiction of village ritual practices is a striking feature of this trilogy. More important is how he communicates the passion of his political, social, and religious convictions. He not only tells the tragic story of the dancer Srintil, but also narrates another larger story: how an entire village, because of isolation, ignorance, and poverty, was left behind socially and spiritually as Indonesia began to modernize, and how its inhabitants had become pawns in the political turmoil of 1965.

The trilogy covers a period from 1946 to 1971, from the end of Dutch colonialism and Indonesia's early efforts to become a democracy under president Sukarno, through the time of his downfall in the aftermath of the bloody 1965 debacle (during which somewhere between 400,000 and one million supposed communist sympathizers and activists were murdered), up to the early years of the New Order regime of Soeharto. These were formative and tumultuous times in the country of Indonesia, not only in terms of its political development but also in the religious direction of its national character. Although the overwhelming majority of its citizens are Islamic, Indonesia remains a secular state, maintaining an uneasy relationship with its religious activists.

One might say that *The Dancer* is simply a coming of age novel, or a love story. It is, after all, about Srintil and Rasus, two orphans of a terrible calamity that struck their village while they were still babies, and how they grew into adulthood. I think, however, it is far more than just about growing up in rural Java. The novel introduces the two characters as young children: Srintil, a little girl who begins to feel the calling of her future profession as a dancer; and Rasus, who feels the stirrings of manhood through his confused infatuation with Srintil. The two find adulthood through tortured paths; she attains her womanly status only after a completing several rituals, including a grueling ceremonial rape, and he by coming to grips with his confused longings for his dead mother and vague feelings of lust and love toward Srintil: in the end rejecting both women.

The story opens in a village of extreme desolation during a period of drought: it is a tiny world of poverty, hunger, and near hopelessness. In the third person voice, the author describes the village of Paruk as a kind of throwback to an earlier, pre-Islamic time in Java, and remaining so into the twentieth century because of ignorance and isolation. The novel introduces the main characters Srintil and Rasus as children: but children teetering on the edge of adolescence and clearly attracted to one another. Despite the harsh conditions of their lives, the two live in an almost idyllic world of childhood innocence and blossoming love. However, for Rasus, their world begins to come apart when Srintil becomes a ronggeng dancer.

Switching to the first person narrative, the story is continued by Rasus. Through the eyes of a confused young boy, we see a young girl become possessed by the spirit of ronggeng. Srintil demonstrates an uncanny ability to dance and sing in the style of traditional ronggeng performance, demonstrating that she has been chosen by the supernatural Indang Ronggeng to become the dancer of Paruk. Srintil is then prepared to enter into the ronggeng tradition through a series of rituals and practices based on ancient animist beliefs. After witnessing several rituals that draw her closer to being a true ronggeng, Rasus realizes that he is losing his beloved Srintil to the fleshy world of adults. His world shatters when he learns of the final initiation ritual in which Srintil will have to lose her virginity. She is to be raped by the highest-paying man. From then on, her life is not only to be the dancer of Paruk but also to become a prostitute.

The author told me that his intent was to describe a community that was entirely without contemporary notions of sin and virtue. His character Rasus learns about such concepts only after he leaves Paruk. Unable to resolve his own feelings of loss over his mother, who disappeared while he was a baby, and the emotions he felt toward Srintil, Rasus decides to escape from his small village and learn something of the world. Departing the morning after his one and only sexual encounter with Srintil, he leaves to live in a nearby town, called Dawuan, and works as a cassava vendor in the market. It is there where he first begins to learn the meaning of sin and about moral transgression.

Rasus eventually embraces the Islamic faith, and joins the army. He finds a kind of stable family life for himself as he grows up among soldiers even while the political situation in Indonesia deteriorates. During this time Srintil grows up as an extremely successful dancer and prostitute, bringing prosperity to the people of Paruk and enjoying local prestige as a kind of celebrity. Like other Paruk villagers, Srintil is illiterate and, without realizing it, she is implicated in the political upheaval that eventually overtakes the country. It is at this point that she, along with her fellow villagers, begins to learn that right and wrong are relative concepts. She begins performing at Communist campaign rallies and, without even realizing it, she is swept up in events that lead to the massacre of 1965. The people of Paruk have become pawns in the struggle between the communists and the Indonesian nationalists. In the beginning of the third book in the trilogy, the Indonesian army comes to Paruk, arresting Srintil and others, and burning almost the entire village to the ground.

The author describes some of the horror that occurred in 1965, but this part of his novel was censored by the publishers because they feared reprisals by the Soeharto government. Thus, 1965 became a national secret, widely known to the people of Indonesia yet rarely openly discussed. Returning to the story, Srintil is held as a political prisoner for about two years during which time she is subjected to rape and violence by her jailers. Even after her release, she, like other former political prisoners, continues to be brutalized by hatred and shame. She is labeled a communist sympathizer and a traitor to her country. She has no rights, no legal recourse, and no sympathy from the people around her. In her mind, she blames her past immoral lifestyle for her troubles and resolves to become a good citizen. Haunted by a sense of guilt, her only wish now is to settle down and establish a family. She gives up hope of ever marrying Rasus, her true love, and is courted by a contractor involved in building an irrigation system in the region. However, she is betrayed by this man whose intent was to pass her on as a plaything to more powerful men and further his own ambitions. Her world now completely shattered, Srintil descends into madness.

One day Ahmad Tohari took me to the place that inspired him to write the trilogy. It was a small hamlet called Pakuncen. He showed me the large leafy bungur trees often mentioned in his novel. We strolled through the village cemetery and on a small hill was the grave of Bandayuda, a local historical figure. The site was exactly like that of the place spirit, Ki Secamenggala, in the novel. In front of Bandayuda's grave was an immense Banyan tree, looming over us with roots reaching down to the ground from the branches, like a ragged shroud, adding to the brooding silence that seemed to envelop the place.

Our voices automatically turned into whispers as we stood there in the cool and gloomy shade of the bungur trees. For the author, the place evoked the island of Bali where spirits seem to roam more freely than in Java. He said that the village and its cemetery represent a vestige of Java's earlier, pre-Islamic past. The grave of Bandayuda was a site of animism and ancestor worship, of *kejawèn.*

As evidence of the sacred power of this place, he pointed to a fallen bungur tree, near the grave of Bandayuda, long dead and decaying. "Nobody will cut up that dead tree," he said, "even though people here are in constant need of firewood. They simply won't touch it."

He told me that he discovered this place when he was a small boy hunting birds with a slingshot. In the years that followed he kept returning and watched the people of Pakuncen as they practiced their beliefs. In the 1960s, Islamic youths vandalized the graveyard and the government refused to protect the people of Pakuncen. Following the events of September 1965, many of the villagers of Pakuncen were imprisoned or murdered for being (or allegedly being) Communist sympathizers. One day, as a small boy, the author himself witnessed a man being executed there in the Pakuncen cemetery, shot in the head by soldiers. He told me that this experience later inspired his commitment to speaking out for the rural poor of Java. In his novel, he wanted to point out the flaws in Islamic belief: the concept of sin does not easily apply to those that have no understanding of it. Villagers of this area not only had little understanding of Islamic law, they had less understanding of the political struggles taking place in Indonesia in the mid-1960s. These were poor illiterate farmers with little knowledge of the wider world. Like the people of Paruk in his novel, many of the author's fellow villagers were jailed or executed in 1965 simply because they were the pawns in larger religious and political struggles.

He argued that, while his trilogy is fictional, the characters are drawn from real people and the events and practices he describes are based on reality. Indeed, the fictional Paruk, where the story takes place, is based on the real village of Pakuncen, only a few kilometers from his home. The events that he himself didn't witness were described to him in detail by older neighbors. For example, he had learned about the opening-of-the-mosquito-net from an old man who participated in the ceremony when he was a young man. In fact, he told me, the competition for the young celebrant's virginity was even more fierce than he described in his novel. According to the old man, one of the competitors was killed during a violent argument over the prize.

When I asked about Srintil and her role in the story, he stated that she is Islamicized, although she does not become a Muslim. In other words, she begins to live like an Islamic woman. After her release from prison, Srintil gives up her profession as a ronggeng dancer. Apparently unable to conceive a child, she adopts a baby and tries to live like any other modest village woman. "After everything she has endured, Srintil decides she wants to be a normal woman," he told me. "She wants very much to become a housewife and mother. From being a ronggeng who tried everything, she decides to become a normal everyday woman. The process here is Islamic."

In a way, both Srintil and her childhood love, Rasus, are able to escape the isolation, the poverty, and the grinding ignorance of Paruk village. However, they come into contact with the outside world in very different ways. Rasus literally leaves his past behind, running away from the village and eventually joining the army. He discovers Islam one day while working in a market; it is revealed to him in a powerful moment when he touches the cheek of a devout young Muslim woman. From this experience, he learns the meaning of sin. For Srintil, on the other hand, the outside world intrudes upon her life, first in the political turmoil of 1965 and later through modernization. Along with other villagers from Paruk, she learns about the concept of shame. She is ashamed of her ignorance, her lack of morals, and her sordid lifestyle. After she is released from prison, she resolves to become a virtuous woman and live (albeit unknowingly) like a good Muslim.

Yet, in the end even this cannot save her from madness. The irony of her tragic story is that, unlike Rasus, Srintil never had a choice over the way she lived her life. As a man, Rasus could leave his past behind. He could choose to embrace Islam. As a woman, Srintil has to live with the shame of her past. She did not choose to embrace Islam: Islam embraced her. She tries to reject her earlier life as a ronggeng dancer by attempting to embark on a new life as a housewife but Rasus rejects her. And she experiences the ultimate betrayal by the only other man in her life, a smooth-talking minor bureaucrat from the capital city of Jakarta who promises her a life of marriage but tries to force her to return to prostitution. Srintil loses her mind in the end, perhaps, because madness offered the only escape possible from a painful past and unendurable present.

The Dancer, then, is a novel about the 1965 debacle and its aftermath. This English translation includes a long passage that was not published with the original Indonesian version: perhaps because this section describes too well the horrors that imprisoned villagers like Srintil faced. Ahmad Tohari feels that, as a writer, he had to tell the story of 1965. Indeed, he believes that it is the moral obligation of writers like him to document and dramatize the events leading up to and following the mass killings of 1965.

In a public lecture he once stated that Indonesian writers have a moral obligation to speak of the past: "The writers of Indonesia are still faced with the challenge of fulfilling the moral debt they owe to the past. They must explore and write about all issues associated with this great tragedy. They carry a heavy burden of moral responsibility to make a record of the tragedy of 1965 become a literary monument that the people of the world can examine. If this moral duty is not fulfilled adequately, the debt will remain outstanding forever. The memory of those thousands of victims that suffered brutal and inhumane treatment will haunt the writers of Indonesia forever. It will haunt us all for generations to come, demanding that this debt be paid in full."

Many people in the Banyumas region are not happy with his writings. They are troubled by his revisionist approach to Islam, his critical attacks on the Indonesian government, and his frank description of rural Javanese life. Many of the Banyumas residents I spoke with expressed outrage at the depiction of villagers as ignorant and primitive, at the explicit sexuality (by Javanese standards) of certain passages, and at the political stand (often implicitly critical of the Indonesian government) he takes in his narration. Indeed, most of the people I spoke with, including musicians and ronggeng dancers, denied that the religious and social practices described in the novel ever existed. What remains unclear to me to this day is whether the outrage they expressed was because people truly believed the author misrepresented the past or because the past he depicted was simply too shameful for the inhabitants of Banyumas to acknowledge.

Anthropologist Stephen Tyler once pointed out, perhaps only partially tongue-in-cheek, that "the meaning of a text is the sum of its misreadings". In present-day Indonesia, ronggeng involves acknowledged professional dancers and musicians who perform for public and private celebrations. Some women and their accompanying ensembles have in fact become widely known throughout the region through locally marketed commercial cassette recordings. Indeed, ronggeng today is an odd mixture of tradition and popular culture, viewed (it seems) with both pride and contempt. On one hand, local fans and even government officials emphasize the deep roots of ronggeng in regional history and pre-Islamic religious practices. They point out that it is an ancient "tradition" of Banyumas, unique to the area, and therefore should be protected and supported as an indigenous art form. On the other hand, ronggeng is also viewed as crude and primitive: crude because the female dancer's movements draw male audience attention to her body in an overtly sexual way; and primitive because it arose out of behaviors and attitudes no longer appropriate to modern Indonesian values.

Local government officials of the former Ministry of Education and Culture (now the Ministry of National Education) have been mandated to identify, develop, and preserve the rich cultural diversity of Indonesia. In Banyumas, as elsewhere, this also means altering traditions such as ronggeng so that they conform with contemporary (government-determined) values. In this same way, past practices that are now considered unsavory are altered or erased altogether in the name of "art" or "tradition", or "ritual". However, when I asked the head of the local office of Education and Culture about the practice of "opening the mosquito net", he gave me two responses: officially, he denied any knowledge of such a practice but, unofficially, he admitted believing that it existed in the past.

Perhaps this last response best exemplifies the uniquely Indonesian problem of old disorderliness colliding with government views of the past. Untidy cultural practices like ronggeng do not easily fit in modern notions of "tradition". Indeed, as Felicia Hughes-Freeland notes, the word "'tradition' should not necessarily be understood as referring to customs [that] are authentic, indigenous, and long-established... but rather as an ideology which attributes precedents to practices which may have recently been revived, recast, or reinvented..." Indeed, "tradition", "ritual", and "art" are themselves problematic terms, invested as they are with government ideology and devoid of messy past worldviews that might contradict present day values and norms. What is left, as anthropologist John Pemberton puts it, "is a purely traditional culture free of political and historical implications..."

In such a socio-political environment, simply invoking the past becomes a kind political act of resistance. The trilogy was not meant to be a titillating coming of age story. The author intentionally wrote it to make his readers feel uncomfortable, to compel them to think about social injustice in rural Java. The poverty, ignorance, and immorality he describes in such detail in his novel form a critical commentary aimed at a state that systematically ignored the needs of its most vulnerable citizenry: those people living without irrigation, without schools, hospitals, and other basic facilities that could have helped them improve their conditions. As he

The Author

Indonesian writer Ahmad Tohari is the author of eleven novels, three anthologies of essays, two collections of short stories, and many individual short stories and essays. His works have been translated into English, Dutch, German, Japanese, and Chinese. Tohari is the recipient of several national and international literary awards, including the Southeast Asian Writers Award and a fellowship through the International Writers Program in Iowa City. He is an experienced and respected journalist who regularly contributes political essays to *Suara Merdeka*. He is also a religious intellectual and leader and he and his family run an Islamic school (pesantrèn) and community center. Finally, he is a well-known expert of Javanese folk arts. Today he lives in home village of Tinggarjaya near Purwokerto, Central Java. The 2011 Indonesian film, *Sang Penari* (*The Dancer*), produced by Shanty Harman and directed by Ifa Isfansyah, is based on this trilogy.

The Translator

René TA Lysloff is an Associate Professor of Music at the University of California, Riverside. He has published numerous articles on traditional music and theater in Central Java in scholarly journals such as *Ethnomusicology*, *Asian Music*, and *Asian Theatre Journal*. His most recently completed work is *Srikandhi Dances Lengger*, a book on shadow theater and music in rural Central Java, published in 2009 through KITLV.